Season of the Witch

Richard Fey is the author of

Mandy's Rules

Available online

Season of the Witch

a novel by

Richard Fey

The Sundown Electric Publishing Company

Third Edition 2018

ISBN: 0615923755
ISBN-13: 978-0615923758

For the Weirdos

David J. Pearson & Gregory C. Hoag

GRATEFUL ACKNOWLEDGEMENT

To Ms. Mia Frances who, serving unbeknownst as the muse on this work, graciously agreed to let me use her charming image on the cover. In the photograph, she had just found a copy of Donovan's *Sunshine Superman* album for a quarter and was thrilled as it was the music her parents had played in her kitchen as she was growing up.

To Mr. Jacob Levy who altered the photograph to place the image in time.

To Kinky Joe Flash who co-wrote two of the lyrics ascribed to Jamey Craig.

To Richard A. Hill and David R. Hicks who are encouraging, thoughtful, and perceptive readers. Their efforts are much appreciated, and their literary advice is represented throughout the work.

And to all my past readers. While I may not retain all or even most of the good advice, many comments have stayed with me and have influenced the present work.

—Richard Fey, Knollridge, 2013

WHAT'S THE HAPS, MAN?

A HARD RAIN

SOUVENIRS AND MEMORIES. Cool is to have been at Woodstock, to have seen Dylan at Newport or in the Village, Hendrix at Monterey, Savile Row for the rooftop concert. In the Valley, a hippie might have seen The Doors or the Airplane at the Fantasy Faire or Hendrix might have been heard wafting up the road to the high school on graduation night.

This one guy knew a guy whose brother was in a band on the same bill with Hendrix. He got invited backstage and ended up smoking a joint with Jimi Hendrix, the brother, that is—not the guy who told me the story. One high school hippie saw Cream at CSUK and managed to cop Clapton's Coke bottle as a memento. A chick with pretty hair and long legs asked if he would lay it on her. As she likely had a better use for it than he, it passed into the land of legend, which she certainly was.

It doesn't have to be rock stars. One old geezer identifies himself hanging out in a famous photo of Mario Savio atop a car in Berkeley in 1964—Savio, that is, not the guy. But he was right there in the crowd. Another guy says it was his car. One dude can find himself in a crowd scene, shaking hands with RFK during the California primary run, both of them passing through the lens of history.

Ephemera lose their meaning as the players disappear behind the screen at the end of a long trip. A Quicksilver Tapestry, but, oh God, I'm getting ahead of myself by a year or two.

THERE WAS A HIPPIE in the Valley in the summer of 1969, a suburban California flower child, a year from high school graduation, a step away from fame. Five-six, shoulder-length full golden hair parted in the middle, pretty green eyes, a sweet, high, well-pitched singing voice, a soft boyish speaking voice, a naturally clear complexion which turned rosy in the summer heat, Jamey Craig believed with all his heart that he was a rock legend in the making.

He played a Fender Precision bass from the late fifties which he had picked up pretty inexpensively because someone had painted it orange. He played through a Fender Bassman, unfortunately with a matching orange speaker box. Jamey had picked up the whole kit for $175.00 after working in his old man's plumbing yard the previous summer. The orange was an unfortunate drag, a hang-over from someone's psychedelic trip—maybe orange sunshine—but that's why he could afford it.

Despite the orange, Jamey was creating his cool and aloof stage manner. He liked to try out his cool appraisin' stare on the chicks that came out to see his band, Crazy Place. His hair was down to his shoulders and he was working on a stache, though it was hard to see—more soft peach fuzz than a manly mustache. Along with playing bass, Jamey Craig did most of the squawking. His beautiful voice, almost chick-like, is what distinguished him. Whether it would be enough to get Crazy Place and Jamey on the cover of Rolling Stone was the question to which his life was dedicated.

During the school year, Jamey Craig was at Knollridge High, hanging out on the quad with the hippies. At school, both the low riders and jocks harassed Jamey and the lads, ostensibly because of their long hair and hippie clothes. Now and again, harassment turned to violence. That mostly happened when Jamey's dismissive attitude toward the unhip nimrods was on display. He and his friend, Craig Roman, the guitarist, were too witty for the occasion, and for these sins, and more, they were labeled queers and fags, though Jamey couldn't get anyone to tell him the difference. You see the problem. And so they were bumped and pushed, and sometimes pounded.

Apart from that, they were well liked among the hippies, and, it being cool times, by many others, too. Their band was getting known around school and around the north Valley. The school year meant curfews, less time to practice, and more time bored to death, sober, and at home. But this was summer, and summertime was freedom. Playing music and writing songs was the most important thing to Jamey, so he relished this short summer as it was taking off.

The idea that Jamey and the band were anything but straight was absurd on its face. Teri Ann Murphy should have belied those charges. In the weeks before, Jamey had become a man, and Teri Ann, through reciprocity, had become a woman. Not that the P.E. teachers and ROTC recruiters who derided Jamey and the boys for their long hair, their drugs, their queer lifestyle, and their dirty hippie ways would have known the intimate details—though there was something a little different in Teri Ann's walk which Jamey particularly noticed as she was walking away after she dumped him just before the summer. It was a case of first heartbreak, and Jamey nursed his broken heart, an inspiration for hit tunes.

Whether anyone really thought that Jamey Craig, Craig Roman, Mark, or Paul were actually queer is doubtful. Looking at a Polaroid of the foursome, their imagined album cover, perhaps Jamey and Craig might have looked a little girly. Craig's mom and dad were really cool, so his hair was as long as any guy's at Knollridge High. In some eyes, P.E. coaches for example, that alone was effeminate. And Jamey's voice had yet to change, so even the band teased him a little on that score. But their sexual interests were not the point. Jamey and Craig were deemed different, and that's what the inarticulate were trying to say. Given the long hair, the colorful hippie clothes, and their pacifist natures, they were deemed pussys. But, they would have it known, they were straight pussys.

The harassment and the put-downs were not the central issues. That was an aspect of their lives that reinforced the feeling that they were exceptional. What did it matter what dip-shits thought? And what did matter was the sure knowledge that Crazy Place was going to be bigger than The Doors, the Airplane, The Forgotten Avenue, and the Orwellian Bards. Crazy Place had gotten quite a few gigs at parties and events, and they were going to make it in the big time and share the stage with their idols—not forgetting all the girls, dope, and money that would come with their success. Majorly straight—sex, drugs, and the band.

But breaking into the L.A. club scene was harder than they had imagined it had been in the olden days when The Buffalo Springfield or The Byrds were on the make. Jamey and the other band members were all high school boys between sixteen and seventeen, not popular with club owners who couldn't have a bunch of kids drinking. The music scene was growing up. Jamey and the boys couldn't get in except with a ticket, which they couldn't afford. And if Jamey waited to turn eighteen, the wave would have passed them by. They would be ancient and unhip. Winwood was fifteen when he was in Spencer Davis. And Jamey didn't have a year or two anyway. Things were not cool at home.

Most of the problems were in his head. He was sixteen and knew very little. The Craigs were leading the good life in the north Valley, and it would be hard to make the case that it was as intolerable as Jamey seemed to believe.

He lived in a spacious rancho style house in the north Valley with a swimming pool and central air. He had his own room, complete with sounds and the requisite hippie style art, posters of Big Brother, Jimi Hendrix, Katy Mondy, and Janis. He had a hookah, hidden from view but easily accessible. He thought he wasn't into fashions, but when the stuff from the stores didn't make it, he would go to Goodwill or Salvation Army to get funky duds. Teri Ann had painted his desert boots for him with suns and moons.

And he had some good stuff, too. Along with his bass and amp, which he kept at Craig Roman's, he also had a nice Sears six-string acoustic guitar, the one that he had had lessons on in his long ago youth, and he had his Gibson twelve-string; not a bad instrument for a kid, and not cheap. Thanks, Grandpa!

It wasn't as if he was in serious want. He ate on a regular basis, and his mother, Margaret, was not only a good cook, but one who catered to his tastes. Jamey got pretty good treatment at home. This included laundry service, sheets, and cleaning. The problem, as Jamey saw it, was the old man.

Jamey's grades had gone down the tubes. He was a smart guy and he used to do well. He was fairly interested. He liked literature and poetry. He had been quick with figures. But, given the choice between taking the algebra final or recording with the band, he had chosen the music and had failed the math course. He bombed most of his classes across the board.

Quite often, Jamey would be blazing, even at school. Drugs of choice included methamphetamines, pot, and LSD. Miss LeAnn Curtis, his recently minted English Lit teacher, summed it up as well as anyone. "Jamey has a good head on his shoulders. It's just that he doesn't use it." She liked some of his poems, his song lyrics really, but Miss LeAnn Curtis was not very influential with college admissions boards. With those grades, UCLA was already out the window and CSUK was rapidly fading. So, if he didn't catch a break in the music scene, Jamey Craig was JC bound—at best. Good thing Jamey was so sure that the lightning would strike! And in those moments when he contemplated the possibility that maybe it wouldn't strike, he shook it off. No sense letting the shadow of tomorrow darken his summer days.

Jamey's dad, Jim Craig, Sr., a working contractor, had laid down the law. He was afraid that Jamey was drinking pot, smoking acid, and shooting up LSD. When he saw the end-of-the-year report card, he knew that Jamey was going up in smoke. Jamey was supposed to have gotten a summer job, but he was shining that on. He was not even trying to play it cool for the old man.

Jim Craig ordered his hippie son to the barber shop. Tomorrow was the Fourth of July and Jim didn't want hippies hanging around the pool on the big holiday. He went to the job, and the boy paid the barber his two dollars, returning home with his split-ends trimmed but no reduction in length, still sporting his rather unconvincing mustache and sideboards.

But this all went out of Jamey's head because, later in the day, the news of Brian Jones' death had come to Knollridge. The band spent the afternoon and early evening practicing their Stones numbers: "The Last Time," "It's All Over Now," "Not Fade Away," and "Mona." So Jamey had been out when the old man had come in from work.

And it wasn't until the next day that Jamey's act of defiance, and waste of two dollars, had come to light. Jim Craig was pissed, but there were people over for the Fourth. The Craigs were taking Super Eight movies by the pool and Jamey was clowning for the camera with his sister, Missy. But as Pabst followed Pabst, by evening the guests had gone home and Jim had been stewing for too long. He just figured the little fag ought to have done what he had been told to do.

The shouting of the old man and the nasty high pitched rejoinders got worse. The old man had tried to take Jamey physically in hand and personally give him a manly mid-western haircut, but Jamey had put up a resistance. His hair was his image, and he couldn't afford to be shorn. "Leave me alone!" he tried to shout, but it came out sounding more like his sister, which always happened to Jamey when he was stressed. He couldn't control it. Jamey retreated to his room.

And the old man walked on down the hall and invaded Jamey's sanctuary scene. His mom and his sister were crying in the background as, scissors in hand, the muscular old man, who must have been all of forty-five, was storming around Jamey's room trying to get hold of the little hippie shit. In the brouhaha, though it wasn't intentional, the old man smashed Jamey's Gibson with his shoe.

There was a stunned moment of silence on both sides. That was an irretrievable act, a break in the continuum. Jamey, driven by equal parts rage and frustration, punched his dad in the face—something he had never done with the football players who had harassed him at school and something he had never contemplated relative to the dad. While Jamey, barely a hundred pounds, couldn't really have hurt the old man, the idea that the bastard hippie prick would strike his pop was beyond the pale. Society had broken down into anarchy and someone had to speak up. No wonder he had voted for Nixon! The generation gap had been apparent in the Craig household for some time, but this was the ultimate uptight scene to date.

Between the smashed guitar and the attack on his father, to Jamey, there was nothing for it but to run. And that's what he did. He left the house with nothing. The old man had yelled after him not to bother to come back, and Jamey had said, "Fuck You Right Now!" The old man pronounced him a hippie faggot. Jamey hadn't bothered to respond. What was the difference between the assholes at school and the asshole at home? Jamey was fixin' to boogie.

FLYIN' HIGH

A N HOUR LATER, having walked around the neighborhood, a little more thoughtful now, he knocked on his sister's window. Missy surreptitiously gathered up some clothes in a backpack and sent that and his guitar case with his six-string through her window.

Missy urged Jamey to give in, to cut his hair, and to behave, at least until he could get to college, but Jamey was too young to know how to be contrite or even to bide his time. She gave him her remaining twenty dollars of birthday money. Her pretty green eyes were glistening at first and then her face had a stream of tears. She pushed back her long blond hair. The two could be mistaken for twins. She was fifteen, pink faced, and things seemed as real to her as they did to him in the dramatic moment. He was running away, but that meant that her life was changing, too. Jamey had always been sweet to Missy. Now, in their maturity, they were allies, even if she didn't share an interest in the drugs and derring-do of her counterculture brother. She would worry about him out and alone making his way in the world. At the open window, Jamey squeezed Missy's hand. "Take care, Jamey," she said, believing that perhaps they would be separated, if not forever then for a long long time.

Then he coolly walked into the night wearing his backpack and carrying his guitar case, knowing that at least until he got to the corner of the cul-de-sac, someone was taking notice of his cool gait as he set out on this next step to his rock and roll destiny. The last occasional bursts of fireworks were going off in various directions with a few remaining pops and explosions in the distance. At first, he just walked around trying to collect his thoughts. He knew the neighborhood of his youth very intimately. He didn't want to get rousted. So he avoided walking on the major streets.

But it seemed that every little avenue and street held some major memory. This was home. He walked by Clarissa's house. Her bedroom light was on, but she had been beyond Jamey for months.

It was in the garage on a Friday night in winter. Jamey had been scheming on Clarissa. He had been getting somewhat insistent, making a serious effort to work his hands under Clarissa's dress. She wasn't opening

7

up like a flower, but Craig had previously advised Jamey to break on through in a case like that. Just keep pushing. "You just have to warm her up," he said. "Get your fingers in her pants."

Unfortunately, when Jamey chanced to see the helpless tears on her face and felt the trembling of her tiny body, it was all too much. It put him in mind of Missy. It was the first time that he connected everything they had been thinking and saying about chicks with actual persons. Somebody was probably scheming to get his hands under Missy's dress. It was creepy! His mind was blown, a common state these days. Jamey's somewhat affectionate aggression against Clarissa ended there. He was a couple of blocks away when he realized that that had been a weird flash.

She wouldn't have been the hottest first time, anyway. She was kind of weird. Kind of cardboard and her body was pretty straight really. Not a lot going on. And it wasn't her personality, either. She hardly spoke. It was all sort of formal. There wasn't anything really exciting about Clarissa except that she seemed to have, at least as a prototype, a feminine nature to some degree, and that was good enough.

Craig Roman had once kissed Clarissa, and, later, they both agreed that her kisses were pretty tame. Craig likened kissing Clarissa to kissing a dead fish. Jamey thought that she actually smelled a lot better. He liked her shampoo or whatever it was. All in all, thinking of the incident, Jamey thought he had been noble. Clarissa had been preserved for a few more months, but Jamey's virginity had been protected as well.

He continued through the neighborhood and soon got to thinking that this running away business was pretty lame stuff. He had no idea where to go or what to do even on this first night. But it would have been uncool to go home and even more uncool to get a haircut in the middle of the summer. Real hippies didn't have buzz jobs. But, if they did, they didn't have hippie chicks.

The night was balmy. Jamey thought about what to do and where to go. He was drawn to hanging out with his band mates at their houses as he would often do on a summer night, but he was sure that his mother would soon start tracking him. The band members would be the obvious place to start. He walked by Teri Ann Murphy's window. There was a light but no silhouette on the shade. She had dumped him, so not much point knocking on her window.

There wasn't any place he could go that wouldn't be a bust, so he got the notion to go down into the wash where he and the boys had first smoked pot. Nobody would find him there. Hidden under a bridge,

Jamey took his first few hours of sleep in the wide world, his head on his backpack.

In the early morning hours, hungry and not well rested, he made his way to Craig Roman's early morning window. He felt as if he were out of options. What could he do now?

When he tapped on the window, Craig slid it open and Jamey came inside. As Jamey had guessed, Craig's parents had gotten the call during the night, and Craig told Jamey that he couldn't hang around because it was a sure bust. The cops were on his case. But Jamey knew that Mrs. Roman always had a layer cake on hand, sometimes chocolate, sometimes butter cream, sometimes a heavenly combination of the two. Craig quietly went down the hall for breakfast cake and Jamey took in his friend's scene. Craig had his favorite albums framed 12 x 12 style: *Fresh Cream, Linda Rondstadt, Surrealistic Pillow,* and *The Forgotten Avenue.*

As Jamey scarfed the cake, he asked Craig to take care of his bass and his amp. It needn't have been said. Craig asked where Jamey was going, but Jamey said that it was better if he didn't tell anyone. It was better for Jamey since he had no answer.

"When it's cool, man, I'll get in touch with you," said Jamey. He tried to get his generally high pitched voice to sound strong and sure. His script was cool and collected, but his delivery was weak. He half-hoped that Craig would decide to join him on the adventure, but that would have been pretty lame on Craig's part since his folks were so cool. Craig had no reason to give up his cake.

Jamey knew he had to get away from his regular stomping grounds. He had often travelled by way of thumb, but that would be an obvious bust. He broke the twenty at a liquor store where he didn't think he'd be noticed because quasi-hippie punks appeared in great numbers on that corner due to the presence of the recently opened Big Boy.

Jamey boarded an RTD bus. A few transfers and an hour and a half later, he finally made it to Topanga Canyon, land of the freaks, where he figured his long hair and mustache, such as it was, would allow him to blend in with the trees and shrubs. By way of thumb now, he discovered that he was heading out to Pacific Coast Highway and the beaches. He knew how to get there.

He was picked up by two cool dudes. Jamey didn't know cars from chemical elements, but he recognized the hood ornament. It was a long white Jaguar four-seater. The three of them were heading north on PCH. On the passenger side was a tall soft featured guy with light curly hair who turned around with a grin. Jamey thought it was maybe Art Garfunkle, but he never sang, so how would a person know? Jamey had a Garfunkle voice, but he thought of himself as a songwriter and rocker, something weighty beyond the sweet voice. He never knew if it really had been the Garf. He jumped ship at Heathercliff.

The day was already bright and sunny, approaching hot. He was getting thirsty, and Margaret's refrigerator was miles away. He stopped at a hamburger joint on the beach at Zuma. It being the July Fourth weekend and sunny weather that wasn't quitting, there were crowds. Jamey was thinking that the cops were looking for him, but they didn't find him in this freak scene. Even walking with his backpack and guitar case, he didn't stand out. There were plenty of guitar punks at the beach.

He had all the time in the world, so he spent some of it watching girls. One young lady, albeit older than Jamey, struck him as at once incredibly absurd and equally provocative. She was taller than he was, and maybe a year or two older, but that didn't explain her fashion sense. Her boxy two-piece orange suit reminded him of the painted Bassman sound box. It rode high, almost to her belly button while the angular dual diamond top hid all signs of cleavage. She wore her dark brown hair in long pigtails sticking off to either side tied with white ribbons. She sported bangs over her extremely made up round eyes. Despite the manifest silliness, he was fascinated by her long shapely legs. There was nothing funny about her stems. As the locker room saying went, he wouldn't kick her out of bed. Not that it was likely to be a decision he would be required to render. She was clearly out of his league and Squaresville besides. Her mod look was straight out of the magazines, and her conservatism was confirmed when her crew-cut boyfriend rejoined her, bringing a rainbow snow cone for her pleasure.

As the morning turned to afternoon, Jamey rambled southbound along a mile of beach. There was no parking except along the side of a narrow access road, so the farther down he walked, the less people he encountered. He knew the territory, especially recalling a memorable night making out with Teri Ann. He hadn't gotten into her pants that night because she was strongly opposed to sand in the nether regions. It wasn't really an argument he could answer, and her breasts in the moonlight were quite lovely as a sweet consolation.

TALES OF BRAVE ULYSSES

HE CLIMBED OVER SOME JAGGED AND SLIPPERY BLACK ROCKS that extended into the ocean, not an easy feat with his guitar case and backpack.

When he got to the other side, to the secluded cove where he had spent many days and nights with his pals, a happening was in progress. Six high school hippie kids were occupying the cove, three dudes and three chicks. The guys were down in the water, bare tops and jeans, body surfing and swimming around like loud mouth kids, which they certainly were. The girls, in jeans, t-shirts, and loose-fitting blouses, were sitting on the blankets, smoking cigarettes with impunity, and watching the boys without wanting to look as if they were. Then Jamey appeared on the beach with his guitar, the beautiful bard, Donovan-on-Blonde.

The cove was an intimate scene, and staying cool and aloof wasn't going to get it. Jamey approached the camp and the girls. The whole scene looked exactly like the scenes he had been a part of, a parallel world. It could have been his people.

Jamey was a little shy about the girls, except when he was on stage. He had never been very aggressive. Putting the moves on Clarissa was about as aggressive as he had ever been. In the case of Teri Ann Murphy, it was she who had sought him out. She had given him the signals, and, slowly, he had picked up on them. He realized later, not yet, that she had wanted someone she could handle, someone who would go just as far as she was ready to go. And, after some months, she needed someone who could take charge, and that wasn't Jamey at sixteen. But he sat down with the chicks when they invited him. He was nice looking with pretty hair.

In the moment, Jamey was aware of the feminine forms, feelings, and pheromones around him. Add to that the loneliness, the home-sickness he was already feeling, and he was quite overcome. The boys in the water quickly returned to the camp site, maybe protecting their interests, though it was more of a tribe than cute couples. Jamey introduced himself and was welcomed. The welcome included a place at the hippie circle and a discount on a hit of the ace that one of the guys had for sale. It was only a buck, at cost. Jamey couldn't pass it up despite his dire straits. They willingly shared their loaf of tasty but sandy French bread from the Trancas market.

Jamey was coaxed to play his guitar, leading the group in a Beatles sing-along. They did a couple of Stones tunes for Brian Jones, RIP. Then one of the dudes got out his bongos and another guy took out his flute. Then Jamey played one of his songs, a paean to the lost love of his life, Teri Ann Murphy.

Now that I shouldn't touch you
It's as if I never knew
And I can dream of your ways
Imaginin' what it would be
To kiss your face
And feel you kiss me
And to reach into your frightened eyes
And somehow make it come alive
Imaginin' (Imaginin')

It went over well with the hippies, especially the girls. The song felt autobiographical, and it sort of was. The feelings of loss and separation were real. The details, he had played with to touch the heartstrings. Jamey played reasonably well, but it was his voice that set him apart. "Man, I never thought about adding a flute part to that song," said Jamey. "That was really far out. It sounded like it was meant to be there. Wow!"

"You got any other songs?" Jamey tried out the one he had been working on, a trippy kind of thing. Jamey played the cords for his new band mates, and pretty soon they were sailing. Even the chicks put together a little harmony under Jamey's voice.

As the freak takes you
Do your own thing
You can stay cool
Be cool and maintain
You say I'm trippin'
I'm on the wing
You're my jewel
Beautiful insane

"Wow, man! Kind of Donovany," said the blonde girl, and this was not meant as a negative criticism of the derivative nature of Jamey's song. She liked it. The youngsters expressed what Jamey had heard before, that he was really good and ought to be in the business. Jamey put away his guitar when he realized that he was having trouble remembering how to play. He was beginning to rush. The fret board was melting in the sun. Every movement had major trails, man.

The familiar Zuma cove scene was taking on a painted aspect, all the colors of the cliff faces pouring down across the golden sand and into the blue and white waters just as they had in Indian times. Jamey knew nothing of Indians, but the image seemed right in his mind. Something ancient. Something timeless. There was a religious aspect to what Jamey sometimes experienced on acid. It didn't cause him to take up churching, but he was aware of a greater power at work in the universe. It was far out stuff, vague, and not easily apprehended when he wasn't zonked.

The obvious visible motion of the atomic world became apparent to Jamey, as it often did when he was blazing. The motion extended to the beings around him in the circle. Even the sand was arranged in an ornate delicate filigree design. Who created this fantastic perfection hidden from the eyes of those who would not see? Was it God? So God drew pictures in the sand? Wo. Far out, man. Or does man draw pictures of God in his brain? Far out.

A girl sat near him. He could see the pores of her face forming beautiful, similarly related designs. The grains of sand on her skin were decorative sequins reflecting the gorgeous life-giving sunlight. Jamey had fallen backward, looking up at the sky now. He saw a girl's smile, her hair brushing over him. Her eyes were beautiful, big, and brown. Her smile seemed well-informed, as if she knew what was happening. She wasn't any older than he was, so from where did her wealth of wisdom come?

"Are you really a dude?" she asked. "Because you're like so beautiful, man. Like an angel or something." Jamey could hardly understand the echoing question, and never even began to formulate an oral response. Then her hair brushed against his face again and she disappeared. There, behind the sky, was more sky, but not the same sky. The clouds were atomic. You couldn't see all that existing in the temporal plane, which he was not.

That is until the blonde girl came back into his focus, towering like *The Thirty Foot Bride from Candy Rock*. She popped her jeans and pushed them down her long pink legs, kicking them off. He was in the temporal world now. Her white top came off over her head and Jamey watched it drop on the jeans. She reached behind and unsnapped her bra, pulling it forward and dropping it on the pile of clothes, her lovely breasts and fascinating nipples exposed, perhaps for the first time, to the warm sunlight and certainly to Jamey's gaze. Jamey couldn't turn his eyes from her. Her skin was *so* beautiful. How many thousands of colors could he discern? She continued, as if nobody would notice, rolling her pretty paisley underpants to the sandy mound of clothes. Jamey was agape now, staring at her curly lightly golden colored hair. She had more hair than he did, and definitely more than Teri Ann. Every other male on the beach certainly noticed. And the two other girls also seemed to notice, though Jamey barely caught the bad vibes. "Come on, everyone!" she cried out, "Let's all get naked!"

Through it all, there was no concern about her indiscretion drawing the rangers or the police. The cove was isolated and not approachable by land vehicles. A hippie could smoke dope, take drugs, get naked, even have sex at the cove, and never have to deal with the man.

The fellows were quick to go along with the suggestion. The other girls were more reluctant, but they didn't delay for very long as the party ran down to the water's edge. "Come on!" the brown-eyed girl called to Jamey. He rousted himself, dropped his clothes, and plunged into the water with the party at the shoreline. The boys were in heaven. It couldn't have been engineered by any of them.

Jamey was still peaking and not able to organize his thoughts, but the water and the sun and the occasional contact with the girls felt profoundly beautiful. Jamey stood in the water, hardly conscious of his own nakedness, and watched his new friends cavorting, with the vast ocean as a backdrop. The girls with their youthful breasts and glorious complexions seemed to be a part of the ocean, like they were lost mermaids home at last.

With the breeze coming in from the ocean, the party was dressed again, forming a circle around a fire. They roasted hot dogs, of which Jamey had two. These helped to calm his stomach and helped him to regain some equilibrium. The hippies had brought sodas and wine, and they shared it with Jamey. Jamey, in turn, shared his music, and everyone shared their love, to a point. They went back to their jam on Jamey's new song.

As the freak takes you
Follow the Tao
Nobody else
It's only for now
I do my own thing
Into your dream
Look at yourself
Don't she make the scene?

14

He was in better shape now that he was beyond peaking. The naked play seemed in the distant past as the evening came on. "It's pretty amazing, man, how the music comes out of these vibrating strings," one of the dudes observed.

"And like the vocal cords are vibrating, too, man..."

"Far fuckin' out! It's all just vibrations..."

"And waves, man," added the flautist.

"I'm diggin' it..."

As the summer sun was setting over the Pacific, the party packed up its things. The girls' parents expected them home by a particular curfew, and if they were going to meet it, they explained, it was time to vacate the scene. The party climbed the trails that had been etched into the high cliffs behind the cove, no doubt by those ancient Indians, leaving a still stoned Jamey on the beach, the sole master of the cove at sunset: A solitary acid head on the beach.

Then it was dark. Jamey kept the fire going for a long while. He was meditating in an acid haze on where to go from here, on missing Teri Ann, on how beautiful the cool night was at the beach. But things never stay the same. The tide was coming in to reclaim the cove up to the rocks. He climbed about half way up the cliff, securing his guitar and backpack against the ocean, to a lookout or make-out spot he knew from previous explorations. The fire was soon washed away. It was a long and lonely night, full of thinking about the past, present, and future. He played on his guitar and sang to the seagulls, just like Joni Mitchell. Jamey had no better idea of how to proceed at the end of the day than he had had at the beginning. But he was resolved on not going back home. He needed an audience for his music.

Even in summer, the night was a good deal colder next to the Pacific Ocean than it was in the warm Valley where Jamey had grown up and had spent the previous night. He was stranded up in the rocks where he shivered and tried to get his sleep under the stars, listening to the waves as the acid and meth continued to turn in his mind. He did finally fall into a light sleep secluded behind the rocks, up above the cove.

BUS STOP

IN THE EARLY MORNING MIST he awakened to a unique unidentified crying sound. It might have been the gulls that Joni had been going on about, but it wasn't. When he looked down from his perch, he found a couple that likely thought they were quite alone in nature. Jamey kept his head low, but watched the two having sex on their sleeping bag. The girl was making all kinds of interesting and wonderful noises as she wrapped her legs around her boyfriend's head and later around his back. They gave themselves over to one another's pleasure, and Jamey couldn't remember Teri Ann Murphy crying out so deeply and with such lust and abandon. Either she had been doing it wrong or he had. Maybe that's why she dumped him, he reflected. There was something more to sex than he had yet discovered, but this pair was on to it.

Jamey was in the ungentlemanly position of spying on the lovers because his appearance now would give away the fact that he had already shared their intimacy. That seemed wrong to him. Teri Ann would have freaked. So he remained hidden as long as the lovers owned the beach. They had fallen asleep entwined. Later, he observed the young woman, now standing beside the bag, her naked back to Jamey. He wasn't sure what she was doing at first when she bent completely forward, but he realized that she was brushing out her hair, perhaps tangled from the misty air of the morning or whatever causes tangled hair. She could have remained in that equally charming and revealing stance with her legs slightly spread for as long as she liked and Jamey wouldn't have given up his seat. But in time she ran down to the water where, shivering, she waded into the ocean. She stayed in the water only briefly. Her man was asleep on the sand and she seemed to feel altogether alone at the seashore, walking slowly back to their bedding, completely naked in the gray morning light.

Since leaving home, Jamey had already seen four completely naked girls, and in marvelous detail. He had seen Teri Ann, but it was usually pretty dark. Her breasts in the moonlight. A flash of the inner thighs. The pink of her bottom. Her pretty legs stretched out as she replaced her underwear before going home.

Had he known about the naked girls part, he would have run away sooner. The young woman was pulling her peasant blouse from under the still body of her boyfriend when he woke up to see her towering over him, another thirty foot lady. He reached for her calves, but she escaped his grab and soon they were running and playing on the beach in the margin of the water. Jamey had to wait for the naked lovers to make out some more. It looked like a love generation poster. If by chance we meet naked on a deserted beach, *go for it.*

Jamey lost sight of the girl and was left with a view of the naked, hairy, and muscular back of the dude. Her arms sometimes rose up his ass or his lower back. Jamey had never experienced this for himself, but his extensive reading of pornography helped him to understand what was happening. Jamey watched the muscles of the dude's ass contract and then relax as he arched his back and looked up to the sky as the morning light shone down behind him bursting in glory over the cliff to find the lovers at the edge of the surf.

They slowly dressed and rolled up the sleeping bag. Jamey had no way to know what time it was. He figured it to be about eight or nine of a Sunday morning. The lovers exited the scene over the rocks that led to the longer beach from whence Jamey had come to this apparently quite busy bit of isolation. Only after they had departed could he finally reclaim his beach. There was just a little of the lovers' dregs at the bottom of the bottle which he used for washing out his morning mouth. He had come down from the acid and was feeling played out. In his previous life, the day after an acid trip might have found him drifting in the pool with a tall glass of iced orange juice. But he didn't have time for a headache now.

Jamey was a lad, and he was hungry again. If the clock could stop and little things like hunger could be put aside, he might have been satisfied to become the beachcomber. But even boney hippies like to eat. Unless he got lucky and another tribe of hippies came along, Jamey would have to do some foraging back in society, but the money thing was getting to be a drag. He could look ahead and Missy's money wouldn't last very long.

Possessions in hand, he went back over the rocks and along the access road that paralleled the long beach. He decided to impose some discipline, so he passed on getting a breakfast at the Zuma stand. It smelled pretty good, though. He hiked up to PCH, put out his thumb, and was quickly riding south toward Santa Monica in a red pick-up truck. Jamey had no plan, and he wasn't rapidly forming one, perhaps due to the dullness in his head after the acid. It takes a little out of a person.

It was lonely out on his own, and hitching afforded Jamey the

17

opportunity to converse. The roughneck asked him if he needed a job, which he did indeed if he was going to live on his own. The man told him that there might be openings at a foundry just east of downtown Los Angeles, off of the 10. He could come in on Monday and see if there were any openings for a beginner. He advised Jamey that he would probably want to trim his golden curls. He would probably take a ribbing if he came in like that. When Jamey asked him what a foundry was, the redneck was at first bewildered. "You don't know what a foundry is?" The bewilderment turned to disgust.

"I never heard the word," said Jamey. "What do you do?"

The conversation just sort of died out after that. Jamey disembarked at Will Rogers's Beach and offered his thanks. He climbed the concrete stairs and took the bridge over to the palisades, catching a whiff of marijuana when three hippies passed him. Two women, maybe a little older than Margaret, were having their pictures taken by one of their husbands, Jamey guessed, with the Pacific Ocean as their background. Jamey heard one of the women saying to the other, "I thought it would be bigger. On the map, it looks so much bigger than the other oceans."

"Fuckin' idiot," thought Jamey, though he was still musing over the question of what a foundry might be.

Jamey was feeling alone and on the edge, and he had only been away from home for a little more than thirty-six hours. He walked along the busy pedestrian streets of the seaside town. He stopped at a coffee shop for breakfast around Fourth Street. It was a good breakfast, but he found it hard to enjoy given that he knew how much it cost. He didn't even like leaving a tip, but he had been raised properly.

Between the two meals, his bus fare, and his acid trip, Jamey's twenty dollars was already less than fifteen. Everything had been a necessary expense, and he had gotten a free meal from the kids on the beach the day before. His last bath was in the Pacific with the naked sirens of the previous afternoon. His hair was increasingly knotted, even matted in places. While Jamey didn't have Teri Ann's most delicate concern regarding sand, some sand had indeed permeated his person. A shower and a complete change of clothes was the obvious solution, but that luxury was not available. He felt somewhat untidy.

After breakfast, a little depressed after the drugs, but refreshed with the food, coffee, and drink, he hitched his way along Santa Monica Blvd. One corner led to another. One car after the other, a Volkswagen beetle, a Corvette, a hippie bus, through Beverly Hills—where a fellow could be stopped by the police in bright daylight just for smiling on a sunny day, to paraphrase The Dead.

At Doheney, Jamey passed The Troubadour, where some of the big names played when they came to L.A. He planned to be on that stage someday soon. In the afternoon July sun, it didn't look so impressive, but places like the Troubadour, the Aquarius, the Whisky, the Greek, and the Bowl were all on Jamey's agenda. And it wouldn't be long because Jamey didn't have any other plans. At that point, he hitched up to Hollywood Boulevard. There were hippies up that-a-way, and he figured that he wouldn't be noticed by the cops if he kept his head down and played it cool. He didn't ask himself if Hollywood was in need of another vagabond hippie. He was reporting for duty like thousands upon thousands of underage runaways and adventurers.

It was maybe two in the afternoon when Jamey arrived in Hollywood, walking the Sunset Strip and Hollywood Boulevard after that. Like the beach, like Santa Monica, there were Sunday summer crowds groovin'. He met a clear-eyed fellow from Scientology who talked to Jamey for twenty minutes. It seemed like an hour. Jamey was thinking that he could get a whole lot clearer on the concept over a cup of coffee paid for by the blowhard, but no such luck came his way. Jamey did allow as how he carried a goodly number of engrams, but he said that he thought it could be worse. His wise-acre persona hadn't been humbled by two nights in the elements. It was his only survival skill, and not very impressive at that, but it was in tact. There was some questioning about Jamey's background, but on that score he lied outright, saying that he had left home when the car they were living in had finally broken down. Whether because he didn't believe that Jamey was talking straight or Jamey seemed like a penniless prospect, he went his own way leaving Jamey to find his.

Jamey exchanged some "Hey, mans…" with a kid on a street corner who wanted to bum a smoke from Jamey who had none to offer. Jamey was out in the wide world on his own, and that was for real. But he still felt like a tourist. Everything was new to him. Ian, this kid on the corner, had been in Hollywood for a while. He looked considerably more beat up and worn down, no longer wide-eyed, but he was hep to the jive. They talked a little because Jamey had wanted to. "Where can a guy crash?" was what Jamey wanted to know. "Are there any, like, you know, free clinics for sleeping?" Where were all the crash pads you heard about in the Hippie Report? Ian seemed to know the streets.

"No, man," he answered incredulously. "They'd have to turn you in.

You're pretty young, no offense, and too pretty for the streets. I wasn't sure if you were a girl pretending to be a guy, like a disguise."

"What are you talkin' about?" Jamey complained.

"You can't go to the shelters, man, 'cause it's a bust. They'll want to help you, and you know that's trouble."

"So what do you do?" Jamey asked.

The kid turned his head away. "I work," he said. "I work at night mostly. You know." Jamey not only didn't know, but he didn't suspect. For all he could guess, the kid worked at the foundry. "I mean, if you want me to connect you to someone. You could have a place tonight. I mean, they'd like *you.*"

"But what kind of work is it?" asked Jamey, oblivious to the obvious. "I mean, I worked in a plumbing yard. I can work hard."

Ian didn't have all day. He shook his head. "I turn tricks, man."

"Magic?"

If the foundry worker was irritated by Jamey's ignorance of the working world, Jamey's present interlocutor was incredulous. "Shit, man," he said, breaking it down. "I stand on the corner and get into cars and suck cock for cash. I'm a fuckin' prostitute! Shit! Don't you know anything?"

Jamey didn't like his ignorance exposed. He liked to think of himself as tuned in and up-to-date, but this was new territory for the Valley boy. It was almost an academic approach. "So it's like homosexual stuff?" said Jamey.

"I guess you could say that, man," said Ian. "I mean. Well, anyway, good luck, man. I gotta get back. But if you ever need work, I can get you connected. You can find me along this block. I really think they'd like you. Pretty hair. Nice ass. No offense."

"It's cool," said Jamey, who usually said it was cool, whether it was or wasn't. Jamey's mind was temporarily blown.

Later in the afternoon, Jamey was sitting on a bus bench, careful to move away if an actual bus came along. But it was RTD and Sunday, so that didn't happen very often. He absorbed sunlight and watched the people going by. There really were all kinds, and this was Sunday, tourist day. He watched the people in the cars as well as walking by on the street. Some were cool, bopping to the ever-present sixties music, presumably, and you could see uptightness on the faces of some others. Well, why wouldn't they be uptight? They were in Hollywood traffic.

Jamey had been to Hollywood, to the Whiskey, to the Troubadour down the road, and to the Aquarius for shows. Usually, he and Craig couldn't get in because of the drinking age, but they would hang around if any of their heroes were playing. Sometimes they hitched and sometimes one of their buddies with a license was driving. Lately, Craig Roman had gotten his license and they would take the folks' blue Volkswagen. But Jamey had never done it on his own. He was a lot less confident, with nobody with him and no home to fall back upon. He was putting off the real problem of where he would be sleeping that night. It was too late to get back to the cove now, but he could get back tomorrow. Who knows? Maybe there would be more naked chicks. But it was cold at night along the cove.

In a sudden vision, a very pretty young woman in a flowing white top and an ankle length skirt with at least one white underskirt sat down on Jamey's bus bench. His eyes were drawn to her bare ankle. The side of her face and the top of her breasts were pink and white. She looked nice to Jamey, like a chicken dinner looks very tasty on the table just before dining. She wore a strong sweet fragrance, suggesting that she had just completed her ablutions and was just setting off for her day, despite the time. She turned to him, and he realized when he looked directly at her that she was not a small boned girl. You could almost put two Teri Anns in her outfit, but that would have been too many. The white girl's face was heavy, but it was pretty and ever so pink. Her arms were substantial, and, reviewing now, even her ankles had a fleshy appeal. But she was just young enough, he thought, that she might be interested in him. Jamey was a very small guy and might have gotten lost in this sweet cream pie, but he was willing to take that risk. He was sixteen, and he still believed in miracles. As it played out, she did, too.

"Have you accepted Jesus Christ as your Lord and Personal Savior?" she asked. Her eyes were bugged, and she was seeing, at least, the illusion of the light. There was a small macramé cross hanging by a string over the parting of her breasts. She was beautiful, he thought. And this missionary business seemed such a waste to Jamey. She was *a darling bud of May* and he could not imagine that she would ever be so lovely and beautiful again if *every fair from fair sometime declines*. He had that one cold because Miss LeAnn Curtis liked to teach it. He realized that he was even missing Miss Curtis and her J.B. Priestly English Lit text. What was Miss Curtis up to?

But there was a question before the bus bench, so Jamey turned the question around. "Do you believe whole-heartedly in the teachings of Don Juan as outlined by Carlos Castañeda? Do you think love is all you need? Do you believe in a beach that never ends 'cause I know one, baby." This sort of response is what used to get him clocked back at the high school. But he soon lost interest in teasing the girl when he saw that she was not diverted from her script, but only waiting to resume.

She was patient with the uninitiated, and she began to tell a story that didn't ask for responses, though she got a few. "One day, you look out your window and there's a man across the street." She had the sweetest little southern accent and a very calming voice. He just wanted to curl up against her breasts and listen to her gentle breathing. "He seems calm and peaceful, so you go on about your life. The next day he's on your own front lawn. And the next he's on your front porch." Jamey couldn't help but wonder how she might look with her knees raised and her thighs spread. Very pink, he imagined. It just flashed as her lips smiled and she continued the rant.

"Then he's in your living room, rearranging your furniture. One by one, he takes out your old shabby things and brings in new and elegant fine furniture."

"And then the cops come because they need to haul him away…" An odd line from the vagabond Jamey Craig, but it seemed right at the time.

"Then he does your kitchen the same way."

"He better stay out of my sister's bathroom, if he knows what's good for him."

"In time, he's replaced every single piece of furniture in your house and made it better than it had been. Then he does the same thing with your clothes and your towels and the food in your kitchen. So, day after day, week after week, month after month, this person has been improving your life in every single way. At first, you were wary of him. You didn't trust him. But, little by little, you saw the results. You knew that whatever he did for you, it would make your life better and better every day, every week, every month, and every year."

"And every lifetime, too?" said Jamey. "Next life, *I'm* going to be the walrus."

"Well, that's exactly what Jesus does for you. At first, you don't know what to think. You've been living your sinful life…"

"Hey! You don't know that…" It was true, of course.

"…for so very long, that you think goodness and light are things to be afraid of. But, as you grow in your faith, it gets easier and easier to just accept Jesus, and live by his guidance, to accept his grace."

"So this is like a Jesus parable except it's about Jesus. That's a pretty good story, Miss," said Jamey. "And I like the way you tell it. Like a tape recorder. Your voice is beautiful. I could listen to you forever. You got any more stories? Like Scheherazade? Maybe we could talk about it over coffee at your place 'til the sun comes up. Mine's being renovated at the moment."

"Well," she said, as the bus pulled up, "You think about what I told you. Maybe Jesus is knocking on your door right now."

"If he looks like you, I'm gonna let him in," Jamey was saying. She had a radiant smile, a gift from the Gods—or a one true God as the case may be. She waved behind as she got on the bus, taking her white shiny ankle with her, and flashing a final smile at Jamey, who didn't want to let her go. "I'd follow her to Heaven," he whispered. He liked that idea for a song. Maybe a repeating hook, and each verse about the phases of life. Noble girl saves dissolute man. Maybe she dies, like "Honey," and he's thinking about suicide. He thought that sounded country-western, and Roman was pretty good on slide.

> *I'd follow her to heaven*
> *I'd leave it all right now*
> *To make love to my Angel---Holy Cow!*

But Jamey thought more about the girl than the song. He was sorry that he had let her get away, but he had to admit that he didn't have anywhere to bring her if she had been hot for him. She reminded him of some songs and that reminded him that he didn't have his tunes. He was missing his record player and his records, just as he was missing his regular meals at the air-conditioned castle he called home.

BEELZEBUB BOOGIE

As the afternoon shadows began to fall, Jamey was afraid that he would attract too much attention hanging out on the bus bench indefinitely. And getting picked up by the cops was a one way ticket back to Knollridge, and to who knows what? Reform school? He wasn't sure what the next step would be after punching the dad and staying away from home for—it seemed like a week—two nights and then getting busted by the pigs: Major uptight scene, and one to be avoided.

So he made his way down the boulevard, fairly directionless, looking more and more the vagabond part and less the day-tripper he had felt at first. An older brother joined him on another bus bench, offering Jamey a Kool, which Jamey gladly accepted. He didn't have the money for a luxury like smoking, but a cigarette was welcome. The man lighted the cigarette for the boy.

"Did you ever eat a pussy?" he asked. Jamey was astounded. As a conversation starter or just a way to pass the time, this was unique in Jamey's experience. Back in Knollridge, it might have been something like, "Hot enough for ya?" Among the guys, it might have been, "Check out those tits…" But this was beyond all of that.

"Not really?" Jamey answered.

"Good. You ever look at that mess? That stuff is ugly!" The gentleman laughed and provided his own "Mmmm…hmmm's." Too much time had passed, and Jamey hadn't come up with a reasonable response. On his own account, especially after the last twenty-four hours and the four naked girls, he was inclined to disagree. But he allowed as how he hadn't really been up close and personal, in a visual sense. He would have to withhold his judgment.

"You look like you need a place to stay," the gentleman observed. "I'm Buck. You need a place?" Jamey looked at Buck's rough features, his graying hair, and the scar on his face He was not giving off a flower child vibe.

"I guess," said Jamey, suddenly wary. He was suspicious, but he was also feeling guilty. He had very little experience with blacks. He hadn't felt like an oppressor, but he did feel uncomfortable. There were a handful of

24

brothers at Knollridge High. One was a high achieving college bound type who, no matter his race, would have had no truck with hippies like Jamey Craig and Craig Roman. He was going with a white girl, a Janis Ian thing, again a girl who would have had no use for Jamey under any circumstances.

Another guy was mixed black and Mexican, Gilbert Jimenez. Jamey didn't really know what the guy's origins might have been, but as he understood matters, Mexican covered anything in the Spanish speaking world. Gilbert had a party band which Jamey had gone to check out at a party on the east side—of Balboa. The genre was so foreign to Jamey that he figured there just wasn't any competition between Crazy Place and Gilbert Jimenez. Jimenez and company played old time dance music, soul classics, and Oldies-but-Goodies. Sort of Ruben and the Jets.

But despite Jamey's effort to love his fellow man, whether it was the blackness or something else entirely, there was something actually unsavory about this guy on the bench. They talked a little, but it was only a few minutes before they got to the question.

"You about hungry?" the man inquired.

"I'm all right," said Jamey.

"Got a place?"

"I'm looking," was the reply.

Buck had more to do in life than sit on a bench like Jamey. "You ever turn tricks?" Jamey was puzzled. He knew what it meant now, thanks to Ian, but he couldn't understand how the question applied to himself. Certain unfortunate girls turned tricks. Even Ian. But not a potential rock star like Jamey Craig.

"I'm not into that."

"Well, how you earn your money?"

"I'm looking for a job," said Jamey, who was beginning to think that none of this was anybody's business. The man was looking at Jamey, more overtly than the way Jamey had been eyeing the Christian chick. "Look, I gotta split. Thanks for the smoke."

"I can get you a place to stay, and you could make thirty bucks a night," he said. "You're *real* nice, honey. How's that sound? I'll teach you what to do."

Jamey's jaw dropped open, which was probably not a good strategy under the circumstances. The idea that he would work as a prostitute was beyond anything he had ever imagined. Who would have any use for him? It was repellant and bizarre at the same time. Jamey was up and walking away with his frayed guitar case and his back pack on his shoulder.

He looked back to the bench where he had been hanging, but Buck had already disappeared. Jamey was creeped out now. First the kid. Now the brother. There is definitely a house in New Orleans, but Jamey wasn't planning to take up residence there.

Jamey spent a lot of his time building songs in his head. He had some chords in mind as he started working out a song to cover this scene. As he worked it out in his head, he kept thinking of the parts that Mark, Paul, and Craig could do. He was even trying to figure out who could do the imagined keyboard part on it. He wasn't used to being a strictly solo act.

The Kool had had a strange flavor as cigarettes go. There was, perhaps, a taste of sulfur. The whole thing with Buck was way creepy. As he turned it over in his mind, his song was taking its form.

The devil, he's got me
He's chillin' my soul
I know I ain't never
Gonna see no crimson and gold
'Cause Mr. Satan, he's comin''
I don't gotta be told
I guess it's all over
Man, I'm feelin' so old...
I'm on my way home

He came upon a corner where some shaved heads were gathered. It was a posse of Hollywood-Buddhist monks. There was an underlying buzz going on as they stood in a circle and made a scene of themselves. One of the acolytes approached Jamey, asking if he knew the Buddhist chant, "Nam myo ho ren gay kyo?"

This fellow was not as pretty as the angelic Jesus freak who had materialized on the bench, but he was not as distasteful as Jamey's most recent smoking partner. Jamey had no place to go, so he engaged these "monks" if only to get the taste of Buck out of his mouth, so to speak. He learned that anything he needed, wanted, or just thought he might like to check out he could have by the daily and repeated recitation of "Nam myo ho ren gay kyo." This sounded like a silly plan to Jamey, but he had been raised to believe that bread and wine was the body and blood, so he didn't cast stones.

"So just straight across," said Jamey, clarifying the deal. "I do the chant, and the stuff comes in? See? 'Cause the problem is I need a lot of stuff. Like, for instance, some place to sleep tonight—that doesn't involve prostitution, that is. Is there some place I can crash around here, man? I mean, I could clean up the kitchen or take out the trash, but I need a place to crash."

He was assured that all would be well and that all manner of things would be well if he took to chanting, though it would be greatly enhanced if he purchased a gohonzon from Nichrine Soshu, Inc. Given Jamey's rather strained funds, he just couldn't raise the capital necessary to bring all of his worldly and spiritual goals into his hands. But it would have been cool.

The monk did mention that Jamey might make his way to skid row in downtown Los Angeles where he might find accommodations for the night. It was kindly meant, but it seemed a long way to go. Jamey knew a little about Hollywood from his occasional pilgrimages with his band mates, but the rest of the city was foreign and frightening. There were hippies here, and here he planned to stay, at least for the night. He was already wishing that he was back at the Zuma cove. But you didn't get discovered sitting on the beach.

Jamey, by nature, was easily swayed. He would fall for most anything. Owsley was a saint. Clapton was a God. Dylan was the greatest poet since Shakespeare, and Bobby Kennedy was a knight in shining armor. He believed in music. He believed in acid. Love is all you need. And he had believed in the love of Teri Ann Murphy. But, even with all of that, organized religions seemed to be so extraordinarily stupid, so completely blithered and brainless, that not even this most gullible boy on the boulevard was tempted. Scientology, Nichrine Soshu, Jesus in white panties—it didn't matter. Jamey was sixteen and far too sophisticated for such myths. He was equally sure that the employment opportunities that had come his way thus far were out of the question. But it was getting darker now, which, on Hollywood Boulevard, meant that the lights were coming on.

There were plenty of bright lights on the boulevards, but there were few doors open to the flower child. He hung out in the record shop, just to groove on the tunes that were playing: Still a lot of Stones with the recent passing of Brian Jones. He got a Coke at the donut shop. He figured that was rent on a table for a good long while. He thought about renting a room. They had one night cheap hotels, but he calculated that that would bring his sum to zero in a matter of a day or two, so what would have been gained? He held onto his money, knowing it had to last him for the rest of his life.

He thought about camping in a doorway, but he couldn't stand a roust. He knew he couldn't crash on the street. He checked out the neighborhoods above the boulevard, but it looked more uptight than his hometown of Knollridge. It flashed on him that no doubt many a homeless vagabond had already tried this ploy and that the suspicious folks were watching him through their windows ready to pounce if he planted his flag. He was a suspicious looking character carrying his guitar case and wearing his backpack, but even Jesus in the white girl's story wouldn't have had any luck with these folks. The second he grabbed their black and white TV to replace it with a Zenith color model, the fuzz would be all over him and they'd nail him to a cross on the front lawn.

Jamey let the time get later because he had that power, if not much else. He didn't want to be noticed setting up his camp. He eventually found an alcove in an alley that had never gone through from block to block. There was a loading dock into a locked-up warehouse. There wasn't a lot of debris, so he put down his stuff to the far side of the trash bins. They were not as fragrant as Margaret's clean sheets, but the price was right on a summer night.

And all of this because of a hair cut? He never could talk to the old man, but he hadn't really been that bad to Jamey over the years. More and more they were at odds, but it was just that the old man couldn't handle the sixties. It was a lot to ask: To just let your kids go crazy and do whatever the fuck they felt like. You keep them safe until they're fifteen, and then you let them play with fire on the freeway? Of course you had to lay down the law now and then. Even Jamey could see it.

He was wavering at times. He wanted to go home. He realized that it was lame. How was he going to make it without any support? But you had to go through some shit to make it. So he decided, again and again, that he had to hang in there. He couldn't go home now. He had to prove something to his pop. He had to somehow make it, even if that only meant getting a job. Getting a job was the new plan and first thing on his morning agenda. And that was kind of a trip since that's exactly what the old man had been telling him to do.

One thing about living on the street that Jamey had never realized was the loneliness. He had talked to various folks all day long, but none of it was real. He was alone in the crowded Hollywood party. The Buddhists, the Scientology freak, and even the white linen angel were all plastic. The girl was very good plastic work, and he really had no complaints there, but she was plastic like most everything else he encountered. She was selling something and not really being straight. Nothing was real in this plastic land.

Well, almost nothing. He had had a burger and a Coke, and earlier he had had some donuts. The food was pretty real. Real enough that his fifteen was now closer to eleven. And each of those stops brought home another revelation. The longer he lived on the street and the dirtier and more disheveled he became, the more the straights were wary of him. Now when he walked into a burger joint or the donut shop, they wanted to see the money up front. And there were no niceties. He may have had the quarter for the Coke, but he wasn't someone they wanted around the place. Take your drink and go, like a stray dog—that had a quarter for a Coke. He was feeling a sense of isolation, poverty's desperate companion.

He never cared in school when it seemed that the hard guys, the jocks, the ROTC's, and the other guardians of societal norms were actively against him. He had had his band mates, his friends, and his talent. He had people who cared about him. But if he tried to see any of them now, the nets would descend. That left him with only his talent, and there didn't seem to be much use for that tonight.

It wasn't like going to San Francisco with a flower in your hair like in the song. There were lots of pretty people and everything was fuckin' beautiful and all that, but the beautiful people seemed to have the money. It was hard and lonely for the lad, and not as groovy as the songs had suggested. But he decided he had just been feeling sorry for himself, which was true, and figured he had to get it together. He tried to sleep, but he didn't do very well. He would sometimes hear persons stumbling by. Once he heard someone rummaging in the cans. He curled up and hid, avoiding any contact. But, as the morning light hit the alley, he had made it through another night, wearier than he had felt when the sun had gone down.

THE UNIVERSAL SOLDIER

Monday morning. He had spent three nights hiding out now. He was hungry. And he was thinking about his mother. She had been cool, he thought. He decided that she deserved to know that he was relatively safe. His dad would be on a job, so he called his home from a phone booth on Hollywood Boulevard. It was Missy who answered, as he had expected. Jamey properly warned her not to react emotionally.

"She's at the market."

"Cool. I just called to say I'm groovin'. I just wanted you and Mom to know that I'm fine. Healthy, really. Thanks for the money, too. It's really helped."

"Healthy, then?" said Missy. "That's what you want to say? Where are you?"

"I'm in, uh, Big Sur. But don't tell anyone. Hippie commune stuff. Smoking pot. Very cool. You can tell Mom that I called, and I know she'll tell Dad. And let Craig and the guys know that I'm groovy. Okay?"

"Craig has been very nice about all of this," said Missy. "He's a good guy. How'd you get to Big Sur?" she asked.

"Thumb ticket," said Jamey. He was suddenly beginning to feel too much. Jamey's voice tended to get too high when he was upset, and he didn't want to let on. "Listen, I have to hang up now. Long distance and all. I just wanted to let you know that I'm cool, and that I love you. And tell Mom the same."

"What about Daddy?" she said. "Any message?"

"Tell him the *queer faggot boy* is fine," said Jamey.

"I won't! Take care of yourself, Jamey," she advised. "I wish you could come home. You know that you can, don't you? You could come home, and everything would be the way it was."

"That's the bummer. It would be exactly the same. Okay, I have to go. Peace and love." Hanging up on Missy was not easy. Her voice was beautiful. She represented home to him, and he was mightily homesick. It wasn't easy to walk down the road to nowhere when each step was away from home. How could people be so cool and calm all the time when there was a world of feeling all around them? It was like oceans of emotions.

The remaining eleven dollars might carry Jamey through two or three more days. He tried to run down some work as a dishwasher, a janitor, or whatever was needed. He tried the carwash. But even if he got through the obvious barrier of his unkempt hippie appearance, he had no phone number to leave for later consideration. Someone would have to hire him on the spot, an unlikely event. It amounted to another day hanging out and getting nothing accomplished. He wasn't looking or feeling as fresh as he had been.

Jamey was seeing the brightly illuminated but seedy Hollywood night life more realistically now. He had been around for a day or two, and it wasn't so dazzling anymore. He paid more attention to the commerce of the street. There were girls getting into cars, and on other corners there were boys. He even ran across his old friend Ian a couple of times. There were plenty of hippies on the boulevard. Jamey listened to some of the street musicians, and, as it got late, he had made a decision.

Exhausted, he stopped at a joint between the boulevards that had a big Rooms-for-Rent sign painted on the side of the red brick building. The man at the counter, Jack, didn't ask any questions except whether Jamey had the money, which he handed over. Jack walked him up two flights. "Noon check-out," he said. "Out by noon."

Even though Jamey was paying fair and square, he still felt like he was some kind of criminal. Jack wasn't going to call the cops, but it still felt creepy. The bed wasn't as fresh as something made by Margaret, but it was a lot nicer than the concrete and blacktop floors he had been sleeping on. He washed his clothes in the sink, took a shower in the communal bathroom, and even shaved his face. He played his guitar for the first time since the beach scene, but he was missing an audience.

Now close your loving eyes
And float away from my heart
You know I've loved you for so long
I've forgotten my solo part
And I know I've done you wrong
And I know that you'd forgive
So maybe it's right your folks still love you
And told you never
Never to see me again
Imaginin'

He slept better than he had been sleeping in the alley, but he was awakened several times by the groaning and creaking of the bed next door. Every hour or two it seemed to start up again until it stopped around three-thirty in the morning.

Early the next day, with his guitar and backpack more or less safe in the room, he tried the job quest again. He had seen hippies working along side the Mexicans and blacks at the carwash, so he tried it again, this time looking a little better for the shower. But he came up empty. He barely got back to Rooms-for-Rent in time to recover his things. With a small meal, the funding was down to two bucks, and he looked about as clean as he was ever likely to look. He made many attempts to get some work, but he looked a little goofy with his backpack and guitar case. He was young, without identification, and, perhaps unbeknownst to himself, he looked a little feminine with his long hair and ruddy summer cheeks. He was just a baby-face and he didn't look as if he were up to a day of hard labor. He had gambled on a shower and he had lost. Except that his butt was better, and that matters. But another night was ahead of him, and he was running out of options.

Jamey had been too chicken to try it before, but he had seen others doing it. In the evening hours, he set up shop on a corner near a club and started playing as a street musician. If he could make a dollar, that would be a burger and a coke or fries. He only had to make a dollar, singing for his supper. He played Beatles, Simon and Garfunkle, and some old rockers just for fun. He tried a few originals to no effect. He was still working on "Imagine Yourself."

You can't take company
She said she always knew
Freedom's kinda lonely
As the freak takes you

Jamey took his courage from the audience. The more the audience gave back, the better he got. But there was no juice out on the corner. He tried to make eye contact, especially with the girls, as he used to do from the stage in the gym, but he was no longer the rock and roll star that he had fancied himself. He was invisible or worse, distasteful. The pretty legs and tiny thin skirts walked right on by with no smile for the troubadour.

Still, after a couple of long hours, he had actually raised about a dollar and a half which did provide a meal for the night. This made him a professional musician as he had always wanted to be. His diet was increasingly limited: donuts, burgers, hot dogs, fries, and soda. He couldn't afford even much of that. The kitty was just over $2.00, so the day had been marginally profitable.

He slipped back into his alley to spend a fifth night on the lam. As was getting to be usual, he didn't sleep very well. It was smelly, uncomfortable, and he was always alert for sounds, for intruders. He realized that these were the good times, summer in Los Angeles. When the fall and winter months came down, with the wind, rain, and cold, it could get a lot worse. But Jamey meant to resolve the job thing long before that happened.

Late in the night, another unsteady walk came along. Another drunk. Jamey scrunched up in a corner in an attempt to hide should someone look to the side of the bin, which they hadn't done to date. This scavenger was lingering and rattling the boxes, looking for what Jamey never knew. "You might as well come out," he said in a calm twangy matter-of-fact voice. "Looks like you and me jumped into the same foxhole. Better show yourself."

Jamey hid his stuff behind the bin and stood up as tall as he could, but he was barely taller than the bins. The other fellow was a big guy, but he wasn't so scary after a moment because Jamey noticed a disabling limp that, judging from the expression that flashed across his face from time to time, caused him serious pain. He sometimes ministered to it with a bottle of wine that was even cheaper than Teri Ann Murphy's Pink Chablis.

"Let me tell you something, boy. Your idea was a good one. You're down at the end and even if someone encroaches on your perimeter, they probably won't never get to you. Problem is that this is walled off on three sides, see? You're in a box. So, if they do find you, you have nowhere to go, and, I'm guessing, no artillery to blow them back, to punch a whole in their line and skedaddle. Am I right?"

"No artillery," Jamey admitted.

"I don't carry none, neither," he said. "I think about it sometimes. I have a weapon. But the point is they got you cornered here from the git-go. You need an escape route. Keep the supply lines open." He added, "I'm Mitch."

Jamey repeated, "Mitch."

"You're supposed to identify yourself."

"Jamey Craig, sir."

"Sir?" he laughed. "That's what we call assholes, Jamey. Right before we frag 'em. Mitch is fine." Every now and then, Mitch took another swig.

It didn't look as if it would last too much longer.

"How'd you know I was here? How'd you know I wasn't a threat?"

"I got eagle ears," he said. "On patrol, you better learn to listen or a sniper can take you down like that." Appropriate snap of the fingers. "Seen it done many a time. I knowed you was here from the right off the git-go. And I know you stuffed some things behind the can. Anything good? Anything I might want?"

"Some clothes and a guitar," said Jamey, resigned to losing his stuff. He knew he could outrun the gimp in the open, but gathering his stuff and breaking out was the problem, as Mitch had pointed out. Mitch looked through the backpack and the guitar case. "Well, sir," he said. "I wouldn't fit any of your gear, even the skivvies. I knew a whore in Saigon could fit some of that, but no *man* I ever met. No room for the balls, ya see? But I do admire the razor," he said.

"You can have it," said Jamey, as if he had a choice. "It's used, though, so watch it."

"Aw, you can't eat it," he answered. "Problem number two, soldier. Logistics. You're carrying too much equipment. You'll start to sink in the big muddy and never make it out on the other side."

Jamey had been feeling the same, bogged down with his stuff, but it all seemed essential to him. They settled down against the back wall against the loading dock. "Between the two of us, I reckon we can handle any incursions tonight. Just follow my lead. When you get the chance, make a break for it. You won't be able to take all your stuff—and maybe none of it. Meanwhile, I'm starved for rations, and I could use a drink, to boot. But we got shit. So why don't you take out that damned instrument of yours and play me some music in this piss hole, and let's see if it's worth keeping your instrument or not. I got eagle ears, you know, so not too loud. I don't mind it's fast, but not too loud. Let them sleeping dogs lay there."

If this soldier was a malevolent force, he had Jamey bamboozled because Jamey felt safer with this fellow than he had felt since he left home. Even the night in the motel didn't feel as secure as having Mitch directing operations. Jamey flipped open his case, pulled out his instrument, and started to tune it.

"Nice fiddle," Mitch said. "Do that one about King and the Kennedys. You know it?"

"Dion," said Jamey. "Not exactly, but I know the song. Give me a couple of minutes." Jamey started noodling with the song, trying out the first line here and another line there. Jamey worked on it for a few minutes and said he was ready, but he didn't know the bridge part.

Mitch was enthusiastic now. "I don't need no fuckin' bridge part! Sing the fuckin' song, boy." So Jamey sang the fuckin' song, and he had the same effect on his commanding officer that he had on most folks who heard him in a fair fight. His guitar was competent, and his voice was unusually pretty and authoritative. Jamey needed an audience to shine.

When they had all four of them walked up over the hill, Mitch grinned and said that Jamey's guitar was mission critical. Then he urged Jamey to play "Louie Louie" since he had some spicy verses to add.

At night in bed I play a little game
I fuck a girl until she's tame
Out of her cunt and deep in her mouth
And for the coupe de grace
I pump her way down south
Oh Louie, Louie

"Now you go home and sing that to your pink ass girlfriend and her prissy mother, and they'll both suck you dry." The vision of Teri Ann Murphy, especially her verifiably pink ass, was appealing, but the evocative image of Mrs. Murphy was something Jamey had not contemplated before. And picturing the two of them together was not for the faint of heart. He was reasonably sure that he wouldn't want Teri Ann's lips meeting her mother's at the tip of his own shaft. And he certainly didn't want Mr. Murphy bringing up the matter via the telephone.

"Now, listen here, Jim Craig, I understand that my wife and Teri Ann were sucking your son's dick. I don't know what goes on in your house, old man, but in my house, that's off limits."
"I'll punch him in the head and smash his guitar," Jim assured Mr. Murphy.
"Well, that's just fine. Just fine!"
"Get together for a drink over the barbeque?"

MITCH AND JAMEY TRIED A FEW MORE SONGS. Jamey knew plenty, and Mitch liked the music from his days in the service and before. Mitch told Jamey about being shot and finally sent home. He had taken to drinking and was generally degenerate and usually destitute. He apologized, but he said that it couldn't be helped. There was a great deal that he would rather forget, but, though he had come home, the war was still with him. "That's why I don't carry my weapon," he said. "I'd very likely use it."

As Jamey understood the matter, the politicians gave lip service to the soldiers who served, but wouldn't lift a finger to help them. Jamey had no idea about the different responsibilities of local, state, and federal governments. But he knew from his counter-culture sources that Governor Reagan was a desperado.

Mitch's talk disturbed Jamey. He was bewildered as his simple vision of the universe was shaken by reality once again. He had thought that "they" fought the war, that "they" were all for it, and that "they" were all of the same mind. Mitch said it was a sad, sorry, mixed-up business that made no sense to anyone who ever really knew what it was like over there.

He said they could never win the war because there wasn't anything to win. He said that he never thought his country could ever do some of the things it was doing. He talked about chemical agents, defoliants, and terrorist practices. For that matter, he never thought he could do the things he himself had done, but he had done them to survive. He was convinced that it would have been better for all concerned if he hadn't. That was heavy shit, man, and Jamey didn't have anything to say.

Mitch then turned to Jamey. "So, why are you out here tonight? If I was you, I'd rather be in a nice bed at home or buried deep in some high school girl's ass. She'll thank you," he winked.

"My shit doesn't amount to much next to your story," Jamey admitted. "I guess it's my pride 'cause it doesn't make much sense any other way."

"Pay a heavy price for pride," said Mitch.

"But, it's probably too late, now," said Jamey. "I got in a fight with my dad, and I took off on the Fourth of July. Been out here ever since."

"Independence Day!" said Mitch, pausing. Resuming after ruminating, "And how's it working out?"

"You can see for yourself," said Jamey. "I'm trying to get some work going, but I'm not exactly looking wholesome and reliable these days. I'm about out of money."

"Damn it!" said Mitch. "Now you shouldn't have said that. Now I know you got some money. Maybe not a bundle, but more than I have, I can guarantee you that. So what's to stop me from stickin' a knife in you and takin' your money?"

"I trusted you," said Jamey. He looked at the soldier. "I still do."

"Well, either you're a decent judge of character, or you're a lucky little shit," said Mitch. "Either way, we better bed down. Keep one eye open for the enemy, and another eye open for me."

"Look," said Jamey. "In the morning, when the sun comes up. Let's go to get some breakfast. I've been holding out on myself, and I'd be honored to fix you up with some breakfast. I don't have much, but we could get some breakfast."

"I take that kindly," said Mitch. "But that don't mean I won't slit your throat in the night. Remember that. Still, I take that mighty kindly." Mitch finished off the bottle, and they settled in to sleep in their less than fragrant bivouac.

Wednesday began with Jamey reconnoitering that Mitch was gone. Jamey's guitar was still there, and his backpack was under his head. He waited around for Mitch to return, but he didn't want to be in residence when the folks who worked the dock by day showed up.

So he took a little breakfast at the donut shop, and let the sun come up over the blurry town. Fellas in trucks, some like his pop, stopped for their morning coffee and donuts on the way to the jobs. He even drew a few dirty hippie remarks and more than a few disagreeable stares. But these guys had jobs, and that was the thing: A job. Jamey needed work, and he was running out of time.

But as he became increasingly distasteful, that job that he needed to pull him out of this was fading further away. He pounded the pavement and knocked on some doors, but he just didn't look like a reliable applicant, even if someone needed an unskilled underage worker. Later, he found a park where he could spread out and take some sleep in the shade of a tree. His two bucks had gotten him some food and drink for the day, and he was down to forty cents. Now even a soda seemed extravagant.

He didn't do his street musician thing in the daytime. There weren't so many hipsters and he didn't want to draw the heat. But at night, everything was different. Most of the shops and businesses were closed, and the ones that were open were of a different nature, serving the cool crowd that had come out clubbing. The night time is the right time. He set up shop on the same corner where he had made the big money before.

He was still trying to make contact with his passing audience. At one point, when he turned around, he saw that his backpack was gone. Like a pro, he knew there was nothing for it, thought of Mitch, and continued the number. When he spotted the pigs, he feigned just playing for himself as other hippies waiting around might do. There weren't a lot of street musicians because there wasn't much support, but there were a lot of guitars and Jamey blended in with the thousands of passing teens on the summer scene.

AS THE FREAK TAKES YOU

He WAS CAUGHT OFF GUARD when, after an hour or more and the loss of his clothes and more of his dwindling pride, another quarter was tossed into his open guitar case. He looked around and saw a trim middle-aged cat with a rough face and a sharp black leather jacket and long hair draped over his shoulders. The guy was well set from his purple shirt to shiny shoes.

Jamey, the performer, played it real cool, and continued his ballad to the end. The quarter would help him get to a burger, and securing some money was make or break for the next day. The dude, obviously a rich guy with hippie leanings, hung around to the end of Jamey's original song, "Blues for a Blue Lady." Then he made his way beyond the front of the waiting line where he was quickly passed in ahead of the crowd.

Jamey went on to play his Beatles, Donovan, and random songs. Jamey hit a hot streak and picked up another dollar in coins, taking the running total to $1.65. The lesson Jamey learned from two nights of this peculiar work was to play more Paul McCartney and less Jamey Craig. This evening, he had made a dollar-forty on McCartney songs and a quarter on Jamey Craig songs. Jamey songs would have to wait.

Jamey, despite losing his worldly possessions and having no place to hang his hat, if he still had had one, had found a career in the music business. No starving with a steady income like a dollar a day. Jamey was a professional musician now, a point of pride where there wasn't any other. Nowhere to go but up through the stars. Now it was time to hit the Big Boy. He had enough for a combo with a coke, and more than enough for a coffee the next day. What more could a guy want, apart from some time with Teri Ann Murphy? Or a bed to sleep in. Neither was likely this Wednesday night, but Jamey stopped at a liquor store and bought a pack of Chesterfucks and grabbed a pack of matches to keep him company during the coming night.

He crossed at a light and proceeded up the boulevard. The Big Boy was about a half mile to a mile away. The pieces of the mosaic were clearer to him now. He could make out the hungry kids, the girls and the boys in the trade, the day-trippers from the Valley or South Bay, the local population of musicians, users, and hopefuls, the amazed sight-seers from out-of-town, and the constant presence of the cops in their cruisers. He always felt that he stuck out like a rube, carrying his guitar case, but there were others doing the same. He was looking like just another hippie street urchin, not so much a disguise as a reality.

Coming upon the next light, a big black car pulled over and stopped. Jamey was no kind of car guy and couldn't tell what sort of car it was, but it was big and shiny. He heard a voice calling out through the open passenger window. Jamey assumed the asshole wanted street directions. He approached, stepping off the sidewalk, and put his face in the window to help out if he could. He recognized the cat with the leather jacket and purple shirt. "I didn't hear you," Jamey said.

"I said to get in the fucking car," answered the dude. He had long Jesus hair with a touch of gray. His eyes were black and he was very intense. His voice was deep and demanding. Jamey could see no reason to comply. "Get in," the man said again. "You'll get me a ticket, or worse."

"It's cool," said Jamey, his catch-all for non-communicative speech.

"I heard your song, man. It was happening. Get in the car. I want to talk about it." Well, what if the movie actress discovered at Schwab's had told the producer to fuck off? You wait all your life for something to happen. Maybe something was happening.

Jamey was a veteran hitchhiker, and he wasn't a girl. He didn't consider himself a target. It's not like Missy or Teri Ann getting into some guy's car. That could be dangerous. But Jamey figured he could handle himself if he had to, if the guy was going to put the queer moves on him. But what made him think that was certainly nothing based on Jamey's history. Back in high school, Jamey was regularly roughed up, and he took no steps to defend himself or to retaliate. The interior was filled with cool air, Joni Mitchell music, and pot wafting out the window. "Let's go," the guy urged. So Jamey put the guitar case in the back seat of the car and took his place in the front seat. It was pretty nice with the windows rolled up tight and the cool air from the A/C. Air conditioning was getting rarer since leaving home last week.

"Where are you going?" asked the driver. "I'm Rick, by the way."

"Jamey," said the youth, shaking the long blond hair out of his eyes. This Rick guy kept looking sideways at him, the way he himself might look at a Christian girl on a bus stop or Teri Ann pretty much any time. Jamey didn't really know if he was just paranoid or if he really ought to trust his gut and make a run for it at the next light. But, meanwhile, he was in a nice car, and Joni Mitchell's second album was on the hotshot sound system.

"Jamey," he said, savoring the sound on his lips. "Pretty name. You into Joni Mitchell?"

"Pretty cool," said Jamey. "The Gallery" was playing at the moment.

"Where are you going?" asked the dude.

"Just going up to the Big Boy. I'm literally starving, man."

"I believe it. Look, I'm going for dinner, too. You want to join me?" Jamey didn't know what to answer, not knowing what the cost might be. "I'm buying," said Rick, lighting a joint and passing it to Jamey. That kept him in the car for a few more blocks for sure. "Enjoy the tunes, Jamey. Enjoy the smoke." They rolled right past the home of the Big Boy.

"Hey! That's the place..."

"Not really," said Rick. Jamey was confronted with the classic problem involving candy from strangers—and this was good candy: Music, dope, A/C, and some interesting company, too. Nevertheless, in all of his experience, little that it was, when had a forty-year-old rich dude just wanted to hang with a sixteen-year-old hippie tramp? It was highly improbable that this Rick fucker was just feeling like hanging out with someone a half to a third his age. Everything pointed to it. The guy was "a homo." Nothing else made sense, but he had said something about free dinner. This was very good candy.

"I heard your song, Jamey," said Rick. "It was really good. You wrote it?"

"Yeah, I wrote it." Jamey knew that he was a good song writer, and Rick was one of the few adults to have noticed the same, Miss LeAnn Curtis being the other. Miss Curtis was barely an adult, and, in this Rick guy's case, it was probably a come-on, the same way Jamey would have said anything to Clarissa if he thought it would have helped to peal the panties. But, still, he liked to hear it, which explained for him something about the gullibility of girls who fell for ridiculous lies, something Jamey thought went on far too often.

Since he had been old enough to know what a homosexual even was, sort of (and he hadn't really learned much about straight sex despite some sessions with Teri Ann), he had been taught to hate them, to be disgusted by the very thought of man-to-man sex.

Lesbian sex was okay, naturally, if it was girly like in the movies or pictures he'd seen, that is to say, if it was done for the benefit of a male audience. But he was supposed to be completely creeped out by man-on-man sex, and Jamey had always complied with that social edict. Never really questioned it. Just took it for granted that it was sick stuff.

A charge of homosexuality was the lowest form of chop in his crowd of otherwise tolerant hippies. At this point, the late sixties, there was some talk of tolerance for homosexuals, but it wasn't real, not that Jamey actually knew anyone who was openly homo. There was a rumor that Mick Jagger was bi, but even that wasn't something that Jamey was ready to consider. In short, he had no intention of giving this guy what he probably wanted.

Still, for all of his concerns, Jamey felt that he was in control. And a dinner, the music, and the smoke were not to be passed up. It was all too tempting, and it would leave him with his buck sixty-five with which to start the next day. Coffee and donuts, together at last!

Rick pulled up in front of an exclusive Sunset Boulevard restaurant called Jack's. It looked like a little wooden house in front, and it was right on the street. Jamey expected to see Ed "Kookie" Byrnes, but the valet was actually Mexican (according to Jamey's classification system) who took Rick's seat. Rick had come around while a second valet helped Jamey out of the car. "Hey, man, maybe I should grab my guitar in case I need to boogie?"

"It'll be safe in the car, Jamey," said Rick, pushing Jamey along by the small of his back. "I really like that name. Jamey." Jamey didn't like to leave his guitar, and he was uncomfortable with Rick touching the small of his back. And one night, very stoned indeed, he and Craig Roman had been reading excerpts from Dale Carnegie, and this repetitive use of his name was sounding like an ingratiating device if ever there was one, but free dinner…

"It's really James, but Jamey is my stage name." He was trying to appear manlier. He expected the hand to be on his bottom in the next instant, but it didn't happen. Rick was reeling him in slowly, but he felt the line.

"When we get inside, Jamey, go wash your face and hands." In the restroom, Jamey took the opportunity to wash his hands and face, even under the nails. Running water and a private space was increasingly rare in Jamey's world. He gave his underarms and his crotch a quick bath. But, in the end, there was only so much a guy could do in Jack's restroom and Jack wouldn't have been too happy with that. The unwashed clothes were as they were. His teenaged fuzz was coming out a little on his face, not heavy but not clean. The bigger problem was to eat or to run? But, like a jerk, he had let his guitar become a hostage for this queer. So he decided on a middle course. He would put his cards on the table at the earliest opportunity. Just lay it on the dude.

There was a long haired handsome piano player with a mighty beard and several beautiful people around the grand piano. It looked like an after-hours Sinatra scene, but the music was now, or a year ago anyway. The singer was doing "Feelin' Alright" and rockin' it very well. A few of the patrons were even singing along, more or less under their breath. Rick caught Jamey's eye as he came into the main dining room. Rick had taken a booth along one side. Jamey approached the table, felt the heat of Rick's eyes as he walked, and pointedly sat down across from, rather than next to Rick, as Rick had indicated with a little pat.

They could see the piano, the bar, and many of the patrons, mostly young, dressed in hip styles, and obviously wealthy accompanied by aspiring women. "That's Mike Carl," said Rick, smoking his cigarette and nodding toward the pianist. Jamey seemed perplexed. "He played piano on 'Little Dreams'? He wrote 'Dancing with Linda', among others."

"Wow!" Jamey was properly star struck. He had never heard of Mike Carl by name, but he knew those two songs quite well. Crazy Place did "Dancing with Linda" in their set.

That's what Jamey really wanted: To occupy some little part of the rock and roll/counterculture firmament. To have played on "Little Dreams" would more than answer. To have written "Dancing with Linda." Anyone who knows pop music will appreciate those Mike Carl piano runs even if they'd never heard his name. It wasn't just the girls, the money, the dope, or the attention. Jamey wanted to be part of the big scene, to do something really cool, and he knew he had the chops. There was just, as he saw it, some shit to go through. He liked school fine, but who had the time? "Listen," Jamey started, trying to execute his new plan.

Rick offered him a cigarette from his pack of Camels, which Jamey took. Never pass on a free smoke, even when you got a pocket full of Chesterfucks. Rick insisted on lighting the cigarette for young Jamey, who was embarrassed. "Listen," said Jamey again, giving out with the smoke. "I have to tell you the truth."

"That's a rare thing," said Rick. "I usually wait for the pictures to develop. But go ahead and try." Rick reached in his pocket and slipped a capsule over to Jamey that was wrapped in a factory sealed plastic pouch.

"What's that?"

"Acid," said Rick.

"Acid that comes wrapped up like Contac? I've never seen it packaged. This is some kind of bullshit."

"It's Czechoslovakian Pharmaceutical Acid."

"Commies drop acid?" asked Jamey, whose mind was already blown.

"It's the purest acid you can get," said Rick.

"How do I know it's not some drug that turns me into a fag?"

"I'm still looking for that," said Rick.

Jamey liked to take acid as much as the next freak, but you have to act responsibly. He didn't want to follow Rick down the rabbit hole. He wanted to stay on his guard. So Jamey left the small package alone. "It's cool," said Jamey. "I'm not trippin' tonight." That wasn't easy for Jamey to say, but he knew things would be out of control on acid. Jamey left it on the table, not really wanting to give it back. Rick put his back in his pocket.

Jamey wanted to make his original point. "You know, I don't know what you think of me. Maybe it's my hair, or, I don't know, maybe my voice. I'm not *that* pretty…"

"I don't agree," said Rick. "You *are* that pretty. And, if you must know, it's your ass. And a cute face, too. But a girl shouldn't fish for compliments. It's unbecoming."

Jamey was turning another shade of pink. "I wish you wouldn't say stuff like that. I'm not a girl," said Jamey.

"Then why does it turn you on when I tell you about your cute ass?" Rick looked at the drug on the table. "Put that it your pocket if you're not going to do it. You want to get us busted?"

Jamey put the package in his shirt pocket. "It doesn't turn me on," said Jamey, but he did feel embarrassed and warm. "Look. Obviously, you think I'm a pansy. But I'm not queer at all. Maybe I look like a queer, but I'm not a queer."

"You shouldn't have to say so," said Rick, nonplused by Jamey's denials. "And four times at that." Jamey thought that Rick was somewhat condescending. But he ignored the last.

"I'm not going to…do anything sexual. I'm not going to do anything like that, ever. You get that?"

"Well, you brought it up," said Rick. Jamey sensed that Rick was hiding his amusement while he tried to play it straight; Rick didn't take him seriously. The waiter brought the wine, and, after Rick approved, poured a glass for Rick and Jamey. "I already ordered for you," he told Jamey.

"See? That's like chick stuff. What if I don't like it?"

"That doesn't happen at Jack's. Cheers. Bottoms up!"

Jamey took a first sip, but carried on his point. "I don't like girls to tease *me*. Too much prick teasing. So I figure I should tell you upfront what the scene is…"

"That's where we differ," said Rick. "I like girls who tease me. They can tease me as long as they like, as long as they can hold out."

"You mean you like girls?" said Jamey, starting to feel like an idiot, and not merely embarrassed to be talking of such matters.

"Don't you?" said Rick.

"I like girls. That's different."

"What do you like best about them?" asked Rick, ignoring Jamey's thrust. Jamey was stumped. There was a lot to like. "I like their clothes," said Rick, savoring the thought. "I like their clothes. Do you like their clothes?"

Jamey didn't have an answer for that. He wanted to make his point clearly. "Well, I told you now. The thing is," he started, always straying from the main road, "But now that you tell me you like girls, I mean, now that I know that, I guess it doesn't matter. What I was trying to tell you was that I'm not going to have sex with you. So, if you wanted to have sex with me, I'm not going to do it. And I'm not a tease. So, maybe you shouldn't waste your money or your time on dinner with me. 'Cause I'm totally straight. I've never been with a guy. Never will."

"Never been with a guy?" said Rick. "Then I don't know how you could be so sure? Did you ever think that when you're my age that you might look back and wonder about that decision? You might think, hey, I should have let that weird guy fuck me in the ass. You wouldn't die from it, you know. And, you're not even the one making that decision, are you? I mean, it's the people around you telling you what you feel, but you don't really know what you feel. You just said you never tried it. Of course, it never occurs to you that you could make up your own mind, based on your own experiences and your own real feelings. You hippies make me laugh. You're so full of alternative lifestyles and cosmic visions, but you're just as two-dimensional as the squares you dismiss."

That was a new thought for Jamey. "Well, a guy knows if he's queer or not," Jamey asserted. "I've been with women, or girls anyway. I like girls. What's to wonder?"

"You think girls are safe," said Rick. "When nothing—nothing could be further from the truth. If all you ever had was vanilla ice cream, if someone offered you chocolate, instead, you might turn it down. But you'd be wrong. Anyway, I'm just talking to your ignorance. This dinner of ours is in no way a quid pro quo. I am treating you to dinner because I liked your song." Rick held up his wine glass and induced Jamey to clink. "And I can see that you obviously have little or no money and no place to stay.

True?" Jamey nodded. "For all we know, you'll be a famous rock and roll star someday, and I'm giving you a dinner because I want to be able to say that I know *you* just like I know Mike Carl over there. Name dropper. Maybe you'll write a line in a song about it someday when you look back on these hard times or on the prejudices that a seventeen-year-old just has to harbor. If I wanted to have a little twit to have sex with, that's a lot cheaper than this dinner."

And it was a fine prime rib dinner with a wedge salad, thin crispy onions, sautéed mushrooms, and too much fine wine for a lad who seldom drank, except to keep company with Teri Ann Murphy, always making sure that she drank most of it. In the midst of the meal, a well dressed man, short in stature, clearly buzzed whether by drugs or by internal energy, nice suit, bare chest, medallion, maybe halfway in age between Jamey and Rick, accompanied by a tall model-like woman on his arm, stopped at Rick's table with a friendly "Hey, Rick! What's happenin'?"

Rick seemed surprised to see him. He reached and shook hands with the gentleman. "Jerry!" he said. "Far out! Didn't see you."

"In the back," said Jerry. "Secluded." Jerry made no effort to introduce the woman, and Rick ignored Jamey in the same way. "You should give the office a call. We're trying to do something with Morrison. Interested? I'll leave you my card. It's the office at the house."

"Sure," said Rick. "Good to see you, Jerry." Jerry looked at the vagabond Jamey who was quietly watching with his mouth open.

"You be careful, Rick," said Jerry. "You're too damned good to go straight to hell. The system hasn't caught up to the new reality. That's why they call it living on the edge." When the couple moved on and out the front door, Rick nodded after him and said, by way of explanation, "Jerry Westerfield. Indus Valley Records?"

Jamey knew of Indus and its stable of stars, and he was, once again, properly impressed. "You know Mike Carl *and* Jerry Westerfield? And when he said Morrison?"

"Jim," said Rick. "He fucked up down in Miami, but I think he's working on it now." Rick flipped the business card across the table to Jamey. "Your ticket to the big time. Now you have Jerry Westerfield's private phone and address. Lot of would-be rockers would love to have that."

Jamey looked at the Benedict Canyon address. He put it in his top pocket, along with the acid. Craig Roman would get a kick out of that! "Fuck! You know all these people," Jamey remarked, considering out loud

"Far out!" Jamey worried about Rick's homosexual intentions, but he was having the time of his life in the scene with Mike Carl and Jerry Westerfield, and who the fuck is this Rick guy?

Rick returned his attention to Jamey, asking questions about how Jamey happened to find himself on a street corner in Hollywood singing for his supper. So the story of the sojourn came out. He also wanted to know about Crazy Place and the music that Jamey liked. Rick advised the lad that he should probably be a solo act. According to Rick, Jamey's special sound wouldn't come through in an electric band. He suggested that it might be a Tim Buckley or Joni Mitchell thing that Jamey had going. Even if he had a band, he would eventually have to go solo. Jamey could weigh the good advice at his leisure, but the fact that someone seemed to be taking his music seriously disposed Jamey to believing that this Rick cat was telling it like it was. More, Rick seemed very curious about Jamey's plans and about how he was living. Maybe he was some kind of producer who could get Jamey into the studio.

Rick had fun making comments about the high level patrons in the restaurant. He directed Jamey's attention to a long pair of bare legs under a table and the hand of a boyfriend between them. "Looks like the cafeteria in junior high," Rick observed.

"I didn't go to that school," said Jamey.

Rick got Jamey to talk about his musical aspirations. Rick mentioned that there was an open mic night at the Troubadour on Mondays and that Jamey should try it. It might be good practice dealing with a more sophisticated audience than that provided by the Knollridge High School gym or the sidewalk in front of the club. Rick hinted that he could help the lad in the industry. Hello, Mr. Wolf! It all sounded like a line to Jamey. He recognized the scene. He was Clarissa to Rick's Jamey, but he had a feeling his tears wouldn't stop the assault.

As the meal concluded, Rick, never looking at the check, pulled out his wallet and dropped two Jacksons and a Ham on the table as if it were nothing. Jamey figured that that much juice would have carried him for two weeks. When Jamey stood up, he suddenly realized how drunk he was. Rick was right there to steady him. On the way out, Rick had his hand on Jamey's lower back, a little lower now, guiding him through the dark room, though it wasn't so dark that Jamey needed to be herded along. Passing the piano, Mike Carl flashed a peace sign at Rick. "How's it goin', man?" said Rick, sort of brushing off the bearded musician. How do you blow off someone like that? "Dancing with Linda" was one of the greatest songs of all time. Jamey was increasingly convinced that Rick was some kind of Phil Spector-George Martin music scene genius.

"What do you do?" asked Jamey.

"I hold the mirror," said Rick. Jamey grabbed a book of Jack's matches on his way out the door.

Stepping into the night air and bright lights of the boulevard, Jamey was struck by the rush of light and sound and the presence of the lost souls streaming by. Pretty good pot, he thought. Got to be laced with something, man. But, through the wine, the pot, and the dinner, Jamey remained conscious of the close proximity of Rick. He could feel Rick's open hand just above his ass. There was no grab, but it felt awkward and foreign. He might have walked with Teri Ann as Rick was moving with him, but no one else had ever handled Jamey like that. He was capable of walking forward without guidance, though, due to the wine, or the pot, or whatever it was, he was a little less sure than usual.

But the hand thing was too much, and Jamey knew this to be a point of no return, as, he reflected, each moment was. No. This was the point of no return. He was not going to be this Rick guy's pussy. Whatever drug it might be, it did not make Jamey a pussy. So he resolved to escape from Rick right here and now on a public sidewalk without an unpleasant incident. He liked Rick. He was in awe of him. And he didn't want any unnecessary bad vibes. He wouldn't mind hanging out with Rick, if he weren't a queer. Rick had been cool, and pretty upfront. But Jamey considered himself savvy enough to sense that he was heading for trouble if he stayed on this ride. It wasn't going to get better than the prime rib at Jack's.

Rick went around to the street side, handed the valet a five, and was getting into his car when he noticed that Jamey was still standing on the sidewalk, neither coming nor going, lost in his thoughts. The second valet held the door open for Jamey. "Get in!" called Rick, over the top of the sedan. "What are you waiting for? Don't forget your guitar. You don't want to lose that, do you?" Rick didn't wait for an answer, but took his place at the wheel.

Jamey couldn't forfeit the guitar. He jumped into the front seat and let the valet close the door behind him. The Bryan Cooper album was playing now. Rick seemed to be grooving, so Jamey didn't let on that he thought it was crap. But Rick could read faces. "What? You don't like Bryan Cooper?"

"When he was with The Forgotten Avenue," said Jamey. "He was the best. But this solo shit is so plastic, man."

"Well, you're the customer," said Rick. "And, to tell you the truth, he isn't moving much vinyl. It was probably a mistake for Indus to let him go solo. The Forgotten Avenue was a solid name."

"He has to do his own thing," said Jamey. "But, the truth is, he's better with the group. He can sing, but he can't write songs. Not for a whole album. And, really, he's obviously too stoned. Too full of himself. He's done."

"Just like that?" said Rick. "One bad album?"

"Who's ever come back from a flop like that?" A few blocks along, Rick managed to turn the car around, slowly retracing all the ground they had travelled, and even more. They passed the corner that led to the alley where Jamey had spent some of his Hollywood nights.

"You're pretty harsh, man," said Rick. "I guess you heard about that scene in Texas when he was getting kind of rowdy on stage and then he missed a couple of dates. Westerfield was ready to kill him."

"He should get his money back. Cooper is done."

They did another number. "What's in this?" asked Jamey.

"Opium," said Rick. "Northern California bud bathed in opium. Not your Valley weed."

"Pretty good shit," said Jamey, hardly an expert. It was the best pot that Jamey had ever encountered. He hadn't known that there were such things. At Laurel, Rick headed up into the canyon. "Where are we going now?" asked Jamey, when he momentarily awoke from his dream.

"My pad," said Rick. "I have some stuff that I really think you'll be interested in."

"Do you know what that sounds like?" said Jamey. "If I ask you to turn around and take me down to the boulevard, will you do it, man?"

"I guess I might," said Rick. "But I really think you'll dig the scene. But, hey, I'm not kidnapping you. You're a big girl. You want me to put you back where I found you? I won't sleep well thinking about you stoned on the street. Come on up to the house. You'll be safe, and it'll be a groove. But I don't have any restraints. You can do what you like."

Jamey perceived that time and distance was on Rick's side. Rick, at the wheel, was racing up the dark canyon. "How do you drive when you're this stoned?"

"Lots of practice," said Rick. The car, at one with Rick, continued to follow the curves and climb the hills into the canyon. Jamey was becoming increasingly stoned, enjoying the trip but trying to be responsible, to take care of himself. The oncoming lights, the reflections in the windows, the sound of Cooper's voice. Jamey wasn't following so well anymore.

"I'm not gonna be your pussy, you know," said Jamey, who was fairly certain that they weren't just buddies hanging out.

"I told you, if I want a twit, I can go down to the boulevard and get as many as I want—boys or girls—or whatever." It was the *whatever* that concerned Jamey.

"It's just a fucking long way to walk back down the hill, man," said Jamey. Stoned as Jamey was, Rick was fascinating company, full of surprises and loaded with dope and tunes. Compared to a dumpster, Rick didn't seem so bad.

THE GALLERY

RICK'S CABIN IN THE SKY was off of the main canyon road and high on a dense arboreal hill, accessible only by a steep narrow road. In the night and in his state, it was all darkness to Jamey. He was trying to recall the major twists and turns, thinking what a long walk that would make down the hill, but he had no idea of where he had come from or where he was going. He was only sixteen. The yard was dark. Once again, the sly hand was guiding Jamey along from behind, and it was getting a little lower.

"I think that's enough touching, man," said Jamey. "I'm not cool with that, okay? I told you I'm not gonna to be your pussy."

"A real man would have punched me a long time ago," said Rick, letting go his hand and getting out his keys. Jamey tried to contemplate that remark and what it might mean, but he couldn't wrap his head around it. Rick pushed the door open, switched on the lights, and waved his arm in welcome, inviting Jamey to take a look around. The lights stunned him after the pitch darkness outside.

While his eyes adjusted, Rick switched on the stereo. The room filled with the music of *Magical Mystery Tour.* Jamey was at home with The Beatles. Looking around now, he was standing upon a polished wood landing that provided entre to an atrium, the center of the house, a mix of indoor plants and trees and wooden furniture. Plenty of polished wood all about, floors and walls, open spaces. The kitchen was visible from the entry as was the stairway, neither the one to heaven nor to the one in your mind.

The house was unlike anything Jamey had known in the Valley, except that most of the world didn't live like the Knollridge Craigs, let alone like Rick the Queer. The ceiling was glass with occasional supports. The décor consisted of clear frames displaying photographic art of various sizes, everywhere.

Jamey was drawn to the many shots of his own rock and roll idols: Beatles, Stones, Dead, the Plane, Country Joe, Janis, Hendrix, Dylan, Martin Turner, Life Force, The Band, The Byrds, The Doors, Traffic, Cream, Kinks, Springfield, Forgotten Avenue, Trudy Lewis, Linda Rondstadt, Katy Mondy, even Zappa and Beefheart! It was a mix of candid very personal shots, sometimes one famous player from one group interacting with some equally cool cat from another group. Jamey recognized some of the original photographs from the magazine covers (without the print), from album covers even, but others were unknown to Jamey. He had never imagined that such things existed. How could they not be made known to the world?

Rick had disappeared out the glass door in the back, but was returning now. "My God!" shouted Jamey, "Where did you get these?"

"I know the photographer," said Rick, rejoining Jamey. Then Jamey flashed. He knew his trivia, and everyone knew the work of Richard Altier. But who knew what *he* looked like?

"You're Richard Altier?" said Jamey. "Fuck!"

"Call me Rick," he answered. "And I wish you would. You never call me by my name. You always call me 'man.' You've been doing it all night."

"I didn't mean to be rude," said Jamey. "You know, guys just play it real cool."

"But *you* don't have to," said Rick. "So, it's Rick. Okay?"

"Rick," said Jamey. "Man! I didn't know who you were, and I still don't know what you have in mind. But, my god! These pictures are incredible!" It was only beginning to sink in, when, once again, by the small of his back, Jamey was guided into another room. The room was heavy with the war theme, and the work collected and displayed like this was a serious bring-down. Some of these photos were credited with the turn-around of public opinion. Altier had raised consciousness of the reality of the war. After the pictures in Life, it wasn't just McNamara and his charts. It was real. Some of these pictures had helped to bring down Johnson, paving the way for RFK—Nixon as it turned out.

Continuing the tour, Rick guided Jamey into another gallery where there were photographic works which Jamey, in his mind, classed as "art" pictures. With his pals, informally, it would have been "naked lady" pictures.

They were strange portraits of women, posed and candid. Very soft lighting. Very small breasts. Black & white and color. Never quite naked, and a lot of pantied ass—but always with the strange timid faces at the same time. Jamey was drawn to the prurient side, but he returned to the eerie faces. The models all seemed a little frightened, a little guarded or unnatural. They were beautiful, haunting, and just a little creepy. But it was Richard Altier, the greatest photographer of the weirdest times ever. The pictures were beautiful, worlds away from rock and roll, politics, and Viet Nam, and Jamey was fascinated. "How do you like these?" Rick asked.

"I haven't seen these," said Jamey. "I mean, in the magazines and stuff."

"It's for a new book I'm doing," said Altier. "Kind of my Sergeant Pepper. You like them?"

"I do," said Jamey. "I mean, who doesn't like naked ladies? But there's something going on here that's way different. I mean, sexy stuff, but it's not like Oui or Playboy. They're more delicate, more beautiful." Jamey was trying to get his head around the feeling that the photos created. "I guess they're pretty young. I mean, it would be pretty stupid for me to say that you do good work. I mean, all of it." There was something he knew he didn't understand about the pictures, and he was intrigued. But he definitely liked the ones of ladies.

"I can show you my political wall. I followed the last presidential election. I don't know if I'll do seventy-two. Pretty depressing. I'm kind of getting into some new territory."

"Politicians are pretty ugly," offered Jamey. "But you knew Kennedy, didn't you?"

"And King and Chavez."

"Wow! I can't believe this. I never knew anybody who was famous before. We talked to a roadie for Cream at a concert once. Got a Coke bottle that Clapton drank from."

"I told you I had something to show you, didn't I? Not unlike etchings."

"I was that close to bailing, but I'm so glad I saw this stuff."

"Find one you like, and I'll try to run a copy for you."

"Oh, man, no."

"Man?"

"I'm sorry. Rick. I mean, that would be pretty stupid. I have no place to live. They stole all my stuff tonight except my guitar. I don't even have a change of underwear anymore. And you want to give me a rare piece of art which I would probably sell for a hamburger or a motel room. But, thanks. I mean, some of these are just incredible." Jamey was lost in a wonderland and had returned to the rock and roll gallery in the main entry and living room. "Look at this one of Lennon! When was this? He's got the Sergeant Pepper mustache and glasses."

"That's about right. It was at a party a couple of years ago."

"So that would be like '67. Amazing!"

"It's my job. I told you. I hold the mirror. They trust me as far as the drugs and keeping stuff cool. So I get the insider's view. I have a lot more. It's a pretty amazing collection. I will some day do the definitive book on the sixties. But it's a little close right now. Still happening. Maybe there's a chapter about Jamey?"

By now, Jamey had sat down on a chair and was looking around the room again and again, finding new photographs and personalities every time he looked in a different direction. To his surprise there was a photo of Brian Jones sitting on a studio floor, playing his guitar with a very peaceful look. "It's amazing that a kid like you can actually appreciate this stuff," said Rick. "A lot of kids don't get it."

"You bring a lot of kids here?" asked Jamey, still on his guard. He felt Rick's eyes upon him, but he was nonetheless glad to be in this place, this holy shrine to rock and roll. Jamey was pretty fucked up. Here he only had to be on guard against Rick. Out in the world, it was anyone and everyone.

"I meant, in general." Rick reached down and took Jamey by the hand, pulling him out of the chair. Jamey expected him to try to carry him off to the bedroom. Rick's hand was powerful, and didn't waiver in its command. "Let me show you the patio."

"Listen, Rick," said Jamey, rising but taking his hand back. "I'm not going to be your pansy."

"Will you lighten up, Jamey?" said Rick. "I haven't said or done anything. That's all you. *The lady doth protest too much, methinks.* Here you are, and what straight-up red blooded guy would have come up here without a fight?"

"Well, I can go," said Jamey, actually doubting his ability to walk.

"But you don't have to," said Rick. "Let me show you the set-up." "I Am the Walrus" was fading out. "But first, let's change the musical mood." Rick put the first Doors album on the stereo. He went into the kitchen and came back with a bottle of wine and two glasses, all of which he handed to Jamey who then followed him to the deck out back. Rick had already switched on the mood lights and the hot tub, and now he laid out some lines on a plate on the patio table. Jamey had never done cocaine, and Rick suspected as much. So Rick showed Jamey how it was done. Rick had a lot of things to teach Jamey, and Jamey gamely wired up. They listened to Morrison: "Break on Through (To the Other Side)."

"Check this out, Jamey," said Rick, who took a finger-full of the powder and, before Jamey could protest, laced Jamey's gums with the residue. "You feel that?"

"Stay out of my fuckin' mouth, man!" Jamey protested.

"Try it yourself, then" said Rick. Jamey did. They did several more lines in quick succession. Jamey knew nothing of cocaine, and Rick was loading him up. Jamey was living like a rich kid now.

Then Rick stood up, took off his leather jacket, and put it across a deck chair. He pulled his medallion over his head and noisily dropped it on the table. He opened his shirt and pulled it off, kicking off his shiny black shoes at the same time. He took down his socks and, never hesitating, opened his trousers.

"What?" said Rick. "Am I doing a strip show?" Jamey had been sitting in his chair, agape. "Stop staring at me with your mouth open. You're giving me ideas. Get in the hot tub."

"It's cool," said Jamey.

"Water's warm. Middle of July."

Rick dropped his pants and put them with his jacket. He was standing now in his shorts, which fell to the floor as part of the natural order. He pulled a joint out of his pants pocket, flashing his ass in the process, and lighted the smoke. He had captured Jamey's attention as much as Jamey tried not to observe. He had seen guys in the locker room, and never thought much about it. But he hadn't seen men. Rick stepped into the hot tub. He was in very good shape for an old guy. The muscles were defined and there was a general lack of flab. But there was hair all over the place, most of it still dark, some a little gray here and there. And Jamey also noticed Rick's crotch. It was not at attention, but it was hanging long until it was submerged in the water. Jamey wasn't sure he wanted to compete with that.

"You don't have to get naked, Jamey," said Rick. He passed the joint to Jamey who had to sit down beside the hot tub to take it. As he toked, Rick poured more wine and handed a glass to Jamey, who had already had more than he was used to back at Jack's. But the wine felt warm and good, and it tasted of grapes, something that Teri Ann's concoction never did.

"I never get tired of hearing this record," said Rick "His voice is incredible."

"Morrison had a great voice," said Jamey. "And a lot of the material was great. The band's a little rinky. I like this stuff, but they're pretty weak these days. And *Waiting for the Sun* was bullshit."

"Well, why so coy?" said Rick. "Why don't you just say what you think?"

"Well, that's how it sounds to me," said Jamey.

"You're the customer," said Rick. They listened to the music and talked a little. Jamey was on his guard, but he was impressed that anyone of his dad's generation even knew these albums and bands, and Rick, Richard Altier, that is, seemed to actually know the musicians. Jamey spread out on the deck looking up at the stars, occasionally taking a sip on the wine or a toke on the J. Richard Altier lived the good life up in Laurel Canyon, and Jamey was getting a taste. The alternative was the trash bin of the night before. If Mitch could see him now!

Jamey returned to consciousness at the sound of Rick's voice behind him. "We better go in," said Rick. "Looks like you're ready for bed."

Jamey turned over and looked up to see Rick's unit as Rick finished off the wine in his glass. This was a new situation, one he had not previously encountered. He thought about the revulsion he was supposed to be feeling, because he really wasn't repulsed. He wondered how it was that he had always been repulsed before when it struck him that he had never been confronted by such a situation before. Rick, putting on a robe, stepped over the sprawled Jamey to get something from his pants on the pool furniture.

Jamey allowed that since Rick hadn't taken advantage of him while he had been spaced out that maybe there wasn't too much to worry about. He had said that he liked girls. But, if he liked girls, he could have had girls up here instead of Jamey. Jamey had heard that girls liked good wine and pure cocaine. He believed it to be so.

He got himself up, rushing all over again, and followed Rick indoors, a little wobbly. Rick offered him support as he returned to the kitchen and walked through the gallery to the wooden stairs. Jamey tried to walk on his own. The stairs ascended to an upstairs landing. Down the hallway from there, Rick opened the door and Jamey was in a bedroom with a decidedly feminine feel, the center of which was a four poster bed with a lacy canopy and a pink princess comforter. There was a French door leading to a small balcony to one side and a full bathroom in similar shades to the other. On the walls were Degas ballerinas, though Jamey didn't know Degas or whether they were originals or prints. The only painter he had any truck with was Dalí. He and Craig, stoned out of their minds on Green Beryl, had spent several evenings looking through a coffee table Dalí book of paintings. That was psychedelic stuff with melting clocks and heavy religious symbolism. This shit on the walls was homo, or, at best, girlish.

"Whose room is this?" asked Jamey.

"It's yours," answered Rick. Jamey was about to say THAT *does it!* when Rick quickly added, "…for tonight. Sorry if it's a little much. It was going to be my daughter's, but she never got to stay here. She's in New York with her mother. She doesn't see me anymore. Her mother, that is. Well—her, too."

"Doesn't sound too good," said Jamey.

"I'm a jerk as far as family stuff goes. I do my work thing and travel all over the world. And that's the problem. And, too, I have sex with strangers."

"But your daughter?"

"Her mom thinks I'm a sick S.O.B., and I don't want to be the story. I don't want to be in the news or to be dragged in front of a judge. I like to take the pictures. I'm not the story. So I give my wife whatever she wants. And, apparently, that includes my daughter." Rick ceased his sad story. "Now, take all those clothes off and give yourself a shower. There's shampoo, towels, razors—everything you'll need. Lose the mustache. Better without it. Shave up to here…" He was touching the top of Jamey's ears.

"I don't need a shower so much," said Jamey. "I had one this morning."

The evidence was against him. "I will personally put you in the shower and soap you up and down if you don't get in there and strip down right now." In case there was any doubt, Rick was starting to unbutton Jamey's shirt. Jamey brushed Rick's hands away, touching the hands in the process. He suddenly turned around and escaped into the bathroom, carefully locking the door behind him. As he began to unbutton his own shirt, he heard Rick through the door. "Don't forget to shave that mustache. Take it from your photographer: You look better without it."

Jamey was beginning to think he had better figure out how to say no to Rick or risk finding himself in a situation which his experience didn't really describe. He stepped into the excessively grand shower. He experimented with the water until it started pouring from the walls, out of the mouths of carved cherubs from a number of directions and levels. The abundant streams of water were warm, relaxing, private, and clean, as well as roomy. The adjustable cherub mouths spouting the water were a little freaky, but surprisingly handy. There was an array of shampoos, conditioners, and lotions. Jamey took a red one and washed his hair and such matters. It was good to be clean again. He knew now that it was not to be taken for granted.

He was drying himself as he came out of the shower. With the wine and the steady stream of heavy pot, Jamey was ready to go back to sleep. But the cocaine made him more alert. He knew he had to keep his wits to fend off Rick the Queer's advances. Too bad Rick was so queer. But, of course, Jamey would never have met him if it were otherwise.

The worry was not unreasonable. He was about to shave when he noticed his wallet, change, his Westerfield business card, the Czechoslovakian Pharmaceutical, his Chesterfields, his matches from Jack's and the liquor store, and his guitar picks all on the marble counter. What *was* missing were his socks, shirt, jeans, underpants, and shoes. Not good news. It seemed like every time he assented to one of Rick's demands, there was another more disturbing one to deal with. This was going to start getting difficult, if it hadn't already. "Where the fuck are my clothes?" he shouted through the door. No answer there.

He looked through the drawers and cabinets, but there was nothing to wear, not even a robe. Though he would have preferred something less gaudy, he wrapped one of the big fluffy pink towels around his waist, holding it in place with his right hand. When he opened the bathroom door and stepped into the bedroom, Rick was in a chair, waiting. There were several sudden bursts of light as the shutter snapped again and again and the flash made its blinding impression. In his stony state, Jamey didn't realize what the lights were. "Not cool!" said Jamey. "Where's my clothes? Seriously, man!"

"In the wash," said Rick. "How long has it been?"

"What am I supposed to wear?" said Jamey.

"We'll find you something." Rick was up from the chair, the camera hanging on his shoulder. As Jamey's eyes returned to him, Rick smiled kindly, or perhaps appreciatively. This did nothing to put Jamey at ease.

"I told you I wasn't going to do anything," said Jamey. "I told you. I was totally upfront, man—I mean, Rick. If you want me to clear out, fine. Just give me my clothes. This is majorly uncool." His voice was cracking again. Just when he wanted to sound harsh, manly, and determined, to himself he sounded like a *pussy*.

"You just took a shower," Rick argued. "You're all fresh and clean. You smell like strawberries, for God's sake." He took a whiff of Jamey's hair, coming way too close for Jamey's comfort. Jamey backed up. "You don't want to put those clothes on. Zulema comes in the morning, and she'll do the wash for you. For now, we'll take some pictures."

Rick opened a drawer of a bureau revealing an array of pink, black, white, and purple apparel, all from the lingerie shop. Jamey was appalled as Rick pulled out a simple straight pink nightshirt which he tossed to Jamey, who caught it with his free hand. The other was still holding the towel in place.

"I'm not wearing chick clothes," said Jamey. A man has his pride, even if he's sixteen and without a place to put his warped head. Rick tossed him some thin pink underwear to go with the ensemble. "I'm gone, man!" said Jamey.

"You have to wear something," said Rick.

"You got clothes," said Jamey. "Give me some of your stuff."

"Oh, but this is much prettier," said Rick, who was looking at Jamey in the way Jamey had lusted after Teri Ann. If she were standing before him wrapped in the pink towel with her bare feet and calves and equally bare torso, Jamey would be thinking about taking her on the bed, just overpowering her if necessary, pushing hilt-deep inside her. Of course, he probably wouldn't really do it, not without her, at least, tacit permission. But who knows what scruples Rick had, if any? For someone who didn't want to be a tease, Jamey and the pink towel-look was probably the wrong message for Rick to be getting. "Listen to me, Jamey…"

"This is bullshit, man!" The same thing always happened when he argued with his dad. His voice went higher as his frustration increased. "This is going to get uncool." His hands were occupied, one with the towel and the other with the nighty, so his intended threat seemed impotent. Richard Altier let out a long, regretful sigh. He picked up his camera and took several quick shots in succession. Jamey backed up and found himself seated on the side of the bed, still holding the towel in place, clamping his knees together. Rick became more insistent now. "Go take off the mustache and put on the outfit. Use the hair dryer. I'll give you model pay. But lose the mustache, and the sideburns, if that's what you call 'em."

"You want to put me on your wall!" said Jamey, coming to another flash. "Those weren't chicks! That's why their faces are so weird. Their minds are being blown! They're dudes. I was checkin' out dudes…" Jamey felt as if he were trapped in a crazy place. "I'm gonna get my stuff and get the fuck out of here."

He was determined this time. He pushed Rick aside, but Rick reached out with one arm, and took Jamey by the neck. He pulled the lad to him. Jamey began to flail, hitting Rick on the chest with both hands, but it seemed as if his blows were nothing to Rick. Rick had his arms around Jamey, holding him in place, and Jamey could feel that Rick was much stronger than he was. Jamey was yelling, and then crying, and then Rick was rocking the naked boy in his muscular hairy arms, kissing the top of his strawberry scented hair.

Rick patted Jamey's bottom. Then he let go. And there was Jamey standing naked with the pink towel at his feet. Rick sighed once more. Jamey knew what it meant; he had become Clarissa. He wiped away the tears that had issued forth, and, bending his knees, he picked up the night shirt and started putting it on. Something was better than nothing. "Don't forget your pants," said Rick. "You absolutely can't go around without pants. I couldn't take it."

"That's okay," said Jamey disdaining. "I'll just wear this until I get my stuff back. And then I'm gone…"

"You already said that," Rick replied. And then he continued more forcefully.

LIKE A ROLLING STONE

"**N**OW SHUT UP, you silly girl, and pay attention." Jamey's skin was turning pink in front of Rick, as Jamey blushed all over. "You have no money. You're going to get yourself out of here as soon as you can—that's what you're thinking. Fine. So what are you going to do then? You're going to rush back down to the boulevard. Great life. But I'm offering you a day of pay, seventy-five dollars. That could keep you alive for a week. And you can spend the night here. So at least you'll be safe and rent-free until morning. If I wanted to rape you, I'd be up your ass already. You *are* stoned, you know. Now I'm not asking for sex. I'd love to fuck you, but I'm not going to rape you even though I can already tell that you'd love it. But what I am asking for is to shoot you for the series. You've seen my work. You know it's what I do. So, you know, on the up-and-up. You sign a release. You shave. And you do everything I tell you to do." Rick was already fixing Jamey's hair. Jamey shook him off. "You know it's legitimate. I'm Richard Altier here. But, to get the job, you have to do what I say. No sex, but you have to do what I tell you."

"What do I have to do?" mumbled Jamey, who could see the point of what was being said, though he didn't believe it was to be a strictly professional relationship.

"Whatever I tell you…"

"That's what I don't know. Whatever you tell me." Jamey's voice was rising again. "I don't know what that means."

"Well, if there's no sex, what's the worst thing you think I could ask you to do? Apart from sex, where's the line? You pose exactly like I tell you. Your pretty little smile. Your sexy green eyes. Your cute pink ass. But I won't fuck you. Unless you explicitly want it," said the photographer. Jamey was listening now, observing Rick's chest hair through his partially opened robe. Jamey averted his eyes, looking at his own knees and the little white lace trim on the hem of the night shirt.

"Seventy-five dollars?" said Jamey, justifying himself. He thought about it. It was much better money than a dollar a night singing for his supper, but he didn't believe it would be that simple. "So what do I gotta do?"

Rick handed him the underwear. Jamey sat on the side of the bed, thinking it over. "Let's go. Burnin' moonlight, honey. Move it!" Jamey sprang into action and felt just the trace of Rick's attempt to slap his backside. Once in the bath, Jamey looked at himself in the mirror. There was also a little white lace trim around the collar. The shirt was tapered at the waist, to suggest the effect. It was short, and barely covered his manhood, such as it was.

He felt like an idiot and imagined the impression he would have made on Craig, or, worse, on Teri Ann—or the jocks or low riders! He washed the red from his eyes and dabbed them with a towel. He shaved his stache and boards above his ears. He put on the second prescribed article. Rick knocked on the door while Jamey was blow-drying his hair. Jamey opened up. "Try these," said Rick, looking Jamey over. It was a pair of white stockings.

"I can't…" Rick opened a drawer and pulled out a lipstick applicator and did Jamey's lips. He pulled out a makeup case and brushed his cheeks. He next put on some eye-liner. "Not bad for a photographer," he commented, standing behind Jamey in the mirror, both of them looking at his face. "Put on the stockings. Oh, and try on these earrings." They were gold clip-on drop earrings with good sized matching pearls. Rick left Jamey to finish up while he got his cameras in order.

After a few moments, Rick called from the other side of the door. "What's taking so long?" Jamey didn't answer, but came out to the bedroom, the stockings hanging from his hand. "I can't make 'em work," he said.

Rick laughed. "On the bed," he said.

"God damn it!" said Jamey, "I told you!"

"Sit on the bed, and I'll help you with the stockings. You look great!" Jamey, wary of course, sat on the bed, his back against the headboard. Rick rolled up a stocking in his hands. "Give me some leg," he ordered. Jamey extended a leg. "Someone needs a pedicure," Rick observed. Taking Jamey's foot and leg, he rolled first one and then the other past the knees and half-way up the thighs, where the smooth material gave way to the tightly fitting lace. Still holding a leg, it seemed that Rick was about to kiss Jamey's foot, but he dropped it. A little professionalism was called for here.

Jamey was embarrassed to see himself like this. Rick stood beside the bed now, looking at the girlish lad. "Now what are we going to do with…" His eyes darted to Jamey's exposed crotch. "…with that? You seem to be enjoying yourself."

"Well, I'm not!" said Jamey, protesting.

"Well, see if you can scrunch that down. And think about baseball or something. Or Nixon, or the war. Medgar Evers."

"William Zanzinger!" laughed Jamey. He tried to comply, though some things are not as scrunchable as they seem.

"There's a good girl," said Rick.

"I wish you wouldn't…" But he knew that Rick did it to a purpose.

Rick laid out a few more lines, and Jamey and Rick did them. Jamey could feel Rick's eyes on him the whole time. Jamey was snorting the coke and trying to manage his nighty and keep his knees clamped all the while. When Rick put the coke away, he checked out his camera and then put a hand on Jamey's leg, raising the knee to show the curve of the ankle. It was one position after another as Rick tried to get the photograph he was looking for.

Jamey suspected that Rick was enjoying his work. Jamey was told to sit, to stretch, to turn over, to drop the panty behind part way. He was induced to touch his own flat breasts, and even to slip a finger into the top of the underpants. Jamey knew it would be pretty sick stuff if it were to appear in the high school yearbook. But Altier was an artist of the first degree, and seventy-five dollars was no less than that. Act like a fairy to please the fairy. And nothing really nasty. Nothing to really be ashamed about; it was art.

Richard Altier got into his work, and was barking orders one moment and cajoling his model the next. He had a way of demanding or enticing poses that should have made Jamey balk. Rick got what he wanted from subjects and models. He encouraged Jamey, telling him that he was doing a great job. He made Jamey feel strange, calling him pretty and beautiful when that was the last thing that Jamey wanted to be. His mind was blown. And he was heavy with the wine, the opium-pot, and the cocaine. And, all around him, the world was bleeding pink. He saw himself in a mirror and wondered who it was.

"I need a break," said Jamey. "I want a smoke." Rick flipped him a Camel, and Jamey lighted it. He saw the red lipstick on the end, and he thought of Teri Ann Murphy and her Tareytons. "What are you going to do with these pictures?" asked Jamey.

"For my wall," he said. "We'll do some formal ones later on, for the book. But, you'll have to dress up for that."

Jamey figured that there was little chance that he would ever do this again. He went back and forth from the reality that he was posing like a girl, like a cute playboy bunny, to more disconcerting thoughts. He thought about whether all of Altier's so-called models were of the unprofessional variety, street kids like himself. Where were they now? Maybe he killed them when he was done with them. The Laurel Canyon house might someday be the scene of the excavation of a mass grave of Hollywood lost boys. Just so long as Knollridge High School never gets a load of this.

"Can you stop fidgeting?" said Rick, going back to work. "Smile as if someone is forcing you to smile. Not really happy."

"I can do that," said the model. Then there was the feeling of stretching and posing on the bed and on the floor. It felt good to use his muscles, to feel his skin against the bedding, and the feel of the sheer nightshirt and underwear on his body. He had recently been used to rougher treatment. He had always liked the feel of the girly fabrics when he was touching Teri Ann or Clarissa, but he had certainly never tried them on. He actually found pleasure in wearing the items, but he wasn't going to admit that to Rick. The feeling was seeping into his consciousness. As a model, he just tried to be as much of a girl as he could be, accepting the obvious differences. "Aren't you done yet?"

"Shut up and smile," said Altier, going from camera to camera. Being on all-fours was particularly degrading in Jamey's opinion. What guy does that? He couldn't even get Teri Ann to do that. Well, it was probably a failure of his imagination. He hadn't really asked her. Sometimes Richard would be behind him, and Jamey suspected that he would be upon him the next moment—but Richard hardly touched him during the shoot, just now and then putting a hand or an arm or a leg just so. The session went on for about thirty minutes. It was more work than Jamey thought it would be. It required more concentration than he expected. "I have enough for this session," said Rick at long last. "You did great. We'll go down, get something to drink, and then I think you should get to bed."

"So where's my cash?" said Jamey.

Altier laughed. "You don't trust me?" Richard reached for his camera case and pulled out a legal document. "Just fill in your name up there and sign down here," he said, tossing the form on the bed. Jamey didn't look at it very long. It said something about being a model release form. He was too tired to read it. He signed at the bottom and left the paper on the bed. Rick pulled a hundred dollar bill out of his camera bag and tossed it into Jamey's lap, taking the release form and stuffing it into the case. "Twenty-five dollar tip. You were very good for a first timer," said the photographer. "We'll do more when I get back."

"Where ya goin'?" asked Jamey.

"New York. Come on," Rick was saying as he was guiding Jamey out of the room and back down the stairs. This time he did pat the boy's pink bottom, ever so lightly. Jamey swished out of the way. "I'm going on an assignment tomorrow morning. Early. I won't see you, unless you want to sleep with me…"

"We made a deal."

"Well, why don't you stay here until I get back? You can have the place to yourself. The housekeeper comes every day, but she won't bother you. She'll cook whatever you want. I'll send my girl, Molly, to check on you. She'll take you shopping and get you your things." Jamey was looking at Rick in a most suspicious manner.

"You look at me like I'm the crook! I should be worried about you, kiddo. You could rob this place blind and I'd never be able to find you, much less explain what you were doing here. Meanwhile, try on different outfits. Molly can take you, to do your hair and legs and stuff. Practice wearing heels." The argument wasn't moving Jamey. "Another payday?"

In the kitchen, Rick opened the refrigerator. Jamey reached in to grab the orange juice, trying to keep the nightshirt in place behind him. He wasn't confident about his success. Rick poured himself a cognac while Jamey poured a glass of OJ. Rick went on, "The next shoot, I want you dolled up. Meanwhile, you have the sound system. You can write your songs. And all the cigarettes you can smoke. This beats living on the street. I've done it, so I know. Try it in Saigon." He pulled out two pills from a small pill case he carried. "Do one of these."

"What the fuck?"

"Thorazine," said Rick. "Take this and you'll sleep like a kitten." He touched Jamey's hair, pulling it away from his eyes. "A very sweet little kitten."

Shaking his hair and Rick's fingers away, "You're so gross," said Jamey. Both Rick and Jamey popped the pills with their respective drinks.

"Cool dreams, kid."

Jamey then looked at Rick as they were standing at the kitchen island. "I can't figure this out. You want me to live like a chick? Why? Why don't you just get a chick? They're good at it. I'm a spaz."

"Jamey, dear, I know you're not stupid. I could tell that from your song. So why not stop pretending? I tell you what I want. You say no. I insist. Then you submit. Is that about it? Because that's all I've seen."

He took Jamey lightly in his power, with his hands on Jamey's cheeks and with his eyes. Jamey trembled. But he tried to look defiant, in spite of the pink. "So, like I said, I want you in drag for this." He patted the two cheeks, and let Jamey go with a smile. When released, Jamey's impulse was to slap Rick's face, but he realized that that would be acting the very role he wanted to deny. That's what the Hollywood starlet whose honor was at risk would have done.

"I'm not going to do it," said Jamey.

He turned away from Rick and broke for the stairs. Rick followed in pursuit, bringing Jamey down on the lower steps. Rick embraced Jamey, holding him helplessly on his lap as he tried to break away. Rick was a lot stronger than Jamey, surprisingly so. "You wouldn't still be here in your pretty pants, would you, if you were this macho guy?" Rick whispered to him, "I love that you think you hate it, Jamey. Now kiss me." He kissed Jamey as Jamey tried to push him away. Jamey could feel his strong arm holding him in place and his other hand running through his long hair. Mitch would have considered Jamey's opposition a piss poor defense, but he wouldn't have thought much of the uniform either. Rick held Jamey in place with one arm and squeezed his ass with the other. Involuntarily, Jamey's bottom contracted at Rick's touch. Rick kissed Jamey on the top of his head and then released his hold, giving the boy his freedom.

"This isn't right," said Jamey, who didn't know what to do now, still sitting on Rick's lap. When he realized that he wasn't being held any longer, he jumped up and ran to the top of the stairs. Rick, walking now, followed Jamey, who had gone back into the bedroom and slammed the door behind. He gathered his hundred dollar bill and the previous contents of his pocket as Rick walked easily into the room. It flashed on Jamey that it probably wasn't the best of ideas to run into the bedroom.

"You don't know what you want," said Rick. "That's what I want for the shots. You hate it, but you want it. You're ashamed, but you're excited. The thing is you're seeing yourself for the first time. You're not as small as you thought you were, even though you thought you were hot stuff. There's more dimension than you ever knew. *Love* isn't just a fucking word the hippies made up. When they say that love is inside you, it means you have to open yourself up to feel it. If it's something safe, it's bullshit. We're all bewildered to find ourselves, and sometimes it's not who we expected. The more you hate it, the better. And that was just the audition. With hair and makeup, you might be the best I've ever had…" Jamey was trying to block it out, and there were tears of frustration welling up again. "On camera, darling."

"Give me my fucking clothes!" said Jamey, as forcefully as he could. Rick's face suggested that perhaps Jamey was more inviting than intimidating.

"Hey! You can leave if you want to. Any time."

"Like fucking NOW!" Jamey screamed. "You keep saying that, but I'm still here. I don't make out with dudes. No way!"

"Well, just sleep here tonight, and the housekeeper will do the laundry, and you can hit the streets in a clean outfit with your hundred and one dollars and sixty-five cents. If you really think living here is such a terrible thing, I can't stop you. But sleep here tonight at least. It must be nearly three, and I think you'll be pretty sleepy with the Thorazine and the wine. I'm going to bed, baby. You know you want to come with me. You're aching to know who you really are, but you can pretend a little longer, if it makes you feel like a dude. I'm gonna crash, kid."

Rick left the room and Jamey locked and closed the door behind him, though he was sure that the lock wasn't going to protect him. He wanted to change out of the girly outfit, but he had nothing. He looked in the dresser drawers, and there was nothing a guy could wear, though plenty for a teen-aged girl. He wasn't a prisoner. He could climb out the window, if not the front door, and walk into Hollywood in his pink, but that was probably not the best plan. And he was very drowsy. There was a calmness coming over him. It crossed his mind that Rick had drugged him, but what could that mean? He had willingly taken everything offered, except the acid. Why would Rick have had to *slip* him drugs? He was a willing user.

He oozed into the bed, and turned off the lamp. Rick was definitely a queer and a perv, besides. He had been ass-grabbed fer sure, man. On the other hand, this nice bed in Laurel Canyon was cool and cozy on a summer night. The sheets were more luxurious than his Margaret-approved bedding at home. He was in the lap of luxury. He may as well be in a nice bed in Laurel Canyon as sleeping in his alley. And Rick would be out of town. He could stay a day or two and then bug out. It would be dishonest on his part, but there was nothing right about any of this.

But, in the bed, he could still see Rick's unit by the spa, and he could still feel Rick's arms, and his hand—in his hair, on his ass. He stashed the wallet with the money under the pillow.

The silky sheets smelled of roses. His hair still smelled of strawberries. He could feel the stockings on his legs and he felt like a fool, a beautiful little fool. But he could still smell Rick cutting through all the feminine fragrances. Rick was a tricky bastard.

Jamey's fingers found their way to his unit, which was now at attention.

Under the circumstances, under the panties, he wasn't sure what to think about. What sort of dream was he dressed for? This Rick guy, likable and famous as he was, was a pervert, and he, Jamey, was apparently a drag princess who would pose on all fours in chicks' underwear and then make out with the photographer. So instead of working himself up to an orgasm, he fell asleep feeling his shame. But the shame was very mellow after all the marijuana, opium, wine, cocaine, and Thorazine. Jamey had actually done pretty well, he thought. What girl wouldn't have caved? He was trying to stay awake, expecting Rick to come back with amorous intentions, but he soon fell asleep, despite himself, and his sleep was undisturbed by the temporal plane.

GOOD GOLLY, MISS MOLLY

WHEN JAMEY RETURNED TO CONSCIOUSNESS, he had enjoyed the longest, deepest, and most restful sleep he had had since leaving home. Jamey Craig, the next Jack Bruce or Bill Wyman or the next Who-the-Hell-Ever, woke up chin-high in luxurious soft bedding in a room so cool and dark that he had no sense of the time of day or the month of the year. It was July, and the temperature should have been in the nineties, at least down on the boulevard, but, even under a comforter, Jamey was cool. When he sat up on the side of the bed, his pink nightshirt and white stocking legs came into focus and he remembered, first, the night before, and then the days and nights leading up to this pass. It was a lot of weird shit going down, but he wasn't ready to say that he shouldn't have run away from home. He had been learning a lot, even about himself.

Looking at and touching his face in the bathroom mirror, there was no visible hair. He determined to go masculine again, to grow his mustache back—even if he was the only one who thought he had one. Good decision when you're wearing pink underpants. It was all very weird, but he wasn't going to live like a chick or like a bird in a gilded cage. This bird shall have flown. Still in stocking feet, he ran down the stairs, thinking to catch Rick before he left. In the atrium, the windows let in the light through the greenery outside. The place was even more fantastic than the night before. The house was more impressive when the outdoor setting was discernable. He thought of his instrument in the back seat of Rick's car, and ran to the front door. The battered guitar case was on the landing. Jamey opened the big front door anyway. The sun blinded him, but he eventually discerned the big black car from the night before, the one with the peace sign on the hood. But there were two other cars on the lot. One looked to be expensive, a white Mustang, the original model which Jamey knew from building models. The other was an early model white Corvair. He didn't know if either had been there the night before, but he didn't think they had been.

The day was beautiful and inviting. He could feel the heat, but it wasn't miserable like it would have been on the Valley floor. There were breezes and there was plenty of shade. He walked out past the porch, toward the greenery. No kind of intrepid explorer or Boy Scout, Jamey was still able to ascertain that it was already early afternoon. It had been a good sleep, especially compared to recent sleeping arrangements. He knew that he had to go back to those unfortunate patterns, but the hundred dollars would help for a while. He told himself that he had earned some money for modeling, not for entertaining a pervert. The argument was a bit hard to make when he looked down at the outfit he had slept in. And that determined his next task.

He ran back up the steps and into the house. He went to the kitchen toward the back. There was a young woman with light skin and blond hair, and beautiful brown eyes. She was wearing jeans and a t-shirt, and she had full shapely breasts that stretched the shirt most obviously. "Are you the housekeeper?"

"Qué?" She had been putting away some dishes that had been out. She looked him up and down and suppressed a derisive giggle. Strange things happened in Mr. Rick's house. Jamey's face turned pink, and probably his exposed thighs as well. She seemed to make a point of looking at his indignity. Or so it felt to Jamey.

"My clothes?" he said, as if that attempt was somehow more communicative. Jamey had chosen French for his high school foreign language, so he had nothing. He pulled on the hem of the nighty. "Clothes," he insisted.

She smiled. "Rosada. Muy bonita!" Her voice was surprisingly husky, and her look didn't match Jamey's idea of what a Mexican maid should look like. But the world didn't really comport to Jamey's stereotypes.

In any event, her comment was not helpful. He pantomimed putting on his jeans. "My clothes. My pants." He was at a loss.

There was suddenly the musical voice of another woman who had just entered the kitchen. "Zulema, dónde es la ropa de…" She struggled for a second, referring with her hands to Jamey. "…del muchacho? Por favor," she added as a courtesy.

"Muchacho?" Zulema replied with a pointed smirk. "Ah sí!" She proceeded to an alcove behind the kitchen where the washer-dryer was situated.

The woman who had intervened introduced herself. "I'm Molly Gifford, Richard's assistant." Her voice was quite gentle and decidedly English, a proper sort, she seemed to Jamey. Since the arrival of The Beatles five years before, Jamey admired the English rock and roll culture. Her English tinted Spanish was charming to the lad, though mighty peculiar to Zulema. "He called me this morning and told me that you'd be here. Jamey, isn't it?" She smiled and he nodded. Jamey, not quite seventeen, was immediately enamored. He pulled the nighty over his pink underwear lest his enthusiasm for Molly show too indiscreetly. She continued to talk, but he got very little of it. "...and he wanted me to take care of you."

Molly was a young woman, but possibly ten years older than Jamey. She was older than Miss LeAnn Curtis, but much younger than his Mom.

Molly wore jeans and a white lace blouse that exposed the top of her breasts sans brassier. She was taller than Jamey, and he thought he might be in love. But then he blushed. How ridiculous he must look in his present pinkness! If that were not enough shame for the lad, he also laughed at himself for even thinking that his clothes might make the difference. Under any circumstances, Molly was obviously light years out of his league. He tried to pull it together, to say something to this bright light of loveliness.

"Well, there's been a change of plans," said Jamey, not sure if he should talk to her as if she were a sexy woman, one of his teachers at school, or his mother. "At least, I mean, *his* plans. Because I told him."

Zulema returned with all of Jamey's items of apparel, clean and nicely folded. She had even cleaned his shoes, as best one might. He took the clothes from her.

"Gracias," he offered.

"You're welcome," said Zulema, with a thick Spanish accent and an accepting smile. It occurred to Jamey that she probably saw a lot of odd things in this house. He also realized that she knew easily enough English to have answered his questions. She was a mean one. She presented Jamey with a plate. "Tostado? Jugo de naranja?"

Jamey took both and bit into the toast at the counter.

"Change of plans?" asked Molly, securing his distractible attention.

"I'm not going to be his little sissy," Jamey insisted, juicing up.

Molly seemed confused by his comment. "You do understand that he wants you to model for him?" asked Molly.

"I did some modeling last night," said Jamey. "I have to get out of here."

"Did he tell you that he's Richard Altier?" If Jamey wasn't going to be impressed, Molly continued to be. "I mean, Richard Altier wants to shoot you? Trudy Lewis has to pay him to shoot her. Trudy Lewis. But he wants you, and you're jumping overboard?"

"I think he wants me, all right," said Jamey. "But, I don't want some guy, famous or not, kissing me, or grabbing my butt, or putting me in baby dolls and high heels."

"You *are* adorable, Jamey. I can see what he sees…" She rethought that. "Sort of. I mean, of course, he's a fucking genius. Nobody sees what he sees. But you are lovely."

"Yeah, well. That's pretty far out. But I'm checking out of the Crazyland Hotel." To emphasize the point, Jamey dashed out of the kitchen, taking his clothes with him, and ran back up the stairs.

Jamey had run into the bathroom in his room upstairs where he had lost the pink which he dropped on the floor and donned his traditional garb. He grabbed the razor, the hair brush, the shampoo, a toothbrush and toothpaste, a pack of Camels that Richard had left behind, and some unused soap. He didn't care what anyone thought about it. He could use it. He tossed it all on the bed. Out of the closet, he took a gray and white canvas carry bag which zipped up square. He stuffed it all into his bag on the bed, including the pink towel.

Molly came into the room and sat on the bed where Jamey had been the night before as Rick had closed in on him. "Let's talk about this a little," she said.

Her voice was enticing, but Jamey went about his business. He went to one of the dressers he had already looked through and took several pairs of underwear and a pink t-shirt, having nothing of his own. He grabbed a couple of t-shirts which he thought weren't too girly. One of them had a peace sign on the chest, but that wasn't too bad in the summer of 1969. He stuffed it all in his bag.

"There's nothing to talk about, really," said Jamey. He put his stuff in his pockets, including his Chesterfucks and his matches. He checked the wallet which still had the proceeds of the night before. "I'm not a fag. It was a mistake. I should never have come here."

"But all he wants is for you to model. He told me."

"Except that you weren't here. Look. I'm not a fag. And why does he want me to be a girl anyway? Every girl in school is more of a girl than I am. He's fuckin' crazy, and it's makin' me crazy."

"He's an artist," Molly was saying. "He sees everything differently from how you and I see the world."

"It's not art," said Jamey. "It's just sex. Weird sex."

"I liked it better when he was shooting objective reality," said Molly. "Now he's putting together his own reality. But you've seen what he does? It's fuckin' brilliant."

"I saw the gallery," said Jamey.

"Then you know he's a great artist," said Molly. "And getting better all the time."

"Hey!" Jamey complained. "I'm a fuckin' artist, too. But I don't…"

"What?" said Molly.

"I don't make people feel like twits. He knows how I feel about it. I can tell he does. He wants to take away my…manhood."

"He thinks you're beautiful," said Molly. "What are you going to do with your precious manhood?"

"I'm going to fuck girls. That's what Jesus wants us to do." Jamey zipped up the soft carry case. "He wants me to dress like a girl. What did that lady down there think of me? You don't see me like a dude. I'm some boy-girl creation. What did you say? Adorable. I don't want to be adorable. Guys aren't adorable. They don't want to be adorable."

"Generally, no," said Molly, thoughtfully. "Dudes are not generally adorable. But you misunderstand him, Jamey." The music of her elegant English accent made it difficult to listen to her words. "It's not really sexual. It's artistic."

"He kissed me," said Jamey. "He kissed me like I was a girl."

"He hasn't kissed me…" she said, a bit envious. She took his free hand. "You don't understand," she began. "If you don't stay, Richard will be very disappointed. For his work, and in me. You are my assignment. I'm to look after you and prepare you. We could have fun."

"You sound like a babysitter," Jamey complained.

"I've already called the salon. We've got a whole day tomorrow. And then shopping for all your things. And he told me you've been on the streets. I mean, do you really want to go back so soon?"

"I would rather be on the streets than be his girlfriend. Is that really so far out? How many guys do you know would go along with what I've already done, no matter how desperate things got?"

"That's the point, isn't it? You've already given in," she answered. "I suppose it's embarrassing, but nobody has to know."

"He's the most famous fucking photographer in the world!" said Jamey. "Nobody has to know?"

"Well, he won't use your name," she explained. "He hasn't with the others. I mean, the less said the better. Nobody really has to know."

"But you know," said Jamey. "Rick knows. Housekeeper was laughing at me."

"She wasn't," protested Molly.

"I'm not going to go through with it. I can't live like a girl. I won't put on a dress. That's…I don't know what it is, but it's sick stuff. I said I was leaving, and I am. And why should you care? He's an artist, okay. But he can get real models. Not punks like me who don't have any options. And you shouldn't be…" He was searching for a word.

"Pimping?"

"Well, why should you care? I don't get why he needs me to dress like a girl when he knows I don't want to, and I don't get why you're going along with it."

"Sex is very strange," said Molly. "And love is weirder than that."

"You love him," said Jamey. "Then all the more reason for me to clear out of here. You know he kissed me last night. Grabbed my ass and kissed me. I didn't want him to, but he just kissed me, as if I were some helpless chick. Why would you want me around? I'm sort of the competition, not that I can compare…but he's a sick guy. You should get the fuck out of here." Frustrated and out of ideas, Jamey pulled away. "Look, I'm leaving. I'm taking what I brought, and, I hope nobody minds, some shower stuff. Okay?"

"You can't go."

The way her *can't* rhymed with *want* was lovely.

"I have to, for my self-respect. This is so queer, man." As a final addendum, "It was nice to meet you. Peace and love, Molly." She was lost in thought as he turned away for the door, carrying his things over the shoulder.

And he was almost out the door when he heard her entrancing voice calling to him, "Jamey!" When he turned around, her blouse was just floating to the floor and her breasts were free from all restraint. He had no idea what expression might have been on her face.

"What are you doing?" he asked, both stunned and fascinated. He could neither retreat from nor advance toward the vision before him. It may as well have been Julie Christie. He read the whole of *Far from the Madding Crowd* just because Julie Christie's tits were on the cover. Miss Curtis had been impressed with Jamey's interest in Thomas Hardy. She recommended *Tess*, but the cover was just blue.

"I'm begging you to stay," she answered. "I can't fuck this up. I need you to stay and do…what he expects." Now she stood up beside the bed.

"Fuck!" he said, not loudly, but convincingly.

"Would you have sex with me?" she asked.

"You're bribing me with sex?" said Jamey.

"What else have I got?" she answered. But she did have that. "Now,

Jamey love. I've never done anything like this before, so you can't refuse me. How will I feel if a high school boy doesn't want to have sex with me? Am I as old as your granny or something? Am I really so repulsive? You can't possibly leave me like this," she said. "No real man would think of leaving me this way." Jamey was sure there was a song in there somewhere, but he couldn't focus on anything but the breasts.

The gravitational force seemed to be increasing. Jamey, having looked at nothing but the pear shaped breasts for the last minute, felt impelled to take them in hand. He had never had an offer of this magnitude. With little Teri Ann, it had been a matter of inches at a time, not a full undraping in an instant. That was how they did it!

"If you walk out on me now, you haven't a heart at all." She invited him closer with her eyes, and he approached her. His hands automatically reached for her, but she met his hands with her own, clasping his between them. "Tell me. Are you a virgin? Have you had it off?"

"I've had sex," said Jamey. "Lots of times."

"How many?" she asked.

"You mean like *all the way?*" he clarified.

"Well, I hope so," she said, laughing a little. "How many times?"

"Like four or five," said Jamey.

"Guys always lie, at least a little, so no more than four," she said. "Right. And that's four different birds?"

"No. Just Teri Ann."

"So, you've had sex with Teri Ann, and that's the end of it, then?"

"Teri Ann is very hot stuff," said Jamey.

"My goodness gracious, I'm sure she is," said Molly, still holding his hands. "And do you think I'm *very hot stuff?*"

Jamey's face was quite red now. He wasn't inclined to talk about it. He wanted to get to it. He and Teri Ann might dance around it for hours, but, when it came to the act, he was quite urgent and quick.

"Well?" she said, seeming more confident now, taking it more slowly. "You're hurting my feelings. A woman wants to be well regarded, you know. You should say something sweet."

"You are the most beautiful woman I have ever seen, I mean, up close like this." His eyes bathed her breasts with appreciation and desire.

"That might have gone better without the clarification."

"I'm sorry," said Jamey. "This is all kind of unexpected."

"And, if we have sex together, you'll be Richard's model? You'll live here until he's got his shots and you'll be under my guidance the whole time. You'll be a good little boy, won't you? No more storming about and threatening to leave. No more boy clothes while you're here."

The "good little boy" talk did not encourage a bold erection, but the exposed breasts kept him from breaking off relations. To Jamey, holding hands with Molly, inches from her breasts, and talking about having sex as if it were a real possibility, it seemed fantastic. "Let's try a kiss," she said to him, dropping his hands and putting her mouth closer to his.

Jamey was confused. This wasn't Teri Ann anymore, and he felt like none of his long history of sexual experience would be of any help in this new mature situation. Feeling compelled to act, tempted by the proximity of the liberated breasts, he leaned up to kiss Molly, but she touched his lips with her finger. "Are we agreed then? We'll have it off, and then we'll get started on everything that has to be done."

"What has to be done?" he asked.

"You have to say yes, and then I will give you a fucking unlike anything sweet little Teri Ann ever gave you." At this, she took his stuff in her other hand through his jeans, firmly but gently, as if she knew her business. He was feeling seduced, as if she were in charge and not himself. His unit was on high alert, but he somehow felt like the girl nonetheless. Molly seemed to be calling the shots. He wanted to break away, but he wanted a taste of the next tease before he left. To see her breasts was exciting. To feel her hand on his crotch was compelling. He was inches from her lips. He wanted to touch her, but he had to promise away his dignity, as he saw it. His very manhood. How could he have sex with this incredible woman and then find himself back in panties? His breath was quite short now, shallow, and his heart was palpitating. She was the ultimate teenage dream. She was so incredibly feminine. He could smell her, and it was intoxicating. He was fascinated to see more of her. He couldn't say no.

But he couldn't say yes. And he just stood poised between the two. He thought of just taking her, but he wasn't really sure that he could manage it even if he wanted to. She had him by weight.

"Jamey," she said, trying to awaken him. "You're distracted, love." She took his hands now and put them on the top button of her jeans. "Say yes. If you want me, sweets, you've only to say yes. Because I want you inside of me, dear. I want all of you inside of me."

But she didn't want him. She wanted him to be compliant. He had received a hundred dollars for what he had done before. It was almost justifiable under the circumstances. But getting an opportunity to have sex with a grown-up woman could never come again, at least in relation to him being sixteen. How much was that worth? Once again, he concluded that the whole affair was sick, which changed nothing.

And, just as his gang taught him that you don't do anything queer, they also taught him that you don't turn opportunities down. He closed his eyes. "I promise," he said. "You can turn me into a twit. But, first, I'm going to fuck you."

"You're quite sure?" she asked him.

"I don't want to talk about it," he said, leaning in to her. Molly was quite as good as her promise. There was none of the tentative Teri Ann. She had always just been on her back with her legs spread in an accommodating A-shape. Maybe, he tried to remember, she lifted her knees sometimes. But mostly she just let Jamey do what he thought was best, and he didn't really know much. Molly was fun, but she was clear about guiding him. Jamey was ready to learn from her. She wasn't going to tell the other girls. He could let her teach him. He learned what experienced hands could do, and then found out about an experienced tongue and lips. He literally tasted a woman for the first time in his young life and thrilled at her responses. Still, he was sixteen, and his patience was soon at the limit. She rocked and rolled and made moaning sounds that easily convinced Jamey of her passion. She squeezed him, allowing him to express himself.

"Just stay where you are," she whispered, collapsing forward on the bed. "Don't move." Jamey was in heaven. Her smells. Her taste. The feel of her contractions. The closeness. The softness of her skin, her flesh, her voice. The accent. "Pretend like you want to be here. I know you'd rather be a thousand miles away now…"

"No…"

"Once it's done, guys are done with it. But just keep your arms around her. You can say something sweet, if you feel it."

"I love you," he tried.

Molly laughed at the absurdity. "No, no," she cautioned. "It has to be plausible." His face was in her hair, his chest on her bare back. "A little bit plausible. Something like, 'you were wonderful' or 'you're so beautiful' or 'I always want us to be just like this.'"

"I always want us to be just like this…" tried Jamey.

"See?" said Molly. "But don't just pull out and go away. It feels like you slammed a door. She just needs a few minutes. Always be sweet afterward, and they think you're wonderful! Good for your reputation. Girls talk." He wondered how long the whole thing had lasted. He didn't carry a watch, but it couldn't have been fifteen minutes.

The two were entwined for several minutes more. Jamey discovered that Molly was right. He did want to move away but he followed her advice. It was she who broke their bond. Molly toppled him onto the bed and sat up. Jamey watched her as she gathered her things from the floor. Before, she had been complete perfection. Now, she was interesting, but he could see flaws—too much flesh here, some imperfection on her thighs or her knees. Everyone's a critic. "I'm going to dress," she said. "And then we'll get started. And tomorrow: hair, nails, and shopping." She smiled at the boy. Now she was unsure of herself.

"Whoopee!" Jamey replied, having sold himself for the transitive prize. Molly had to flash her ass for Jamey as she dashed into the bath. She was a good looking woman, but he could see that her particular ass had more wrinkles and bumps than Teri Ann's or any of the girls at the cove. Molly's was a very firm ass, but, at sixteen, Jamey was used to the natural perfection of his high school sweetheart, usually draped in illusion and half truth.

As Molly disappeared into the bathroom, Jamey made a split second decision that took him by surprise. When he had agreed to her terms, he had no thought of deception. It was worth it to have her. But, having had her, he nevertheless abrogated the agreement with hardly a thought. He jumped off the bed, quickly pulled on his clothes and his shoes, grabbed his carry bag and made sure of his wallet. He heard the shower come on behind the closed door, and he quietly but hurriedly left the room. He was down the stairs and to the front door landing in a flash, picking up his guitar case. He took one last look around the gilded cage.

He looked back at the fantastic atrium scene, the polished wooden walls and floor, the indoor plants, and the photographs that represented his generation so artistically and so completely. He grabbed his guitar case and was planning to run like hell down the road, but it crossed his mind that he could handle this with a little more ease. He found a stick on the ground and used it to deflate one tire on each of the cars. And then, guitar case in one hand and carry bag on his other shoulder, he booked it down the shady road toward the canyon below.

He thought maybe she would call the cops and accuse him of something outrageous, but as he made his way down the labyrinth of paved trails, he thought about it and realized that she wouldn't bring in the cops to catch an underage run-away who had just had sex with her. He realized that he was now in the clear. That made five naked girls since leaving home and a really cool fuck, as well as Jamie judged such matters.

CALIFORNIA DREAMIN'

THE AIR WAS HEAVY WITH SUMMER, but there was plenty of shade, enough to keep it bearable. He couldn't remember the way from the night before, but he continued his way down, and, within half an hour, he was on Laurel Canyon itself, carrying his stuff, and making his way along the side of the narrow road. The cars were racing by, so he kept close to the curb. He went by the store. He watched to see if any of the Laurel Canyon celebrities would show up: Frank Zappa, Joni Mitchell, Sean Nichols, even Jim Morrison. No such luck.

Richard Altier might be a sick bastard, as the evidence suggested, but he was a great photographer, thought Jamey. Mick Jagger might be bi, according to the stories, but he was a great lead singer and songwriter. Maybe a lot of these stars were assholes or creeps in real life. But they were artists on the stage or in the studio. So maybe Jamey fucked up sometimes, acting like a fairy for a night, taking a whack at his dad, breaking his mother's heart by disappearing, even being a liar to Molly, but that didn't mean that he wasn't going to make it as an artist.

On two different occasions drivers pulled their cars over to offer him a ride, until they discerned that he was a guy and not a girl. Both had sped off leaving him walking. At this point, he really didn't want a ride anyway. There was a lot to consider. He didn't relish another night on the streets, but he was glad to be out of Rick the Perv's place. He didn't like to think of posing in pink the night before, and he was not proud of breaking his agreement with Molly. He had deceived her like an asshole. But she had been asking for a lot. She must have known that chicks shouldn't flash their tits like that and expect a reasonable response. She wasn't the sixteen-year-old kid. Jamey was.

NOW IT WAS TIME to think about the immediate future. Maybe it was, but his mind kept returning to Molly Gifford. She had given him head. He had tasted her. He was still picking out an occasional hair from his mouth. It had been that recent. And, Buck, for the record, up close and very personal, Jamey thought it very beautiful indeed! He wanted to try out that new skill on Miss T.A. Murphy. And he thought of Molly on her knees, receiving him. Craig Roman would never believe any of it. He'd be calling bullshit about the scene at the cove and the idea that a grown woman got on her knees to suck Jamey would never fly. And an English chick besides.

But, returning to reality, where was he to sleep? Staying in a cheap motel would have him flat broke within the week. How beautiful her pussy between her legs! On her knees! He had to think. But sleeping among the trash bins in his favorite alley after the night in the luxurious pink rose petal sheets was a radical come-down. He thought about actually going up to Big Sur, and maybe on to San Francisco. All he could see was her hair as he felt her mouth engulfing him. He could find work up there as easily as he could down here, which wasn't easy. He thought about going back to the beach, maybe for a night, and then hitching up the coast highway. It smelled so nice, and tasted like nothing he knew. And such a thrill when she had shivered and held his head down. It had been seven nights now. He doubted that the cops could keep their minds on him for that long. He should be able to hitch up the coast without being picked up. The purple paisley panties. The blond bushy mound. Even a contact with the cops might not tip them off, if he played it real cool. But Frisco nights were colder than Hollywood nights. Maybe he should go back to street singing? The feel of those beautiful tits! Street singing had paid him close to three dollars in two days, and it had gotten him noticed by Rick—but was that a good thing? Rick had provided a prime rib dinner, a nice bed, really good drugs, and the fuck of a lifetime. Her murmuring voice as he fucked her! And he provided a hundred bucks for a few hours in panties. Squeezing everything out of him… And, with nobody else around to hear him, he had to admit that he liked how it had felt, if you really want to know, even if it looked damned silly. Molly!

After he had traversed a couple of miles of the winding canyon on the Hollywood side, he did start actively trying to attract a ride with his thumb. And he eventually succeeded. He picked up a ride from a square, a dude who seemed to want to go hip but who had too much invested in the system, man.

"I can dig it," said Jamey. "I mean, you got a car and a place to live. I don't."

"But you're like totally free, man," said the dude.

"Free to beg a ride," said Jamey. "I'm carrying everything I own, man."

"See what I mean?" said the dude. "That's what I mean. That's really cool."

"But you have a regular paycheck," said Jamey. "You can make plans. You can put your stuff down and it's kind of safe. You can have underwear for every day of the week, man."

"But all the responsibilities and all of the hassles," said the dude. "I just don't want to be hassled by everything. I just want to blitz out sometimes and do my own thing."

"The weekend or vacation. You got it made, man," said Jamey. "Are you married?"

"No," said fellow.

"So everything you make is yours," said Jamey. "You got it made, man."

Whether he had it made or otherwise, he did take Jamey down into Hollywood. Jamey offered his thanks and returned to the street scene. He hadn't been missed by anyone at all. The Hollywood scene was a giant Knollridge High School quad peopled by squares, hipsters, users, and fucked-up throw-aways like Mitch.

He encountered the carwash that he had visited twice before, and he saw the same manager with whom he had talked. He reintroduced himself and once again pitched the job idea. Given that he was a repeat applicant, that he looked a lot better due to the clean clothes and the showering, and that two of the crew had not shown up, Jamey Craig was given a shot. He was employed at the minimum wage of $1.65 per hour. The number one rule was that if a guy missed a shift in the first three months, he was out on his ass, no excuses. It wasn't the music business, but it was a job, just like the dude in the car who wanted to be free. Thanks to the Perv, Jamey had enough to make it to payday, whenever that would be, so he thought he should go about finding a more decent place to sleep and maybe some clothes after that. The California dream was happening, man. Fuckin' Molly!

Jamey remembered the place he had stayed one night. Why he chose to go back there, he never really understood. It had been musty, very noisy with the prostitute next door, and the bathroom had been communal. But he knew that the desk guy minded his own business and didn't call the cops on teenage runaways. So he figured Rooms-for-Rent would be his new home. He went inside again, more confident than on the first night. He waited at the small front desk until Jack came around and Jamey inquired.

The manager was closer to fifty, actually older than Jamey's old man, if such a thing were possible. He had a red nose and fuzzy eyes and a ragged beard. His hair was not long, but it was curly and full, though graying. He didn't get around quickly, but everything seemed to be working. "What can I do for ya, Miss?"

"I'm a guy," said Jamey, even though Rick had told him that a guy shouldn't have to tell anyone.

Jack's look in response was nonplussed. He explained that the rooms were by the day or by the week. Six bucks a day, thirty bucks a week, all in advance. The elevator was for show, and there was no discount for its inactivity. They climbed the three flights. Halfway up, they met a tiny Chinese looking girl with straight black hair, an oval face with olive skin, and a sharp intelligent smile. She wore heavy black glasses that automatically added points to her already Oriental IQ. Her light brown cords were low on her hips but loose and comfortable. There was no attempt to draw attention to her shape. She was small, shorter than Jamey, but she carried herself as if she were older. Her attitude suggested that she might be all of eighteen years, though her physical appearance was less convincing. She wore a black boy's t-shirt and no bra because there wasn't any great weight to be constrained. She eyed Jamey and his guitar case and carry bag as he followed up the stairs behind the proprietor.

"Hey hey, Jack," said the girl, by way of greeting. Her voice had a husky tone to it, but it wasn't unpleasant. "What's happening?" She ran, smiling at Jamey as she went, looking him up and down. "Cool!"

"Hey yourself, Mona. What's happening?" Jack replied, in a most blasé voice. She was already long behind him, bounding down the stairs. Jack unlocked the door and Jamey took a look around. The room had a bureau with a cracked mirror, a bed, a chair, a large sink, and an overhead light with a pull-chain. No fan. The room was hot and a bit smelly, with dark green floral wallpaper long past its best, some of it hanging from the wall in strips. Jamey made sure the window would open. He looked down on the alley behind the building, the sort of place where Jamey might have been sleeping if not for his model's pay from Rick the Perv. Aside from the open door where Jack was standing, there was a second door leading, he presumed, into another room. He tried the lock. It seemed as secure as anything in this milieu. He listened at the door but heard nothing.

"I'll kick you out if you're doing the dope or having the pot parties. Got me? No guests, if you know what I mean. I'll call the fuckin' cops. No refunds. Rent due before noon or out on your ass. Got it?"

"It's cool," said Jamey.

"Not really," said Jack with a smirk. The twelve dollar weekly differential was tempting enough that Jamey committed to the weekly rate.

Big spender. "Let's go sign you up," said Jack. "Bathroom's at…"

"I know. End of the hallway."

"We're all hippies now," said Jack.

It was about four by the time Jamey found himself ensconced in his luxury suite and once again considering his situation. He wanted to be practical about this. The one hundred bucks was a gift, something with which to get started. He wanted to take care of it, to be careful. He had been dangerously close to zero on more than one occasion, and he had spent a lot of time living on less than two dollars. But, apart from rent, he determined that there had to be some immediate expenses.

He needed a few changes of clothes. He had been to a Goodwill store in the Valley looking for cool clothes, so he had a sense of what it might cost like two or three changes might cost him ten or twelve. Anyway, that was how much he figured he could let go of, so he would make it work. Margaret had always seen to the basics, but Jamey was on his own now. He might have to go to a department store to buy socks and underwear, but that wouldn't kill him.

He was calculating to determine whether he could afford one or two meals a day. A guy would need a couple of meals if he was going to work all day and maybe rock at night. Three bucks a day would come to a little over twenty a week. With thirty for rent, he would be up to $50 a week overhead. He figured the carwash was good for that. Pretty basic, but not bad for a punk runaway. Jamey finally had a plan, and that felt good. And no cock-sucking with Ian required.

He hadn't intended it, but he fell into a nap. He was in a relatively safe place for it. He awoke when he heard a commotion from the adjoining room. He was a tolerant fellow, so a little neighborly noise didn't bother him. He hoped that his neighbor would feel the same about his guitar. He had no idea how much time had passed. It was still sunny and hot outside, but it didn't get dark until after eight.

He awoke thinking of food. He hadn't had much. He was getting used to less of it, but he was no ascetic. He was thinking of a burger and fries. It was hot out there and a little stuffy inside. He was waiting for the day to cool off. He pulled out his instrument, and he opened the carry bag to take out his Camels which he laid beside the Chesterfucks. The guitar, the smokes, the contents of the bag: It was all he owned. If he someday became a millionaire rocker, he could look back at this moment and remember what few possessions he had had. He flipped the strawberry scented hair out of his eyes, and he began strumming and singing one of his own songs, just

82

to satisfy his urge to play. It was nice behind closed doors. He was backed against the headboard, eyes half closed, singing the bridge part.

> *You can't take company*
> *She said she always knew*
> *Freedom's kinda lonely*
> *As the freak takes you*

At the root of it all, he was doing what he was doing, living as he was living, for the music—if you believe Jamey's rationalizations, which he sort of did. His dad was pushing him to bear down in school, to get into the university. Everyone wanted him to decide on his life, but neither his teachers nor his parents took his music seriously. To him, that meant that they didn't take him seriously. It wasn't about the long hair. It wasn't about dope. It wasn't even about sex with Teri Ann Murphy. He kept thinking of Molly from behind. It was really about doing his own thing in his own time.

There was some pride at work, and he knew it. He couldn't go home again because he wasn't going to submit to his father's unreasonable demands.

> *"As long as you're under my roof…"*
> *Well, I'm not.*

Jamey was somewhat pleased with himself. He had run away from home with twenty dollars in his pocket. Six days later, he had $71.65, a job, and a bed for the next seven nights. He was providing his own roof now. He had enough for dinner and breakfast. He was doing very well, by his lights.

But he was not even seventeen, so his judgment might have been suspect—given how he had earned the money. He had been kissed by a pervert who had squeezed his ass with impunity. He could still feel Rick's fingers. On the other hand, he had seen a total of five naked ladies, and, one of them, a full grown woman, he had nailed, paisley underpants and all. He could now say that his love affairs included someone other than Teri Ann Murphy. So, on balance, he decided that he was doing pretty well.

He had about made up his mind to go splurge at the Big Boy, but he was momentarily happy playing his guitar and singing his song. A job, prospects for tomorrow, a bed, dinner—all of that was in his grasp.

Dreaming was becoming reality.

She's down when she's up
Turn it on now
I'm over there
But I don't know how
Imagine a freak
In someone's view
I'll take the air
As the freak takes you
Imagine Yourself
As the freak—takes you

He was playing, but his mind was turning on the events of the night before. If you had asked Jamey a week ago what you call a guy posing in pink underwear, he would have said *pussy*. He didn't know why he had done it, no matter how famous the guy was. And why did it excite him as well as creep him out? He sort of wanted to try it on again, without the pressure of the perv looking at him. It was exciting. He was pretty sure he was supposed to be repulsed. That's what they had told him. That's what he had believed. And he knew he wasn't that way, queer. A gentleman has no business telling stories, about Teri Ann, about Molly. And if you don't tell the one, why tell the other? Both Molly and Rick would have to remain private matters. He put the guitar down and unzipped his appropriated carry bag. He looked at the pink underwear again. The touch excited him. He had paid for the privacy, but then his stomach growled a little.

Thinking about that burger again, nothing but toast and orange juice for breakfast, he flashed that he could go to dinner and leave his guitar case in the room in relative safety. He didn't have to carry it up and down the boulevard, drawing attention to himself. He could walk with his hands in his pockets, the young freewheelin' punk. But where was his Suzy?

MONA

H E HEARD MORE NOISES in the room next door, quite a bit louder now as if furniture were being moved. He wiped his brow with the pink towel beside him, and went back to his music. Shortly, there was a scraping sound on the other side of the door. Then there was a rattling, presumably the lock. Next, a quick knock as Jamey looked up. And finally Mona, the girl in cords from the stairway, popped her head inside. "Hey, girl!" she said. "Jamey, right?"

"Jamey," he answered, trying to make his voice manlier.

"Listen, I'm sorry to mess with you. How do you like that lock? Sometimes I'm in there and it's some weirdo pervert dude in here, and I don't know what he's doing." Mona was already completely in Jamey's room. "Jerking off probably. I know how easy it is to get in. You just saw. So I put the bed against the door, but it's kind of lame, isn't it? If I can move the bed, he can't? So I'm really glad *you're* here. You have any Kotex? I'm hemorrhaging like a hemo."

"I'm a dude, you know," said Jamey, still sitting on the bed and holding the guitar.

"Ooo, sorry," said Mona. "Well, you look kind of…well, your towel is hot pink, you know. And…" She held up the pink underwear that had been on the bed. "What's a girl to think?" Jamey grabbed his things and stuffed them back in the bag. "Don't be uptight about it. I'm always getting into trouble with my mouth. I checked out your card when Jack was sweeping out front. He got you down as female. Well, get real! You have beautiful hair and your voice is so sweet! Which is why I came over, too. I wanted to see the angel who was singing that song. But maybe you're a boy angel. I think angels are boys anyway. Gabriel. Maybe they're fags. Where'd you get the song?"

"I wrote it," said Jamey. Complimenting Jamey's talent would quickly get you on his good side. He would assume that you were a very perceptive person with good taste besides. "Are you a musician?"

"I have a band. I'm the bass," she said.

"Far out!" said Jamey. "I'm the bass in my band, back home, that is."

"Where do you gig? We have a gig going at The Contortionist."

"Well, I'm kind of going solo right now," said Jamey. And it hit him that Crazy Place was a long way and a long time distant. If he was really living on his own now, on the lam, he wasn't in a band anymore. That was the old Jamey Craig. "I guess I don't have a band any more."

"Bummer." Mona really seemed to understand, but she didn't stay on one point for very long. "I need a Kotex," she announced. "I hope you don't mind. I mean, some guys get all creepy about it, but you're not a creep, are you? Would you go down to the store and get me a box? I'd go, but I'm really starting to slosh. I was on the bus, and I just got back. I thought I had some, but the box was empty. I'm going to go in my room and stick my legs up in the air. Don't you hate periods?"

"You want me to go and buy girl stuff?" said Jamey, who put the guitar aside on the bed. Mona picked up the instrument. She played the chords for the tune Jamey was just playing. He was blown away. Chick knew her music.

"You don't need a license to buy Kotex. You don't have to be twenty-one." Jamey was not comfortable with this, but Mona didn't let up. "Pretty please, with sugar on top? Don't you dig Paul McCartney? I mean, I know he's square, but I love his songs. And his voice is so pretty, and, I hate to be a teeny bopper, but he is cute. And he's one of the best bassists I know."

"Some of his stuff is pretty square. 'Your Mother Should Know.' *He* should fuckin' know. But I like a lot of his stuff." It was difficult to follow Mona because there were so many balls in the air. Now she was looking at Jamey, calculating something he didn't know. He caved. "So where's the store, and give me some money."

"Yeah. When you go outside the building, go left about two blocks. There's a little market on the corner, near the hot dog joint. I asked him if he could sell me like one or two at a time, like he does with cigarettes." She saw Jamey's Camels and Chesterfields. She went for the Camels, lighting one with Jamey's matches. "Jacks? Looks classy. Anyway, he makes me buy the whole box. Like I'm a zillionaire. But chicks need this shit, and so he's got us by the balls. You have any money?"

Jamey wanted to react to what she had just said, before the question, but the pace was pretty intense. "A little, but, I mean, it has to last. It's all I have…"

"I'll pay you back, but this really can't wait. This underwear is gone, and I only have…"

"Okay. Okay. Okay," he tried to cut her off. He didn't mind thinking of Molly's paisleys, but he didn't want to know about the bloody mess in this new chick's pants.

"And don't forget the M&M's. Two bags. Gotta have the chocolate. And a jug of orange soda. A big one. It gets hot up here, man. You don't want to dehydrate."

"It's cool," said Jamey. "I dig."

"And some TP? I don't know if Jack's too cheap or just too lazy, but it can get kind of hairy in there. It's better if we just bring our own."

"Our own...?" Jamey set off on the mission before Mona could add anything else to the shopping list. He could hear Mona working out his song on his guitar as he descended toward the street. Mona was a fast operator, and she seemed to be a rock and roller, not a folksy Judy Collins chick. He looked through the market crowded with merchandise, and he found the section with the appropriate box. He grabbed a four pack of toilet paper from the shelf, a cold orange soda from the cooler, and at the counter he found the candy rack. He was wondering if she was upstairs going through his things and stealing him blind. He just had to laugh. What things were these that she was ripping off?

Blushing, he presented his purchase to the cashier. Jamey was thinking that he ought to say that it was for a friend, but he thought it really should have been obvious. The clerk regarded Jamey, scanning his appearance and pausing at the breasts, or lack thereof. The charge was $4.48. This middle class Squaresville lifestyle that Jamey had moved into was no free ride. How quickly $71.65 becomes $67.17, unless he considered that he also had the asset of Mona's bond for a large portion of the cost. Somehow, he didn't really think she would come through. He had to at least operate as if she would never pay. "There you go, Miss," said the gentleman. Jamey flicked his blond hair out of his eyes and paid the man his money, a little exasperated but following Rick's advice: You shouldn't have to tell.

Jamey returned to Rooms-for-Rent, thinking again in his paranoid mode that this chick might have stolen his guitar. The guitar might be worth something. But, toward the top of the stairs, he heard her playing and singing, "Sweet Little Sixteen." As he came in, he pulled the orange soda out of the bag and put it on the bureau. He tossed the bag and its remaining contents toward Mona. She got out one of the four rolls of paper, ripped open the Kotex box, took out a pad, picked up a pair of fresh underwear that she had already secured from her room, and ran down the hall to the bathroom.

Jamey went into Mona's room for a look-see. It was well lived in, and she was no housekeeper. Her open closet—there was no door—was spare given that much of her wardrobe was on the floor. Her things were spread all over the room like a kid without a monitor. Underwear, tights, jeans, shoes, t-shirts, and dresses, presumably ready for the laundry, but maybe not, made up a thick carpet. When Jamey ventured in deeper, he had to be careful not to step on stray shoes or Mona's guitar, cast on the floor.

The bed was tossed and now at an angle to accommodate the open door. There was a little pink bear near her pillow. She had strung a line by the alley window for the drying and airing of her in-house washing. Venturing deeper, he looked in her sink and found Mona's laundry, soaking and floating in a bath of soapy water. This is more than he had wanted to know, but that's what you get when you're too nosey.

On the bureau in Mona's room, plugged into the wall, was a little Tele-Tone portable record player suitable for playing children's records. The speaker was under the tone arm and was covered by the *Retrospective: the Buffalo Springfield's Greatest Hits* album that had last been played. There were quite a few albums, most of which Jamey had in his collection at home including *Disraeli Gears, Mr. Fantasy,* and *Revolver.*

There were three pieces of art on Mona's walls. One was the dark silhouette poster from *Bob Dylan's Greatest Hits* album, with the psychedelic *Yellow Submarine* style colors swirling on his head. In the mirror was the cut-out sheet from Sergeant Pepper. And the inside of the *Sergeant Pepper* cover was displayed over the headboard. Mona had talked about him, so Jamey couldn't help but notice Paul in the middle with biggest head. Teri Ann had once told him that she liked to look at a certain picture of Bryan Cooper on her wall, so he guessed that Mona liked to look at Paul when she fingered herself.

Girls were weird, if you asked Jamey. Bryan Cooper was cool because he was a great rock-blues singer. He had a cool, rich, powerful voice, and his group, The Forgotten Avenue, had made about eight top forty hits over the last few years. Not the bubble-gum teeny-bopper shit, but really good records that rocked. The fact that he had taken to wearing tight leather pants and low cut shirts with gold medallions just seemed lame to Jamey Craig.

Teri Ann didn't care about his music. She even liked his new psychedelic solo album, *Translucent Curtain.* Jamey and Roman had checked it out, on Teri Ann's two-ninety-eight, and they pronounced it barfable. It was pretentious, overdone, and it lacked the musical power that made Bryan Cooper who he really was. Of course, Teri Ann didn't care about all that. She liked his eyes on the cover. She just thought he was sexy. But,

Jamey allowed, that picture of Bridgette Bardot in the magazine had kept him company on more than one occasion. It wasn't her acting; he had never seen one of her movies.

On the shelf of the closet were several fancy pairs of leather pants with metallic studs, a cool wide brimmed cowboy hat, and, hanging, under the pants were a couple of shirts that went with the rock-western look. These blouses were out of proportion to Mona. Some of the more personal clothing on the floor was also a little big for Mona to have worn. Detective Jamey determined that another girl had been living here with Mona. The archaeological record didn't say exactly when, but in the recent past.

He was back in his own room when Mona returned. "I feel better," she announced, running through Jamey's room to her own to put another item in the wash soup. "I hate my period. I wish I was a dude. Don't you? Well, you are a dude, so okay. But I wish I were a dude." Mona took on a dude persona, tightening her muscles and using a husky oafish voice, sort of dragging her knuckles. "I'm a big strong man and chicks play like girls." She switched back in an instant. "But I really wish you *weren't* a dude."

Now she was half kneeling on the bed, her bottom resting on her calves. She had poured out the M&M's, both bags, and begun to sort them by colors, but popping a few before the count was finished. "Chocolate! Have some!" Jamey passed. "Okay. I get it," said Mona, "You *are* a dude. No chick could have resisted. But when I heard you playing, I was thinking that you would be great for the band because, like, we all rock real good, but your song was like really trippy and quick. And it would round out our sound, as long as you can rock when it's time to rock, which is most of the time, but we could have more dimension, like, you know, with your voice. And you said you played bass?"

"Thumpin'," claimed Jamey.

"Because that would be so cool. I'm the bass. I told you. But I'd rather play guitar, because I'm better at it. I just do bass because it's like so important. It's really a big part of the sound, and you need a real musician on bass. So I always do bass because, well, you get it. But if you could play bass, then I could play guitar. Denise is rhythm. Karen is drums."

"It's a girl band?" said Jamey. "I never heard of a girl band. I mean the Supremes or the Shirelles, or something."

"That's the deal," said Mona. "We're good musicians. I think we're better than a lot of dudes, but we're chicks. All the dudes think chicks are good for is like chick vocals and tambourines banging on our hips. In other words, tits and ass stuff, and I don't have a lot of tits, maybe you noticed. That's why I thought you were a chick. I thought you were like me. Just no tits. You have a nice ass, by the way. I wouldn't mind having your ass. Well, that didn't come out right. Well, it sort of did, but we're room mates so forget about it. Is that okay, Jamey? I don't like it to get weird where I live. But we could be really good friends."

Mona had an attractive face. Everyone was posing, but her pose was a pretty good one. It was a nice offer. His friends had all been guys. He liked some girls, but it always came down to something romantic. He didn't really think he could be friends with a girl, the way he was friends with Craig. But he went along with the idea.

"You have any pot?" Mona suddenly asked. "It helps me through my period. And pretty much everything else."

"No," said Jamey.

"Oh, it's like that, huh?" said Mona. "It's cool. I was just checking it out." Mona was clearly disappointed and she showed some measure of hurt.

Jamey sensed the sudden chill. "What are you talking about?" He asked.

"Well, I guess you mean except for that lid in the pocket of your case where you keep your capo and picks and stuff. I was checking out your stuff while you were gone. I'm nosey, which you'll figure out. You don't have any clothes, by the way. I mean, except for the chick stuff, which I don't ask about. But, anyway, it's cool. You don't have to share your stuff. It's not a commune."

Jamey looked in the case and found the lid. "Damn!" he said, truly blown away. And that wasn't all. He found the five by seven photo of John Lennon that he had admired. It turns out that Jamey's previous inventory had been insufficient. He had had unknown resources. "Mona, believe me, I didn't know about it. This guy I met last night, he must have turned me on to it—like a surprise. I wasn't holding out. Let's blow some reefer, man!"

"I wouldn't blame you if you were holding out. You don't know me."

"I buy your fucking period stuff!" said Jamey. "I hate to tell you, Mona, but you're my very best friend. I don't know anyone else around here except for one homo creep up in Laurel Canyon and a really cool English chick who I kind of fucked over."

"So, what's that picture?" Jamey smelled the bag of pot. Then he looked at the picture of Lennon. On the back was Richard Altier's autograph and comment: "*For Jamey who's leaving home…bye bye.*" Mona whistled a fragment of a familiar Beatles tune.

It was like a Christmas stocking. One thing after another. Jamey found Molly Gifford's business card. Mona asked about Molly, and Jamey explained to Mona a number of the particulars of the recent night and of the recent week. He also showed her his genuine Jerry Westerfield card. That impressed Mona. Jamey was telling his story, but he could never finish a whole sentence and certainly never a whole story because Mona was constantly interrupting and redirecting, but she got the big picture.

Mona understood that Molly was the contact for this Richard Altier guy, and, obviously, he wanted to stay in contact with Jamey, plying him with gifts as if he were the Sultan of Brunei. Mona, generally frenetic, ran back and forth from room to room, this time bringing back some papes to roll a couple of joints along with a recent Rolling Stone magazine. "Check it out. Here's a couple of shots by your boyfriend." There was some cowboy on the cover and a big spread of Yoko and Lennon inside. But Mona directed Jamey to some photos of Trudy Lewis and The Forgotten Avenue with credits to Richard Altier. "He's a big deal, man. Hey, let's go for a walk and blow some weed. By the way, did you catch the other thing? Why don't you have any clothes, girl?"

"I'm a dude," said Jamey.

"So no clothes?"

"No. You called me *girl* again."

"Everybody says *hey, man* all the time. Sorry. Did you catch the other thing?" Mona eyed the guitar case again. Jamey looked inside the compartment where the photo had been. "You didn't know about any of this, did ya, chick?" Jamey rolled his eyes. Mona didn't let up. He found the pair of golden pearl clip-on drop earrings from the night before. They looked genuine to both of them, but neither knew how to judge or value the quality or origin of pearls. Mona picked them up and looked at them in her hand. On her knees on the bed, she leaned over to clip them onto Jamey's pink ears.

"What are you doing?" he complained. Still, he let her clip them on for the pleasure of her proximity and the nearness of her tiny breasts. After Rick had dressed him and checked him out like he was a girl on a platter, he didn't really mind Mona playing with him.

"I just want to see," said Mona, backing off once the earrings were attached. "Cute! They're definitely the real thing. I mean, like maybe a hundred bucks, or maybe two. They look antique. I don't really know. You could have them appraised. They're nice on you. Are you sure you're not a chick? Because you would really be a cool chick." It just kept happening.

Jamey was distracted for a moment. "What?" asked Mona.

"Well, I never took these off," said Jamey. "I went to bed last night with the stockings and the earrings and the whole thing. I never took them off."

"So?"

"So, he came back in the night and took them off," said Jamey. "I don't think he did anything to me."

"I think you'd have a feeling about that," said Mona.

"So he came in the middle of the night. Why?"

"Maybe he tucked you in and gave you a kiss good-night," suggested Mona.

"Maybe he did," said Jamey.

"That photographer guy is really hot for you. All this stuff. You didn't even know about it. Good thing the pigs didn't check out your case. You'd be in jail, and you are way too pretty for jail. I know he's got money, but this is pretty excessive. Jamey has a boyfriend! Jamey has a boyfriend!" Whether he did or not, he wasn't amused. Mona rolled on. "And then there's the card from Jerry Westerfield."

"I met him with Rick," said Jamey.

"I've been in Hollywood forever, man, and I haven't met Richard Altier or Jerry Westerfield, the biggest fucking producer on the west coast. You are magical, girl. I'm gonna stick with you."

"Good to be loved," said Jamey.

Holding up a joint with a wink, Mona told her new found friend, "Jack doesn't like drugs in the building, at least when he's awake. So you either have to go out or wait for him to go to bed, usually around eight. He drinks now and again. That guy wanting you to be a girl—it gives me an idea."

SWEET LITTLE SIXTEEN

MONA QUICKLY CHANGED and put a gold chain around her neck with a peace sign medallion. She grabbed an orange bucket hat with a floppy brim. "That's some style," said Jamey, hardly a critic, but one can't help but notice. For a second, Mona reminded Jamey of the girl in the orange two-piece on the beach that first day. With some trouble, Jamey took off the earrings and put them on the bureau. As they were heading out the door, Mona swept them into the purse she carried on her shoulder.

They walked in the late dusk through some streets up above the boulevard where they hoped they wouldn't attract police attention. "I want you to join the band, Jamey. Maiden Head. See? 'Cause we're maidens, sort of, and maybe we give head? And maybe we're virgins, like maidenhead. 'Cause we're like a chick band. And we're a head band. I mean, we do some psychedelic stuff. So Maiden Head."

"I can dig it," was Jamey's claim.

"We were gigging three nights a week at The Contortionist, but we're advertised as a girl band. That's the attraction. And we lost our lead guitar, so that's on hold."

"Well, there's an obvious problem, Mona," said Jamey, shaking his hair out of his eyes. "I would love to gig. I miss the band as much as I miss anything, but you see the problem."

"Whatever you say," said Mona.

"What kind of stuff do you guys play? You guys write your own shit?"

"I have stuff you could wear," said Mona, solving what she thought was the obvious problem. "Our lead guitar, Leslie, she quit. And she was really really good. I can play lead, but not like she can. I'm like old fashioned George Harrison and she's like fuckin' Hendrix or Clapton or fuckin' Jorma. She really is somethin' else. But if I'm the guitar, then we need a bass—and that's you. You could use mine. We keep our stuff at the studio because we don't usually have a car to get around. Sometimes Denise's brother helps out. You should join the band, Jamey. Make it in the big time!"

"Hollywood is so weird," said Jamey. "Everyone either thinks I'm a chick or they want me to be a chick. This never happened to me in the

93

Valley, man."

"Never?" Mona was doubting that claim.

"Never," Jamey asserted.

"Hooray for Hollywood!" said Mona. "What the fuck does it matter, Jamey? It's about the fuckin' music. You want to play, and we need a bass. Pretty simple. I mean you have to meet Denise and Karen. Denise'll have to check you out. I mean, I don't know how they'll feel about you being a dude in a girl band, but we need a fourth and we'll lose our connections if we don't get it together. Fuckin' Leslie."

"I don't know your shit," said Jamey. "That would take a long time."

"For a retard. Are you a retard? It's rock and roll. It doesn't take any brains. It's a feeling. And we're practically roommates. We'll go over it and practice. It's not really that hard to get through. It's like oldies and some recent shit, all covers for the gig because who wants to hear original music? And we practice at this studio. But it's ten bucks a night, so we don't practice too much when we're giggin'. But the equipment's safe. Isaac is really okay, and he watches out for our shit. This is Thursday, right? So we could have a practice tomorrow and Saturday, and they could audition you. We don't have to be *that* good for the gig."

"I don't know my work hours yet," said Jamey. "I'm starting tomorrow at the carwash. That's why I figured I could rent the room."

"You got a gig going? That's so cool!" When they had done the two j-Bob's, they returned to the boulevard, respectably stoned. Mona locked her arm with Jamey's as they walked up to the Big Boy to have dinner, on Jamey's dime.

Mona said she did tutoring and Beverly Hills baby sitting during the regular year, but there was no babysitting and no tutoring in the summer. Instead, she had a half-day gig at a summer camp that paid forty a week, so she was getting by. But she didn't get paid until tomorrow.

She scammed the gigs by going into the jobs office at the local college and claimed to be a student and got a referral. On the interview, she had worn her intelligent glasses. Her conservative look, her industrious Asian features, and the imprimatur of the college made her a shoe-in. And, Jamey could only suspect, she was probably really good with the kids. She had the energy to keep up with them. They probably scammed her for chocolate milk and she scammed them for nap time so she could do whatever it is Mona liked to do when she wasn't scamming.

They were almost to the restaurant, such as it was, when Mona stopped Jamey on the sidewalk. She pulled out some eyeliner and delineated Jamey's eyes. Jamey was embarrassed, but he didn't fight back. Same trick. He liked being handled by her. She seemed safe. "What the fuck are you doing!" he protested, with his usual ineffectualness. But he kept his face still. She applied some lipstick and then some patchouli to his wrists and neck. "What are you doing?"

"Let's see if you pass," she answered, taking off her chain and putting it around Jamey's neck. She transferred the silly orange hat. "Oh!" said Mona, taking out and clipping on the earrings. "And the finishing touch." She handed her purse to Jamey, who put it over his shoulder. "Your ass in those jeans'll take care of the rest. Even I'm interested, and I don't do sex."

Jamey didn't have time to wonder what that might mean. He was too busy feeling ridiculous, not completely trusting his new best friend. If Craig and the guys could see him made up like this, they would be laughing their asses off. Jamey expected ridicule and derision upon entering the restaurant, but nobody questioned *the girls*. It was Hollywood anyway, and '69, but nobody seemed to even notice. "Jamey, party of two." He did get the once over from a couple of guys. "Don't look back," said Mona. "You look right through them."

They settled into a booth, face to face, on the center aisle and perused the menus. "I got a lot of threads, you know, but you'll need to get some stuff."

"Stuff?"

"You know. Well, you can wear my panties but you definitely need your own bras." Jamey was inclined to protest rather forcefully, but the waitress in her brown skirt, nylon legs, white blouse, and Big Boy nametag: Carrie, came along to take their order. "I don't know how you can wear pantyhose in July," said Mona, sympathetically.

"Tell me about it," said the waitress. "It's the regs."

"Jamey here got fired for not wearing them," claimed Mona. "It was just too hot. Right, Jamey?"

"Well, there was more to it," said Jamey, amazed at Mona's tentative relationship with reality.

"I don't blame you," said the waitress. "But I can't afford to quit. Look at those pearls! They're so cool. Are they real?"

"Present from her boyfriend," said Mona.

"Wow, man!" said the waitress. "I need a new boyfriend."

The waitress went about her business, and Mona turned to Jamey. "So, you're wearing completely boy clothes, down to your shorts. The only thing is the earrings, a little eyeliner, and a hit of patchouli, and she'd have you over for a slumber party. No tits. No hips. But she bought it. She liked you. And, let's face it, dudes are a whole lot lamer. They could be in bed with you and never catch on."

"Jesus!" Jamey complained that Mona could even think of such an image. "That's so gross! You say this stuff as if I should be glad about it. How am I supposed to pick up girls if everyone thinks I'm a chick? What would Lorenzo the low rider or Jack the jock have to say about this? Or Teri Ann Murphy for that matter?" He put the hat to the side of the seat in the booth, and shook his hair out. Mona smiled as Jamey removed an element of the costume.

"I know the other guys, but who the fuck is Teri Ann Murphy?"

"She was my girlfriend. She broke my heart at the end of last semester."

"You liked her?" asked Mona. He nodded. "Why did she break up?"

"I guess she was bored," said Jamey.

"With you or the sex?" asked Mona. "Tell me there was sex."

"We had sex. Molly says I should have given her head…"

"That's the chick that you fucked this afternoon?"

"Right," said Jamey.

"Well, you can hardly go wrong with that advice," said Mona. "So. Being a macho guy, are you getting a lot of action?"

"I fucked a twenty-five-year-old chick this afternoon!" said Jamey, his voice louder and more animated. The white haired gentleman who was reading at the next table suddenly looked up.

"Lucky break," said Mona, whispering now. "Once in a blue moon. Once in a solar system! She was trying to keep you on the line." Mona stayed with her point. "So are you in? I mean, Denise and Karen have to go for it. But, are you cool with the plan? I mean, you don't always have to be a chick—just for the gig. It's like a gimmick."

Jamey noticed that two dudes were across the aisle, and one of them was eyeing Jamey with appreciation. It was the blond look because Mona obviously had more to offer. Jamey averted his eyes, but that just made him more chick like. "I don't like the way dudes look at me. Like I was a hot chick."

"You mean your boyfriend," said Mona. "But, according to your story, he had you pegged before he had you dress up. He knew you were a cat, so he's a perv. But I'm talking about customers at the gig. You just have to pass."

"But dudes will come on to me, and, when they find out, they'll beat the shit out of me. You might know about chick stuff, but this is dude stuff. They'll kill me."

"The point is that they'll never know. I mean, you don't want to date the customers anyway, do you? So you stay out of that situation. I don't fuck the bastards who come to the gig."

Jamey and Mona went back and forth, and covered other topics along the way, particularly talking about their musical tastes and experiences. Concerts they'd seen. Musical collections. Instruments and sound equipment. But Mona always brought it around to what was really on her agenda, as far as it affected Jamey.

To their surprise, they were suddenly joined in their booth by the two hippie dudes who had been trying to get their attention through the meal. "Who's up for some sweet dessert, ladies?" The big guy squeezed closer to Jamey.

Jamey was going to say, "Fuck You Right Now!" as was his wont, but Mona said, "Hot Fudge Cake?"

"Go for it!" said the dude who had moved in on Mona. During the wait for the cake, Jamey was surprised to feel the creeping hand of her new-found partner on the inside of his thighs. Jamey pushed the hand away and closed his legs. He held Jamey's hand for a moment, squeezing it tenderly. Jamey turned pink all over again. He was going along with Mona's plan, but it seemed crazy. He could have paid for the cake.

When Carrie came around with the desserts and coffee, Mona made sure that Carrie put them on the boys' check. "I'm not supposed to mix up the tables," said Carrie. "But…" she winked. She couldn't argue with Mona and Jamey getting some free dessert, so she left the check with the Hot Fudge Cake with the boys.

"So what are you two chicks doing tonight?"

"Well," said Mona, "If you must know, I'm having the worst period I've ever had. My Kotex is already saturating, and I just changed it an hour or so ago, right, Jamey?" If that didn't affect his amorous feelings, Mona went on. "But the chocolate is really good for it, so thanks, man. And, later, I'm going to shave Jamey's balls…"

"What's that supposed…?"

Jamey's new sweetheart quickly moved his hand off of Jamey's. He looked at Jamey closely for the first time, and, coming into focus, he saw it. "Holy shit!" He and his buddy were up in an instant.

"What the fuck? You bitches…"

The manager came running from across the store. "Oh, no. This is a family place. You'll have to leave."

"No, wait!" he said. "You don't know what's going on…"

"I know you're leaving, sir. I'll call the police if I have to. Why don't you just move on?"

"This is bullshit!"

The brouhaha made its way to the register and then out the door. The clientele at Bob's pretended to be shocked, but they had enjoyed the ruckus in general. Mona was finishing her cake, dipping her fork into the chocolate syrup and bringing it dripping up to her lips. She was amused by it all. Jamey was still a little shocked.

"What if they wait for us and beat the shit out of us?"

Mona shrugged. "It's not usually a problem. But, you're right." This hardly comforted Jamey. Mona went back to what she was working on before they had been joined by the good company the gentlemen had provided. "Maybe we could go to Goodwill and get a bra, and I could sew in some padding. Give you something of interest. I could paint your toe nails and you could wear hippie sandals. That's very feminine. Now we're probably going to have shave your legs and things. Show me what you got."

"Things?"

"You know, arm pits." Jamey was relieved, for a second. "…and stuff. Show me your legs."

"Back in the room, okay?" said Jamey, who wasn't inclined to show off his ankles. "What other stuff?"

"Just things," said Mona.

"I have hair. Not a lot, but, like my arm." He rolled up one sleeve. It was silken and airy, almost a fuzz. It wasn't particularly masculine.

"Soft!" said Mona. "Feels nice. But we probably need to defoliate you."

"That sounds like Agent Orange," said Jamey.

"I don't know what that is. Is it like Nair?"

"This guy, Mitch, told me about it. They use it to burn down the forests and crops in Vietnam."

"I'm talking about shaving your legs," said Mona. "Is this Chink related?"

"No!" said Jamey. "I just thought of this guy I met. Whatever. Do you shave *your* legs?"

Mona laughed. "I forget that you're sixteen and sheltered," said Mona. "Girls do a lot of stuff that you probably never thought about. I mean, even your precious Teri Ann pulls hair out of her nose and shaves her armpits, and trims her bush. Being pretty isn't pretty. There's a lot to do. It's like mowing the lawn every Saturday. There's a lot of shit. Like I'm wearing a diaper because of this fucking period. Sexy stuff. I hope you like patchouli," Mona went on. "The olfactory sense will be very convincing, and nothing says hippie chick like patchouli. These earrings are probably too classy for our show, but you don't need to get your ears pierced right away. You can wear clip-ons. That Rick guy is so thoughtful. He realizes you aren't pierced. Most guys know nothing." Mona had moved on. She was assuming now that Jamey was on board to join the band, in drag. "When we get beyond the gimmick thing, we can just be a real band and you can be any way you want to be. But we get gigs because of the chick thing which gives us a chance to play."

"But you should get gigs because of your music," said Jamey, the idealist.

"And we should be able to join bands with dudes, but being chicks works against us. So, it's only fair that we should get some chances because we're chicks."

"I never realized that chicks didn't get a fair chance. I just thought they liked to sing and play tambourine. I mean, they're good at it."

"Right. And blacks really dig sitting on the back on the bus and Mexicans like stoop labor. Like I said, sweetie, you're naïve. Do you really think it's an honor to suck the lead singer's cock?" said Mona. "Who wouldn't want that? How about you? Do you think that cock sucking is anatomically appropriate to chicks and not to dudes?" Mona was looking at Jamey's hands. "I guess the short nails are okay. You're a guitar player, so that's not so weird. But we need to clean them up, maybe some polish, just a gloss, not a color. And some rings, too." Jamey was looking at his nails. He had never considered these sorts of issues. How would that look at the carwash? That he didn't absolutely refuse, sock Mona for denigrating his manhood, and leave the table was a clear signal that he would eventually be persuaded. Jamey was feeling like an easy mark, whether Mona or Rick. Jamey didn't say no.

Finishing her cake, Mona asserted, "I'm the smart one." Jamey looked at her in surprise, not doubting her, but surprised she would feel compelled to make the claim. He was willing to allow that between the two of them she certainly was. After all, she was eating for free. "Because I'm a Chink. I don't mean that I'm the smart one really, though I guess I probably am, because I'm a Chink. But that doesn't matter. I'm talking images. Like Paul is the cute one and George is the serious one. I wear sexy dresses, but I also wear glasses on stage so that I look like the librarian, in a general way. Not the lace collar librarian."

"Marian."

"I don't know that chick," said Mona.

"Marian the Librarian," said Jamey. "Shirley Jones? We did it last year for the spring musical. *The Music Man.* Trouble in River City. The fuckin' Wells Fargo Wagon…"

Mona was baffled. "Try to stay with me," she said. "Denise is the sexy one. She's got a great shape and she dances to show it off. She does this thing with her lips." Mona imitated her friend, and got a laugh out of Jamey. "Karen is the drummer, so you'd think she'd be all butch and stuff, but she's *so* pretty. Guys just drool over her. She has this long full blond hair and pink skin, a little like you, but she's taller. So she's like the pretty maid all in a row. Truth is that she's Denise's sweet tart. They're like a team, and you don't want to get between them. Whatever Denise says, Karen will go along with. They like it that way, and, really, it's kind of easier. I just have to get Denise to see things my way. She'll take care of Karen. Leslie was the psychedelic one. She had a country leather thing going on, but her music was strictly rock virtuoso stuff. I don't know why she quit. I'm going to make it. We'll be on the cover of Rolling Stone. Maybe your boyfriend will shoot it."

"He's not my boyfriend," said Jamey. "I'm a dude."

"If you say so," said Mona. "She said it was all bullshit. She just wants to play. There's a song in that somewhere. Want to write a song together? Maybe we'll be like Lennon and McCartney. Paul's my hero. I know that sounds teeny bopper. So we have to think of who you are. Like your song is so sensitive. Maybe you're the poet girl. Like black leotards and smoking like Mrs. Ferlinghetti in a coffee shop, but you rock, too. A freak poet who rocks. Is the world ready for that?"

"I really don't think there's a Mrs. Ferlinghetti," said Jamey.

"He had to come from somewhere. Whatever. Or you could be like…" Apparently Mona could just wind it up without really knowing what the end of the sentence might sound like. "…you could be like *Sunshine Daydream.* Like the cool hippie chick, all natural and full of love and peace and stuff like that." Mona considered that for a moment. "You know, but, if you're like the natural hippie girl, your tits have to sort of hang out, at least on the sides, you know, so I guess not."

"That's good," said Jamey. "You know, you're assuming that I'm going to do this. I don't want to be a girl."

"Right. And Nick doesn't want to be Santa Claus. Okay. But if the red suit fits," Mona explained. "At least you won't have to wear a diaper. Am I your typical girl? Come on! But, ya know, you play the hand they deal. I want to be a rock and roll star, but I have tits, sort of, so I have to go for it with tits. I can't do the dude thing."

"But there are chicks who make it big. Gracie, Janis…"

"And for every one of them, there's a hundred one-hit wonders or just singers with tambourines. Brenda Lee. I'm Sorry…" said Mona. "And Leslie Gore. Marcie Blane. Shelly Fabares. Merilee Rush."

"But like Joni Mitchell and Katy Mondy," said Jamey. "That's for real. They write their shit. They call the shots. They have pussys and tits. So you have tits, but I have a dick. Hand you're dealt."

"You don't have to get all gross about your weenie," said Mona. "You guys…"

He liked it when she said something like *you guys*. It made him feel like one. "I can't be a chick any more than you can be a dude."

"When we get up, we'll go into the ladies' room. If anyone even bats an eye, okay. If they look twice. Even though the only thing you're wearing is the earrings, you will automatically pass."

"And the hat?"

"Okay. Maybe if you had a mustache or sideboards, it wouldn't happen. But I'm telling you, you'll pass, with pastel colors. If I'm wrong, I don't know what. But, if I'm right, then you have to stop whining. It's so feminine. Deal?"

"No way!"

"Then I win by default."

"Why can't I back you guys as your bassist? I don't have to be part of the chick band."

"No," said Mona. "Won't work. We're a chick group. If we have dudes, people will think we're not really in charge. It'll be like Mr. Jamey and His Jammin' Jamettes. Fuck that." They appeared to be at an impasse, so Mona tried a different approach. "Pretty please, with sugar on top?" It worked last time.

Jamey paid the check, and they were next walking toward home. Mona kept up the pressure. "Just shake your ass a little, Jamey. Give it some swish. Guys will be like following you, and girls will be like jealous." Mona leaned close to Jamey's ear and whispered, "You really do have a sweet little ass, baby. I want some of that…if I had a dick. Which I don't."

WORKIN' IN THE COAL MINE

JAMEY WAS A LITTLE WARY as they left the home of the Big Boy. He was expecting to be confronted by their erstwhile suitors. As they walked back down the boulevard, he was less concerned about it. Soon enough, he had shaken them off completely.

The streets were the same as ever—warm, sometimes breezy, crowded, hep, hip, and now. The difference was that Jamey had found a friend. He couldn't say that she didn't want things from him. She seemed to take everything she could get, and then demand more. Not unlike Rick the Perv in that way, although, he knew very well, Rick had been extremely generous and considerate with him whether Jamey let Rick turn him into a fairy or not.

But Mona didn't frighten Jamey as Rick did. She fascinated him. He wanted to be in her band, if not in her dress. And he wasn't at all convinced that he couldn't get between her legs. Maybe not when she was indisposed. But, in a few days, in a week. She'd be in a better mood and more likely to want to put out. After Molly, anything was possible. He liked the immediately intimate way that they seemed to connect. He had to consider that perhaps she was that way with everyone. They promenaded down the busy boulevard, singing "For the Benefit of Mr. Kite" for starters and then just trying out some lines, Jamey singing in a smug Dylan voice and Mona doing a Jagger.

Mona and Jamey laughed. Then Mona, stopping, looked at Jamey with more thoughtful eyes now. "We're primo, man!" she said. Jamey was still calming down, but was arrested by Mona's sudden intensity. "I'm really into you. I was missing Leslie so much. I really love her, even though she's a skank and a heroin freak. You really are my angel." Embarrassed by Jamey's bewildered silence, and with restrained affection, Mona socked Jamey in the shoulder, like a guy, but kind of cute about it.

Jamey wasn't sure what to do about any of it. Despite parading as a chick, he was quite smitten with Mona. He thought he ought to respond to her remarks. He bent toward her lips to kiss her. She turned away. "I'm no Lesbo," said Mona. "And the blood is starting to run down my legs. Want some?" Jamey didn't have an answer. "We go home now."

"Say good-night," Jamey replied. Mona took him by the arm.

IT WAS ONLY THEIR FIRST NIGHT TOGETHER, but the loneliness was gone, at least for the nonce. Mona was on her bed listening to *Crown of Creation* on the Tele-Tone. Through the opened shared door, she could see Jamey who was on his bed, apparently spacing out. He was calculating under the influence of marijuana, meditating on his finances. After dinner, his fund had been reduced to $64.25. They had stopped at a record shop, and that hadn't cost anything, but at the head shop Jamey had to spring for papers. Jamey figured that the job at the carwash, if it was forty-eight hours, should net about $67 a week. That meant that there would be about $37 a week after rent. The bottom line here was that Richard Altier paid pretty well compared to real work, but a person could survive at the carwash rate, if the person played it cool. But Jamey's mind continued to roam. "What ya thinkin'?" asked Mona.

"Money stuff," he replied.

That didn't interest her. "What else?" she said.

"Did you ever butt-fuck?" Jamey asked.

Mona laughed. "Can't say I've had the pleasure."

"Do you think it hurts? Everyone says it hurts, but nobody I know ever got fucked in the ass."

Mona was about to answer when it apparently crossed her mind what Jamey was actually contemplating. "You miss your boyfriend?" asked Mona.

"He's not my boyfriend," said Jamey. "He's a perv."

"Then why do you ask?"

"I don't know," said Jamey. "I just always heard that it hurt like hell, but I never heard it from anyone who really knows anything about it."

"Well, don't look at me," said Mona. "You could ask Karen. I bet Denise does her with a dildo."

"Really?"

"Like I would know," said Mona.

Being that he had a job in the morning, Jamey said that he was going to go to bed. Mona didn't object, but she didn't go away either. There was not a lot that Jamey could do relative to changing for bed. He eventually took off his socks, dropped his pants, and hung up his one shirt. Mona was quite blasé as she made no pretense of hiding the fact that she was checking him out in his tight, relatively clean white underpants. She didn't seem to tremble in fear or excitement at the sight of his almost naked

103

body. There was practically no hair on his upper body except a little peach fuzz on his arms. His legs were hardly hairier. His body blushed under her scrutiny, and he wished he had a woody to hide, but his member appeared to be AWOL, which Mona, he was sure, observed. No wonder she wanted him to be her girlfriend. He quickly got into bed and pulled up his covers.

"You'll lose your earrings," Mona reminded Jamey. "And no perv to kiss you good-night." With some trouble, he unclipped them and put them on the nearby bureau. Mona went down the hallway with some things. Jamey caught a whiff of his wrists with the heavy fragrance. He liked it. He looked around the room and through the door to the next room. His room was still relatively uncluttered, but Mona did leave a trail.

When she returned, she locked the door behind her. She was now in a red robe and slippers. She dropped the robe and rested it across a chair. She was in a blue t-shirt now. Perhaps betraying a lack of good manners, Jamey watched as she adjusted her underwear. Mona showed very little modesty. She gave the impression that Jamey really was her sister and not some possibly horny dude whom she had just met. But she did seem to like him.

Her body was tight. She was tiny, but she was in good shape. Her legs were smooth and muscular, and her dark skin fascinated Jamey. She was no pink assed Teri Ann. Mona strolled into her own room. Now he felt the woody. She was on the rag and not a likely prospect in any event, but Jamey, despite the opinion of apparently the whole world, was just a guy, and she was a fine example of what it is that most guys were looking for. Mona came back into Jamey's room, brushing her straight hair, bending over as the girl on the beach had done, though not visible from behind. She looked like a dark haired Cousin It. When she was done, she tossed her hair over her shoulders, poured a final orange soda into her plastic cup, and drank it down in a rush. "Well, this Buddha head is off for bed. I could close the door if you want to jerk off or something."

"Not on my account," said Jamey. "I told you. I had sex today. But if you have plans…"

Mona switched off the light in Jamey's room. "I'll leave it open, then. It makes me feel less claustrophobic, and I think we get a little cross breeze. I love having a friend here." She bent over the bed and kissed his forehead. She went back into her room, still speaking as she climbed into her bed and cuddled with her little bear. "Good luck in the morning, working stiff. Leave me a few dollars for breakfast and for the bus, will ya?" $61.25, if she didn't think of something else.

In the morning, Mona was already out. Checking his wallet, she had only taken the three dollars. It could have been worse. Like any working man, Jamey got donuts and coffee on his way to the carwash. He was there when it opened, and he was immediately put to work getting the materials and solutions ready for the day, along with some brushes and towels. It was serious muscle work, on his feet the whole day, running from car to car, window to window, going for towels, scrubbing, cleaning, struggling to keep up, especially in the latter part of the long hot day. "Easy money!" said his fellow—but more experienced—laborers. "Easy money!"

He had worked in his old man's plumbing yard to earn a buck or two toward his bass, but he had never experienced work like this. He could barely lift his feet when he was ready to head home, but the manager said he had done okay for a first timer. He was encouraging, telling Jamey that he would surely do better when he came back on Sunday, Monday, and Tuesday, and on and on. Now it wasn't a matter of counting the money in his mind that he would earn. It was a matter of counting the minutes while he was working.

On the way home, he stopped at a Goodwill that he had scoped out. Jamey was five and a half feet and not very big at that. But he found two pairs of pants that could fit him along with three shirts. He also picked up a beat-up but functioning backpack to carry his purchases and to replace the stolen article. $57.25 remaining in his pockets. At this rate, he would soon be back in Rick's clutches. That was unlikely as he would have to go through Molly to get to Rick.

It was almost five-thirty when he arrived at home. "We have a lot of shit to do." Mona had been procuring clothing as well. "I know I owed you some, so I spent it on your get-up for the band." This sounded both unreasonable and suspicious to Jamey, but he went along with his best friend in the world on that point and to the bathroom. "Get in the bathtub, Jamey."

"Mona, I told you…"

"We have to practice at nine. Let's go. They want to see how you'll look on stage. If you can carry it off."

"I don't want to…" Mona clapped her hands in rapid succession.

Jamey laughed. "What's that move?"

"My mother used to do that when it was time to get serious. And she usually thought it was time to get serious. You practice piano *now*!" The quick claps.

"You did piano?"

"You get in shower *now!*" Jamey, exhausted, rinsed in the shower and found himself sitting lifelessly in the bath. While Mona shaved his legs, arms, and underarms bare, Mona explained that she had done piano from the age of four through sixteen. She was a competition player and once had a shelf full of first place trophies. Her mother had thrown out the seconds, thirds, and fourths. There was always practicing, recitals, and homework, homework, homework. Mona had Jamey stand and turn around while she defoliated his bum. She had him bend over for some rather delicate matters. She had him face her and she proceeded to remove much of his pubic hair. "You better do something about your woody, Jamey."

"Well, if you'd stop handling it," he replied.

"Oh, it's like that, is it?"

"I told you I wasn't a chick," said Jamey.

"We'll see about that," Mona replied.

Back in their rooms, Jamey was on the bed in just his towel, and Mona had a flash. "I understand that dudes don't operate so well on speed."

"Huh?"

"No hard-on," said Mona. She gave him three double-cross whites, a manicure, and a pedicure. She painted his toes and cleaned, clipped, shaped, and glossed his fingernails.

"Now turn over on your front, but don't mess with the nail polish."

"This doesn't sound right," said Jamey.

"Keep your feet up," said Mona. "Don't ruin the polish." Mona gave him a treatment with a moisturizing oil. She was all business, but it felt sensual to Jamey, back and front. "I'll get your new outfit."

He felt his arms, his legs, his pubic area, and his ass, all of which were now as smooth as Teri Ann Murphy's. He smelled like a chick. He was still engaged in this audit when Mona burst back into the room. "Everything copasetic?" she asked.

"Well, what if it wasn't?"

"Costume time!" She pulled the pink underwear from Rick's bureau and tossed it to Jamey. "Put these on." He looked at them as if they were foreign. "Excuse me, Jamey," said Mona. "I did not bring those into your life. You had them before you ever met me, so don't blame Mona."

"I needed a change of underwear. I only had one pair."

"And you chose pink," said Mona.

"It's all they had." Jamey pulled the little pants right up tight over his smooth bare legs and snapped them in place, feeling more like an idiot than ever. "Now," said Mona, "This gets a little personal. We're going to do the trick."

"This does not sound good."

"Believe it or not, you can scrunch your balls…"

"No no no," said Jamey. "Scrunch and balls do not go together. Suck and balls. See? Goes together. Scrunch doesn't make it."

Mona explained that a fellow could push his balls back up into his abdomen from whence they had first burst forth. With the balls out of the way, the unit could be pushed back between the legs, the tight pants holding it all in place. No visible manliness. But, she pointed out, none of this worked if he started out with a hard-on.

Jamey had asked if this were some sort of Oriental mystical practice out of the inscrutable Chinese past, something the Great Helmsman had come up with perhaps? She said she had met some transvestites who had shown her. She assured Jamey that there was no pain involved. That part was not altogether true. It didn't have to be painful, but neither Jamey nor Mona had any experience in the matter. They weren't sure that they did it right, but there was no visible bulge when they were done, though Jamey walked a little more carefully, which didn't hurt the effect.

Mona had been busy between the time she got off work and the time that Jamey arrived. She had a light duty black lace embroidered brassier. "See?" Mona was proud of her stitching. "I put in some padding so you'll have some shape, more than I have anyway. And, see? It's nude on top. So, if something shows, at least quickly, you'll be all right. And, check this out. There's a little slit on the inside. You can hide your money or your dope or whatever."

"So now you're Q?"

"What are you talking about?"

"James Bond…never mind."

"Now, turn around, Jamey." In spite of booking it down the shady lane, leaving Molly in the lurch, Mona had him deeper down the trans-hole than either Rick or Molly ever had. "Put up your arms." She slipped the bra in place and fastened it. "How's that feel?" The bureau mirror told the story. Jamey had arrived, framed in the mirror in bra and panty. It could have been Missy, but she wouldn't have looked so silly.

Mona gave him a t-shirt, boy style, and the shape of the bra and the faux breasts came through just as Mona had calculated they would. She reached into her bag of tricks and pulled out some denim short-shorts. Jamey pulled them on and Mona buttoned him tightly. A little bit of the pink showed through the frayed denim, a very young and effective casual/

professional look. She squeezed his ass to assess the fit. Put on those thongs. There was a pair of woven flip flops that showed off his colorful toe nails. Then she brushed his hair again and crowned him with a tie-dye head band. "I don't think the pearls," said Mona. "I found these big old hoops. They have clips. We might need to get you pierced, Linda." She did a little work on the face and sprayed him with a fruity fragrance. "Hot stuff, Jamey! Now we have to get your cute ass to practice."

"What if I have to piss?"

"Sit down to pee, in case anyone comes in," said Mona. "I ask you again. Don't you hate your period?"

"I hate everything about this…"

"So you say," said Mona, some laughter and doubt in her voice.

Jamey and Mona on parade arrested the consciousness of more than one young hippie dude, to say nothing of the gentlemen passing in their cars whose eyes were momentarily diverted by the vision of the *young ladies*. Mona and millions of other girls lived with this invasive attention, but it was all new to Jamey. There were also the older chaps, who were also on the alert for young, or any girls. They ranged from furtive to blatant in their ogling, and left Jamey with a doubly creepy feeling. But women suffered such fates daily. "Stop turning around and looking at them," said Mona. "You're making a scene. Of course they're checking out your ass. You don't have to wonder about it. Don't acknowledge it, and don't give them an opening." She added, "And your ass is natural. We didn't do anything to it."

"You put it in short-shorts and pink underpants!"

"Your underpants…"

"Ow!" Jamey felt a sudden pinch on his bottom. He turned around to fire on someone, but he couldn't be sure who among the crowd had taken the liberty. "I don't even have fucking hips!" Jamey complained. "Women are supposed to have hips. What are these jerks thinking?"

"But scrawny young girls don't always have hips. And you're definitely a scrawny young girl." On the way to the practice studio, the *two chicks* stopped for dinner. "I spent a lot more than the five bucks I probably owe you on your stuff, but it's cool. You can buy the dinner and we'll be even." Cha-ching. $54.45. Jamey was innocent in some ways, but he noticed that none of the stuff Mona provided had labels, price tags, or even store shopping bags. He didn't know how, but it was pretty clear that Mona had stolen the clothes from who knows where? Someone's dryer? The Goodwill? Laundry lines? Jamey didn't buy the story, but he didn't mind it either. Perhaps it was the intoxicating perfume of new love. His big made-up eyes were open. It was Rick's dime.

The chief and best feature of the practice room in an old studio warehouse building down the block from the boulevard was that it locked-up pretty well. Maiden Head kept its stuff in a locked closet and set it up on the practice floor when they had the room. Isaac, the enterprising landlord, didn't guarantee anything, but he was reasonably watchful. He was quite attentive with Mona. When she and Jamey arrived, Karen was setting up her drums and Denise was tuning her guitar. "Hey, Dee. Hey K. What's happening?" Karen smiled timidly and waved. Denise played the chords to "Mona" by way of greeting. "This is that girl I told you about—Jamey. Let's try her out. She can play. Karen and Denise," said Mona, as an introduction. There were more *heys* and *what's happenings.*

Jamey had been under the delusion that Mona had told the rest of the band that he was really a dude. Jamey questioned Mona with *her* eyes, but Mona telegraphed a "maintain and be cool" vibe. Denise bought the story, having no reason to suspect otherwise, other than knowing Mona to be a liar. Karen hardly raised her eyes; it made no difference to her as long as Denise was cool with it. Denise gave Jamey the once and twice over, maybe a little suspicious, not of *her* gender but of *her* person.

"Take a picture," said Jamey, who felt the eyes. He thought he must look ridiculous, and he was still waiting for Mona to come clean. It wasn't in her nature to do that.

Isaac, a long haired dude, came into the room. "So where's my ten bucks, ladies? Hey, Mona." He nodded to Mona. Her eyes darted back and forth and she faked a smile for Isaac. It was more than she gave most guys.

Mona looked to Denise. Denise replied verbally, "I paid last time. It's Leslie's turn."

Mona turned to Jamey. "Well, we do like a merry-go-round. So—just to keep things fair, I guess it's your turn, Jamey. Cause you're filling in for Leslie." Jamey was not fooled by the argument, but he nevertheless reached into his tight front pocket and pulled out his decreasing wad of money and paid the piper. $44.45 remaining, but who's counting?

Maiden Head played rock classics, a lot of hippie stuff, and a couple of moony-eyed ballads. They rocked like Eddie Cochran, Chuck Berry, and Elvis Presley. That was an advantage for Jamey as he already knew the material or could rapidly pick it up. He was a good musician, better than your average sixteen-year-old, if not exactly Steve Winwood at sixteen. The bass parts were fun, and easy for Jamey to work out. The more difficult matter was the back-up vocals. Mona's voice was a little rough for a chick which allowed her to do the material more convincingly. She traded lead vocals with Denise, who could power it up. Whoever wasn't singing lead would sing back-up with Leslie, now Jamey, Beatles style. So Jamey had to go from harmonizing with Mona to Denise, and back again. Jamey didn't have any songs yet, but they let *her* do the new one. Jamey didn't think it worked with a quartet. He liked the flute and bongo sound from the beach. Maybe Rick had a point about not shining in an electric band. On the other hand, he loved the feeling of playing bass in a combo.

Karen didn't sing, but she nailed the beat. Jamey found that Karen grasped his musical ideas very quickly and backed them up. With time, they could become a hot rhythm section. Denise was more than competent in her musical ability, and she brought a lot of life to the show. But Mona was a revelation. She was into the music and playing the old style rock and roll lead guitar, imitating the classics and adding some of her own, trying to bring it up to the late sixties. They were a classic garage/bar band, and surprisingly good for kids. Mona was eighteen, if one could believe her, and Denise and Karen were twenty. Jamey had to play up to their level. They were clearly better than Crazy Place and a good deal better looking.

A LITTLE HELP FROM MY FRIENDS

THEY NEVER SAID SO, but Mona was the leader of the band. She had the ideas for the arrangements, but she had to go through Denise, who usually just didn't care about the little niceties. She wanted to rock. Denise sometimes glanced at Jamey, perhaps jealously, but Jamey didn't necessarily understand.

Jamey fit in quickly. He was all business, trying to learn the parts, and the specifics of the arrangements. Both Mona and Denise were very physical on stage, if the practice was any indication. More, Mona was a very strong rock singer. Jamey thought it was a pretty good band.

During a break, Jamey, a fairly sheltered boy up until this week, couldn't help but observe Denise and Karen in a long passionate kiss that involved Denise feeling Karen up and down. Mona stepped out the back door leading Jamey by the hand into the alley where they did a couple of Chesterfields. It was cooler out there. "She's marking territory," whispered Mona. "You stay away from Karen, she's telling you. Lezzy stuff. But, you have to admit, they're pretty good musicians, especially Karen. Hard to get a really good drummer, and a chick besides. She's good. So how do you like being a hymen?"

"Why didn't you tell them?" asked Jamey.

"I wanted to see if you could pass," said Mona. "And you did. Denise was kind of checking you out, and she likes girls. Anyway, they're so lez. They don't really want anything to do with dudes. Just by being a dude they think you're a rapist. I just think dudes are assholes, but it's not like a religion with me like it is for them, which means Denise, you know. But I don't care what people are or what they believe. I just want to make music, and I want to make the big time." Mona sensed that Jamey was getting moony. She rolled her eyes. "What are you fucking thinking about, chick?"

"Teri Ann," said Jamey. "I know it's kind of weird. I had sex with that Molly girl, and I would do you in a heartbeat, but I still miss Teri Ann, even though Molly was kind of sexier."

"You're probably hotter than Teri Ann," said Mona. "Your first fuck?"

"Yeah."

"Blind leading the blind. Strictly missionary. 'First Boy I Loved.'

That's a good one for you, Jamey. You got that Judy Collins thing going. Pretty hard song for the band, though. Hard to live up to Stills, even for me. Leslie could do it, if she held back a little. And not really for The Contortionist crowd, but we won't be there forever. So you guys fucked straight up? Boring missionary stuff?"

"Mona!" he complained, suggesting that she could be too intimate.

"Oh, right," said Mona. "I shave your fucking ass, and you're too delicate to talk about positions? The main thing is that you had a good time, and learned a little something—and nobody got hurt."

"Other than she dumped me, and broke my heart," said Jamey.

"Should have given her head. Adds months to a relationship. But, were you really thinking of having grandchildren on your knee, then? We need a clarinet for that. Can you blow clarinet? I bet you could. You're fucking sixteen. You're not getting married, are you? Where could we get a wedding dress?" Mona was thinking that it could be very easily done, but that was neither here nor there.

Mona and Jamey became itemic, spending all of their time together when they were not working. What Mona did during the day between her camp job in the morning and the time that Jamey came home was beyond Jamey's ken. Jamey dressed fem for their three practices during the following week, and Mona encouraged him to dress fem at first whenever they went out, but later even around their rooms and to sleep. Jamey felt that there was something Mona wasn't telling him, some kind of punch line to all of this, but he went along with her. He said it was because he wanted to be in the band, but it was fun, too. He had never had a girlfriend. Not like a Teri Ann girlfriend, but a Mona girlfriend.

Mona was instructive as to how a Hollywood chick ought to behave, and Jamey made a quick transition. His face, his hair, his voice, even his manner naturally lent itself to the part. Mona taught him about makeup, hair care, nails, and maintenance of his smooth girlish skin. He didn't color his fingernails because it would have looked weird when he worked at the carwash, but a definite change was coming over the lad.

Jamey had taken to organizing their clothes. He washed, dried, and even ironed what he could at home. The rooms were looking more like a place to live and less like the floor of a kid's closet. Mona complained that soon there would be lace curtains at Rooms-for-Rent. Mona played the guitar and sang while Jamey organized their things. "You are so domestic!" Mona exclaimed. "I'm gonna get you an apron." It sounded okay to Jamey.

But, Clark Kent style, by night Jamey was a chick, playing in the band, cruising the boulevard, one of the girls. By day, Jamey was a laborer at a great metropolitan carwash, and then he wore his boy clothes. "Easy money!" was still the watch cry, and Jamey racked up the hours. But they had spent most of his money by Thursday morning. Jamey tried to be frugal, but it cost big money to work and to live, especially with Mona who was a major leak in the money boat.

"Rent's due, kids," said Jack.

"Eagle flies on Friday," said Mona. "Big money from Jamey and me. Give us a day?"

"You know the rules. Pay up, or you don't sleep here tonight." Jack was their buddy, but he answered to higher powers and he never let it slide.

Mona proposed that they pay the day rate on Thursday and the weekly rate starting again on Friday. That was fine with Jack, but the best Jamey could come up with was $11.54.

"Which ain't twelve," said Jack.

Mona was not stumped for long. "Okay. How about this? Jamey and I move in together. Six bucks."

"Nine bucks," said Jack. "You both use the bathroom, I'm guessing. There wouldn't be enough hot water if everyone doubled up. So nine bucks for double, and forty-five for the week. Nine bucks today and forty-five tomorrow. And move your shit so I can rent the room."

"A girl this time?" said Mona. "I'm sick of perverts next door." So they had $2.54 for the two of them for the day. And, despite all of Jamey's work, they had to quickly move Mona's stuff onto Jamey's side, totally making a wreck of the room. Jamey barely got to work on time. They were flat broke by Thursday evening, though the ship was due on the morrow.

Mona was proposing that they go out for dinner. Jamey thought it was an unreasonable suggestion. Mona won that disagreement. "Bring your guitar."

They set up on Jamey's old corner and did some Chuck Berry, Buddy Holly, Everly Brothers, and Lennon-McCartney stuff. They gave each other confidence. They were good musicians anyway, and they appeared to be cute chicks.

It took Jamey a while to get what was happening. Some guys were attracted to him because they thought he was a chick. But other guys were attracted to him because they knew that he wasn't really a chick, which meant he was some kind of fairy, and an attractive fairy at that. Whatever, they did far better than Jamey had done, scoring six bucks, three of which went to dinner and the remaining three was split between them for busses and donuts in the morning. The eagle was flying Friday night, and they were having their first gig since Jamey had joined Maiden Head. They'd even get some cash for that.

So Jamey went to work on Friday, confident that he was going to get a fat check for all the hours he had put in. And these had been long hard hours on top of practicing most nights and not getting a lot of sleep in Mona's company. It was only the whites that kept Jamey going, and they did help to keep his Jolly Roger in check.

On the bright side of the road, the carwash cashed the check right on the spot. The bad luck had to do with their pay schedule. By the end of Friday, Jamey had put in seven working days out of eight possible. He calculated his take-home at roughly seventy-five dollars. He was good at his numbers, and he would have been right. But he discovered that they only paid him from Sunday to Saturday, with a week delay. In short he was paid for his first day of work only, $11.16 after taxes, nothing like what he had expected to have. The big money wouldn't come in until next Friday.

Walking home, he was contemplating living in the garbage again. Mona had received her forty dollars, so *the girls* had about $51. They paid up the $45 rent and had about six dollars left to live on—for the week. It wasn't so bad. They expected a little income from the gig, and the first gig was tonight. But it goes to show that these plan things didn't really work so well.

FOR THE GIG, Mona had them all wearing short sexy dresses. Mona's was red and Jamey's was a dark green with reflective spangles. Mona had heels, but Jamey couldn't do a whole show in heels yet. It was 1969, and anything went, so he wore sandals.

They got to the practice studio to load up their shit and they met Denise in her leather and Karen in her virginal lace collar. Jamey and Mona went into roadie mode. Isaac was around, but he didn't get too physical. Even Jamey could read that there was something between Isaac and Mona, at least on one side of the street; Mona was inscrutable. And soon they drove down the boulevard a good long way, not exactly the Sunset Strip, and finally pulled into the lot in back of the club. Looking up at the sign, Jamey learned for the first time what it was all about. XXX GIRLS! GIRLS! GIRLS! XXX. "Well, what did you think?" said Mona. "Did you think it was the Hollywood Bowl with Leonard Bernstein conducting?"

Mona and the band set up in a crowded corner near the stage, but not on it. That was reserved for the dancers. Maiden Head provided the interstitial music between the strippers' sets. "What the fuck!" said Jamey. He had pictured a music club where folks sat at tables, drank liquor, and checked out the music.

"This is commercial work," said Mona. "Just follow my lead." Jamey always did.

The manager, a pony tail and beard by the name of Tony, came over to check them out. "I should have fired you," he said. "You're nothing but trouble."

"Bullshit," said Mona. "How many customers asked for us while we were away?"

"Not enough to get you a raise." He looked at his girls, but he didn't recognize Jamey. "Hey, who's the baby?"

"Leslie," she said.

"Let's have it," Tony demanded. Jamey flashed the license given to her by Mona. "Not so fast." Tony took the ID and looked it over. Jamey didn't look a thing like Leslie King. The date appeared to be correct, so he returned it. "Can't be too careful around here." The drinking age and the serving age in the joint was twenty-one, but the dancers, and, presumably the musicians, only had to be eighteen. Hard to say who was being protected.

Karen had disappeared before the show but had soon returned with a banana which she put beside her drum kit. She sat down on the stool and took a few whacks at the snare and the toms, adjusting the snare here and tightening the cymbal there. Mona tried out a few runs while Denise provided some chords to work against. Jamey came in with his bass sound, locking eyes with Karen to get to the same place. Jamey found Denise a little on the distant side, but Karen was easy to work with musically, though she never said much to anyone other than to Denise. Mona was a lot like her Beatle hero, always trying to put on the show. Back in the practice room, Jamey had heard a few discussions in which Denise claimed that Leslie had been right about too much show biz and not enough music. Mona was on the other side of that debate. Jamey knew that bands were seldom easy relationships. Everyone wanted to be the star of the show.

They started the night with "Sweet Little Sixteen." The beer began to flow more readily, and Mona and Denise held the attention of the patrons as well as they could. They couldn't compare to the dancers who came on the stage. This wasn't a burlesque, strip-tease, drop-a-glove kind of place. It was more a bump, grind, crawl on the floor, lie on your back spreading your pussy kind of joint. Jamey had never been to such a venue in his young life, and he watched in fascination. This was not how Teri Ann Murphy behaved. Mona had to inch over to Jamey. "Your clit is showing, Jamey. Maybe better if you don't watch. You got enough to think about." But it was hard not to watch. Teri Ann had said he was boring, always doing it the same way, all four times. These dancing girls knew quite a bit that Teri Ann didn't even suspect yet. And, before the night was over, Jamey had lost count of how many naked girls he had seen, intimately, since running away from home.

The dancers got tips, especially when they interacted with their clients. Mona had put out a tip jar, but there wasn't much action there, though a few bucks had turned up. Some pervs liked the band. It was a long hot night. They played between the dancers, and kept the crowd revved and rockin'. It stretched out the show for management and built excitement for the next act, and the next, and the next. For Jamey, for the whole band, it was fun, though hot and tiring. Nobody but themselves noticed the subtle mistakes and sometimes just plain clinkers that he or the band made. It was not, perhaps, a musically discerning audience at The Contortionist, but, at the same time, it was the best band by far that Jamey had ever been in, and he was loving it. It was just a matter of moving the show to Winterland.

Toward the close of the first set, Mona was seriously putting out on guitar and vocals. Every now and then it was almost as if Mona would forget her pose and just play the music. That was the most fun for Jamey. And just playing in the band was a trip. Jamey was digging it probably more than the less than discerning audience. The song was a Mona original, the obligatory introduction of the band members, and now it was charging to its climax:

From Tuscaloosa to Arizona
Ain't nobody tighter than your little...Mona!

On the name, Denise had cut in while Mona tossed her guitar behind her, still on the shoulder strap, and, to Karen's rim shots, Mona lifted the hem of her hot red dress, flashing her tiny underwear with a lengthy shimmy that got some of the audience out of their seats and shouting. Jamey's mouth was wide open at this display. Mona was all about the show biz. The dudes couldn't do that. The band picked it up only long enough to build up to the same point in the song:

Some girls give you a little squeeze
But you get it all with sweet...Denise!

Mona's hand offered the audience Denise, who made a similar move with her instrument. She ripped open her blouse, flashing her black brassier. Of the four, Denise was the only one with breasts that would be of interest to this crowd, and she didn't mind flashing them, what one might catch through her bra.

Jamey realized now that Mona had done it again. She tended to leave out key bits of information that might be controversial. When it was Karen's turn, she didn't expose herself.

> *You won't be askin' what she's wearin'*
> *When it's all inside of…Mistress Karen!*

Instead, she pealed the banana and took the whole of it into her mouth, licking and tonguing to wild cat calls. As that died down and the band resumed, it was time to continue the introductions. It wasn't a bright crowd, but they could just make out the pattern. All eyes were turning to Jamey. He was not inclined to do what either Mona or Denise had done; the equipment was faulty in both areas. As always in life, there were only so many measures to think about it.

> *Once you may have been in love with Amy*
> *But that was before you encountered…Jamey!*

Jamey turned beet red and away from the audience, which was perfect when Denise on one side and Mona on the other raised the back of his dress. "Jamey! Eric Clapton, please!" Jamey got the applause that he had always wanted and the rowdy cat-calls that *she* had hoped to avoid.

Then the band pulled it back together and finished the number, slipping into the "Kansas City" intro, their closer. The tip jar got more action than it had all night, which is why Mona developed this part of the show. When he asked later, Jamey learned that the previous guitarist, Leslie King, who was all about the music, wouldn't do it. She would play for the others, but she herself never whipped anything out except for her exquisite riffs. But Jamey seemed to fit right in. "Give the folks what they really want," said Mona.

There was a short break which they took in the back alley with beer and cigarettes, and then three more sets of roughly the same material. They planned to expand the set list as they worked Jamey into their arrangements. Into the third set, Jamey's pick-up started buzzing and then cutting out. He was able to fix it on the spot, but it was only a temporary fix.

The band had made twenty dollars in tips, mostly for shimmy work, and thirty dollars from the management. Ten of that had to go to Denise's brother for the van. They kept their equipment at the bar when they had consecutive nights, probably a risky business, but they couldn't get the van every night. The girls went out to a coffee shop and spent eight dollars, which was more than they should have spent, but they all had a good meal. They divided the rest of the money. So Mona and Jamey, with what they had left from the Eagle and with the money from the show, came away with $22.00, rent paid for a week, and a dinner that would tide them over until the morning. Show business. You're down and you're up.

Denise and Karen dropped Mona and Jamey off at Rooms-for-Rent. As Jamey was getting out of the van a little unsteadily, Denise said, "You were pretty good, woman. Wear some pettipants tomorrow. Mona's the pussy. I got the big-girl tits. And you're a cute little ass if I ever saw one." Denise looked back at Karen, who was getting out of the side door. "And she's the magic mouth." Karen didn't blush, but she ignored Denise as a wife might ignore her loutish husband.

Mona was talking to Denise when Karen whispered to Jamey in passing, "You're a dude?" Jamey blushed and looked for Mona, but Mona was on another case. Neither she nor Denise seemed to have caught the exchange. "It's cool," Karen assured Jamey. "I don't put you down for what turns you on. Do your own thing, man."

"See you at the club tomorrow," said Mona, sliding the door closed. Once up in their single room, Mona and Jamey played records. This covered the sound of the creaking bed next door. And they smoked some of Rick's dope into the wee hours. Saturday was Jamey's day off.

"What are pettipants?" asked Jamey.

"I'm very glad you asked," said Mona.

REVOLUTION

J AMEY, WHO WAS BECOMING A PART of the great working class, wanted to do something fun on Saturday, his off day. Mona wasn't inclined, but, after repeated suggestions and some pouting on Jamey's part, Mona sighed and allowed that they ought to do something out of their normal. She suggested an art faire over at Barnsdall Park, but Jamey was set on getting away from Hollywood.

"I may as well have a fucking girlfriend!" Mona complained, unable to understand how traveling around L.A. would get them on the cover of Rolling Stone. Nevertheless, she patted Jamey on the head, saying, "If it'll make you happy…"

They split the cap of Czechoslovakian Pharmaceutical that Rick had given to Jamey that night at Jack's figuring that half a hit was just the thing. It was certainly sufficient. They hitched across Beverly Hills to Santa Monica, down Lincoln, and out to Venice Beach, all the while coming on. On a map, it seemed like a long way without a car, but Jamey was in short-shorts and Mona was in her cords and t-shirt, and they had no trouble attracting rides. Hitching had never been like that for Jamey and Craig back in the Valley. They had been known to wait hours while thousands of cars had passed the hippie ruffians by. Mona sat in back and always thought she had a plan. Jamey was up front being cute and shy, which is what he was. They were both blitzed by the time they arrived on the busy Venice boardwalk.

Jamey had done some hanging out down at Venice, so he knew a little of the area. Before the summer of 1969, Jamey's idea of going to Venice was taking in the freak scene and watching for girls in bathing suits. His perspective was somewhat altered now.

He had hoped to hitch up to Zuma, to show Mona his cove, but she was pretty wiry and really didn't know much about relaxing and grooving on nature. The end of Venice Blvd. was as far as she was willing to take this ride. But it was a groovy sunny scene and there was a lot to look at. The colors on the sand, the movement of the ocean, the reflective sidewalks, the oozing liquid glass on the windows of the shops forming puddles at the base of the old frames, the thousands of winged-eyes floating around the boardwalk, and a whole lot of other stuff. And there were freaks and there were girls, more than usual.

They had had no idea of it, and the psychedelic posters did nothing to make it understood, but they came upon a growing crowd farther down the beach to the south. They were gathering in front of a temporary stage. It was to be a free concert with Martin Turner and Life Force. Even Mona wanted to stick around long enough to see if Martin Turner's voice was as good on stage as it was in the studio. *The girls* were relatively tiny and had no trouble slipping into the crowd and moving up little by little toward the front. Someone even passed Mona a J which she shared with Jamey.

Life Force was a local L.A. band, but they had made some national waves with their first album, *Eat Your Plate*. They were in the psychedelic vein, and it remained to be seen if they had any staying power. They had a number one hit, but they had missed with their follow-up. Still, in the summer of 1969, they were pretty hot, especially for a free concert on the beach.

Martin Turner had already shown his keepin' power. He had had some dance singles in the early sixties, a really big ballad in 1965 called "Your Love" and everyone figured he was washed up with the arrival of the Brits and the stoners. Not so. He came up with a combination plate of soul, psychedelia, and positivity with *The Turnin' World* from 1968. It's what Bryan Cooper's *Translucent Curtain* should have been, but definitely wasn't.

Life Force went on first, but the crowd was pretty rowdy. There were shirtless hippies and halter top dancing girls. There was a lot of drinking and a cloud of puff drifting from the beach to the sidewalks. Life Force was really pretty light weight and, beyond the single, it didn't really catch the imagination of the discerning crowd. One big asshole threw a beer bottle just up in the air with little regard for Newtonian physics. This caused an injured skull, and that in turn precipitated a fight. Mona and Jamey scooched away from the center of this activity. Another bottle flew onto the stage. It didn't hit anyone, but it was certainly uncool.

When a second bottle hit the stage at the feet of the tambourine shaking lead singer, he stopped the show to address the rowdies. "Okay, man. It's all about peace and love, right? That's what we're talking about, man. Everybody's having a good time and just groovin' to the music on a sunny afternoon in Venice, man. But we gotta keep cool. We gotta dig the vibe. Let's not get so rowdy, man!" It had like no effect on the crowd, man. Most of the hippies were there for a good time. It was only a few loud mouth drunks who were ruining the party, and the lead singer's speech had no effect on them. "Hey, come on, people! You want to see Marty Turner, right?" That was an applause line. "Okay. Right. So do I. So we have to maintain and keep cool. We're gonna finish our set now. Hope you can dig it." It was not to be dug.

What most of the crowd didn't catch was that the Los Angeles Police Department was also making the scene. There was a black and blue line in riot gear, spread out along the shore line and in greater numbers on the margin of the crowd. The alleys were being sealed off by combat ready cops. When the third bottle hit the stage, the officers moved in, forcing the crowd up the beach, toward the sidewalk, to the right of the stage. They were creating a bottleneck which was manned by more officers with night sticks and handcuffs. A cop came on the stage and ordered the crowd to disperse.

But there were cops at every exit and they weren't letting anyone through, so even willing dispersers were caught in the push. Mona took Jamey by the hand and pulled him along through the crowd which was picking up speed in the panic. Heads were being cracked behind and ahead. Anyone who resisted or who looked like he might want to resist was arrested and stuffed into waiting police vans. Hippie dudes were trying to protect their ladies by covering their heads and taking the blows in manly fashion. There was no way out of this crazy place that didn't involve getting your head busted. It was a full-on police riot because it wasn't the audience that was out of control. Mona and Jamey held back in a doorway as the crowd pushed through in front of them. Jamey, still stoned, was frightened. A head cracking seemed like a sure thing.

THEIR DOORWAY RECESS was NOT FAR from one of the alleys that led up to the street and away from the riot, but two officers in riot gear were manning that egress, preventing refugees, including our girls, from escaping their just fates for grooving on the beach on a Saturday afternoon. Three burly dudes in denim jackets with uniform insignias on the back figured they could take the two cops with the batons and thus effect their exit, so they went for it, rushing the two cops head-on. Up went the day sticks, and Jamey, wide-eyed and open mouthed at the impending gladiatorial match couldn't tell you how it ended because Mona dragged her through a doorway and up a flight of stairs. The stairwell was dark and Jamey couldn't make out who Mona and she were following, but there was somebody leading the way.

"Gonna get your fuckin' heads spit, man!" That had been a concern, so this savior, whoever he was, was welcome at the time.

On the third floor, they followed into a smoky room. It was the classic bare bulb in the middle of the room look, but it was out of the police riot, so it looked relatively inviting. There were posters on the wall that gave them the first clues as to where they had landed. They weren't posters of Katy Mondy, Donovan, or the Beatles. There were impressive black and white shots of an armed Huey Newton and Bobby Seale. Jamey didn't know the two gentlemen from anyone else, but he recognized the black power look in a general way. There was a black power poster with Angela Davis in all her Afro glory.

There was also a disarranged metal office desk against a wall with a Malcolm X poster looking down over the work space. On it there was a manual typewriter and a hand gun, which Jamey had no way to identify. It was heavy, though, under the purple haze of smoke and acid. Oddly, there was a name plate on the desk: Saul Gary, Deputy Minister of Defense.

"You know what's going on out there, you little white bitches?" It was a big man, black, and over two-hundred-fifty pounds, with a wild Afro and a mustache. And the gun on the desk.

"Cops are trippin' out," said Mona. Jamey didn't know what was going down but the vibe was most uncool. It didn't make any sense to Jamey, especially in his psychedelic state.

"The capitalist pigs have identified still another nigger: The Hippies!"

"Maybe they just don't like Marty Turner," said Mona.

"Martin Turner's an Oreo, white in the middle, just black on the outside. He's not with us. He's one of them. Part of the machine that wants to grind down his own people." Jamey began to feel a little more oriented when he realized they were dealing with a rougher, realer version of Clarence Williams III from *The Mod Squad*.

"He sounds pretty black to me," said Mona. "I dig soul music. That sweet soul music…"

"It's all the Man's music, you little white bitches," said their friendly host. "What do you know about music? You think your white long haired freaks made up rock and roll? What do they know about the blues? What do they know about real life, life on the streets, man? Life on the plantation! You a couple of Sunday trippers, and you think you know where it's at. You don't know shit."

Jamey didn't know what was going on really, but he thought that maybe Mona was playing it a little more cool than usual which was a good thing. She wasn't pissing off the guy too much. Jamey was pretty sure he didn't want to go back out to the riot any time soon. "So is this your crash pad?" Jamey suggested.

"It's my office," he said. "We're a department of the Black Panthers. You ever hear of the Black Panthers?"

"Is it a band?" said Jamey. No doubt they jam at *The Foundry*.

"It's an organization that represents the interests of blacks in this racist white society, and if it means violence in the streets, then let the blood flow and wash away the sins of the world to reveal the shining light of black justice underneath!"

Mona and Jamey were both speechless at this latest turn. They were about apolitical. Jamey didn't approve of the war, thinking of Mitch and the possibility that he could be drafted, and he generally went along with the pronouncements of his rock and roll idols, but they didn't say much except that love is the answer. John Lennon was writing songs about revolution, but as long as you're writing songs and selling vinyl, the status quo is generally safe. Everyone knew Nixon was bad, Reagan was bad, pretty much all politicians were bad except maybe the Kennedys or good old Eugene McCarthy. But Jamey didn't have a deeply articulated or well considered political outlook. As far as the black question went, they went along with the late Dr. King. Violence was never the answer. The gentleman at hand took a different position.

"You little bitches should read…"

"White bitches," put in Mona. "Which, you know, you really need better lighting in here. I'm an Oriental bitch."

"You got that right, bitch. Have you ever read *Soul on Ice* by Eldridge Cleaver? That'll set you straight on this white society in which you dwell in comfort, power, and privilege. "

"So you don't like white people?" said Mona.

"I don't like the Devil, either."

"Okay," said Mona. "So are you planning to kill us?" They had had this one-way discussion all on their feet. Nobody had offered anyone tea or cocktails, not even a seat.

"Now is the time to kill the pigs!" he said. "I'm not interested in killing a couple of whores like you. I might split your little asses with my black cock."

"I think that's Jamey's department," said Mona.

Jamey was tripping on the cover of the *Soul on Ice* book. The guy didn't look friendly at all. "You're going to do what?"

"I'm gonna bend you over, stick my foot on your head, and my cock up your ass until I split you in half."

Jamey was at a loss.

"So, how do we get out of here man?" asked Mona. "It's not that we don't appreciate your help, but, you know…"

"What if I put this gun…"

"Okay. Okay," said Mona. "Is there another way out of here? Because I think my mommy's calling."

"First, I think you should make a contribution to the Free Huey Newton Fund."

"You want money?" said Jamey.

"Revolution ain't cheap," he told them. "Give me your money, bitches, or I'll find it myself." He was a peculiar fellow. Jamey was in no condition to decide one way or the other as to how dangerous he was going to be. Mona wasn't inclined to be searched, so she nodded to Jamey.

"I think we better free Huey Newton, don't you, bitch?"

"That," he mentioned. "Or I'll split your ass with my fat black cock."

"I think you said that," said Mona. "Jamey, we better pay the man."

So Jamey was turning away and reaching into his bra for the cash. Jamey turned over the whole twenty-two dollars and put it on Eldridge Cleaver's image on the book.

Mona showed him her wallet, and there wasn't any money in it.

He pulled back the heavy curtain, opened a window, and pointed to the fire escape. "Cops in front. Empty alley in back. But you better educate yourselves, girls."

"Bitches," Mona corrected him. Jamey started through the window while the panther held the curtain for her, slapping Jamey's ass on the way out. There are some universals. Mona had spilled her wallet by the corner of the desk, so she couldn't protect Jamey just at the moment. She gathered her things and was next to the window exit.

"Because you will someday be serving your black masters."

"At the IHOP," said Mona, who followed Jamey through the window and back into the sunlight and Venice beach sea air three stories over the alley. Mona quickly followed down the metal stairs. When they looked up, he raised his right arm in a fist, the symbol of black power. Mona did the same in reply, sort of shoving it upward. Perhaps a different message.

"Get yourself a copy of *Soul on Ice* and learn about your white racist bullshit!"

"Is it in the library?" called Mona, as they made their get-away. "Because I owe some fines."

"That was a trip!" said Jamey.

"You can close your mouth now, Jamey," said Mona, leading the way, holding Jamey's hand as they crossed the open alley to a parking lot. They, and a stream of others, were more or less safely out of the bloody net. Some of the hippies had been whacked by the cops and blood was still pouring down some of the faces. Women and girls were still crying, but there was less screaming though still some obscenities.

Mona stopped Jamey when they came to the boulevard. She stuffed some cash back in Jamey's bra.

"How'd you do that?" asked Jamey.

"I knew he'd go for your ass," said Mona. "I would, but it would give you the wrong idea. So, when he was going for it, I went for the cash."

"You ripped off the Black Panthers using my ass as a diversion? I mean, they shoot cops and stuff."

"We're chicks, Jamey. An oppressed minority if ever there was one. Nobody's threatening to split his black ass."

Jamey and Mona distinguished themselves from the general crowd through their youth and the fashion statement they seemed to be making. In their summer costumes, they didn't have any difficulty attracting rides along Santa Monica Blvd., though extricating themselves from the vehicles was always the trickier matter. They arrived home by late afternoon. Their little vacation had cost them nothing. But Mona was pissed that she didn't get to see Martin Turner, even if he were an Oreo. And that night, it was back to The Contortionist and back to Rooms-for-Rent to sleep for the Sunday morning carwash gig. It was like a routine, man. Déjà vu, but not in a cool way.

EVERYONE'S GONE TO THE MOON

WHEN JAMEY'S EYES FLASHED OPEN, he immediately felt weird. The room was too bright and sunny, and little Mona was still there beside him. Jamey jumped out of bed. He checked her watch on the dresser, no doubt lifted at a department store or from someone's jewelry box. It was almost noon. Jamey had missed his shift. "Shit!"

"Now we can do your fingernails red," said Mona, not even opening her eyes.

"You knew?" said Jamey.

"It's no place for a girl to work," said Mona. "We'll find something for you."

Jamey shook his head. "We're gonna miss the money," he said. "Not that we've seen any yet."

"If they fire you, they'll give you all your money at once, and we'll be rich!"

"You can't miss a shift," said Jamey. "I'm fired, fer sure, man. I only got the job because someone missed their shift."

"Good!" said Mona, herself out of bed. She squeezed Jamey's upper arm. "I don't like these muscles you've been growing."

"All the better to toss you out the window," said Jamey.

Mona pulled a pair of panties from the drying line in the back of the room and tossed them to Jamey. "Moment of truth, Jamey. You can be what you want to be. If you want to go straight, cool. Put on your boy clothes and that's it. If you put on the panties," she said, "then we're going for the big time together."

"So you just did this, I mean, cost me my job, just to turn me into a chick—more of a chick?" He stared at Mona. She remained inscrutable. Now that he was jobless, Jamey's options were considerably reduced. He pulled the nylon undies right up tight, and *the girls* did their morning ablutions. It was a day for casual jeans and tops. Jamey's was pink this time. The ladies went out on a laundry mission.

Mona let Jamey do most of the sorting and loading while she roamed the mat sometimes quite stealthily and other times in quite a gregarious manner. Waiting for the laundry to dry, Jamey had stepped outside to sit on a nearby bus bench, taking in the afternoon and smoking. Jamey was picking up on a vibe. There was an excitement, a communal feeling, a thrumming happening. People were talking in crowds, some shouting from the cars and the windows, a general feeling of the out-of-the-ordinary, like the squares were tuning up. It was quite a while before the news reached Jamey's consciousness.

The Moon was no longer virgin. Men—big strong American men—had now befouled it. Kennedy's great challenge for the decade had been met. And a triumphant Richard Nixon was leading America in its celebration. It was on the televisions, the radios, and coming out of everyone's mouth. It was a strange feeling on the Sunday street, and there was no acid involved, at least for Jamey and Mona. The closest thing Jamey could think of was the day Bobby Kennedy died. Everyone was coming together with the same feelings. But this was a groovy feeling, not a bummer. None of the usual expectations prevailed. Jamey had been psychedelicized too many times to remember, but this was a weird vibe. When Mona came out to join him, Jamey excitedly told her the news. "They fuckin' landed on the moon!"

"Then we ought to be able to get on the cover of Rolling Stone."

"They're on the fuckin' Moon, Mona. That's really far out stuff!"

"I guess," said Mona.

"How can you not think that's a trip?" said Jamey.

"We didn't go to the moon, did we? When we're on top in the music biz, that's news! Then I'm on the moon..." It was remarkable. Jamey and Craig had built their rock and roll dreams perhaps beyond reasonable expectations, but Jamey realized that this chick was dead serious; nothing else mattered to her.

As Jamey was folding their things, she noticed that Mona was still all around the joint. She wasn't naturally that friendly, but she interacted here, there, and everywhere. Every now and then, she came by and slipped a garment under a towel in their pile or deep into the basket that Jamey was sorting.

"Oh shit!" a woman shouted across the laundry. "What the fuck? It's all soapy!"

"Too much soap!" said a helpful gentleman.

"Fuck that!" said the woman. "I didn't use too much soap! It's all sudsed."

Mona was looking away. "Oh here..." she said to Jamey. "I borrowed your soap."

Jamey was folding the t-shirts and rolling up the socks. "What'd you do that for?" he quietly asked.

"Last month, I was in here and it was really crowded, and she cut me off and took my dryer. I don't think she'll be needing a dryer any time soon."

"You got yourself a list," said Jamey.

"Karma," said Mona.

When they got home, they had picked up a nice towel, a t-shirt, and a pair of tennis shoes that were almost small enough for Mona and too small for Jamey. Mona didn't say anything, but smiled with some satisfaction.

On their way to the The Contortionist, Mona and Jamey went to the carwash. At first, the manager didn't recognize Jamey in drag. Jamey convinced him that it was herself. The manager, trying to maintain a straight face and not easy to shock anyway, said that Jamey had been a good worker and that he was sorry to let him go. Jamey suggested a simple solution, but his policy was that missing a shift in the first months was an automatic firing. Too many unreliable types.

He said that he was also concerned that Jamey's nails wouldn't survive another day at the carwash anyway. Mona and Jamey had to hang around while the manager had his girl cut a check for Jamey. Jamey felt exposed and kept crossing his legs. The fellows with whom Jamey had been slaving at first appreciated the young ladies in the waiting room, as working gentlemen tend to do. Then one of them figured out who they were admiring. They were appalled to recognize their once trusty colleague. The cashier handed out the $66.96 that was due to Jamey. Easy money! "Nice nail color," she said, most sincerely.

"Thanks," said Jamey, with a friendly smile, and a flip of his hair. "Tee ya."

"How come you never got any tips?" asked Mona, as they were walking away. "People tip at the carwash, don't they? What happens to the money?"

"I always figured I'd get my share…"

"You got screwed, chick," said Jamey. "You need me."

"I know that," said Jamey. "You don't need me, but I need you."

"There's our next number one hit," said Mona.

Now they were rich! Richer than Jamey had been after the night with Richard. Including the Sunday night, Jamey and Mona picked up about $40.00 on band income. With Jamey's carwash income and the twenty-two they already had, less hot dogs and laundry, they were in possession of $127.00. America was indeed the land of opportunity, and Hollywood was a magical Emerald City.

They had two weeks rent, after the week already paid, and, with Mona's income, enough to live on. They could even do some street musician work, to stay above the water line if they needed to. If only they could keep Mona's spending in check. Jamey kept the money on his person, with the cash in his pants, because one didn't leave money around Mona. Mona didn't mind. It was nothing for her to extract cash from Jamey when she wanted it.

On Monday, Jamey tried looking for work, this time as a girl. Mona had given him a fairly conservative blue dress, with stockings and short heels. Whether Jamey was successful in drag might be a question, but there was no question that, no matter how conservatively Mona dressed him, he still had a definite hippie thing going on. Jamey tried the shops, the restaurants, even the bars. The liquor license was too expensive to risk on her fake ID. In short, no luck. Dejected, he hurried home to meet Mona when she arrived. And, as was sometimes the case, Mona was quite late. Next door, the springs of the bed could be heard working overtime. Apparently, another prostitute had moved in. Jamey was glad that he had the musical trade. He practiced his guitar and tried to write a song.

"WHERE WERE YOU AT?" asked Jamey.

"Are you my fucking mother?" Mona fired back. "Or my miserable wife, maybe?"

Jamey, his head bitten off, just stared at her. She went to the bathroom down the hall and returned in fifteen minutes with her hair still damp from washing. She was wearing jeans and a tee, as was her usual. "I found you a job!"

"You got me a job?" said Jamey. "Like at the camp?"

"Good idea, but they don't have anything right now. No. You're going to work at the theater down the street. It's near-by, and it pays the same as the carwash."

"Nothing," said Jamey. "The porn theater?"

"The straight one. The one that's playing *Charly* and *Planet of the Apes*. You just have to go over there and sign up. It's all set."

"What do you mean *it's all set*?" said Jamey. "How can it be *all set*? They never met me."

"I talked to the manager, and he said he'd hire you. Let's go. Fix your hair and your face. You have to look pretty. I told him you were a knock-out. You're going to be sitting in the glass ticket booth on the sidewalk. Like a go-go dancer in a cage at Gazzarri's. You just sit there and take the money and give them their tickets. *How many? Four dollars, please. And one for change.* This is so easy, Jamey. And it's close by so you don't have go all over town. And you can sit on your ass. Now you only get four nights, Monday through Thursday, so you can do the gig on the weekend. You know we can make up whatever we need to. This is so perfect, sweetie. And it's so much better than the car wash."

"And I'll never have to dress like a boy again?" said Jamey, sensing his fate.

"Well, you have to be a chick for the job, and for the band, but you can do what you want…"

"So, I'm still not clear, Mona," said Jamey. "How did you do this?"

"I'm your agent," said Mona. "I take care of things. I told you that. You need me. You're my ticket to the big time!"

T HAT NIGHT, Mona and Jamey made their way to The Troubadour where there was a Monday night open mic, the gig that Rick had mentioned. They signed up in the late afternoon, walked around the area, and showed up again for the show with their guitars. They sat through several acts, solo guitar folk singers a la Joan Baez or Joni Mitchell, a Chad and Jeremy type duo, a girl with a dulcimer who didn't impress Mona as much as Jamey who liked the look, and still another next Bob Dylan with a harmonica holder and everything.

The emcee returned to the stage. He was Leo Banks, the one-hit wonder who recorded the quirky "San Francisco Saturday Afternoon Happening." This one had gone gold, crossing between the hippies, the day-trippers, the bubblegum set, and the squares who were listening from the side lines. Jamey had always considered it a joke with its cliché harpsichord and reverb vocals. But, like Mike Carl, Banks was part of the scene. The song would always evoke the period for millions of music fans.

Mona and Jamey stepped up with their guitars to the stand-up microphones. They were in cords and t-shirts, not doing the sexy thing for their folk set. This was to be more serious.

Banks lowered the mics for *the girls*, almost seeming condescending. The lights from the back of the room on the stage were blinding. It was as big a room as Jamey had ever played but it was effectively empty. The audience was dead, barely applauding the previous acts. "Here they are," echoed Leo

Banks. "In their Los Angeles premier, The Hollywood Virgins—if you believe that!" Hardly even a laugh, but not altogether tasteful had it gone over. "The Hollywood Virgins, everyone!" The guitars were surprisingly competent, and Mona's voice was more interesting without the electric band to compete with it.

> *As the freak takes you*
> *Do your own thang...*

It was a nice hep acoustic rendition that got a few claps, but little enthusiasm. This wasn't a crowd at all, and they kept their participation to a minimum. It was good practice for Jamey. The sidewalk crowds had ignored him cold when he was doing his street musician thing, but this audience paid just enough attention to be bored. The focus was on being cool and not digging the music at all costs. It was almost hostile, but Jamey soldiered forward. Mona didn't feel it. The audience was there for her convenience and she was practicing her cool. Jamey sang the lead for the second song, an unexpected number that was familiar to the audience, "The Elusive Butterfly."

They got nothing back from the audience. The Hollywood Virgins had done a total of four songs when Mr. Banks returned to the stage, exhorting the audience to applaud. "John and Yoko!" he quipped in a put-on English accent.

"She's a Jap," said Mona. Loudly. Over the mic. "Do I look like a Jap? I'm a Chink. Get it right, loser." Mona didn't take a lot of shit. "I never liked your fuckin' song. It was bubble-gum crap." They weren't invited back.

Returning home, Jamey was still wondering about the employment situation. He was pretty slow, but not as lame as he had once been. "Does this involve either you or me having sex with this manager dude at the theater?"

"Well, what do you take me for?" asked Mona.

"I hope I haven't offended your refined sensibilities, milady." Mona never answered the question, but, starting on Tuesday night, Miss Jamey Craig became a fixture on Hollywood Boulevard, selling tickets from the glass booth in front of the El Portal, and from that point, Jamey was in drag full time. He might complain to Mona that he had to do it for the band or for the job, but he did it whether he was working or not, and even when nobody—not even Mona—was around. Jamey was dressing, acting, and feeling like a girl as much as he could. He missed Mona when she was gone in the mornings, and he waited for her to show up. Some days, that was around two in the afternoon. On other days she didn't come home until after Jamey had gone to work. But whenever she came in, Mona would find that Jamey had cleaned the place after the night before. He did their laundry and put up their things. He washed and folded Mona's clothes and placed them carefully in drawers. Mona had shown Jamey how to sew a little, and Jamey spent some mornings working on repairs and refinements. More often, he played guitar and worked on his songs.

When Mona did come home, they might play tunes, whether on the Tele-Tone or on their instruments. But, Monday through Thursday, Jamey was off to work by the four o'clock hour.

The highlight for Jamey and for Mona was playing in the band. Maiden Head was getting tighter and improving the harmonies. Crazy Place would have been annihilated against Maiden Head in a battle of the bands, but, on another hand, The Contortionist was no place to be discovered. They were going nowhere and getting nothing back.

The El Portal was easy money, though not much of it. It was time away from Mona. He never knew what Mona was doing when they were apart, but he didn't imagine that she did nothing. That wasn't in her nature. Jamey was trying to get on the day shift so that he could spend more time with her, and the manager, rubbing his chin thoughtfully, said that he thought it could be very easily done. He implied that it might require Jamey coming upstairs to the manager's office. If this was how he distributed the hours, Jamey had to wonder to what lengths Mona had gone to get him the gig.

Though Jamey was chiefly assigned to sitting in the glass cage where he was supposed to look pretty and sell tickets, he was sometimes privy to the rest of the theater. Late one night, when the manager was out, one of the ushers beckoned Jamey up the stairs to the office next to the projection room. "Want to see something weird?"

"I see a lot of weird stuff," said Jamey.

"Not this weird," said the usher. He unlocked the room, switched on a light, and stepped back. Jamey looked along the back wall of the small office where, at ceiling level, there was a long row of panties hanging on the wall.

"This is certainly weird," said Jamey, taking it in.

"So, if he invites you up here, well, you be the judge…" This sort of thing had never happened at the carwash. And, having met the manager, it wasn't clear that it happened at the theater either. Could be that Mona had some competition in the used clothing market. But, to the usher's point, it was weird. Jamey didn't go upstairs with the manager.

As the weeks went by, Jamey found that his check came in at $35.64 a week, like clockwork. Mona was still making her $40.00 at the camp. Their combined share of the band's take, after costs, was about $55.00, bringing the weekly total to about $130.00 between them. Rent was still $45.00, so they had $85.00 to live on, a princessly sum. Of course, there were expenses. They ate well at donut shops, hot dog stands, and the Big Boy. It averaged about six bucks a day, costing them around $150.00 during the month for food. Mona needed bus fare and traveling money, which came to about $60 over the same period. She also invested in various items necessary to the trade such as makeup, hair and nail products, vast quantities of baby powder, hygienic aids, and even, to Jamey's utter bewilderment, fashion magazines. Indeed Jamey added to the costs by purchasing some cleaning aids. Over the next four weeks it amounted to another $170.00. Mona bought some pot and some whites, not quantities for sale, but additional costs. Jamey, who had a sense of the money more so than Mona appeared to have, realized that they were spending just a tiny bit more than they were making. Having started his new job with about $126 in his panties, that sum, despite their great riches was now a mere $86.00. Miss Curtis had introduced Jamey to Mr. Micawber, but they were some distance from calamity according to the financial forecast. Mona would have claimed not to know the dude.

They were into dressing up, but, to that end, they didn't spend money on clothes. Jamey came to learn that it was a point of honor with Mona. And she could steal anything. Jamey was into Mona, fascinated, and, though there wasn't any sex, he was in love with her. He'd be platonic if she wanted. He'd be lez if she liked. He'd give her cock if she chose, but there was no sign that Mona wanted any of that. He constantly puzzled over their relationship. Mona said they were best friends, stoning partners, adventurers, and musicians. For her, he was hiding his balls and redirecting his unit. It was a crazier place than ever he had dreamed. Sometimes when he fantasized, and he did, he couldn't fantasize about having sex with Mona because he always saw himself as the girl. If anyone was going to be dominant in their world, it was Mona.

Playing with Denise and Karen and watching their relationship where Denise was clearly dominating, Jamey began to see them as a model. Living in Hollywood, where there were all kinds of shops, Jamey came up with a plausible fantasy which he suggested to Mona. It involved a device he had seen at a store on the boulevard, though he had never imagined such a thing before seeing it. It was a dildo that a girl could strap on and use wherever it might find a soft spot. When Jamey suggested this idea to Mona, Mona cracked up. "You're more perverse than I am, Jamey!" she said. "What's in it for me?"

"You like to dominate?" said Jamey.

"I already dominate you," said Mona. "It's not pretend with me. You do what I tell you to do, and that's how you like it."

"Well, maybe I would like…"

"Sex is bad for friendship, Jamey. I told you that. I know what you want…" Oh, Mama!

"Sex with Teri Ann Murphy?"

"If she'd dildo you, but not from what you told me…"

"So you said you knew what I wanted?"

"You'll get mad at me," said Mona. Jamey said nothing, but stared at her, demanding an answer. "Okay," she said. "What you really want, what you're most curious about, what you can't forget…"

"Mona!"

"It's your boyfriend," said Mona. "You never forgot that kiss. You never forgot what it felt like to be in his arms. You want your boyfriend to have sex with you. You can deny it all you want. But you'll figure it out. You've never forgotten him."

"I'm a transvestite," said Jamey. "I'm not a homo."

"I'm not judging, sweetie," said Mona. "Not into labels. But you don't want *me* in your ass. Well, maybe you do. But only because you can't have what you really want. But, maybe there's a way that you can have him…"

"What does that mean?"

"You're not less attractive than you were. You're ten times the girl you were when he knew you. He'd be all over you if he got the chance. Maybe we just have to give him the chance."

"I think I burned that bridge, honey," said Jamey. "He and Molly Gifford would want exactly nothing to do with me."

"You don't know your own power, Jamey," said Mona. "Love is crazy shit."

"That's what Molly told me. Anyway, I'm not a queer. I was just thinking, you and me, you know. We neither one of us has sex." It was almost a question, but Mona was impassive. "That I know about, I mean."

Through his skirt, Mona touched Jamey's vestigial manhood. "I think

134

you're a nasty little girl who wants to have sex with her boyfriend. It isn't me, baby."

"Didn't Dylan write a song like that?"

"Voice of a generation?" said Mona.

JAMEY

Maiden Head spent the Woodstock weekend working at The Contortionist. Jamey and Mona forced their way into Jack's apartment at Rooms-for-Rent to watch the Dick Cavett Woodstock episode. They had heard that Hendrix was to be on, but he had been too zonked to make the scene. They weren't disappointed with Joni, Crosby, and the Airplane.

Information was slow to come at first, but over the next few days, they gathered news about who had played, how many people were really there, how many folks died, and what the conditions were like. *Watch out for the brown acid, man…* The moon shot hadn't much impressed Mona, but Woodstock caught her imagination.

At one point, she even blew Jamey's mind. She was talking about the bummer that they hadn't been there. Jamey was agreeing that it would have been cool, when it slowly dawned on him that what Mona meant was not that she should have been in the audience but that she should have been on the stage. Jamey could see that she wasn't going to spend the next six months, year, or five years at The Contortionist. She was ready to bust out. Jamey had no idea what kind of move she could make, but she was going to do something. Nobody came into The Contortionist who could do them any good. By playing the regular gig, they weren't getting around to any other clubs. It was fun to play, but it wasn't going to get them a rep and it wasn't going to get them on the cover of Rolling Stone. Talking with Karen, Jamey learned that it was most likely that Leslie had left the band because she didn't think it was going anywhere either. Leslie was majorly talented, but she had other interests, Karen explained.

"Like a boyfriend?" suggested Jamey.

"Kind of," said Karen. "But *her* boyfriend is heroin."

As the newspapers and then magazine shots came along, Jamey noted with some pride and Mona observed with some bemusement that Richard Altier had been at Woodstock, too. His photos were being widely circulated. "You can't get away when your boyfriend's famous, Jamey."

"My *boyfriend* hasn't exactly been banging on the door…" said Jamey.

"Well, does he know where you are?" said Mona.

As it was for a lot of hippies, there was pre-Woodstock and post-

Woodstock. They had been thousands of miles away, but the vibe had hit them like a wave. Mona was ready. Maiden Head could only stay together if they began to happen.

THE THURSDAY AFTER WOODSTOCK, when Jamey returned from the El Portal about 10:30 PM, Mona was reading Jack's paper in the lobby of Rooms-for-Rent. There was a long investigative article on the bizarre hippie-inspired *Helter Skelter* Benedict Canyon murders. Maybe the city wasn't living in fear, but there was some discomfort. Nobody had been arrested, and it could happen again at any time. The good news was that the targets seemed to be rich folks rather than hippies. On the other hand, it could give hippies a bad name. "Weird shit going down," observed Mona. "You want to get a hot dog? Get out amongst them?"

"I'm tired. Let's just crash, man. We have to gig tomorrow. I need my beauty sleep."

"It's so fucking hot," said Mona. "Too stuffy up there. We should go out," said Mona. "The weenies are waiting."

"Come on," said Jamey. "We're always going out." Mona took Jamey by the hand and led him up the stairs.

"Easy for you, Jamey. I wait here for you all night, all by myself, and I like to go out a little and have fun. But you come home all tired and bored, nothing to say…"

"Oh, please…" As Rick had correctly expressed it more than a month before, Jamey could say no and protest as much as he liked. Nobody really objected to that, and it was kind of cute. But, eventually, he would do what Mona wanted.

"We're going Catholic tonight! Look what I got us." They dressed in gray pleated schoolgirl skirts with knee socks and white collar blouses with pockets, all the details down to the gold crucifix chains.

Jamey had to wonder where and how Mona had procured the outfits. Did she get them out of someone's dryer? Did she steal them off the line? Did she do some B&E to get them? It would have been pretty aggressive to have actually shoplifted them from a uniform store. And they weren't exactly new. Not ratty, but not fresh off the rack. Then it crossed his mind: Were there two schoolgirls locked in a closet over at Immaculate Heart shivering in their underwear due to an encounter with Mona?

"Where are we going?" was Jamey's suspicious question, as if Mona might respond. They carried their I.D.'s and individual keys in the skirt pockets. Jamey had most of the money in his bra, and a little in his pocket.

Nothing was going to happen in their hot stuffy room and something could happen down on the street level. That was the plan as far as it went. And the costumes added to the likelihood that something would happen. They walked arm in arm to the hot dog joint and sat at a stone table in the light. There was some motion to interest Mona. It was a pretty hot night and the air-conditioning provided by the skirt felt nice to Jamey. It was still relatively novel to him.

Mona decided it would be fun to get someone to pay for their late chilidog dinner. Two younger guys checking out the summer scene approached the stand, Mona made her move. "Hey, guys," she said. "We're hungry. Can you give us a quarter or two?" She didn't want to sound intelligent or engaging, just pathetic and vulnerable enough to con some quarters. Jamey decided that had he been one of those dudes he would never have fallen for it. Just because she was showing some leg was hardly reason enough to open the vault. On the other hand, had he thought about it, this was in fact the same Mona who had been living off of his money for a month, and that didn't take into account that she had talked him into hiding his balls and wearing a skirt out in public to beg money from boys. What wouldn't he do for her? And while Mona was having her fun flashing enough thigh action to get a response, the boys gave her a quarter each.

But then they wanted to sit down and get their money's worth. The guys felt invested and certainly had no better prospects—unless it was a question of paying for piece work or an hourly rate. So it was Mona and Jamey who pushed on down the boulevard on the summer night. Next, Mona and Jamey encountered from the opposite direction a trio of very young guys, maybe fifteen and sixteen. Jamey was sixteen, but his birthday was September. These guys were younger than that, and working on their hair. It was getting good in the back.

The first lad, Nick, definitely not old enough to drink, and posing as a Hollywood hipster, sported straight blond hair parted in the middle. He had fashionable flared trousers and Beatle boots and an Errol Flynn style puffy shirt with French sleeves. With open front buttons, he was flashing his chest, which had barely sprouted hair. The second, Chris, was tall with a round face, heavy black glasses, and black curly hair, in the fashion of a fro but not so stiff. The third had brown hair, parted on the side, just over the ears. He had a few noticeable pimples, but what are you going to do? He was heavier than the other two, but not too far gone. None of them appeared to be in very good physical shape, even at this tender age.

But they were loud and laughing as they made their way along the boulevard, and they certainly regarded Mona and Jamey in their costumes and bare knees as the two parties approached. Mona struck first, approaching Nick, the one in the middle, the best dressed, and obviously the leader of this tiny tribe. "Hey, Mister," she began in her pathetic voice, "We're hungry. Can you give us a quarter?"

"Tell ya what," answered the lad. "Why don't you give me a buck?" Mona took that as a FUCK YOU and pulled Jamey along, trying to go around the trio. "Hey!" called Nick. "Don't go away mad! Just having a little fun. How much do you need?"

Mona turned back to the boys and smiled in a friendly way. He was on the hook. "We just need something to eat for supper. You want to buy us dinner at the Big Boy?" Jamey was dumbstruck. Was there nothing beyond this girl? Caging quarters seemed passable, but squeezing into a booth with sexed-up teens in exchange for dinner was prostitution, and not very lucrative prostitution at that.

The three lads looked the ladies up and down, mostly down. "I was thinking maybe we could have some fun first," Nick suggested. Jamey could not immediately recall any young lady who referred to having sex as *fun*. Nick, it seemed to Jamey, was not only obnoxious, but he was stupid as well.

Even Chris, in his department store checked button-down shirt and pool faded denim, looked uncomfortable. "It might be nice to get to know each other," he said, softening things up.

"She doesn't want to get to know us," said the third, Harry. "She wants dinner, and who knows what else? Either you want to buy her dinner or you won't. That's what she wants. You don't get much for dinner."

"No bullshit here," said Mona, looking Harry over. "Don't you want to spend some time with us?"

"I think it's the money. It's not the time," Harry was saying, as if analyzing a specimen with a tricorder.

"Shut up!" said Nick, to Harry. "What are you doing? You got two hot chicks here and you're talking about them as if they weren't here!"

"You tell 'em, Moe!" said Mona.

"Hey, I'm Nick. This is Chris, and this idiot is Harry. We're the Big Three! So who the hell are you?"

"This is Jamey," Mona started. Jamey's eyes had been downcast and demure, actually embarrassed to be begging, especially since there was some sense that they were trading in sexuality if not actual sexual favors. Jamey was, perhaps, a free thinking fellow, but he had his concerns about delivering the goods as he didn't actually have any goods for which the Big Three were in the market.

"…and I'm Mona."

"Mona!" said Nick.

"If you do the song…" Mona threatened.

"Oh, a mind reader, eh?" said Nick. "Because I would like to tell you what I want to do."

"Story of my life. They want to tell me. But do they ever do anything about it?" Before he could answer, Mona was moving on. "What about Jamey?" she said. "Got a song for her?" Harry was ready:

> *Oh…legs so long and lovely,*
> *A heavenly design—*
> *The Lord must love His labor*
> *'Cause he made Jamey sweet and fine, fine, fine…*
> *well, Jamey…*

Joined by Chris in a dialect,

> *I'm certainly discussing Jamey…*

"I always liked that song!" said Mona. "You got a good voice, Harry. I'd let you buy us a burger even though you think we're whores."

"We can get you burgered up," said Nick. "But let's stop by the car first. We could do a little makin' out." Jamey remarked to himself that Nick really knew how to sweet talk the ladies. Hard to keep the panties in place with talk like that.

"So you want to have sex in your car?" said Mona. "Let me ask Jamey. You do want to have sex with Jamey, too, don't you?"

"I wouldn't want her to feel neglected," said Chris, looking at Jamey again. Jamey was quite uncomfortable.

Mona drew Jamey aside. They watched the boys as the boys watched the girls. It looked like Nick was urging Chris to take up the slack with Jamey. Harry was overheard to say, "What do you need me to keep watch for?" and, "You can't guarantee that they'll suck me off…"

Mona was very animated while talking to Jamey who seemed to be hesitating to a great degree. "There is no way I'm going to do this! Why would we do this?"

"But make sure you get his pants off," said Mona. "Because that's where the money is."

"You want me to let him…"

"Maybe it's his birthday. Surprise of his life!"

"You are *so* sick!" Jamey complained. The observation had no effect.

"I'm not the one who wants a dildo up his ass…"

Nick broke from the huddle as Mona returned to the field. He could barely keep his hands from reaching under her skirt. Jamey followed Mona, and the boys were with Nick, like at a junior high dance. "Well, we could have sex if you guys had a place," said Mona.

"Mona!" Jamey complained. "We really couldn't."

"Wow, man!" observed Chris. "How about the back of the square back? We're parked a few blocks that way…"

"It'd be all right with me," said Mona. "But Jamey wasn't brought up that way. She's a good Catholic girl, and she won't just spread 'em in the back of a Volkswagen. Would you, Jamey?"

"I should say not," said Jamey, not really in a position to spread 'em under any circumstances. "We should go home," said Jamey, tugging at Mona. "Homework! Sister's expecting that paper tomorrow…"

Mona replied, "Sister can lick my pussy…"

Nick was engaged now. Just the words coming out of Mona's dirty mouth seemed to excite him. Chris and Harry were a little less sure of themselves, and Jamey recognized the feeling. If Teri Ann hadn't picked him out of the crowd, he'd probably have finished the eleventh grade a virgin.

Harry clearly thought the whole thing was crooked. "If you could buy chicks for a burger and fries, you know…" Nick and Chris were not listening.

"But there's the problem of the odd-man-out," said Mona, referring to Harry. "You guys are, what did you say, the Three Musketeers?"

"The Big Three!" they all said in unison.

"Ah yes! All for one and one for all, except—uh oh. We're only the Tiny Two. One extra dick, by my count."

"You don't count so well," mumbled Jamey.

"So which one of you gets Jamey?" asked Mona. "And which one gets fucked, meaning not fucked?"

"Wow, man!" said Chris. "Ultimate dilemma. Sacrifice a fuck for a friend or a friend for a fuck? Heavy."

"This one's a poet," said Mona. "Better take him."

"I can't choose," said Jamey. "I like them both too much. It just isn't

141

meant to be. Let's get out of here, Mona."

"Well, what about us two?" suggested Nick, apparently referring to Mona and himself. "You know you feel the electricity with me, Mona. It's a fuck-accompli." Jamey was amazed at the poetry.

"This is getting hard to resist," said Mona. "He's so sexy."

"I'm resisting just fine," said Jamey.

"Your head says no," said Chris. "But your heart says yes." His arm was around little Jamey's shoulders and his hand was reaching toward his breast. Jamey was feeling creeped. Not like with Rick. It was just being handled like that.

"We'll walk with you," said Nick.

"I won't be able to beg any money that way," said Mona.

"Take a break," said Chris.

"What are you?" said Nick. "A taxi?"

"Dinner's covered," Chris assured her. Jamey was trying to extricate *the girls* from the boys, but Mona had taken an interest in them. Jamey could see no gain in fooling with the lads, but Mona was clearly having fun. Jamey wondered at the whole affair. He had concluded that Mona didn't like sex. He suspected that she might use it to a purpose, perhaps, like getting Jamey a job, but Jamey was convinced that she didn't like sex. It was the only way Jamey could explain them sleeping together and never having any sexual contact despite their intimacy. But would Mona go to this extreme for a case of petty robbery?

And Mona wasn't the only mystery. He really didn't know what the guys were thinking. Did they really imagine that it was every girl's dream to fuck strange boys in the back of a Volkswagen on a Hollywood side street? What romantics they must be! Mona was in motion walking on the sidewalk. Nick had his arm around Mona, squeezing her midriff and drifting here and there on her little body. Harry and Chris were on either side of Jamey, sometimes handling him from one side and sometimes from another. "I don't know about this," Mona was saying. "Do you guys pick up girls every night? I don't want to be just another link in your chain."

"Oh, baby!" said an incredulous Nick. "What do you take me for? You know there's nobody else but you, babe."

"Well, if you don't have sex all the time, then maybe you're all virgins?"

That was a momentarily uptight scene, but, intoxicated with the beautiful reserved Jamey and the saucy Mona, Nick quickly recovered his obnoxious self. After walking a few blocks, Chris pointed out that the car was down the street.

LITTLE SISTER

JAMEY WAS FAKING THE GOOD FEELING, because he did not have a good feeling about any of this. He felt the eyes lapping up his feminine form. That was sometimes exciting, but, in this case, he was feeling at some risk. Arriving at the blue square back, there was an awkward moment, among many, that had to do with separating into couples.

Nick was suggesting that Mona might like to climb into the back, and Mona seemed tempted. Jamey still couldn't understand her thinking, but that was often the case. And there was a little jealousy, too. Mona better not make love to one of these jerks, for any reason, since she had consistently spurned her own room mate, the ever-loyal Jamey. The street was dark, but there were a lot of apartments on both sides of the block. Mona's back was against the side of Chris's car and Nick was in front of her, holding her, feeling her up, kissing her. Jamey was shocked to see this infant having his way with Mona. He was also envious. He had never gotten to hold Mona in like manner.

Mona extricated herself momentarily from Nick's amorous embrace. "I better see about Jamey, or no go for anyone." Nick was reluctant to let her out of his claws, but it was the way with girls. When she broke away, Mona took Jamey aside. "I'm just teasing him," said Mona. "Giving him a thrill. You should pick one and give him a thrill. Go with Chris. He's a believer."

"Mona!" Jamey complained, unable to even form the words to protest against this ridiculous idea. "I'm not making out with a guy."

"Saving yourself for Rick?" said Mona.

"We broke up," said Jamey. "But, listen—for once. Please, Mona. I can't make out with these guys. I hate that prick tease stuff, and it's gross."

"When that Chris guy gets into your pants, his mind will be permanently blown!"

Jamey was shocked on shock. "You expect me to let a guy—a boy—into my pants…"

"You have to separate him from his pants, and then let him finger your pussy."

"I don't have a pussy," said Jamey, a little more regretfully than he intended.

"Right, and when he gets a handful of your ding-dong, they'll throw us out the car so fast! It'll be hilarious, and they'll remember it for the rest of their lives. But we ought to get a wallet or two out of the deal."

"But the trauma to Chris..." said Jamey. "And they might kill us. Might beat the shit out of *me*."

"Not these boys," said Mona. "Some guys, yes. Not these babies."

"This is a very bad idea, Mona. Can't we just go home to bed? I'm tired and hungry. Let's just go..."

"I'll get in the front with Nick. There's no way he can get to me with the stick shift and steering wheel. There's just no room. And you get in the back with Chris."

"Mona, I really can't do this..." Mona clapped her hands, mom-style, no more nonsense. Behave. From the distance, the boys saw what they wanted to see, Mona talking Jamey into putting out over her reticence to do it in the car on the street.

Harry agreed to be the look-out. He had expressed his doubts on the whole affair. But, now, it looked as if he had been wrong. Chris put down the back seat, so there was a small bed in back. Jamey climbed through the hatch, against his own advice. Chris followed Jamey. There wasn't much headroom, so all they could do was stretch out in back. Chris was uptight because he could see Harry, observing and grinning. Chris pounded on the window to shoo him away. Jamey was listening to what was going on up front.

"Your tits are nice," Nick remarked, so Jamey presumed that he was in some way able to observe or otherwise handle them. Nick was not a romantic lover. He had a sense of humor about the matter that didn't lend itself to setting a mood of passionate abandon.

"Oh, darling!" cried Mona. Her blouse fell behind her into the back. Jamey could only speculate that she was totally faking it. Jamey could hear Mona murmuring her excitement and thrill at being handled by a fifteen-year-old boy. Mona kissed him now and then to keep him going. "Oh, Nicky!" She was, apparently, a nasty girl who couldn't get enough of his touch.

"Oh, baby!" Nick was replying. It sounded ridiculous to Jamey, what he could hear, but it was probably typical stuff. He couldn't hear the other couple anymore when Chris moved in on him, kissing his tender face and holding his "breasts" through his blouse. They didn't feel anything like breasts, but Chris was no expert. His lack of experience kept the illusion going. Jamey didn't dare permit him to open the blouse or even to get too close, though Chris was working on it. The blouse was out of the skirt now. Jamey pushed the boy's curly head down his body where he was kissing her now bared belly.

"You smell so nice," he remarked. That was sweet, thought Jamey—and after a long day. The windows had gone steamy and Harry had had his last look. Wanting to get Chris out of his trousers according to instructions, Jamey whispered, "Chris? Would you mind if I…"

"Anything, Jamey," said Chris. "Tell me about it, honey."

"Can I touch it?"

"You want to touch my…?" Jamey, under Chris's weight, groped between them for Chris' crotch. Chris adjusted his weight to let Jamey explore at will, not sure at all what he should do.

Jamey laughed. "It's a little cramped," he said, slipping from under Chris and, awkwardly perhaps, trading places with him. "Now, just be a good boy, and let me…"

"I'll definitely let you," Chris agreed.

Jamey seemed to be getting into it, which was funny. He wasn't who Chris thought he was, and he wasn't who he pretended to be. Nevertheless, he opened Chris' belt buckle and then popped the buttons on his jeans, one after the other. There was some strong evidence that Chris approved of *her* efforts.

Jamey, kneeling and crawling to the back, unzipped the black boots, and pulled them off one at a time. Then, he started tugging on the jeans. Chris quickly shoved them down his thighs and Jamey did the rest. Chris had never encountered anything approaching this situation before, but he gave himself over to Jamey who seemed to have good ideas.

Jamey was beside him now, his bare leg across Chris' naked somewhat hairy leg. Jamey reached into Chris' shorts and began to touch him here, there, and everywhere. Chris made some noises of approval, and, at the same time, he reached for Jamey's bum which Jamey didn't resist. As Jamey worked his fingers up and down, Chris was reacting appropriately.

Before very long, Jamey was holding a pulsing Chris in the palm of his hand. Jamey had very little frame of reference, but Chris seemed surprisingly well hung for a kid. The enthusiasm that Jamey exhibited was beyond Mona's instructions. Jamey was forgetting himself.

Jamey moved down Chris' body and put his lips at the tip of Chris' unit. Jamey had no experience with this sort of thing, but he had seen a couple of dirty movies down on Ventura and had seen some sexy magazines that Craig Roman kept hidden in the garage where they practiced. He had always pictured himself as the guy to whom the girl was giving face. This was reversed, and he was surprised at himself by his willingness to do Chris in this manner. Tentative at first, he began to take Chris into his mouth after the fashion of Molly.

However, most suddenly, just as Jamey was wondering how long this business was going to last, Chris suddenly threw Jamey off balance and onto *her* back. He pushed open and got between Jamey's resistant legs. Jamey released a plaintive, "Chris, no!" But Chris was intent on his mission. He kissed Jamey long and deeply, pushing his almost naked body against *hers*, rubbing crotch against crotch. Jamey was physically resisting, but it was too subtle for Chris to notice. He was heavier than Jamey and much stronger. This didn't seem odd to Chris, assuming that Jamey was a chick. He read her resistance as excitement, as *she* squirmed. Chris reached under the skirt and began to remove the last barrier to the passing of his virginity. Jamey tried to hold him off, but the panties were being pealed nonetheless. To the rescue, perhaps, but most inconveniently, out popped Jamey's prick, and there was a definite spring to it. Jamey hadn't gotten off since Molly.

"What the fuck?" whispered Chris, momentarily contemplating the sudden arrival. Chris was totally confused, but only briefly. When it hit him, he automatically pulled away and saw what he had felt inside Jamey's clothes. This was the response that Jamey had been unable to summon when Rick had kissed him. Slamming his head against the roof of the car in the rush to get away, Chris released a blood curdling cry of alarm that shook Nick and Mona from their romantic reverie. She was getting tired of stalling him anyway.

"What the fuck?" Nick remarked.

Chris was jumping out the side door of the square back in an instant. Chris had the presence of mind to grab for his trousers, but Jamey took hold of them and kicked Chris out, quickly locking the door. "You better see about him," said Mona, pushing Nick off of her.

"What the fuck?" Nick reiterated. He was not at all dressed for it and was obviously most unwilling to give up his hold on Mona. She was braless and vulnerable, but he was compelled by duty to see about his friend. "What's the matter?" he called, opening the door to see about Chris. "Mousetrap in her cunt?"

"She has a dick!" bawled Chris. Mona kicked hard against Nick's back. He lost his balance and tumbled onto the sidewalk. Jamey reached over and locked the door behind.

146

"Give me his fucking pants!" Mona checked for the keys, as Jamey climbed over into the front. Now the boys were trying to open the car doors. Mona started the engine, roughly popped it into gear, and jerked her way onto the avenue and down the block. Chris, in his checkered shorts and his button-down shirt, and Nick, in nothing but his socks and white briefs, chased the vehicle down the street, yelling and screaming after *the girls*, their first fucks, Chris's dad's car, and their pants and wallets driving off into the Hollywood night.

Mona, who was no kind of driver, began a short wild ride through the area, frightening any number of drivers on the tight streets. Mona managed to get over several blocks and charged head first into a parking spot, with the rear end of the square back sticking out into the street. Jamey and Mona replaced their clothes, and then they checked the boys' trousers. They came up with about eight bucks and three scumbags between them. Harry must have been the one with the big money. Right. Mona stole Nick's fancy puffy shirt and put it on over her blouse. She also put on Chris' glasses. "This guy is blind," she said. "No wonder he couldn't find your dick." They also took the boys' cigarettes. They left the car locked up safely with the keys inside.

Back on their boulevard, Jamey started to tell Mona what she really thought. "I can't believe you!" said Jamey. "That was *not* nice."

"You're the little slut!" said Mona, buttoning her blouse. "You were so into it."

"I was just doing what you told me to do," said Jamey.

"You sure were. Did you suck him?"

"I was starting to," Jamey admitted. "Well, I was more than starting. I just wondered what it was like. You get to suck dicks if you want to and nobody complains."

"They better not!" said Mona. "Anyway, now you know. It's like sucking cock. Which you're a cock sucker."

"I would have sucked him off, if I didn't gag or choke or whatever. But, instead of letting me suck him, he decided to pants me. He was going to get off anyway. Why did he do that?"

"Did you think he wouldn't find out?"

"But it's better to find out after you get sucked off. Isn't it?"

"I really can't answer that, Jamey. It's sort of philosophical, isn't it? Hey, but it was fun," said Mona. "They won't forget us any time soon."

"It was horrible," said Jamey. "I would have sucked him or jerked him off, and he would never have known, and he would have been happy. Now

I think he's traumatized."

"Believe me. It's a hassle for them now, but they'll be telling this story 'til the day they die of boredom from their brainless pointless useless plastic pathetic lives. This is probably the funniest thing that's ever happened to these suckers. So they'll take a little shit now from the cops and their parents, but it'll be a high point."

"We did them a favor? No pants in Hollywood?" said Jamey. "Stolen car. My dick in his hand? I can't even figure out how this will end for them. The cops'll get 'em for being naked on the street. Their parents will ground them for years. But, really, they might have killed us. Or ripped off my dick. Don't do shit like that!" Mona was looking at Jamey, laughing. "Please don't do that?" Jamey tried. "Pretty please, sugar on top?" Mona just smiled. "You're not promising anything, are you?" She shook her head. Mona, having had her fun, now wanted her hot dog. They had made eight-fifty since setting out, and none of it taxable.

T HEY CROSSED THE BOULEVARD at a light and continued on their way. Mona saw him first, and then Jamey, who froze. Harry was coming out of a liquor store. The girls slipped into an alcove to avoid being seen, but it was too late. Harry ran up to them.

"You little bitches!" he complained.

"Why are you pissed?" said Mona. "We proved you right. You said they couldn't get fucked for a burger and fries. You were right. So where are they?"

"Before you turned the corner, the cops came up behind them— running down the street in their underwear. Took them away on the spot." Mona thought that this was funny stuff. "But it was my ride. How am I going to get back to the Valley? I don't want to be mixed up in this when the cops call their folks."

"So you just kept walking the other way?" said Mona. "That's so cool! Well, if you go that way," she said, pointing. "Quite a distance really, you can pick up the 101 into the Valley, man. Or you could go the other way and try to pick up the 405, but then you have to go through Beverly Hills, which is a bust."

"There's no bus?"

"At this hour?" said Mona. "RTD? Your best bet is to hitch over to 101. What else can you do? Maybe you know someone you can call?"

"You little bitches! Or," looking at Jamey, "Whatever you are…"

"Hey!" said Mona. "Don't we owe you a blow job? For keeping

148

watch?"

"I think I'll pass," said Harry.

"Jamey's really good at it. She likes it. Don't you, Jamey?"

"I would like to go to sleep."

The girls and Harry parted, Harry seeming to be ready to take Mona's advice. Jamey was pretty sure that Mona's advice shouldn't be followed.

They were walking back toward the hot dog joint and Rooms-for-Rent. Jamey was still ranting. "We're practically prostitutes. We have to be careful. I feel sorry for that Harry guy. If something happens to him, it's our fault."

"You're so domestic, Jamey," said Mona. "You will make some guy a cute little wife someday. Look at you. Putting aside money for a rainy day. Worried about little Harry. You have good feminine instincts. A fine little wife." Mona quickly lifted Jamey's skirt and dropped it. "Maybe Ricky? You like him, don't you?"

"He's a dude," said Jamey.

"So are you. Doesn't mean that you aren't curious. Did you like Chris?"

"That was disgusting," said Jamey.

"Oh, really? You were pretty into it. Jamey has a new boyfriend! Jamey has a new boyfriend!" said Mona. "You liked the way he touched you, like you were so special to him, which you were. You were gonna be his first, like you and Teri Ann."

"It was fake," said Jamey. "That was a terrible trick. I loved Teri Ann."

"They were egocentric assholes," said Mona. "They just didn't know it yet. If the right set of circumstances had been in play, they would have raped us, if they thought they could."

"You don't know that," said Jamey. "You sound like Denise. I thought you didn't believe all that."

"I believe it," said Mona. "But it doesn't control my life. But, come on, it was hilarious!"

"My balls have fallen," said Jamey.

"Good thing your tits are sewn on," said Mona.

A YOUNG GIRL

As *THE GIRLS* BEGAN TO CROSS at a corner, a black and white cut them off. "Shit," was Mona's first remark.

A husky light skinned red faced young officer was out of the driver's side. The sidekick, a darker type, sitting shotgun, was at the microphone. Under the red faced officer's badge was the name Tanquerson. He flashed his light in their eyes. Their eyes were pinned from whites. Mona tried to back off, tugging at Jamey, but the officer was on the case. "Stick around, little lady," said Officer Tank, addressing Mona. "What have we here?" He referred to Jamey, a reference to his rather youthful appearance. "How old are you, kiddo?"

"We're both eighteen," said Mona. "I'm Mona Ming and this is Leslie King." Mona pulled out her ID card and nodded for Jamey to do the same. Jamey reached in the pocket and pulled out the ID card. Tanquerson handed them to his partner who ran them on the radio while Tank attended to *the girls*. "We're just out for a stroll before going home to study, officer," said Mona. She was glad for the glasses, adding to the studious illusion. Tank wasn't buying.

"The reason I stopped you is that you two fit the description of a pair who stole a car a little while ago. You wouldn't know anything about that, would you?"

"You'll notice that that's a California ID, not a license," said Mona. "I'm afraid I never learned to drive. We obviously don't have a car, which is why we're walking."

"And does your baby sister talk yet?" asked Tank." How old are you really, little girl? I'm pretty sure that you're not eighteen, Missy. You two holding?"

"Holding? You mean drugs? Oh, no, officer!" said Mona.

"You know, your eyes are pinned. We can't search your pretty pants out here on the street, so maybe you two better get in the back of the car. How's that sound, little girl?" He focused more on Jamey, probably because Jamey was obviously scared and Mona was playing it cool.

"You don't have cause," said Mona.

"An attorney, huh? How about solicitation and prostitution."

"As if!" Mona complained.

"How about you fit the description of the car thieves? How about whatever you're carrying in your pants?" Tanquerson looked confident to Jamey, especially when he turned to him. "How about you, sweetheart? You carrying? Because it looks like you'll be turning eighteen in jail." Jamey bit his lip on that suggestion. "And this one," turning back to Mona, "If you really are eighteen, then it's big girl jail, only you ain't so big, girl."

"This is all bullshit," Mona complained.

The partner, getting out of the car now, was tall and thin with dark hair. "I.D.'s are clean," he said.

"Sure they are," said Tank. "Give 'em back. I have an idea." His partner seemed to understand then. "Cuff 'em. We'll take 'em in, and sort it out."

"You can't do that!" Mona asserted as the taller of the two officers locked her hands behind her back while Tanquerson did the same to Jamey. Mona was wriggling and trying to pull away. Jamey was helpless and scared.

"This is just bullshit, and you're a pig," Mona continued to rant. Jamey wasn't convinced that Mona was taking the right approach, but it was too late now. As the cops stuffed him into the back seat of the Plymouth, Jamey felt a surreptitious swat under his skirt. Mona was put in the back along with Jamey and she apparently felt some similar treatment when she yelled, "Hey, watch it! Son of a bitch!"

Once secured in the cage of the back seat, Jamey and Mona looked to each other in amazement. It was at this point that Jamey spied among the assembled crowd the person of pimply faced Harry. He had somehow managed to escape any involvement. Being the odd man out had worked for him so far. He apparently hadn't taken the girls' advice about the direction of the freeway. His lips were saying something. Jamey thought it might have been something about Karma.

Jamey was on a bummer now. A search of his person in the jail would not produce drugs, but he wasn't sure what cops did to boys who dressed as girls. They probably wouldn't be that stoked on it. And, if they discovered who he really was, he was probably on a list somewhere as a runaway. He could find himself returned to Knollridge before the sun came up, but wearing a skirt, with his body shaved, with smeared lipstick and stale perfume, and a court date for solicitation and grand theft auto. The old man might object to one or more parts of that; he might just leave Jamey in jail to teach him a lesson. And any time in Juvy, a stretch or even a night, would reveal his hairless body and painted toes, to begin. Jamey had not come to terms with how he felt about what he was doing, but Juvenile Hall wasn't the place to discover his true soul, feminine or otherwise.

The sixteen-year-old brain has peculiar priorities, and Jamey was thinking at an intense speed. A bust might mean the end of Maiden Head. They could lose their house band status at The Contortionist if they missed the gig messing with the cops. He looked again to Mona for guidance as the car headed up the avenue, away from the traffic of the boulevard. She was his big sister, but Mona, for the first time, looked concerned. "Where the fuck are you going, asshole?" said Mona.

The ambient radio became louder and more discernable with the competing sounds fading away. Tank's partner, riding shotgun, seemed to monitor the radio and occasionally to respond. Tank was driving, a big burly blond whose head was almost as bare as Jamey's ass. Jamey was thinking again, disorganized process that it was. Once they pegged his age, it would be all over. He realized that it wasn't just Maiden Head that he might be losing. He and Mona would likely be separated now and forever. This trip was way too cool to come down yet. Maybe he loved her.

"We got time for a stop?" asked Tank.

"Nothing going down," was the reply.

"It'll be *groovy*, Missy." he laughed, as the car made a series of turns, winding up and up into the canyon above the boulevard. They passed through a neighborhood of nice houses, recessed from the road, and they finally broke onto a winding narrow lane up into the hills. The vehicle lights went down as the car followed the twists and turns, beyond the land of houses and lawns and up a deserted stretch for maybe a quarter of a mile. The darkened car stopped at the end of a cul-de-sac, well beyond the nearest residences, a future development. The place was deserted. It was a few days short of a full moon, and that was the only light. Jamey hadn't come to grips with what was going on.

"I'm sorry, Jamey," Mona whispered. "I've been through this. Just do what they want. No reason to get beat up."

"Oh, shit!" said Jamey, now instinctively trying to free his hands, to no avail. It was finally dawning on Jamey, who didn't go through life expecting to be raped or taking precautions against it. But cops didn't bring girls to secluded places with the intention of giving them avuncular advice. The menacing officers had gotten out of the car, leaving their doors wide open. Jamey couldn't see the pigs, but he could hear their rough voices mixed with the radio crackle, though not their words.

"I'm sorry I got you into this, Jamey," said Mona.

"What happens when they find out?"

"Not really cool," said Mona. "Maybe he'll be satisfied with a blow job."

"That's the best advice?" said Jamey. "Suck his cock?"

"If you fuckin' get the chance," said Mona, very forcefully.

"I don't know how to suck cock," said Jamey.

"You were doing fine with the kid," said Mona. "Breathe through your nose."

The boys in blue approached the car from either side. Tank's partner was standing around by the shotgun door while Tank opened the back door and roughly pulled Jamey by the arm out of the vehicle. Jamey, arms behind his back, was then pushed to the front of the car where Tanquerson gratuitously slapped him, and Jamey leaned against the warm hood of the car, facing away.

He couldn't see Mona, but he could hear a string of curses coming from her that suddenly stopped with a final cry. Tank pulled a joint out of his pocket and slipped it into Jamey's bra. "When we take you in, guess what they'll find? So, how about it, honey?"

He was looking up to Tank with no idea what to say. He was standing rather close to her face, and Jamey was thinking of Mona's advice. "You want me to…suck you?"

Tank laughed. "Well, don't say it like that. I'm sure you suck cock all the time. He pushed Jamey onto his knees, shoving his crotch toward Jamey's face and taking a handful of the *girl's* hair. Jamey, who had had a little practice earlier in the evening, began to work on the officer's unit. The effort culminated in Jamey's now sticky face hitting the dirt when Tank finished and toppled him.

From the ground, Jamey could see the other officer out of the car, straightening his uniform. Mona was crying somewhere, maybe still in the back seat. The radio traffic was tilting up. The boys were off their beat, but they had to sound responsive. Tank was zipping up his trousers. "How was the Chink?" he called. "You want to trade?"

"Shots fired. 9300 block of Sunset. All available units respond. Shots fired."

"Shit! Tank! Let's get the fuck out of here. Shots fired!"

Officer Tanquerson lifted Jamey from the ground and threw him face down against the hood of the patrol car. He unlocked the cuffs to reclaim them. He couldn't resist rubbing his hand across Jamey's bottom, and deep into his rear cleavage. As his cock had been liberated by Chris, the officer didn't discover the truth about Jamey, though he was dangerously close.

He tossed Jamey several feet to the side and back into the dirt. "It was beautiful," he said. "Like a rainbow."

The girls were tiny compared to the officers and flew relatively well. Mona also landed in the dirt. The cops climbed into their vehicle and kicked up a dust storm with the tires as they pealed out and rolled down the hill leaving Jamey and Mona in the partial moonlight covered in the dust of the deserted field and the remains of the officers.

HANDS FREE NOW, Jamey pulled himself up and dusted off some dirt and debris from his uniform, wiping his face, and spitting out what was left of Tank. The taste remained. He straightened his clothes, as if he were to meet someone. He had no labels for his emotions. Anger, impotence, rage, humiliation, hatred, self-loathing, and a new sense of fear that he had never known were in the rush of emotions he was using to rebuild his sense of self. Another emotion overcame him when he heard Mona somewhere nearby, now in tears. She was restarting her life as well. Jamey found her and knelt on the ground next to her, taking her in his arms, kissing and then cradling her head. "Are you okay, Mona?"

Mona looked up at Jamey. "Am I okay?"

"I mean, are you hurt? Can you walk? Do you need to get to the emergency room?"

"It's just...I'm okay," said Mona.

"We have to get out of here, Mona," said Jamey. "What if they come back?"

"I think they're done with *us*," said Mona. "We're just not done with them. Are you cool?"

Mona was dazed. Jamey helped her sit up. He wanted to get them both the fuck out of there. "Where's my underwear?" Mona was looking around, as if that were the important point.

"Oh, my God!" said Jamey. "Let's just get the fuck out of here, Mona! You don't need your fucking underwear. You have to get up, honey." He helped Mona to her feet and brushed off her clothes and her skin.

Mona tried to collect herself, but she was not herself. "Where's my underwear?" She was only able to remain standing because Jamey held onto her.

"Did he...did he rape you? I mean, like all the way?"

Her face answered in the affirmative. "What about you?" said Mona.

"Come on," said Jamey, leading Mona by the hand, one step and then another. "We have to get away from here."

"Doesn't work," said Mona. "I did that."

"Shouldn't we get you to an emergency room?" said Jamey.

"Do you need a doctor?" asked Mona.

"He just slapped me around a little and made me go down on him," said Jamey. "I mean, I don't think a doctor can do much for that."

Mona looked at Jamey's face. "You'll need some makeup for the show."

"You're tripping on the show?" asked Jamey. "You got your to-do list in order!"

Jamey started to walk Mona down the deserted hill. Jamey was mothering Mona, keeping her moving, holding her hand and sometimes supporting her. They walked downhill along the twisting turns of the dark streets, never letting go of one another.

Mona could hardly move, feeling a real pain inside and several aches on her arms and legs where the officer had roughly restrained her. She explained that she had been fighting him until he got serious. "Hard to fight when you're half his weight and your hands are locked behind your back."

"You told me not to fight," said Jamey.

"You shouldn't," said Mona. "But I had to try. As if it did any good."

When auto lights flashed coming up the hill, they quickly hid in the shadows. It might be the cops. "Cops never picked on me when I was a dude. Let me sleep in the garbage all I wanted."

"I know," said Mona. "Sorry I made you into a chick." It was more Mona now, but still tentative.

"I never realized being a chick was so gnarly," said Jamey. "I mean, we weren't very smart about our little outing tonight, but, still in all, being a chick is gnarly stuff." They walked quietly sometimes and talked at others. "Do you want to see a doctor?" Jamey asked again. "I mean, any broken bones?"

"Just brutalized," said Mona. "I hope it doesn't show. We have a show tomorrow."

"Fuck the show," said Jamey. "You were fucking raped. I mean, he raped you. You can't be okay. We should get some help. Like that clinic doctor of yours. Maybe she would know what to do."

"Doctor can't fix it," said Mona. "Fuck him. What about you? Did he rape you?"

"I did what you said."

"You sucked his dick?" said Mona.

"It's still in my mouth."

"And on your face," said Mona, cleaning Jamey's face with spit on her fingers, mom style.

They were still alone, walking by the houses as they descended the hills. They walked hand-in-hand toward the safety of the crowded city and lights below. "What did you mean when you said that you had been through this before, or something?" Jamey asked.

Mona almost always lied in some way, deliberately, by omission, obfuscation. But she sounded like she was hitting the note quite sincerely on this occasion. Jamey had no filter for bullshit, but maybe it really was true.

"Last summer. I got a ride from these three surfers I hung out with at the beach. I was already drunk, I guess, and they poured more down my throat. At first, it was just come-ons and some pats and grabs here and there. Like our boys tonight. I wasn't putting out. I really felt sick anyway. But, I don't know if they had planned it or it just happened, but, eventually, they took turns with me in the back of the van. Really gross stuff. Tossed me out at three in the morning on our neighbor's front lawn with my bikini top in my hand and my bottom on backwards. I was like seventeen. Nice impression for my uptight and super square mom and dad. Did I mention they were Chinese?"

"I'm so sorry, Mona. Bastards!"

After a pause, Mona continued. "I just can't look at guys the same way. I mean, Paul McCartney's cute, but I don't have to fuck him. I don't want to fuck anyone. I'm kind of a bring-down that way. I know it's the love generation, free love and all, but I'm kind of uptight about sex, I guess you know that. Miss Buzz-Kill of 1969. Guys don't interest me anymore. Except that they're creepy and scary. I mean, when they get the chance."

"But you're not afraid of anyone," said Jamey. "You're like a chick Paul Newman or something."

"I don't let it control me," said Mona. "But, that's why I fucked up on you. I should have been more careful. I should have played it cool, like other chicks do. But I spend a lot of time *not* being afraid. So I do crazy shit."

Jamey ignored that line of thought, though, later, he would reflect that Mona had probably been right. "But you were nice to *me* right away," said Jamey. "And I'm a dude." He flicked his curled hair out of his face.

"I didn't fuck you," she said. "I don't want to hurt your masculine pride, Jamey, but I liked you because I just knew that you weren't like other dudes. Don't get weird about it. I don't think you have a lot of testosterone.

156

That's what makes guys assholes."

"What the fuck is that?"

"An asshole is..."

"Mona!"

"It's the chemical that makes a guy a guy. Like chicks have estrogen. That's why they grow tits and get all gooey about babies. I mean, you have some."

"Estrogen?"

"The other stuff. You have some. Like you fucked that Molly chick. You get boners and stuff. But I don't sense that you're all that aggressive. You would have raped me by now, as close as we live. That's what testosterone does. It makes you get all like a dude. But you don't have hair all over the place. Your voice is sweet. It's why you sing like an angel. It's why you like dressing up. You were embarrassed, but not really. Most guys wouldn't have the balls. From the first time I saw you, I didn't sense all that man juice in you. I felt good about you from the start."

"Sounds like a song," said Jamey, storing away Mona's observations for later reflection.

"Maybe," said Mona. "If you're Gary Lewis and the Playboys." She sang with a Freddy Mersey accent.

I felt good about you
Good about you from the start
Up to then I never knew
Just what I'd do with my heart...

"We should write that down when we get home," said Jamey. "You know, you can make big money just writing shit. We don't have to do it, but some bubblegum band would dig that shit. We could start a revival of Herman's Hermits." They were laughing, but continuing slowly to walk down the hills. "So, since I didn't have—what do you call it? Testosterone. So you turned me into your little sister?" he asked.

"No," she said precisely. "I turned you into a chick because I need you in the band. But you weren't hard to turn. But the band is the most important thing. I had to keep the band together after Leslie walked out on us."

"And you fucked with the Big Three 'cause they reminded you of the assholes who gang raped you?"

"I don't know," said Mona. "Maybe. Yeah. Probably."

By this point, they had made it back down to the boulevard where they had been picked up. Mona looked around for signs of black and whites, but, seeing none, she proceeded. There were dirt stains on their socks, legs, and clothes. Their hair was in disarray. They were used to getting attention, but this wasn't the norm. They dragged themselves through the extended neighborhood, closely entwined, feeling like everyone could see exactly what had happened.

"Let's get home and get you cleaned up," said Jamey.

"Where's your tits?"

"What?"

"You're acting like a mom."

HONKY TONK WOMEN

MONA WAS AGREEABLE and holding onto Jamey as they walked. Suddenly, Mona swerved, dragging Jamey up against a building. "Shit! What the fuck is up with tonight?"

"What?"

"That guy who just came out of the liquor store," said Mona. "Let's just say we don't want him to see me."

Jamey saw the guy. He had a short beard and mustache. He wasn't a stylized fashion follower like so many Hollywood types, but he was no square. He looked to be twenty, twenty-four, not thirty. Jamey wasn't good on age. "Let's just let him get the fuck out of here."

When the guy was no longer visible, Mona guided them into the liquor store. She bought some M&M's which she stuffed into her inside skirt pocket. The cashier regarded Jamey, and *she* felt, whether correctly or not, that *she* had been downgraded in his opinion. Mona, walking close to Jamey, holding his arm, stepped out into the night and they made their way down the street.

"I want my hot dog," said Mona.

"Are you crazy?" said Jamey. "Let's go home. We should never have left."

"So I have porcine cum running down my leg. But I'm hungry. That's why we went out. I want my hot dog! And no asshole cop is gonna stop me."

The girls were approaching the hotdog stand when they were confronted by the young man they had tried to avoid. He had apparently gathered his courage. "What are you doing here?" said Mona, who liked to shoot first.

"You have your nerve!" he said.

"And you're starting to piss me off, Jerry," said Mona. "I was arrested and raped tonight, so I don't really feel in the mood for listening to you."

"Gary," he corrected her.

"I don't care who you think you are," said Mona. "Get the fuck out of my life!"

"I think you owe me something, Lisa," said Jerry, or Gary. "I mean, how much is rent? So like three nights. You owe me fifteen dollars for sleeping accommodations, maybe fifteen bucks for meals and wine, and the twenty bucks you stole from my wallet. So, that's fifty dollars, Lisa. I think you owe me fifty dollars. I'd let you work it off in trade, but I really don't like you anymore."

"So send me a bill," said Mona, who had apparently been Lisa not so long ago. "Now get the fuck out of here unless you have something else in mind. I mean, hit me. I dare you! Get a garnishment on my wages. I can't stop you. But get the fuck out of here."

Neither Larry nor Gary had much choice. Even Jamey could see his frustration. He was not the sort to physically attack anyone, and certainly not women, or girls. Jamey would agree that Mona probably required a spanking on any number of accounts, but this wasn't the kind of guy who would do it. This Jerry-Larry-Gary guy was more like the old Jamey, just a puppy to be kicked around. Lisa, or Mona, obviously had that figured out. She didn't have to hide from him or even sneak out on him. It was just easier than looking at his pathetic face as he turned red in front of her but realized that he had no options for making things right, for making her see it from his side, or for regaining a little of his lost self-esteem. Acting like the little bitch she obviously was, for whatever reason, could eventually lead her to a dangerous outlier, some major bad ass, but Gary or Larry wasn't it. He left the open space, repeating and repeating, "I don't think I like you at all. I think you owe me fifty dollars."

"That was the weenie. Now let's get a hot dog." Mona and Jamey made their way to the window and ordered. The Coke was revivifying after the very long walk. As sweet as it was, it didn't seem to wash away the taste of Tanquerson. Between the M&M's and the hot dogs, they dropped three bucks out of the eight. Adding the remaining five to the eighty-six and the running total was up to $91.00.

"What was that guy?" said Jamey.

"Jerry was my boyfriend."

"You had a boyfriend? Out here?"

"Well, he wanted a girlfriend and I wanted to stay somewhere," said Mona. "I let him handle me a little, but, with my period and one thing and another, we couldn't go all the way. I stayed with him for three days, and I borrowed some money from his wallet when he was sleeping, which was enough to get me into Rooms-for-Rent. They're all so sensitive," said Mona, finishing the hot dog and dipping fries in the chili. "I guess he has a case," said Mona. "But he was kind of a pussy, and I doubt he'd have the balls to wear a dress."

"That's not really how you tell if a guy's got balls," said Jamey. "You might be surprised. Most guys don't wear dresses."

"Then he shouldn't act like a pussy," said Mona.

"So some guys rape you because they have too much testosterone, right? Those are assholes. But a guy who's civilized, who wouldn't think of hurting you, even when you stole his money and let him think you were his girlfriend, then he's a pussy."

"What would you call him?"

"Me. A month ago."

"He can't play bass," said Mona. "He's useless. Let's go home."

Once in their apartment, Mona fell on their bed, face up, just still and apparently exhausted. Jamey kicked off the shoes and the dirty white socks. He looked at himself in the mirror. There was a noticeable red spot on the side of his face where officer Tank had slapped him. He was worried that it would bruise for the occasion of their Friday night gig. Who wants to look at girls with bruises on their pretty faces? Vain little thing.

He dropped the white blouse to the floor. He turned the bra around and unhooked it, dropping it to the floor as well, putting the money and Tank's joint in the stash drawer. He unbuttoned and unzipped the skirt and dropped it to the pile on the floor. Lastly, he rolled the underwear down his legs and kicked it off.

At the sink now, he washed his face clean of makeup, dirt, and Tank. He paused to look at himself. Taking a quick inventory, it looked as if his unit was in fact shrinking, probably due to the speed. He took off his earrings. For a moment, he was neither the one nor the other.

"Come on, Mona," he said. "Let's take a shower. I'll wash your back."

"You go ahead, sweetie," said Mona. "I'm wiped out."

Wearing the red robe, Jamey made his way to the end of the hallway, encountering the next-door whore and her John, leaving what used to be Mona's room. "Evening!" said Jamey, friendly to the neighbors. There were some mumbles.

In the shower, never seeing it coming, Jamey started to cry and cry, out of control crying. There wasn't any sense in it. It was just a reaction to the events of the night, to being cranked on whites, to the lack of sleep, to the craziness.

Jamey tried to think what to do next, in the big picture sense. Being a chick had turned out to be less froufrou than he had previously supposed, and he was thinking of being a dude again. But giving up his girlhood would mean giving up the two things that meant anything to him: Mona and Maiden Head. Giving up Mona might be the safer, saner course of action, but she was also the life of his party. Giving up the band would be very hard. What was he going to do as a dude? Get another gig at the carwash. He could be the square in the plastic box instead of the chick in the glass cage.

When Jamey had collected himself and returned to their rooms, Mona was sitting naked on the side of the bed. She looked shell-shocked. Nothing ever seemed to phase Mona, but there was some phasing going on here. Jamey was only getting his head around the rape. He slipped on a dress and gave Mona the red robe he had been wearing. He went along with her to the shower. Jamey waited with her until she was ready to return to their rooms, both clean but neither feeling so. Jamey could still taste Tank in his mouth and Jamey had to wonder if Mona could still feel the officer inside of her, if she could still feel the beach bums. Does it go away?

Mona climbed into the bed with her pink teddy-bear and lit one of the boys' cigarettes. Jamey had one, too. He shut off the light and slipped under the sheet with Mona. They were smoking away for a long moment. "I sucked his cock," said Jamey, beginning again to cry, but not sure why.

"You did what you had to do," said Mona.

"I could have bitten it off," said Jamey.

"You had no choice," said Mona. "You did the right thing. You have to survive."

"But, Mona, I think I was good at it..."

"What the fuck?"

"I mean, I was kind of into it. Into seeing what would happen. I did things with my tongue, like that Molly was doing."

"I think I've created a monster."

"It's so creepy," Jamey agreed.

"Jamey," she said, holding him now, "I think it's just shame talking. You'll go through a lot of shit with this. I did. I think it's just the shame. Don't blame yourself."

The waves of tears still welled up from moment to moment. Pulling himself together, "Can't we report them? They can't get away with shit like that. What about all the other chicks?"

"They're cops," said Mona. "They can get away with anything. Suck it, or I'll send you to jail or back to foster care or back home. They can get away with anything. Fuck anyone in the back of the car."

"But we could press charges," said Jamey, who had a television view of justice.

"You're a run-away sixteen-year-old transvestite. And I'm a slutty Chink. We just have to stay out of the back of cop cars." Mona continued to smoke. Jamey was curled up in the bed. "I'd like to nail them," said Mona. "But we have to let it go. You were lucky to escape with your life. If they had found your little wee-wee..."

"Is it so little?" said Jamey.

"Dudes are so sensitive," Mona answered, rolling her eyes in the dark.

"Maybe, in a weird way, I was lucky. I mean he didn't find out."

"Well, pretty *damned* weird way," said Mona. "But, look, I totally understand if you want to go home or go straight, I mean, like a boy again. I wouldn't hold it against you. This is heavy, and I got you into it."

"I got me into it when I ran away from home," said Jamey. "It's not your fault. It's fuckin' theirs."

"Same to you, man." There wasn't much daylight between *the girls* on a regular night, but this night Mona turned affectionate. She reached around Jamey and embraced him, resting his face against her chest. Jamey didn't know what to do, not used to affection from Mona. He clung to her and listened to her heart's beat and her lung's rhythm. Neither Mona nor Jamey was anywhere close to sleep, so there they were. Morning was just a few hours away.

WHEN JAMEY OPENED HIS EYES, Mona was already dressed in her summer shorts and short-sleeved buttoned blouse with a pocket and everything, putting on her backpack and heading out to camp. "Hey, Sunshine," said Jamey.

"You should really think about it," said Mona. "You still have your boy clothes. You look good in your boring boy uniform."

"What are you talking about?"

"I feel responsible," said Mona, sitting on the bed. "I don't want anything else to happen to you. It could have been much worse."

"That's the craziest line you've tried yet," said Jamey. "Are you kicking me out of the band? Is Leslie King back in town?"

Mona paused a moment, surprised by the comment. "What'd you say that for?"

"What'd I say?" said Jamey. "I'm totally in, Mona." Jamey threw back the sheet that he had been sleeping in and stood up, still neither fem nor fowl.

Mona remarked, "I think you really are turning into a girl. It's not the makeup or the clothes. I think it's in your head now. Pretty amazing."

Jamey didn't grasp Mona's meaning until months later. But, in the moment, it didn't matter. He was decided. Jamey put on a little fake-up over the bruise along with some eyeliner, blush, and lipstick. "Not very hippie natural," said Jamey. "But fuck 'em. I'm in *all the way*."

The *two girls* came down the stairs together. Jack was at his counter with a bowl of Cheerios. "Rent tonight, kids, or I'm locking you out."

"We're loaded," Mona replied to Jack. "Aren't we, Jamey? And the Eagle flies on Friday."

"Easy money!" said Jamey.

"But those Cheerios look pretty good," said Mona.

"Oh, no you don't!" said Jack. "You two are getting kind of fat anyway. Eating too regular."

"Maybe she's preggers," said Mona, nodding at Jamey. Mona wasn't able to cage a breakfast off of Jack, but she did take over his newspaper. There was an article about the Tate and LaBianca murders. There was increasing speculation that the two gruesome scenes were linked. Also in the Times' Metro section, there was a piece on the shooting spree on the boulevard the previous night. A Vietnam veteran, a Private Mitch Poplar, had gone off the deep end and had started shooting up the place like an old west cow town. He wasn't aiming at anyone in particular, and nobody was hurt on the street. Still, shooting off weapons was bad policy, so the police had been required to take some serious action as he refused to stand down. The cops shot him and hauled him off to the hospital. Mona mentioned to Jamey that some military guy had been shooting up the joint last night, referencing on the sly their situation with the officers.

Jamey never saw the article, and Mona never mentioned Mitch by name. Jamey, in a summer dress, walked with Mona to the bus stop and saw her off to work. He would have kissed her like Donna Reed if she would have permitted it. Jamey was in love with Mona.

He picked up his pay from the El Portal. He didn't need much from life, but he was on a shopping spree this morning. He forked over for two sets of guitar strings at the music store, one for each of them, and he admired a bass, even taking the opportunity to try it out. Mona's was fairly junky. The pick-up was getting to be intermittent and the pegs couldn't seem to hold a tune. But a new instrument was out of their range. Mona liked to pick up clothes at a bargain, but Jamey had never known her to rip off a musician. Of course, there was a lot that he didn't know about what Mona might do.

They didn't usually spend money on smokes, but he was in the mood. He picked up a pack of Tareytons. He preferred Pall Mall's, which he used to steal from Jim, but Teri Ann had smoked Tareytons. He figured if anyone knew what a girl would do, it would be Teri Ann Murphy. He opened the pack and smoked one, noting his lipstick on the filter, just like Teri Ann. He tried to hold the smoke as he remembered Teri Ann holding it.

While window shopping on the boulevard, finding himself looking at the women's shops, he was unable to build up enough courage to enter without Mona to support him. He wondered at himself, catching himself thinking that this would look pretty or that would make him look terrible.

He bought two packs of M&M's for Mona at the liquor store. Her period was long past, but she liked her M&M's in any event. Nearby, he went into a head shop. They were playing music and the song at the time was the new Rolling Stones' single "Honky Tonk Women." Jamey stopped in mid-motion and listened to the song all the way through. It wasn't Brian Jones. He liked Brian's sound, but this was different. "That's a pretty good record," Jamey observed when he came out of his head. Jamey picked up a pack of Zigzags.

He turned about to leave, but noticed a girl coming out from some hanging beads in a doorway. There was a boutique sign, and Jamey passed through the beads and down a single step into an adjacent room, a hippie chick boutique, if ever there was one.

Jamey was looking at the dresses and blouses, holding them up in the mirror. "You should try that on," said a lady, who had been sitting at the counter observing Jamey. "Definitely your size."

"I'm not buying anything today," said Jamey.

"You have a lot to learn," the woman replied. She had partly gray long hair. It used to be raven, but times change. She had had a pretty face, but she looked pretty cool to Jamey now. "Chicks try on stuff just for fun, man. You don't have to buy anything. How long have you been in drag?" Jamey was going to make a claim counter to what must have been obvious to the woman. "I dress women all day long. I think I know a dude when I see one." Jamey smiled. The woman wasn't threatening anything. "Transvestites have to buy clothes, too."

"Well, I never buy anything. Yet," said Jamey. "My friend helps me with all that."

"Your friend?"

"Mona," said Jamey, as if he assumed that everyone knew Mona.

"Ah!" said the woman. "So your girlfriend dresses you funny? You're very beautiful. She's right. You're a natural young lady. Bring her in if you need *the approval of your mistress.*"

"Oh, no! It's not like that...not exactly," said Jamey, on reflection.

"So I know your girlfriend's name. What's yours?"

"Jamey," *she* said.

"I'm Barbara." They smiled at one another. "That one would look good on you." She held it up to Jamey's body. "How do you feel?"

"Pretty."

"Well, you don't have to pay for that," said Barbara. "You brought the pretty. Oh, try this one!" It was a purple flower print dress. Jamey went into the dressing room. The woman stood just outside talking to Jamey. When Jamey had some trouble with the zipper, she was there to do her up. Jamey tried on several dresses and tops. She liked trying things on, and the hippie lady knew her stuff. Jamey liked one dress very much and wanted to buy it, but he thought it better to run it by Mona first.

"So not very long, then?"

"What?"

"How long have you been dressing up?"

"I don't know. A month or more..."

"Oh. Then you're still trying it out," she said. "Take your time. Enjoy yourself."

"I don't know," said Jamey. "I mean, guys are like invisible. Who cares? Who notices? It's like they're nobody, unless they have a bunch of money. Then they're hot shit, all powerful and stuff. But chicks are like special. People pay attention. You feel like you're pretty and cool. But then, since they get noticed, they get fucked over. Like they beat you and rape you and fuck you over. It's like they act like you're so special and then they fuck you over like you were nothing at all. So, I don't know. But I decided to be a chick anyway. I don't want to be invisible."

"Take it slowly, Jamey," said Barbara. "You're very young. You have time."

"But that's just it. I don't think I do have a lot of time. Everything rushes along, and, you never know what will happen. I only know that you have to make it happen."

Barbara made Jamey promise to bring Mona to the boutique, but Jamey said that Mona would probably end up stealing all of the merchandise.

Later, he stopped by the record store and picked up the new Stones' single, the first one with Mick Taylor, the guy who replaced Brian Jones.

It was hard to imagine the Stones without Brian Jones, but this was a very hot record and the guitar lick was cool. He couldn't determine if it was Richards or Taylor. And he was still contemplating such matters when Mona came home during the early afternoon. "Got you some strings," said Jamey. "And some M&M's."

"Cool! My busy housewife!"

"Give us a kiss," said Jamey. It was not forthcoming. "This song is great!" he said, and check out the cover. "You and me. We should be doing this in the show. You could play this stuff. Let me put on the record. Mick Taylor's really good. He's like a musician."

"Just fancy!" said Mona. Jamey put the record on the Tele-Tone. Mona looked at the cover of the single as the cowbells and guitars started getting funky. "Kind of a baby to be hanging out with that group," said Mona.

"The girl?" said Jamey, doubtful.

"Girls'll be okay," Mona laughed. "I was thinkin' of Mick Taylor." The Tele-Tone was not exactly a studio monitor, but Mona quickly got stoked on the idea. "Perfect for the bar. Think Denise'll let me sing it?"

"You'd both be good," said Jamey. "Trade verses? That's hot."

"Maybe," said Mona. They jammed on the tune for the better part of an hour. There was no talk of the night before. They were apparently avoiding any downer talk. No bummers, man. Mona wanted to stuff it away with the other business, and Jamey was still thinking it over. Is it really rape if you get raped under false pretenses? The girl who got raped by Tank didn't really exist. So how was it that *she* could still taste him, even after tacos and Tareytons?

"Why the fuck are you smoking Tareytons?" asked Mona, lighting one.

"I'm a chick," said Jamey. "Should I be smoking Lucky Strikes?"

"I'd rather be a dude."

The gig at The Contortionist was going as smoothly as ever, but, in the last set, the pick-up on the bass went on the fritz for good. It was no longer intermittent, and they couldn't fix it now. It was just buzzing. There was a short or a bad connection. They managed to get through the rest of the night, but it was a bumpy ride. The bass either needed repair or replacement. If they had to buy a bass, they would be majorly fucked, but Mona remembered that Jamey had been a bassist in another life. He had an instrument out in the Valley, and it was time to get it.

Altogether, including Mona's morning money and Jamey's lunchtime tacos, Jamey's extravagant shopping binge had set them back $13.84, eight of it going for guitar strings, a cost of doing business. Out of his pay, he was down to $21.80, but, added to the previous sum, the running total was $112.80. When Mona came in the afternoon with thirty-six of her expected forty dollars, the number spiked to $148.80. It was rent day, however, so the total ebbed to $103.80 when they paid off the insistent Jack. The gig was light that night. Between tips and their usual pay, less ten bucks for Denise's brother and eight bucks for dinner, the band netted $27.00 split two ways, $13.50. So, when the sun came up the next morning, *our girls* were in possession of $117.30 and a bass that didn't work so well.

CELESTE

MONA WOKE UP with a plan. She usually had a plan. Talking it over, they decided that they had to contact Craig Roman, to get him to bring Jamey's instrument. Mona called Craig's house, introduced herself as Mona from English class at Knollridge High, and asked to speak to Craig. Jamey was listening in. Mona was very convincing with Craig's mom, just as she was at the college employment office, or with her employers and campers for that matter. She knew how to be square when the time came for it. She just didn't do it for cops or asshole announcers. Mrs. Roman could be heard calling Craig to the phone. "It's your little friend, Mona, from English class."

"Thanks, Mom," he was heard to say. "Hey, this is Craig?"

"Hey, man. It's Jamey. Maintain and be cool at all times."

"It's cool," said Craig, obviously taken by surprise but duly slipping into cool mode. "Where are you, M…Mona?"

Jamey and Craig set up a meeting late in the afternoon, when the car would be available. The usual donut shop near *the girls'* room was the place. The less that Craig knew about the exact location of the digs, the better. Craig was Jamey's best buddy, and he was cool people. He undertook the mission. He wanted to see Jamey anyway, but Jamey cautioned him that it was strictly secret agent stuff.

Mona and Jamey spent Saturday morning at the Laundromat which, with drinks and a bit of breffy, brought their combined cash down to $110.75. Mona kept an eye on the washers, dryers, and stacks and baskets of folded laundry. She picked up a t-shirt, a day dress, and a pair of socks on the sly which she tucked into Jamey's pink towel. On the way back, Mona bought some chemical crème hair removal goop and some Sally Hansen products. There was more work to do on Jamey. They redid their toe nails and fingers. It was all very well, but Jamey was annoyed that Mona had spent another fifteen bucks. Their net value had now dropped to $95.52. Hanging with Mona was no cheap date. She went through money as if she had some. "Being a chick isn't cheap," Mona argued.

To meet Craig, Jamey determined to wear his boy clothes. The chick thing would be hard to explain. Jamey knew *he* didn't understand it yet.

169

Still, he had sort of wanted to show off for Craig. Mona was back in her favorite loose fitting low slung cords and her new-used black t-shirt. They put their night costumes in Jamey's backpack, and went to the designated donut shop to await Craig's arrival. Later than expected, with Mona getting antsy, Craig carefully pulled into the parking lot in the folks' square back, reminding Mona of The Big Three. "Who's the chick?" asked Mona.

"It's my sister, Missy. What's she doing here?"

"What the fuck kind of name is Missy?"

"Melissa," said Jamey. Missy was out of the car as soon as she saw him. She ran to him and wrapped her arms around him. He embraced her. Craig was out of the driver's seat and standing opposite Mona. "You were supposed to come alone, Craig," said Jamey, over Missy's shoulder.

"I had to fill her in, man. She went inside and talked to my mom about sewing and cake and shit while I got your shit loaded. Anyway, I couldn't go see you and not tell her." Jamey didn't grasp what he was saying. "Missy's my lady, man. I couldn't go see her brother and not let her know what's happening. I'm not gonna lie to my special lady."

"Don't get on Craig's case," said Missy. "He's my old man now. I won't blow it. I can maintain."

"He's like a whole grade ahead of you, Missy," Jamey was saying, really thinking about all of the rather crude conversations that he and Craig had had. But that had all been speculative. Still, Jamey wondered, maybe through Mona's eyes, what sort was Craig Roman really? A peculiar question, given that Craig and Jamey had been tight since junior high.

"Like *that* matters," said Missy, standing closer to Craig now than to Jamey. "You should understand more than anyone. Age and school status are like these artificially imposed structures, man. He's your brother, man. I'm your sister. You should be happy for both of us." Craig now put his arm around her shoulder, showing possession of his old lady, who was all of fifteen.

"I'm sorry," said Jamey, coming to his hippie senses. "I guess I was uncool. I just figured everything back home stays the same as it is in my mind. Nothing here stays the same, so why should you guys?" Then he turned to Craig and gave him a hug. "You better not do her dirt, dude."

"It's cool," said Craig.

"Hey, what's going on with Crazy Place? Did you get anyone to play bass for you yet?"

"There is no Crazy Place," said Craig. Mona didn't agree. Craig continued. "Mark and Paul joined up with Steve Forest from Chatsworth.

170

You're out here. So I'm kind of going solo, except for Missy." They squeezed hands.

"Wow!" said Jamey. "I'm sorry. I can't believe they dumped you for Steve Forest."

"Steve's brother is the lead guitar, so they don't need me. And The Foresters get good gigs, so, who knows? If they had asked me to join, maybe I would have left you guys. It's cool. You gotta do your own thing and follow your own rainbow, man. I don't hold it against anyone."

"Ahem…" It was Mona. Jamey stopped blathering, and introduced the parties. "Okay. Great!" said Mona. "Let's get the bass to the club."

The AM was playing Elvis's "Suspicious Minds." Mona liked Elvis, even though she said he had turned into Sammy Davis, Jr. She wanted to do an Elvis song in the set. "Marie's the Name" was Jamey's suggestion.

"We could try "Little Sister." That's the flip," said Mona.

"She knows stuff like that," said Jamey. Jamey was trying to talk with Missy. Mona's suggestions seemed meant to distract him. It was transparent. He knew she didn't approve of him getting all caught up in the home front. Missy explained that the old man was gyrating back and forth between *I'll kill that little hippie fag when I find him* to *I'm worried sick about the boy*. Both were probably true, but Jamey thought the old man was a Squaresville Nazi bastard. But when Missy explained that Margaret was very upset, that got a different response. Missy suggested that Jamey might at least call Margaret. Mona was all like, "I don't know…" but Jamey was hearing his sister. It was the price that had to be paid for the bass.

Missy and Craig appeared bewildered when they arrived at The Contortionist to see the XXX Girls! Girls! Girls! XXX sign. "We're a bar band," said Mona, as if that was all the explanation that was needed.

"Are you like the chick singer?" asked Craig.

"Yeah, right," said Mona. "It's like Spanky and Our Gang. I got my tambourine in my little backpack here."

Craig took her at face value, and replied, "That's cool. Say! When do you go on? Can we see your set?"

Missy blushed, "Craig! It's a stripper bar. I can't go in there."

"See? That's what I'm talking about," said Jamey. "You have to think, man! You can't bring chicks to a place like this."

"What am I?" Mona complained.

Craig refused the money that Jamey offered for the gas. Craig was willing to carry the freight for his buddy. Mona thought they would never leave, but, eventually, Craig and Missy said good-bye, Missy hugging her brother. "Why are your nails painted so pretty?" she asked him. "And you smell good."

"Oh," he stumbled, "We went to a costume party."

"And you went as...?"

"This was really fun," Mona announced. "But Jamey and I have to get going. Thanks a million. Very cool of you two to come out." Mona was not allowing any more conversation. Craig and Missy exited the lot, back onto the boulevard.

"That was weird," said Jamey, still hanging in back of The Contortionist and looking at his nails.

"Nosey little thing," Mona allowed.

"Smart kid," said Jamey. "She doesn't get loaded. So she's got all her brain cells clicking."

They waited another hour, smoking cigarettes and hanging out. Mona hung Jamey's earrings, femmed his hair, put on the head band, and brushed on a little makeup. When they thought they were unobserved, Jamey slipped off his boy shirt and put on a padded bra. When he replaced his shirt, he looked like any androgynous hippie kid. Finally, Larry, the manager dude, showed up with the key to the locked closet where they kept their equipment.

It was still a few hours before the gig. The place was open, but dead. There was a bored girl on the stage doing her thing to the juke box for very light tips and a few hapless dudes who were just as interested in the beer. "This is pathetic," said Mona. "At least we make a party out of it." Jamey was always drawn to the women on the stage.

There was one barmaid in shorts servicing the clients. "You could do that," said Mona. "You'd have to score some new ID, but I know a dude, Sam, who says it could be very easily done. This probably pays better than the theater. Lots of tips."

"El Portal's pretty close to home," said Jamey, "Like I want asshole squares pinching my bum all day at work. At least at the theater they're all in a cage."

"There's a case of perspective," said Mona. "Hey! It was just a flash, man. I'm not saying you should be a dancer."

"Wrong club," said Jamey. Jamey was looking from across the room to the reasonably pretty dancer whose feet were presently pointing toward the back of the stage while she touched her toes and smiled, albeit upside down, at the rather small audience. In that one move, she showed that she was infinitely more of a girl than Jamey could ever aspire to be, all of

Mona's work notwithstanding.

When Mona declared that it was time to get into uniform, Jamey's costume was a yellow A shaped micro-mini with matching bikini undies. It was, thought Jamey, possibly the most ridiculous outfit that Mona had yet concocted for him, but Mona assured him that he looked bitchin'. And, checking the mirror, he rather thought he did. But Mona observed that it might be too much. Just hanging in a hot room like The Contortionist might give him away. He had been through it before, and he knew what she would do. Closer to show-time, in the ladies', Mona got out the gaffer's tape. "So you can shake that money maker with confidence."

"I hate the tape, Mona. Like you hate periods. What if I have to *pee?*"

"*You can't do that, Dave.*"

And the Saturday show began, Jamey on his new old bass. Mona and Denise interacted with the audience, while Jamey tended to the side, facing the equipment, sometimes catching Karen's eyes to facilitate their pairing as the rhythm section. But Jamey was required to do back-up vocals with either Denise or Mona, so he crossed the small space from one side to the other as necessary in the George Harrison tradition. Mona monitored the scene, checking out the audience, and encouraging them to attend to the tip jar by directing their attention to it, but she was only having minimal success.

Jamey happened to look over to Mona and saw her face suddenly change. He followed her line of sight. Scanning the back of the hall, Jamey caught the person of Craig Roman hanging back, far from the stage, paying close attention to the band. By his expression, clearly Craig's mind was blown.

Well, let him see the band! Whatever he thought was happening, he had to know that Jamey's musicianship had improved. Jamey had always been the best of the bunch, but he was playing even better than he had with Crazy Place—and it had only been six or seven weeks.

Jamey looked around for Missy, but there was no sign of her, which was a relief. Maybe Craig had left her outside in the car or maybe he had dropped her at home and come back to Hollywood to see the set. He wondered if Craig would spill the beans. When the band did their set closer, announcing Jamey's name, Jamey shimmied for all he was worth, which we know to be a fifty percent share of a sum that was less than $100. When Jamey looked out at the audience again, Craig Roman was on his way out the door. No pillar of salt was he. Mona looked across the stage to Jamey. Jamey gave her a blasé what-the-fuck face

After the show, *the girls* rode with Denise and Karen in Denise's blue beetle up the boulevard. Jamey and Mona were stuffed into the back, hot and close, and not altogether fresh given the four sets that they had played. When they got to the Big Boy, Jamey ran to the ladies' room. An intense blond woman, maybe about Molly's age, was still as she gazed in the mirror. Jamey, confident now as his womanhood had seldom been challenged, nodded to the woman, but rushed into a stall without delay. There was a sudden and soulful outpouring of intense non-verbal vocalizing when Jamey ripped the tape off of his crotch. In a relatively public setting, he sat down so that he could, at last, pee. The lady who had been fixed before the mirror casually remarked, "You better make an appointment at the Free Clinic, dearie."

From the stall, "You mean me?"

"It's just us two," said the woman. "I'm a doctor and you need to get that looked at."

"It's cool," claimed Jamey.

"No. It's not cool. When it hurts like that, sweetie, it's not cool. Make an appointment. It's free."

"Whatever..."

When Jamey fixed himself and came out of the stall, checking that his dress fell properly around the back, the restroom door was just closing behind the doctor.

When he returned to the band at the table, he remarked, "I apparently have a social disease!"

"My money's on that Molly chick," said Mona. "But maybe your precious Teri Ann..." Mona suddenly stopped. She had blown Jamey's cover. "Sorry, honey. Being clever again."

"S'cool," said Denise. "I've known for weeks." Denise looked to Karen, who shrugged her apology. "I got it out of her. I couldn't figure out why my little slut here hadn't come on to you." Denise laughed. "Well, there was only one explanation, and I made her tell."

Karen shrugged once more to the assembled. "I'm sorry for blowing your cover, Jamey. That's why I was checking you out."

"It's cool," said Denise. If it was cool with Denise, then it was cool with Karen. So it was cool with Mona which meant it was cool with Jamey. The members of the band had a laugh and ate their combos. Jamey was a little more freaked now. Who else knew?

The kids were loud and rowdy, and sometimes ill-spoken. For all of their crudity, they were young, beautiful, provocatively dressed, and generally forgiven for their sins and their residual perspiration, at least by the many boys and men who observed them.

When the divvying was done, Mona and Jamey's share was nineteen bucks, better than the night before, but they had sounded better with Jamey's Precision bass, even if the color clashed with his outfit. Whenever they received income, Jamey proposed frugal and far sighted measures to which Mona paid no attention. Mona, and life in general, kept urging more spending. Mona's whole life was an investment in her rock and roll future. She was not going for small time investments like a box of Cheerios against hard times. Walking home, Jamey was carrying $114.00 and some change.

"Watch for the Adam 12 boys," Mona cautioned. "We have to be cool." Jamey found that remark from Mona peculiar on two accounts. First, given their outfits, playing it cool was a ridiculous notion. Second, it was heavy that Mona should reference the incident. Mona didn't show her paranoia or her feelings in general. With their jobs, the band, maintaining Jamey's fem, and keeping the scene together, Mona didn't talk about it. That was two days ago, man. So Jamey had followed her lead. It had been scary stuff: Jamey, helpless and kneeling before the pig; Mona, cuffed and helpless in the backseat. But there wasn't much point in articulating their feelings. Now, Mona wants to be careful.

"Fuckers got to you!" said Jamey. "Maybe we *should* go see that Doctor. Doctor to the Hollywood sluts."

"I know you are," said Mona. Jamey didn't laugh. "What?" said Mona. "I'll spread my legs on the table and she'll look at my pussy. What do I need that for? I'm fine. She can't help what's really wrong which is that there's assholes everywhere who fuck with chicks because they can. I'm gonna make it, and then they can't get to me. I'll be in charge. And I don't think you want your feet in the stirrups. Okay. Maybe *you* do."

"I just heard that chicks get fucked up when they get raped, and it's maybe a way to get some help for your head. But, look, if you want me to play it cool, you got it. I'm playin' it real cool," Jamey assured Mona.

Mona stopped short, in front of the record store. Jamey thought maybe Mona had seen another boyfriend or Officer Tank, the way she was suddenly arrested. A new Beatle album? Eric Clapton walking down the sidewalk? Mona backed Jamey up against the window glass and kissed Jamey, hips against hips, a long deep searching kiss. When Mona turned Jamey loose, Jamey, blown away, asked her, "Why'd you do that?"

"That's what Jesus said to Judas," Mona replied. "Your clit is showing."

"Girl can only take so much," said Jamey.

WHO AM I?

THE KIDS WERE LISTENING to *Mystery Tour* on the tiny speaker, a different trip from hearing it at Rick's, but Mona caught the vibe listening to "Hello, Goodbye."

"You want to split, don't you?" said Mona, curled on the bed and hugging her teddy with one hand and smoking a cigarette with the other. "I totally get it. That's why I split my scene and came down here from Portland." It was the first Jamey had heard of Portland. "I wanted to get away from where it happened. It doesn't work. I still think about it all the time. Sometimes I wake up shaking from it…"

"I know," said Jamey.

"You're like the only person who would know. You've been really cool about everything," said Mona, taking Jamey's hand. Despite Mona having been raped, despite having been forced to have sex himself, Mona's proximity in her bare thighs and braless t-shirt arrested Jamey's attention. Mona continued to gush. "Any other guy would have pounced on me, the way we live together, especially the way I carry on. I'm a cock-tease," said Mona. "That's one of my powers. But you've been really cool about everything. I wish I hadn't fucked it up for you, Jamey. It takes your peace of mind. You don't look at people in the same way. But you can't get away from it by going away somewhere. I know you want to scream, but there's nothing for it. And where would you go, Jamey? Home to papa?"

"I can't go back home," he said.

"I'm sure they miss you," said Mona. "You've made your point about being independent. You even have a job. You could go home if you wanted to."

"I don't care about the shit that went on at home, like haircuts and curfews and grades. As if that matters. But there's a lot going on that I don't understand, and I can't work it out at home. It's too freaky for my Mom and my sister. I mean, *here*, I could stop being a chick tomorrow—today—if I wanted. I could walk away, but I could come back. But, *there*, I have to decide and stay with it. Who am I kidding? I would have to be a dude, in full drab, man. But I know I'm nuts, Mona. I would never have let you do all of this to me if I didn't want you to do it. If I didn't dig the chick trip…"

"Duh," said Mona.

"You already knew." Jamey was wondering if that was just Mona bullshit, but he realized it wasn't. "You always knew, didn't you? Hell, if I never met you, I had already gotten into the car with Rick the Perv. What else could he want? My brilliant conversation? I liked the feeling of getting attention, from the very first time he touched me. Everyone knew but me. The fucking jocks in high school knew. My dad knew. I think Teri Ann sort of knew. I mean, she didn't know what it was, but she sensed something about me. That's why she dumped me. I don't know who I am anymore."

"There's a whole generation like that, Jamey."

SUNDAY MORNING, Jamey made good his promise to Missy. He called home and spoke to his mother. He wouldn't tell her his location, but he told her that he was safe and playing in a band, just as he had always wanted. She invited him to come home on any terms, but he was adamant about maintaining his hard won independence. Her voice was not strong and she was clearly holding back her tears. He felt selfish and foolish to hurt his mother, but he was committed to his life in Hollywood. He asked her not to worry, but that was probably a brainless suggestion. He told her that he loved her, and that was a better choice. He was about as teary as she by the time they said good-bye.

When he hung up and stepped out of the phone booth, Mona said, "That was good, Jamey. I probably should call home, too. I've been putting it off, but I think it's time now." Mona had never mentioned home except in relation to having run away. The occasional jokes about her Chinese mom drilling her head when she didn't practice her piano scales were all that Jamey knew of Mona's home life, assuming any of it was true. So this sudden reach-out to her home folks came as a surprise. But Jamey thought it was a good thing. Might start the healing, at least for the first rape.

They did a groovy Sunday, wildly spending money on little things like hot dogs and laundry, and they were down to $108.37 by the time they hit the stage on Sunday night.

Jamey never suspected that anything out of the usual was going on, but he did see that Mona was checking out the audience, and watching the door more acutely than usual. During the break, Jamey was cooling off out in the alley, smoking with Karen and Denise. "So are you like really into being a girl," Denise was asking, "Or is it really just the band thing?"

"It started out as the band thing," said Jamey. "But I do it all the time

177

now. That's how I feel…"

"Like a pussy," said Denise.

"Denise!" said Karen.

"I *am* a pussy," said Jamey. "I mean, in my head. Of course, I sort of wish I really were."

"It's cool," said Denise. "I was just wondering. We're all pussys. Sometimes I'm kind of John Wayne pussy. Ask Karen." Karen seemed to hope that nobody would ask her. They presumed that Mona was in the ladies', such as it was. When she joined her band mates, she had Molly Gifford with her. Jamey's mouth fell open in surprise.

"Who's the square?" said Denise. Molly was dressed nicely, especially compared to the band.

"She works for Jamey's boyfriend," said Mona. "He wants to see you again, Jamey."

"Well, I don't want to see him."

Molly cut in. "You are a bad little girl, Jamey," said Molly, in her lovely English tone.

"I'm sorry about that, Molly," said Jamey. "I just couldn't…"

"You're not the first little twit to tell a lie."

"So what are we talking about? Why are you here?" He hadn't yet come to the question of how she had gotten there.

"I understand that you and your mates are looking for a break. You'd like to get something a little better than a strip club. You'd like to make a record." Molly said this for everyone's benefit.

"So?" Jamey played it as cool as he could, but the lure was having its effect.

"So, darling, Richard can't promise to make you a star. You'd need a modicum of talent for that, which I sincerely doubt. But. He can get you to some important people, people you will never meet but for him."

"Like who?" said Denise, doubtful of this story. A lot of stories are told, especially to girls.

"This is for real," said Mona, to Denise, but also for Jamey. "I mean, you already met Jerry Westerfield. You know this is for real."

Jamey understood now that there had been a conspiracy. "You want me to do this, Mona?"

"It's for the band, Jamey," said Mona. Jamey had expected more, but that was Mona's advice: It's for the fucking band.

"He wants to spend some time with you," said Molly. "We obviously don't have a problem with—what we talked about before, do we?" She looked at Jamey in his get-up. "So, if you want to help your mates—if you want to help yourself—he still wants to see you." She added, "I hope you say no because you don't deserve the help he can give you. But it's not up to me, is it?"

"How do we know he'll come through?" said Jamey.

"Richard's been nothing but open and kind, giving you all the room you could ask for. You are the one who can't be trusted. You are the one who doesn't keep his word!"

Jamey knew what Mona wanted. Richard Altier could save them years of struggle. Jamey didn't have the aversion to prostitution that was built-in to the average middle class chick, but he did have years of training to avoid all semblance of the queer life. That was a laugh, given his wardrobe on this particular night, his jewelry, his makeup, even his patchouli, not to mention the events of the recent past. Mona had him living his whole life in drag. He flashed on that. Was this her plan all along? How long had she been cooking this up with Molly? Since she first saw Molly's card, and the card from Westerfield? There was never time to reflect, though. The bus kept rolling.

He remembered Richard kissing him and grabbing his ass, guiding him around as if he were some kind of show boat, the way Richard looked at him as if he were already on the bed. He remembered Richard buying him for a hundred bucks, dressing him up like a girl freak, posing for the camera, for the perv. He had already sold himself to Richard Altier for some dinner and some cash. Now he was to sell himself again, maybe for a chance to make it in the big time—for himself, for Mona, for the band. And he pictured what would happen if Molly split the scene without his agreeing to the terms. The other girls might understand the decision, but it would fatally deflate them. In short, sometimes a girl has to do what a girl has to do.

"Okay," said Jamey. "I'm a whore. When does this go down?"

Karen turned away and went back to her drums, fiddling with the pedals. Denise soon followed her, retuning her guitar. Mona stayed on. Molly continued, "I'll take you around tomorrow and get you fixed up."

"I can get her ready," said Mona. "You don't…"

"I don't trust either one of you," said Molly. "I will pick *you* up tomorrow, Jamey. On your own. Rick will be in town on Tuesday night, so we'll have to get busy. He's taking you on a trip, but you'll be back in town on your own by Friday. He has a gig on Friday night on the east coast. Is that understood? You belong to Rick until we bring you back on Friday?"

"I get it," said Jamey. "Whore until Friday."

"No, darling. Once you're a whore, you're always a whore."

"That's kind of bourgeois," said Mona.

Molly didn't engage Mona. If she had used Mona to get to Jamey, that was accomplished. Mona, for her part, was surprisingly quiet. Jamey surmised that Mona didn't want to blow the deal. "And you," looking at Jamey, "You better not have any attitude, young lady." It almost sounded like Jim Craig. "Smile like you enjoy it, which I suspect you do. In exchange, Rick will use his influence to get your band an audition for touring and for records. There's no guarantee what will come of it. That's really up to you and your mates. But he knows a lot of people, and he's a man of his word. So, Jamey, do we have a shopping date for the morning?"

"I already said yes."

"Right. And you never lie," said Molly.

Jamey was going to apologize again, but Molly wasn't interested. So Jamey asked, "What should I wear? Should I bring anything?"

Molly looked *her* up and down, not with approval. "It doesn't matter. We're going shopping." Molly sniffed disdainfully. "Leave the patchouli at home. Maybe take a bath." So it was arranged to pick-up Jamey at the parking lot of the donut shop. "See you in the morning," said Molly. "Oh, look at that, ladies. Seems as if your van has a flat."

Maiden Head finished their Sunday night gig. After paying the tow truck to fill the tire, paying Denise's brother for the use of the van, and dividing up the proceeds, Jamey and Mona's share was $17.50, making a grand total of $126.00, less thirteen cents. Jamey would be gone for several days, and Mona would need money to live on. She couldn't be trusted with the whole caboodle, so Jamey split it down the middle, giving Mona $63.00 and keeping $63.00 for himself, against paying the rent should it not have been paid, a very real possibility. This arrangement probably meant that those who liked to look at Jamey in the glass ticket booth cage would be disappointed.

Since Jamey and Mona would be splitting up for a few days, Mona proposed that they get snockered. They didn't usually get boozed up by themselves, but this was an occasion. Mona tried to pass as twenty-one, but it was doubtful that she was really eighteen. The liquor store clerk kicked her out. Hanging around out front, they coaxed a dude to buy them some Southern Comfort. "I already put the cash in my pants," Mona explained to Jamey. "I'll pay you back." It came out of Jamey's share. After some cigarettes and candy, Jamey was in possession of about $57.00.

Back in the room, Mona poured the drinks. "You still don't have to go through with it, sweetie. You don't have to show up, and that's the end of it. They don't know where you live."

Jamey didn't know what else to do except to take a strong drink. "If I don't give him my ass, we could be at The Contortionist for the next five years. I mean, actually, I kind of like it there. It's good for us to play for people, especially like people who don't really care about the band. They're there for the drinks and the girls, so, if we can entertain them, we're pretty good. It makes us tighter. It makes a band a lot better, like The Band or Creedence, but who has ten years to get where we want to go? This is the lightning—maybe. So I have to do it. Don't I?"

"You're right about everything you said, but none of it means that you have to do it. Do you want to go through with it?"

"You would do it, wouldn't you?"

Mona thought about that as she poured another set of drinks. "Nobody asked *me*," said Mona. "He wants *you*. You're the lightning."

Jamey shook his head. "He wants my ass," said Jamey. "It's the lightning rod that I'm worried about." They giggled as they sipped. "But you would do it. Wouldn't you?"

"I don't know. I probably would. I would do whatever I had to do to make it. But that's *my* dream, isn't it? Depends if it's your dream, and if this is the way you want to make it." For the first time, the bullshit seemed palpable. Mona was obviously just trying to get Jamey into Molly's hands in the morning. That's how it felt now.

"I don't know that there's another way," said Jamey. "I'm going to have to be a man about it. Look at everything that's happened, everything I've done. Why *wouldn't* I do this?"

"You were in handcuffs and scared shitless. No handcuffs this time."

"Back of the Volkswagen," said Jamey. "I think what I'm afraid of is, maybe I want to do this. I've been living like you, and I like it. I feel good about it. But, of course, I'm not you. I don't really have a pussy."

"I barely have tits," said Mona. That called for another drink.

"But you do. And cute hips. But I can't be a regular chick. So maybe guys like Rick are the answer, for me. I'll do whatever, like you say, for the band. But what I don't like, or what I don't understand, is that I feel kind of excited about it, which is just gross. I feel like a girl getting ready for a big date."

"It's way complicated shit," said Mona.

"But I like girls, too. I like you. Not to freak you out…"

181

"...no freak taken..."

"And Teri Ann. And that Molly bitch. I like girls."

"Sure you do," said Mona. "It's fuckin' complicated shit, man. The thing is, you don't have to do it unless you choose to do it." Jamey felt the tears welling up, more afraid and confused than he had known. The whole charade had blown his mind. They did a good job on the Southern Comfort.

Intimate as the two had been, the nearness of Mona was almost painful tonight. It was hot, at least in their third floor Rooms-for-Rent suite, but Jamey held the sleeping Mona, unable to fall asleep himself. Her touch, unconscious as it was, was animating his physical desire. He didn't want Mona to wake and discover his erect prick. That would be too queer.

He tried to take his mind off of Mona's body, and he tried to think clearly about the events to come. He was looking at some kind of destiny, a salvation for the band. Where had Molly come from? Duh. Judas herself had kissed him just the night before. The passion is prelude to the crucifixion. What was Jamey afraid of exactly? Was he afraid of being taken or afraid of wanting it and becoming something he hadn't been? Was he taking an irrevocable step? Or was it just the usual fears? If girls can take it in the mouth and in the ass, was he really so different?

Rick had kissed him. Rick had held Jamey in his hands, strongly taking possession of him and kissing Jamey's mouth. He remembered it vividly. It had never been far from his mind. He had been still until it was over, and then he had feebly run away—to the bedroom.

His restlessness continued. He was ready to sit up, but where would he go then? He resettled, but his mind continued to race. Would Rick have him give head? Thinking about it, his unit was getting out of hand now. And he hadn't really been thinking of Mona at all. He had been imagining taking Rick in his mouth. He wished he had been thinking of Mona.

And how painful was this other business going to be? Humiliating, without doubt, beyond redemption, an offense to his core. But here he was, next to the lovely Mona, and he was thinking of cock. This Gethsemane would have gone on if not for the dimension of time that kept him moving right along toward his continuing destiny. He fell heavily asleep under the booze.

JAMEY CAME AWAKE. Mona was dressed in her camp clothes, the shorts and the dark blouse, with the little backpack on her shoulder. She always managed to look fresh and clean for her camp work. What was she really like at camp? Who, apart from Mona, says there really is a camp?

"Better get going, Jamey," she said, as if they were parting for just another work day. It was obvious that Mona couldn't face Jamey, and Jamey was already ashamed of himself. It would be easier if Mona knew nothing about it, but she had set it up. He didn't care what Rick thought of him; he knew what Rick thought of him. He didn't really care very much about Molly; he had burned that bridge. But knowing that Mona could picture him dolled up and giving head and having Rick take him from behind, he wished that she would go. "Jamey?"

"I'm cool," said Jamey. "I'll be back in time for the Friday night gig. Take care. Oh, maybe you should try to square it at the theater. I mean, I hate to lose my job, but..."

"I'll try," said Mona.

"If he fires me, he'll never get my panties on his wall."

"Jamey, I have to catch the bus. And you gotta get to the donut shop in half an hour. Take care of yourself, honey. You know I love you."

"Go. Educate the fuck out of those kids of yours. I don't have much getting ready to do. I think it's a rebuild. No sense dressing up now."

"Okay. Peace." Mona wanted out as much as Jamey wanted her to go. They didn't want to face each other. Jamey was intrigued. Maybe it was imagination. Did Mona's voice seem to be cracking, a little out of control? Was there a little tenderness there?

BRAND NEW ME

JAMEY WAS LATE, but only by moments. He made the scene wearing the yellow dress with matching underpants. He had bare legs and sandals. He had a handbag with a few items, including the $57.00.

At the outset, they were quiet as Molly drove, but the quiet didn't last. Molly was clearly resentful, but Jamey was willing to forgive and forget. He figured she thought him an ass and a shit, and that he had taken advantage of her. It was a funny idea: A sixteen-year-old kid taking advantage of a grown-up woman in the music scene. It wasn't something he could have imagined a couple of months ago. She was ten years older and far more sophisticated and experienced. She had some right to feel ill-used, he admitted to himself, but he doubted that he was the biggest asshole she had ever encountered.

When she saw him glancing at her legs as she drove, she tried to fix her skirt to deprive him of the pleasure. Jamey noticed how she guarded her legs. He was amused. Living with Mona, he knew the feeling all too well carrying his guitar case on the boulevard with an occasional breeze under his short dress. Still, for all his crazy thinking, he was still hot for Miss Molly. He sensed that she didn't really like him, and his green ignorance and asshole brown arrogance didn't make him more attractive. He felt like a kid around Molly. Mona made him feel like he was in the game. Rick made him feel kind of funny inside.

Jamey and her new best friend toured Beverly Hills on Rick's dime. Like the twelve Herculean tasks that Miss Curtis had referenced, Jamey had much to do. The first stop was Exfoliation Station. Jamey's peach fuzz didn't challenge their skills. They daily encountered women who needed their services far more desperately than Jamey. When he took off his things, it was apparent that he was a special cause. Molly directed the skilled labor, referring specifically to his and that.

Jamey was exposed and somewhat embarrassed, but living in a dress and shimmying his pantied ass in the band was much more public and potentially humiliating, though it had dawned on him lately that the humiliation had passed. That was the hippie philosophy, wasn't it? You don't have to be a plastic man. You could be whoever and whatever turned you on. And being a chick was turning Jamey on. As he had realized the night before, none of this could have happened without his willing participation. Having the hair on his balls as the topic of conversation shouldn't have phased him. The ladies spreading his legs to do the intimate work caused him to blush, but he was okay with it really. They threw in some skin softening into the process. It smelled good, and it felt very good as they rubbed it into his skin, all over his body, front and back, and every little corner. He was totally into it, enjoying the sensations.

Molly knew how to tip with Rick's cash, and Jamey replaced his outfit and he metaphorically walked on down the hall and went into the room where his sister lived…

His coiffure was the topic of the next stop. With smooth and creamy skin and back in the yellow dress, getting a buzz from the feminine smell, he was hoping to con the girls at the salon. He made a point of crossing his legs and reading Vogue and Seventeen while they worked. When at length he was turned to face the mirror, there were pretty ringlets throughout the hair and rounded curls that turned up on either side of his mouth. While the hair was in process, Jamey had a full manicure and pedicure. The little high of excitement was grooving inside of him, somewhere near where his pussy ought to have been.

The third stop was a boutique that specialized in makeup and the decorative arts. During this session, while waiting for an application, Molly explained to Jamey. "You'll be travelling with Mr. Altier." Her accent was ever so musical.

"You mean Rick the Perv," said Jamey. "Where did Mr. come from?"

"You need to button those painted lips as much as possible when you're with him, and you could practice being quiet now. You do look pretty, but you are so crude," said Molly. "You'll be staying at a nice hotel. I'll call the concierge and make arrangements for you to get into a salon where they can help you with the makeup and hair if you need it. But you've got to learn some basics."

"Mona does my makeup," said Jamey.

"Mona's obviously a prostitute, like yourself," said Molly. "It's like a three-year-old doing makeup."

"I've been learning," said Jamey, almost with pride. "My hand is steadier. I used to look like Bozo. But I can do lipstick and blush. Mona showed me." Molly tried out a few ideas in the shop, and they bought a bagful of the necessary articles for Jamey's transformation. Molly also selected some fragrances for Jamey, more or less to Molly's taste as Jamey had none of his own.

At the land of foundations Jamey's eyes were opened just a little wider. Mona had been putting Jamey in sheer panties and not so fitted padded bras, and hoped that Jamey would pass. It was sort of a *take-it-or-leave-it* proposition, and Jamey's youth and the strange times carried the day. It was the best they had in the Rooms-for-Rent closet. But these shop brassieres were more proportioned, more elegant, and much prettier. Under certain circumstances, it was possible to flash a little of the bra for effect without giving away the secret of his abject flatness. Jamey also acquired some underwear of a nature he had never imagined. These articles were strategically padded to create the shape of feminine hips and an enhanced rear and profile view under his outfits. Jamey had never posited that the beautiful feminine form that he so admired was in need of such deceptions to the degree that an industry could be supported in the design, manufacture, distribution, and sale of such articles. His mind was further blown when it was explained that some of these necessaries could pocket and redirect any suspicious bulge, creating a flat smooth credible front. Molly selected several pieces of lingerie for Jamey.

"It's ridiculously expensive!" he remarked, looking at some of the prices. "But what good is this stuff, Molly?" he asked, not too loudly. "Who wants to see padded bras and fake hips and puffy asses at the moment of truth? There goes the illusion."

"It has to do with the occasion," said Molly. "He's just another man, you know. He can't play *pass-the-parcel* all night. The rest is dancing and dinner and showing you off."

"To whom?"

"That doesn't matter really," said Molly. "What was that girl's name? The little slut you were shagging?"

"Teri Ann. But I don't think you could say…"

"Tell me you didn't like to show her off to your friends, or just to anyone who happened to see you together. You were proud of her, weren't you?"

"Okay," Jamey allowed. "That's true. Maybe that's what hurt most about breaking up. It turned me back into a nobody." He thought about that, and reconsidered. "No. It was losing pussy access."

"And, then," said Molly, "When it *is* time, you go in the bathroom, change into some real underwear and a little whatever. He knows who you are. He can turn out the lights if he wants to—but I don't think he will. He rather likes the view."

By early afternoon, Jamey, who hadn't really slept, last night and in general, just wanted relief. He suggested going up to the canyon and hanging out in back, smoking a joint, and drinking some of that fancy wine stuff. But Molly was all about the bulsiness. There was a quick salad lunch. Molly insisted that Jamey didn't need to get any fatter, but he ordered a Coke nonetheless. As long as Rick was paying, what the hell? When they got to the jewelry store, they picked up some mid-range pieces. "I saw *My Fair Lady*," said Jamey. "I don't get to keep the jewels, do I?"

"You don't keep anything unless he gives it to you," said Molly.

Next, they hit the clothing stores, and Molly dressed him, with his hips and breasts in place, to Rick's taste. Mona would have loved the casual way that Molly was spending for Jamey's honeymoon trousseau. He acquired jeans, shorts, and tops to go with them. She said he would need a sweater. There were two short dresses, a long dress with bare shoulders, which he wasn't sure he could do given his limitations up top, but Molly was convinced that the dress was just right. Jamey found that, exhausted as he was, he was enjoying his Beverly Hills spree. The pampering, the attention, the smell of the perfumes and the feel of the fabrics on his baby soft skin all made him feel on the one hand ridiculous and, on another, high. The dresses and various outfits were of a different style from Mona of Hollywood. He twirled and flounced and was very much at home in his gender switched clothes. He liked how he felt, and he liked how he looked. Just as he and Mona had made a striking impression on the street crowd on their boulevard, so Molly and especially Jamey were turning heads in the classy and cash-laden part of town.

The seventh task of the day was shopping for shoes. He had practiced walking in heels, but it was not his strength. There was some danger. He couldn't afford a broken ankle, but the shoes added to the overall effect. In any event, some of the dresses demanded the heels. What could one do? They walked out with several pairs, including some sandals and pumps, along with stockings, garters, and belts. "I'll show you how this works," said Molly. "This is why you needed several days, which is what we would have had if you weren't such a liar." To be fair, under Mona's tutoring, Jamey had been practicing.

By six in the evening, eleven hours on the job, Jamey had received a one day crash course in dressing for his new boyfriend. On the way back, they drove close by Jamey's stomping grounds near the boulevard. Jamey wanted to check in on Mona, but Molly was clear. There was no time for Mona. But Molly did have her weakness. It didn't take much for Jamey to convince Molly that they had to stop to scarf some dogs, fries, and shakes. Jamey looked for Mona, but she didn't happen to show. Then it was up to Laurel Canyon.

Jamey had thought of Rick's beautiful pad many times, and it didn't disappoint him. Set rustically, but with all the modern amenities, it was a palace to Jamey. He didn't even think to compare it with his shared chamber at Rooms-for-Rent. When Molly pulled into the drive, the place seemed familiar and Jamey was happy to see it, even if he had been running for his life the last time he had been there or, specifically, to protect his threatened manhood. The heels he was wearing this evening would have made such a run down the hills rather difficult.

It was just after seven, and Zulema was checking the kitchen and preparing to boogie. She waved her finger at Jamey when she recognized him. "Why you do that to my car? Why you back here? Stupido. Ay dios mío!" Zulema quickly left, probably to return on the morrow. "Un lugar loco!"

Jamey and Molly hung out smoking pot and drinking wine on the patio in the late evening summer breeze listening to music over the sound system. They turned down the lights and watched the occasional stars over the LA night sky. The moon looked full. Their animosity had subsided. Working together can have that effect, and Jamey wasn't whining tonight. He sometimes had thoughts about having sex with Molly, but his outfit seemed to limit the likelihood of that happening again, ever. And he had other concerns. In the warmth of the wine, he asked Molly, "So, have you ever taken it in your ass?"

"Excuse me?" she reacted.

"Well, have you?" said Jamey. "You're a girl. You must have been curious. And you have a nice…"

"Perhaps I should thank you," she said.

"So, you must have been asked."

Molly laughed. "They don't usually ask, Jamey," said Molly. "You just sort of let it happen."

"So, what's it really like?" asked Jamey.

"Oh, my! Aren't we a pair of girlfriends?"

"You taught me almost everything I know about sex."

"You knew nothing," said Molly. She collected her thoughts. "You still don't. It's not something one talks about." Molly held her glass in hand. "I don't know what to say. It's, it's…well, at first it's a little shocking, isn't it? One doesn't really expect that sort of thing, does one?" Molly poured more wine for herself and for Jamey.

"Does it hurt like hell?" asked Jamey. "They say it's really painful. Can't sit down for days. I don't know why girls do it."

"Exactly. If it were so painful, why would so many girls, and guys, mind you...why would so many do it? Just to please their partner? Does that strike you as human nature?" Jamey didn't know. Molly could sense his concern. He was on the menu for the next night. "Jamey, it's painful if you fight it. Look, it's making love. It really depends on who your partner is, doesn't it? If it's a crude bastard with no feeling and no sensitivity, then, yes, it hurts. If it's someone loving and knowledgeable, and sensitive, then, it's a little shocking, but only for a moment. And you think it hurts, or that it's going to hurt, but that's really nothing. It passes, and then, while he's in you, it can be very very nice. You're a boy, so your equipment is connected elsewhere, and I've only heard. But a woman's equipment is connected just so, and it's nice because everything is involved. It's some of the best fucking I've ever known. How's that for girl talk?"

"But everybody says how horrible it is," said Jamey.

"Everybody in your crowd," said Molly. "Morons, no doubt. I mean, if you're talking rape, then I imagine it's painful. Any kind of rape. But I don't see why a guy wouldn't experience something very much like what a woman would experience, if he were open to it. I mean, if it's some manly John Wayne type of guy, assuming he's not gay, a guy who couldn't imagine giving himself over to another man, then I guess it would hurt him. But, in your case, I don't think it would have to hurt. It's supposed to stimulate your prostate— if it's done correctly. And I think he'll do it correctly. He's had enough practice."

"What's a prostate?"

"It's part of what makes you a man. Well, what makes a man a man. Not sure what you are, Jamey. Anyway, the thing to do is: Be open. Be open to your feelings. Let yourself go. People have done it for thousands of years, and they've done it willingly, and they've done it again and again. Of course, don't forget the lubricant. You can rub it on his penis and you can put it in your virgin bum yourself. Lots of lubricant because, well, it's not a pussy, is it? It doesn't make pussy juice."

"Do we have that?" said Jamey.

"I'll see to it," said Molly. "So my little girl is almost all grown up..."

"I'm sorry about before," said Jamey. "When I promised to stay, I was planning to stay. I was going to do it. I don't really know why, but staying up here sounded good to me. Food, dope, and even sex with you. I really didn't have any better offers, you know. Even when you went into the bathroom, I didn't know I would make a break for it. I just decided to get out of there, and I did."

"You are very sweet, for a little liar. You don't have to worry about me. I'm a big girl." She pulled herself out of the patio recliner. "And you're here now, and Rick will be back tomorrow. Maybe you need some sleep tonight."

"So you actually like getting ass fucked, by the right guy?"

"Bed time," Molly insisted. Molly walked Jamey up the stairs to the bedroom. She had given him some downers in the wine to make sure that he didn't bolt again. He got to bed safely in the pink chamber reserved for his like. As to apparel, there was nothing boyish about anything. He could go naked or stay in drag. He wore a nighty to bed. One of the things he most loved about Rick's place was the air conditioning. It was so comfortable and cool in the scented sheets. He only enjoyed it for a moment before succumbing to the drugs.

Tuesday involved practice applying makeup, fixing his hair, rolling stockings up and down his hairless legs, and walking on the heels, up and down the stairs and on various surfaces. They packed two suitcases. Zulema had arrived about ten. She had made a brunch for Molly and Jamey and gone about her business. Her eyes were always mocking Jamey, so it seemed to him, so he tried to avoid making contact with her. In the early afternoon, Molly split the scene, confident this time that Jamey would stay. She realized from talking to him that he was not only interested in whoring himself to advance the band, but that he was increasingly obsessed with his feminization, eager to learn all that he could. He seemed to feel that giving himself to Rick was a part of the process. It made all of Mona's work go from being just costumes to an essential, if transitive, reality— as Jamey perceived it. Mona's street fashions had gotten him started, but Molly was taking him into the wider world.

BREAK ON THROUGH (TO THE OTHER SIDE)

J AMEY HEARD A CAR ARRIVE in the later afternoon. He jumped off the bed and stepped onto the balcony to spy on the arrival. Rick had caught the motion and looked up to see his Juliet, who timidly waved. Rick smiled quickly and went along indoors. Jamey's fear and confusion from Sunday night had turned to excitement, almost a giddy feeling. He was full of the romance, of the illusion. Perfumed, in a sweet summer dress with sandals, Jamey ran down the stairs to meet Rick, to show him his new hips.

Jamey expected an affectionate hug, a kiss perhaps, a squeeze on the bottom, but Rick was cold. "Wait upstairs," he said, hardly observing him. "I have to make some calls." He brushed Jamey off as he looked through the mail. Jamey had just stood there, bewildered at the cold reception. Rick picked up the phone and was dialing out when he noticed that Jamey was still about. He mouthed the word "Upstairs" to Jamey, and then turned his back, entering into conversation. Jamey was deflated now, passing Zulema, who carried a drink for Mr. Rick. Jamey made his way up to the bedroom to wait. He checked his outfit and his hair, but there was nothing more to be done on that score. He was agitated now, excited, but with nothing to do. He wished he had brought his instrument. He couldn't keep his mind still, and there was nothing to read, not that he was in the habit of late. Drugs.

Three times, out of boredom and curiosity, he opened his door and listened. He could hear Rick talking down below, presumably on the telephone. It sounded like business to Jamey, but he didn't know anything. He was inclined to run down and present himself again, but he remembered Rick's irritated dismissal. Jamey was apparently not the most important thing on Rick's agenda. He waited for him on the bed.

And the mood turned again. Of course he wasn't important. Jamey was hardly the first boy Rick had seduced. This seemed to be out of a pattern, if he believed what Molly had said about Rick doing it correctly because of all the practice. He had to believe it. Jamey realized that he was just another piece of ass. He reminded himself that this wasn't love.

Whatever happened would take him to the next phase. Wasn't it all about helping Mona and the band? It was a shot to get Maiden Head a ticket to the big time. It was just a crazy chance, and it fell to Jamey to take it.

It was about ninety minutes of sitting and thinking, getting up, walking around, sitting down again. Jamey's confidence had been severely depressed. He heard another vehicle on the driveway. When he checked, it was a big yellow taxi. The driver was approaching the front door. Rick, now in purple shirt and blue jeans with a medallion around his neck and hanging over his hairy chest, appeared in the bedroom door as Jamey returned from the balcony. Jamey was unsure about how he should behave now. He had thrown himself at Rick, and was ignored. He didn't know what Rick wanted or what he, Jamey, was feeling now. "Twirl!" said Rick, using his director tones.

Jamey gave it a tentative twirl. Rick encouraged a little more animation with his gestures, and Jamey responded with more enthusiasm. "Good girl!" said Rick. "Very pretty, Jamey."

Jamey, out of his manly habit, felt shamed by Rick's words and by his tone. But he had said that Jamey was pretty, and Jamey did like that. He thought it so. "Thanks," he said. "You like my new shape?" He flounced the dress a little for effect.

"I like you the way you are," said Rick. "But we're going out, and you have to look right."

"So where are we going?" asked Jamey.

"Get your things together." He called out the door, "Zulema!" He picked up one of the suitcases, and Jamey carried the other, until Zulema took it, leaving Jamey to act the lady as they headed down the stairs and out to the taxi. Rick already had his bags in place but the taxi driver managed to place Jamey's items in the trunk.

Once on the road, they returned to the Hollywood side of the canyon. Rick smoked a cigarette in the car, glanced at some proofs, and left Jamey to his thoughts as the taxi toured the familiar boulevard. The car ride was relatively quiet. Jamey was looking out the window, maybe hoping to find Mona among the lost souls, and he was hurt that Rick seemed to be ignoring him and even unhappy with him. Jamey slid over beside Rick as Rick had seemed to want him to do the night they first met. Rick wasn't buying it.

Jamey couldn't stay quiet. "Well," he began, "Do you like the dress? Do you like my new figure?"

"You look fine," said Rick, lacking all enthusiasm for the topic.

Jamey waited for a few moments and then tried again. "I'm wearing your earrings. Thanks. I found the picture, and the pot, too. I felt kind of bad about it, I mean, since I made a run for it."

Rick didn't respond. Jamey had no idea what was on Rick's mind. "Did I do something to make you angry? Is it because I ran away? Do you want to call it off? I can get home from here, if you're disappointed."

Rick rolled his eyes. "You're not going home," said Rick. "You don't have to babble incessantly, and neither do I. Peace comes from the calm." Rick had been nicer the first time they had been together, and Jamey was hurt now.

This time he was going to try to wait for Rick to start the conversation, but his resolve didn't last. "Why are you doing this?" Jamey asked. "If you're trying to make me feel like a piece of crap..."

The taxi continued on and made its way to the Aquarius Theater. "I have to work a little," said Rick, getting his equipment boxes out of the back, and handing a couple to Jamey. "So you're the photographer's helper. I think you'll like this."

He walked Jamey to the stage door and the two were passed inside without hesitation. There were beautiful people gathered about. Jamey, being new to the scene, was attracting attention, furtive and not so furtive glances. Rick put Jamey on a chair in the wings. He had a good view of a rock band's equipment already in place. There was a keyboard, a guitar, drums, and a microphone at a stool for a lead singer. "Watch the equipment," he was ordered, meaning the camera boxes. In this, Jamey was scrupulous. He wanted to be a part of it, to be of some service or use. But the pretty photographer's assistant was taking in the scene all the while.

While Rick was getting his bearings, an army of men including roadies, electricians, engineers, and sound recorders were doing their final checks. Rick was looking through his lenses from various angles and places. He spent some time preparing, calling for the stage lights to go up or down. People listened to him, and Jamey noted that he wasn't an asshole about it. He might be an asshole to Jamey, but he was good with the people.

Some hipsters were crowding in now, but the house wasn't filling at all. Several different guys took a shot at talking *her* up. Jamey learned that this was not a typical concert show. No general audience was to be there, but some industry main men were expected. Jamey was wondering who might be playing under such peculiar circumstances.

During the hour of wait time, Jamey recognized Jerry Westerfield coming down the main aisle and taking his place in the front row with a new model on one side and another guy to the other. At one point, Rick went out to talk to them. Then there was a sudden buzz, and Rick went to work.

When the house lights went down and the stage lights came up, Jamey, from the right wing, saw Bryan Cooper seated on a stool in front of the microphone stand. He was uncharacteristically bearded, maybe trying to be invisible or maybe making a statement about being a new man. He was wearing denim working clothes—not the fancy leather pants with the bulging crotch he had become known for. Cooper had always been a little heavy, not being a pretty boy. His face was expressive, even with the beard, and his eyes were big and brown. He tried the mic, and made a few comments to the soundman up in the booth, but not in the shitty way he would have been known for several months before when it was spinning out of control.

To Jamey, Cooper looked like a real guy, not the caricature that he had become in the press. His days of fronting The Forgotten Avenue were over. He had earned his permanent place in the rock firmament. It was a question of *what does a guy do now?* Cooper was known for his deep, mellow, sexually provocative voice, and great A&R. Guys liked his tough sound. Girls loved his sound down to their souls, and they creamed for his eyes.

But Cooper's drinking, drugging, and partying picked up speed with the flop, and it was all in the public eye. Crazy Place had done two Forgotten Avenue numbers, and they had always gone over well. Jamey had been sorry about Cooper's slide.

Now Bryan Cooper took his place at the stool and the microphone, speaking with his deep clear manly voice. "If you came out tonight to hear The Forgotten Avenue, you're living in the past, man. No such thing. And if you came to hear psychedelic bullshit, which the record company guys say you didn't, sorry to disappoint you. That bullshit is over." Even his speaking voice was magical. "Come on out here, guys!"

"Guys," Jamey remarked. Mona had a point.

He called his back-up band onto the stage: A guitarist, a drummer, and, on keyboard, Jamey recognized the long bearded Mike Carl. Jamey was thrilled to be on the scene. Bryan Cooper was making his come-back play, and Jamey Craig was on hand.

"Now, listen up, people. This isn't a concert. It's a rehearsal. Me and the band have been putting together some music the last month or so. We want to try out some material and we thought some of you might like to hear it. Check it out, man."

He hadn't sung a note, and Cooper had already established that his voice was still strong and compelling. As the rehearsal opened, it had an informal, relaxed feel—nothing like the frantic high pitched concert performance The Forgotten Avenue had generated or the overblown psychedelic sound he had been fronting. If it had been a standard concert, they would have opened with "The Brick Layer's Son" but they were not playing The Forgotten Avenue's set. It wasn't exactly new either. Cooper had gone back to his beginnings as a blues-rock interpreter. And, of course, he knew how to put it out for the chicks.

They went through a blues based set that didn't feature very much of the music that had made Cooper famous. They were doing some covers, including "Break on Through," "Gloria" and "House of the Rising Sun." There had been rumors going around that Cooper's voice was shot, but not tonight. He was theatrical because he was Cooper, but not to the extreme. His penis was not once presented during the program, and he didn't even drink water. He sometimes took to shaking the maracas. More often he would play mouth organ, and, on several occasions, though the audience didn't know what he was looking toward, Jamey felt Bryan Cooper's eyes all over his body. He seemed to indicate that *she* could make him feel all right. But it was all Cinderella. Jamey couldn't show his true colors.

It wasn't hard to understand why the chicks loved Cooper. He had fairly charmed the pants off of Jamey who crossed and re-crossed his legs several times trying, in vain, to seem unaffected. As with Rick, he was feeling a mixture of shame and excitement. He didn't want to put any limits on himself, but he couldn't show too much of himself and still keep the illusion going.

It was getting warm here, and Jamey was forty feet away. Cooper was magnetic that night, maybe because he was more vulnerable and less of the superstar and exhibitionist that he had recently been. Rick worked throughout the show, occasionally going back to his photography boxes for film, for lights, for lenses, for cameras. He seemed hardly to notice Jamey when he was working. Jamey was feeling ignored by Rick, but there was some balance as a number of guys, including Cooper, were expressing some interest in the new chick.

After the show, Rick went up to Cooper and they did a few "Hey, mans!" From across the stage, Jamey could see that both men were looking to where Jamey was sitting, legs crossed, glued to the chair. He never knew what they said, but they were both laughing. He assumed it had been crude. He blushed anyway. Many people were now milling on the stage, and he lost sight of both Rick and Bryan. When he was able to see the stool again, he perceived that the star was no longer on the scene.

Rick was putting his gear away and packing up. Jamey took a couple of the cases with handles and followed Rick across the stage to the stage door. Jamey cried out in surprise when he felt his ass being intimately explored. Jamey first paused, his heart stopping, and then he turned and found himself surrounded by Cooper's arms. There was no stage light between them now. "How'd you like the show, little girl?" It was really a gorgeous voice. And he smelled quite manly having just done the show. He was beautiful, a true Olympian of rock and roll. Jamey just stared at him dumbly. "What are you doing tonight?" Cooper pressed it. It sounded to Jamey like an invitation. Rick had turned around and come back for Jamey, pulling him away. "Later, Bryan."

"Rick." Jamey looked back at Bryan Cooper who smiled and wet his lips with his tongue. Just as Jamey was pulling himself together to face Rick, Cooper was joined by a tall woman with long blond hair. It looked to be Katy Mondy, and she took Cooper by the arm, giving a quick look across the stage to Jamey who was just disappearing.

When they were alone in the alley, having loaded up the trunk, Rick slapped Jamey across his pretty face. It hurt, and Jamey was stunned.

"What the fuck are you doing?" said Rick who apparently tripped out very easily. Jamey cried, but only for a moment. Rick didn't seem interested.

Soon they were back in the taxi retracing their way. The car went up Laurel, so Jamey assumed that it was time to go home, and probably to bed, the moment of truth.

"Was that really Katy Mondy?" asked Jamey.

"She's a slut," he said. "Like you. I had her. Twice."

The car sped past the turn-off for Rick's house. Jamey tried to talk about his excitement at having seen the rehearsal show, but Rick was not in the mood. Rick had put some distance between himself and Jamey now.

They were soon descending into Studio City. Once the night driver turned north onto Hollywood Way, Jamey determined that they were going to the Burbank airport. The taxi proceeded to a reserved area near a hangar for small planes and business jets. Jamey waited in the back seat while Rick made arrangements. He was borrowing a Learjet25 that belonged to Westerfield. When he signaled for Jamey to join him, the driver opened the taxi door, and Jamey emerged, a center of attention on the lighted tarmac. There were two multi-million dollar Learjets and a world-famous artist, but the eyes, even of the rich and powerful in the next jet, were on the appearance of a sixteen year-old runaway who played weekends in a bar band on the east end of Hollywood. The porters and the millionaires, of course, noted the short dress, the round bottom, and the well formed top. Jamey sensed the attention, but that only made him concentrate all the more on the task of walking in heels without falling over. To some eyes, it enhanced the picture as he appeared to be unable to walk and think at the same time. To complete the picture, the evening breeze had come up and Jamey was required to brush the back of his dress into place again and again, with each flurry causing the onlookers to hope that he would fail in taming the hem of the dress.

The discussion between Rick, the pilot, and the co-pilot was momentarily befuddled as Jamey approached the three men gathered at the base of the short boarding stairs leading up to the cabin. Taking Molly's advice, Jamey said nothing. The best he could have managed was, "Far fucking out!" As he joined them, Rick put his arm around Jamey's shoulder at first, and then, apparently absently, he patted Jamey's bottom. Jamey felt shamed with Rick pawing him publicly, but, given his outfit, there wasn't any room for protest.

Rick dashed up the boarding steps. The pilot indicated that Jamey should follow. With a little care, Jamey was able to prevent bottom exposure, smoothing his dress behind as he entered the cabin. The pilots came on board and went into the cockpit and closed the thin door between it and the main cabin, which had a configuration of beige leather seats, a small table, and a couch against the cabin wall that could accommodate two more notables or perhaps a romantic tryst. The floors were carpeted and there appeared to be a number of compartments, one of which served as a bar which Rick was getting into as the pilots were checking out the systems. He poured a bourbon and soda for himself and for Jamey.

They were belted into the table seats for the smooth take-off. They were soon aloft in the Tuesday night sky, northbound, quickly leaving the basket of jewels of the Valley floor behind. Jamey, who had never flown, was looking out the cabin windows and trying to identify landmarks. The country below was indistinguishable in the night. Rick was taking his drink slowly, and Jamey was now and then returning to his own. Rick moved to the couch and motioned for Jamey to join him, putting his drink in a holder. They did some Maryjane in the clouds.

"I can't believe you know Bryan Cooper," said Jamey.

"It's my job," said Rick, seeming to be speaking conversationally to Jamey for the first time tonight.

"I got a job at the carwash," said Jamey. "But I didn't know Bryan Cooper. Thanks for taking me to the show. I can't believe I saw him like that. That's so far out. Not that anyone would believe the story, but who cares? He was really good. His voice is right back where it was."

"He liked you," said Rick.

"He liked what he saw, but he didn't see everything," said Jamey. "I'm a put-together girl." Jamey's legs crossed and the dress rode up on the thighs.

"You were flirting with him," said Rick. "You've been a chick for a month, and you're already two-timing." Was he actually angry that Cooper had mistakenly given him the eye?

"What was I supposed to do?" said Jamey. "I would have done whatever you wanted, if I knew. You said to stay in the chair. I never touched him, even when he grabbed me. I just stood there. I don't think I smiled at him."

"He fucked you with his eyes!" yelled Rick. "And you fucked him right back." Rick's hands were clenched in anger. This was unexpected turbulence. There seemed to be a lot of anger when it came to pretty young runaways. Jamey thought of Officer Tanquerson, and went on a campaign to calm things down.

"I'm sorry, Rick," he said, putting out his hands, but not touching Rick. "I'm sorry. I was into the music, but that's it."

"You're a lying slut," Rick remarked. "You would have done him."

"I'm a dude. He likes girls," said Jamey.

"You don't know Bryan," said Rick. "He would do you either way. Well, you are a pretty little piece." Jamey took that as a compliment and as a sign that the storm was passing. Rick readjusted, settling his head on Jamey's lap. This was unexpected, but what wasn't? Unsure of himself, he caressed Rick's unshaven face and long hair with his hand, guessing that he should. Rick closed his eyes, and perhaps smiled. As the jet cruised, Rick loosened his own shirt, dropping another button, exposing his chest. Jamey took it as an invitation. Soothing the savage breast with a gentle touch. Just as he had tried to subtly go for Teri Ann's tits, as if she wouldn't notice, his hand was soon feeling up Rick's chest hair. In this manner they traversed the night sky. Jamey was slipping into a peaceful reverie when he noticed that Rick was now opening his pants.

"Oh, my goodness!" said Jamey. Rick pulled Jamey's face toward his own, and they kissed. "Far fuckin' out!" Jamey said, as their lips disengaged. Rick had a definite and insistent idea. As the jet eventually began its descent at San Bruno, Jamey was using what he had learned from his various experiences and Molly's advice. He had the use of his hands this time and he wasn't afraid of being found out. It wasn't smooth, quick, or easy, but Jamey was dedicated. A more experienced *girl* might have brought it off more quickly and more sweetly, but Rick was satisfied exploding in Jamey's mouth and on his face.

IF YOU'RE GOING TO SAN FRANCISCO

IN THE RESTROOM at the little airport, Jamey stopped to collect himself and fix his face. He looked at himself in the girls' room mirror. Bizarre! With the taste of Rick still in his mouth, as he cleaned his face, Jamey remembered flashing on seeing five naked girls in the first week of running away and thinking that he certainly would have run away sooner if he had known about that aspect of being on his own. Since then, of course, he had lived rather intimately with Mona and had spent many a night watching the stage at The Contortionist. But now he was realizing that, since running away, he had now sucked a total of three different dicks. Not too much in the way of bragging rights there, he figured.

Rick picked up a car and drove it into the city. He pulled into the parking garage at the St. Francis in the late hours. Assuming that the moment of truth was upon him, taking Molly's advice, Jamey retreated to the bathroom with his things. Jamey discovered that Molly, who had done such a careful job with everything else, had not included any lubricants on the packing list. That seemed intentionally bitchy.

Rick was in the bed, naked as it turned out, smoking another joint, when Jamey returned from the bathroom in his nighty. He tried not to show his fear. He joined Rick in bed, reaching for the joint. Rick, who took a major toke, supercharged Jamey, exhaling the pot into his lungs during a kiss. When the joint was put aside, Rick began to make love to Jamey, kissing his face and feeling his bottom. Jamey was telling himself over and over to just let go. Just be the girl. Be whatever Rick wanted. It was all very new to Jamey being treated this way. Rick seemed to like that he was a boy, judging from his touches.

Then there was a knocking at the door. Jamey froze as if Teri Ann's parents had just shown up during a make-out session. It was the hotel. Rick had called down for some wine and Italian bread. Jamey pulled up the sheet and Rick put on his robe and quickly completed the transaction. Then Rick poured a glass of wine for each. Jamey, at sixteen, was getting more alcohol than he was used to. This wasn't Teri Ann's Gallo Pink Chablis, and both of them were tired anyway. Rick had blown his top in the plane, had had plenty to drink, was well stoned, and he had put in a night's work.

They had their wine and did a joint. Things had become mellower now. "Why were you so mean to me?" asked Jamey. "Why were you so quiet and distant? And you hit me!"

"You're mine," Rick declared. "So don't ask stupid questions."

Jamey reflected. "But you're not mad at me, are you? You were just fucking with me!" he complained. "Because you can."

"That's what you're here for, girl," said Rick, who began to spank Jamey until his cheeks turned as pink as he was feeling. Jamey squealed a little and wiggled appropriately, but he didn't really want Rick to stop. It made him feel wonderfully helpless in Rick's hold. At the same time, it was threatening. He knew that Rick was going to take him from behind, sooner or later. But Rick eventually fell asleep atop his youthful sweetheart. Jamey, who was being crushed, was able to quietly slip out from under Rick and fall asleep beside him. Given the pot and the alcohol on both sides, they slept well into the morning.

When Jamey came around in the morning, it took only a few seconds to recall that he was in a San Francisco hotel with a man who liked boys. And there wasn't much doubt about who the boy was. Two months before, this was unimaginable. Jamey had no sense of the time of day. Time was a Squaresville concept anyway. He hesitated to open his eyes. He realized that he was ass-up without any bedding covering him. As best as he could recall, he hadn't gone to sleep that way. He slowly realized that Rick was not in the bed. Jamey turned over, pulled up the sheet, and looked around the room. Tumbler in hand, standing naked by a sunny crack in the curtains, stood Jamey's big, strong boyfriend.

"I must look awful!" Jamey said. As it came out, he wondered where such things came from. Your average guy didn't think that first thing in the morning, but your average guy wasn't wearing a negligee and stale perfume.

"Not from behind," said Rick. "Very pretty, even in your sleep."

"I'll go get fixed up," said Jamey, getting out of bed. He reconsidered, and turned back to Rick. "I mean, if you think I should. Whatever you want. Your dime, right? Well, let me go in there anyway…" Jamey dashed to the bathroom.

When he returned, Rick met him at the bedside. Jamey was compliant. He tried not to look. He didn't want to show any attraction to the naked man in front of him. Rick's skin was darker than Jamey's. From Jamey's perspective, sixteen and hairless, Rick seemed to have a lot of hair, front and back, with a little gray coming in here and there, even at the temples. His long dark hair draped his shoulders, and his body was more muscular than Jamey had expected. His biceps, his pectorals, his abdomen, and his quads were all defined—not to an excessive degree, but clearly defined. If you were going to have a boyfriend, Rick was good looking, rich, connected, and artistic. And he was apparently well hung. His cock, even at rest, was hanging tautly between his legs. He drank quite a bit and liked to do drugs, Jamey was learning, but that was what grown-ups did. Even his dad drank as much and as often as practical.

"Go ahead," said Rick. "You're obviously a slut. Go ahead and touch it if you want."

"Mind games?" said Jamey.

"Touch it!" he commanded sharply. Jamey did, with both hands gently stimulating Rick. "Six weeks ago, you were running for your life. Now you can't take your eyes—or your fingers—away."

"You're kind of naked," said Jamey. "I mean, who wouldn't notice?"

"A guy knows if he's queer or not," said Rick. He reached out and pulled Jamey to him, Jamey's head buried in Rick's chest, Rick's hand on Jamey's ass, under the nighty. Rick's exposed physique suggested that Rick could have taken Jamey that first night with minimal effort. "Don't worry, little girl." That's what Bryan Cooper had called him. Had Cooper known who he really was?

Up until the fourth of July, any admonishment from the old man was unacceptable, an affront to his manhood. Now, he was a different girl. Jamey sat on the bed next to Rick, and Rick put his arm around Jamey's shoulder, letting him nuzzle in his chest. Jamey was studying Rick closely. It flashed on Jamey that Rick and his own dad were about the same age. He was the girlfriend of his father's contemporary. In Jamey's mind, there was really no comparison between Jim Craig and Richard Altier, but they were of the same generation.

Rick had meant to get going early that morning, but Jamey caused him to be late. He seemed to have grasped what Rick liked. He had a handle on it, so to speak. Rick found a use for the extra olive oil from the bread plate, and Jamey soon found himself in a most compromising position on the side of the bed with the naked and aroused Rick behind him.

Instead of hurting, as he had imagined, as he had dreaded, it was a surprising pleasure. The moans of anxiety and then of pain had changed now to gasps and squeals of excitement and release. Jamey didn't want it to end, and it didn't end quickly. When Rick had reached his climax and release, Jamey felt him beginning to slowly withdraw.

"Please stay," he cried. "Just stay for a moment. Please…" He had liked the way Molly had said that to him. It had made him feel manly, and he was playing the part for Rick. That, in part, and he didn't want Rick to go.

"You like that?" suggested Rick.

"Just stay. Don't move."

Rick remained with Jamey for enough time to bring his heart rate back down. When Rick did pull out of Jamey, bestowing a final crack against his naked ass, they were both exhausted. Rick rested on his back beside Jamey who was still face down on the bed. He turned his head to face Rick. "Oh, my goodness!" said Jamey, still breathless. "Far fuckin' out, man! I never knew it was like that. Oh, my goodness!"

"I said you were a slut," said Rick. "I can pick out a slut from a crowd."

"Oh, my goodness me!" And they fell back into sleep.

Season of the Witch

LET'S GET TOGETHER

JAMEY COULD HEAR THE SHOWER RUNNING, but he could barely move. He could smell and taste Rick, which he didn't mind. His muscles were tight. His abdomen was sore. His inner thighs had been stretched. He hadn't been physically prepared to have his body used like that. He eventually turned onto his side, but that was as far as he had made it by the time Rick returned, dressed in his street clothes. It being San Francisco, he put on a leather jacket.

"Where are you going?" Jamey murmured.

"Listen, I'm going out today. I have to go down to Daley City to check out the venue. It's pretty dull stuff." Rick tore off another hunk of the bread which he dipped into the garlic and vinegar sauce.

Jamey suddenly came awake. "You want me to wait here?" It didn't sound bad to Jamey. He had been going pretty strong.

Rick pulled out a handful of his money and threw five twenty dollar bills onto the bed. "I'll be back for dinner. Why don't you go sight-seeing, if you like? Have you been to the city?"

"No," said Jamey. "Where's Haight-Ashbury? Where's the park? Where's Winterland?" These were the places of hippie legend, and Jamey wanted to see them.

"Ask that queer down at the desk," said Rick. "I'll see you later."

"Kiss?" said Jamey, climbing onto his knees on the bed. Rick bent over the bed as if to kiss *her*, but took a very powerful whack at his bottom instead. He squealed. It would likely stay red for some time to come.

"You're leaking," he said. "You should take a bath, anyway. Wash that stuff out. What were you thinking? Buy something."

Jamey was about to say that Molly…but Rick was going by then. After he left, Jamey took a long thorough bath. Skipping the shaping foundation of the day before, at least in the lower regions, Jamey wore a red-orange short dress with thin white stripes bordered in black. It covered the brassiere and shoulders but left the arms bare while exposing his legs slightly higher than midway up the thigh. He wore a necklace of lapis lazuli baroque beads which paralleled the scoop of the dress. Sandals and a straw hat with a flat top and a wide round brim made it all the more now. He hid

204

most of Rick's money in his personal handbag along with the fifty-seven he had salvaged from Mona. He put twenty in his mod fashion purse for traveling and lunch.

He descended to the lobby and located the concierge desk. This was a nice looking young man, Craig, in a dark suit. He offered his services matter-of-factly, but he was apparently disinterested until he took a second look at Jamey. "Sir," he said, "How can I help you?"

"Sir?" said Jamey.

"Whatever you prefer," he replied. "You look great, Miss!"

"What was the give-away?"

"I was here last night. I saw you check in. I always notice the celebrity parties. Your figure has changed, for one thing. No more hips." He looked at Jamey again. "And the tits aren't right. Nice work, but I can see through it. But, ninety percent of the time, people see what they expect to see. They're not looking for anything out of the ordinary. Anyway, I'm sort of an expert, if you know what I mean. Love the lapis."

"Well, please don't tell anyone…" said Jamey. "I mean, my boyfriend knows, of course. But I don't want to draw attention." He looked from her hemline and back to her eyes. "I mean, I don't want to blow my cover."

"Discretion, my dear. Not to worry," Craig assured him.

Craig tried to dissuade Jamey from taking the public transportation. It was obvious that Jamey had no sense of the city. He opened a map and tried to orient the traveler. Now, armed with some understanding of his whereabouts, Jamey put the map into his silvery but semi-transparent acrylic-linked bag, the coolest thing in the store. Molly had been thrilled with it. Jamey was glad to have something more to put in it. He didn't carry much. The whole thing seemed an artifice, but he slung the bag over his shoulder and stepped bravely out into the bright July Frisco morning. He proceeded along the busy pedestrian streets toward Market.

Jamey wasn't sure that this expedition would be successful. He had expected that his bottom would be terribly sore and in pain, and that he might be unable to walk about in comfort. But, though there was the definite feeling that Rick had been there, there was no pain or discomfort associated with the affair of the morning. He thought it a peculiar matter to be concerned about, but it turned out to be a tempest in a teapot, so to speak.

Before reaching the streetcar line, he stopped at Zims. Where else? For breakfast. He hadn't eaten much the night before. There was still some Italian bread in the morning, but something about the olive oil made it seem less appetizing. He had a burger and a Coke in lieu of coffee. He was attracting attention, almost expected it by now, but he didn't have any encounters. He was learning to be more aloof. Or maybe, he flashed, he wasn't that pretty today. So sensitive!

Following the instructions, he rode the streetcar along Market until it turned by the Civic Center and eventually proceeded along McAllister toward the park. He did attract attention on the streetcar, but it was early afternoon and relatively safe. He kept his knees together and his eyes away from the onlookers.

When he realized that he had missed his mark, he got off. He crossed over to Fulton and walked along the edge of the park. He used the map to reorient and to guide him on his quest for the well-spring of hippiedom, the corner of Haight and Ashbury, where he may have been hoping for a psychedelic fountain to be pumping far out three-dimensional paisleys. Along the way, he did find Stanyan Street, and several other sorrows seemed to be hanging about. The neighborhood wasn't all that appetizing, but there was a lot of hippie action, including a whiff of marijuana in the air. Hippies yet abounded in great numbers, but Jamey didn't connect with the magic. He didn't feel the love that was all around.

When he found his destination, there wasn't much to it. He was thinking that Rick would have known where to go for the cool scene. He had probably photographed the place during the Summer of Love and also for the Moratorium. He had no reason to think that, but Rick seemed to know everyone and to have been everywhere, making Jamey wonder why he wasted time with him, other than his ass. Then he realized that there didn't have to be anything other than his ass. He was Rick's piece of ass for this week, and not a thing more.

THIS UNPLEASANT REVERIE was shaken when, most unexpectedly, Jamey was roughly jostled on the street, turned around by the jolt, and taken completely by surprise when the shoulder bag was ripped from his arm. The thug, who looked like a hippie but who apparently lacked the necessary love, pushed Jamey to the ground and ran around the corner, purse in hand, along Ashbury, across the street, and then up Page, away from the park. Sitting on the floor at Haight and Ashbury, the short dress had exposed his intimate fashion, though not to the extent that his physical gender was obvious. But it was the thought that counted, and several gentlemen were helping *the lady* off of the pavement and even going to the trouble of smoothing her dress in various sensitive places.

"Wow, man!" said one brown-haired fellow with long locks. "Bummer! Are you all right, man? We saw the whole thing go by in a flash!"

"I'm all right, man. But he stole my purse," replied Jamey, not unfamiliar with the dialect.

"Uncool!" said a second hippie, one with similar brown hair, but a beard besides, picking up her hat and handing it to her. "Like where are the pigs when the people actually need them?" Jamey replaced the hat.

"Right on!" said a third, who was about Jamey's height. He had a fairly clear complexion, thin pretty brown hair, and blue eyes. Jamey flashed that this one could pass for a chick, if he were inclined. Jamey was already figuring on what it would take to make it work. Not that much.

"Hey, man! Your shoulder's like bleeding, man," said the first, who Jamey thought of as the King of the Hippies. It had been scratched by the chain on the bag.

"Bummer!" said the bearded philosopher, also noticing a scratch on her knee.

"It's cool," said Jamey, looking at the cut as best he could through the corner of his eye.

"My old lady can take care of that, man," said the first hippie.

"It's cool," said Jamey. "It's just kind of weird. That was a really expensive bag. I mean, it was worth ten times what was in it. Do you think the guy knows? I hate for him to grab the money and then toss it."

"I'm not into material stuff, man," said his majesty. "How much bread are we talking about?"

"Only like twenty bucks or something in the purse," said Jamey, the "only" sounding a little on the elitist side.

"Twenty bucks is pretty handy around here, man," said the shorter fellow. "I'm Danny. The guy with the beard is John. And that's Sky. We're The Trousers!"

Jamey busted up on the spot. "Grrreat name! I'm Jamey. I'm a musician, too. I play bass and guitar. I'm in a group called Maiden Head. We play at a naked lady bar."

"That's so cool," said Sky. "Listen, why don't you come over? The old lady can fix your cut. You can get cleaned up. And we can jam a little. Danny's the drummer. I play rhythm, and John plays lead. We have a bass sometimes, this guy in the neighborhood plays with us. We want to get a keyboard player. Come on. It's just over on Clayton, the next block over. You can call home, or whatever you want to do." Danny nodded his head, giving Jamey the OK.

Sky's old lady was Tawny who was tall and dark haired. She was hippied out in a very loose fitting granny dress and flat sandals. Unlike the trio of hippies, Jamey sensed that Tawny regarded him as a shallow refugee from Carnaby Street. It was one of those hallway style apartments, and decorated with blankets and pillows. There was a noticeable phallic drawing on the wall spurting out its product, which, on closer inspection, turned out to be the members of The Trousers. "Nice," said Jamey. "Album cover material."

Tawny cleaned the cuts, which really weren't so serious. She explained that band-aids would only keep the germs in. Band-aids were a conspiracy by Proctor and Gamble or Johnson and Johnson to achieve some rather unclear nefarious goal. Jamey insisted that it was cool; everything seemed to be.

Jamey was at the wooden kitchen table. Tawny was setting out the cups for the tea which was steeping in a pot on the table. Jamey was no speedball, but he eventually noticed that Tawny had quite the tummy, and you don't get that big on vegetarian dishes. "You're pregnant?" asked Jamey.

"Six months," she answered. Sky then held her from behind, putting his hands over her belly, making a charming picture for Jamey to take home. It struck Jamey that Mona, for all her illusions, could never make Jamey pregnant. He was just a pretty fake. Tawny was a woman.

While Tawny had been working on Jamey, Danny had been working at the table. He had been busy sorting some small squares of cut paper with blue dots on them into several envelopes. He had a lighted joint in his mouth as he was trying to put the papers away now that there was company. "Pour the tea, Danny," said Tawny, who was now chopping tomatoes on a cutting board by the sink. Danny put aside his papers, spilled the last envelope, collected its contents, and then poured the tea into cups for himself, for Jamey, and for Tawny. Danny took another hit and passed the J to Jamey. As he began to account for his paper squares, he realized that one was missing. He was next crawling on the floor under the table.

"Danny, that's pretty low," said Sky, coming into the kitchen. "You tryin' to look up her dress?"

Danny would have laughed, but he had real concerns. He announced that he had lost one of his little squares. "They're like two-fifty apiece retail, and a buck and a quarter wholesale. Fuck!" Even having sustained a loss, Danny contributed to his poor business practices by chewing on one of the little papers himself.

"I don't want that stuff on the floor," said Tawny. "The baby'll be crawling…"

"The baby won't be crawling for almost a year," said Sky. "I know we're hippies, but we sweep the kitchen more often than that."

In the end, the missing paper was never found on the table or on the floor. Jamey sipped the cup of lavender tea, and Danny finally put his stuff aside. "You've been so nice to take care of me like this," said Jamey. "I'm glad I met some cool heads up here as well as purse snatchers."

"When you say *up here*," asked Tawny. "Like where's *down there?*"

"I'm from L.A.," said Jamey. "I live in Hollywood. I flew up here last night. This is my first time in the city."

"Oh, no. L.A.?" said Tawny.

"It's not catching," said Sky, aware of and perhaps sharing the prejudice.

"Hollywood?" said Danny, intrigued. "I mean, like The Whiskey and shit. That's a trip. Do you ever get to see any L.A. bands?"

"I saw Bryan Cooper last night," said Jamey. "It was a rehearsal or audition or something at the Aquarius. And Mike Carl was in the band. And Katy Mondy was there, but she didn't sing or nothing. She was with Cooper. He was pretty good, not like the Psychedelic Curtain stuff. More of the old time blues. He did "Gloria." It was great stuff. Better band, too."

"You were at a Bryan Cooper rehearsal?" said Tawny, her suspicions showing. "You don't have to put it on around here, chick. Just be straight. It's ego, and that's the root of materialism. It's not about the stuff. Like a two hundred dollar purse? You could feed a lot of people on two hundred dollars. It's not about the scene that you're in. It's about who you are and what you're about."

"I said last night that nobody would believe it," said Jamey. "It's cool."

Tawny basically shut down on Jamey and went back to work. Danny was clearly still interested, even if her story stretched credulity. Sky seemed to have his doubts, but was obviously disinclined to contradict. There wasn't anything to be gained by it, and it takes all kinds to make a scene.

Danny had been thinking. "So, Hollywood, huh? Gazzarri's. Pandora's Box. Sounds like a cool scene, man."

"I don't know Pandora's Box," said Jamey. "You know The Contortionist? That's where we play. It's not famous. Naked lady bar."

"That sounds groovy!" said Danny. "Hey! Let's jam!" he announced. Everything he said seemed to be an announcement. Jamey finished the tea. "Thanks, Tawny. Good tea."

"It's cool," she answered, a bit of an echo.

"I can dig that," agreed Jamey. Now the three boys—and Jamey—went down to the basement that was somewhat soundproofed. When Jamey opened the case, he found a white Fender Jazz Bass with a red tortoise shell guard. "Pretty nice!" said Jamey.

"It's Hal's, but Hal works all the time," said Danny. Jamey strapped it on and plugged it in. Despite her neo-mod-a-go-go expensive plastic look, The Trousers discovered that she was surprisingly adept and funky with her instrument. She could tell that there was some recalculation as to *the girl* being just a poser from L.A. Danny had been crawling on the floor, checking some lines. He switched on the reel-to-reel deck and began recording the session. "In case we come into a groove we can use."

"It's cool," said Jamey, situating himself on a speaker box and trying out some bass lines on the unfamiliar instrument. The Trousers had a rowdy rag-tag sound. John played well and had a good tone. Sky's rhythm guitar and Danny's drums were not so tasteful or precise. They might not be able to keep up with Crazy Place, let alone Maiden Head. They started off jamming on "Who Do You Love?" Jamey's power lines were impressive and caught John's attention right away. He smiled at *her*, and Jamey sensed that John had been hungry for some musicianship. Jamey also felt John's eyes on *her* legs. He had perhaps never worked with such a lovely bass player.

John was singing the lead. They played the song through, including an extended jam and variant lyrics taken from other songs. It was loose, but Jamey was grooving on the low-key jamming. When they finished the tune, Jamey said that it had been a lot of fun, not commenting on the band's proficiency. He was not feeling himself, but that had been the case since he had started wearing dresses. He had sucked a dick several miles in the air and had been ass fucked this very morning. What the fuck was normal? Still, he was feeling a little on the queasy side. Quietly, in the interstitial hubbub, he mentioned to John, "Nice sounds, man!"

"You play a mean bass yourself," said John, smiling again. Jamey had seen the look, in Rick, in Chris, and in some imperfect strangers. John was smitten. Jamey had to admit that he himself could easily fall in love at the drop of, perhaps, a hat.

THE TRIP

"A CTUALLY, I CAN BARELY KEEP UP with my band, but they need a bass, so I'm lucky to be in the mix," said Jamey. "So what else do you guys do?"

"How about "Season of the Witch?" You know that?" suggested Danny.

"Duh?" Jamey replied, beginning to pump a bass line which was soon joined by John and Sky on the *fore-bó-ding* guitars, and then Danny. John urged Jamey to the microphone to sing the lead. He slipped from his perch and took the microphone.

Jamey's voice was practiced and haunting, and The Trousers were impressed. After the song, Sky suggested, "You wouldn't want to join The Trousers, would you? I mean, that's the sound, man."

"And the look," added Danny. "This is just what we need!"

"I'm sort of L.A. based," said Jamey. It had been a long shot for the lads.

"Let's do *Heroin*," said Danny.

"I don't do the heavy shit," said Jamey. Sky played the opening chord. "Oh!"

Replicating The Velvet Underground was right up The Trousers' alley. The Trousers liked to jam. The fourth piece was what Danny called a raga. There was no song, just a lot of jamming on a very simple theme with some George Harrison flavors, not well reproduced, but fun. By the time that was done, Jamey was distinctly uncomfortable. He wondered if he was going Linkletter on them.

"It's getting kind of weird around here, man," said Jamey. "That was some kind of tea," he said. John started in on some musical figures. He was quickly joined by Danny and Sky, and then by Jamey, who didn't know the song at all, but was following John's lead. John was singing something. The lyrics sounded a little T.S. Eliot mixed with Owsley, something about a transitive nightfall or diamonds or something which sounded to Jamey, in the moment, like a plan.

His legs were getting rubbery. The jam was getting stranger. And there was definitely a plethora of people to be. He pulled himself up and onto the peaker box where he seated himself, completely forgetting his lady-like responsibilities until he saw Danny's probing eyes. Mixed with the residual feelings from the morning, the vibration of the speaker on his ass was satisfying. But the colors of the basement walls began to melt and run onto the floor just like at the cove, and Jamey, never very quick, understood that he had been psychedelicized. When he looked over to Danny and saw him playing now with his eyes closed, a bright red face, and a shit eating grin on his face, she remembered something about the blotter paper on the kitchen table. Sky's rhythm guitar was slightly out of time and out of tune. Jamey was having a harder time of it. John was into the guitar groove, but he eventually broke a string, and that was the inconclusive conclusion to the session. Danny switched off the reel-to-reel as he got up from his drum kit.

"I think I found the missing paper," said Jamey. Danny seemed baffled at first, and then a light came over him. He laughed wildly, or so it seemed to Jamey. "Did you guys write that shit?" asked Jamey.

"It's the Dead," said Danny. "We've seen them whip it out a few times and we're trying to figure it out."

"Far out!" said Jamey. He barely put the instrument down without dropping it. He jumped down from the amp, caught by John who gathered that *she* was not stable. Jamey ascended the stairs in wobbly fashion, followed by John who seemed to be watching out for Jamey's safety.

Jamey was on the couch in the living room now, coming on in a rush. Jamey knew acid and its effects. This blotter was apparently very pure, of a high dosage, and an excellent style. He hadn't been expecting to fly, but Jamey could maintain. He had maintained in Miss LeAnn Curtis's English Lit class while blazing. His on-the-fly oral commentary on Rhyme of the Ancient Mariner had been somewhat difficult to apprehend, but he was clearly moved by the material. He always associated Green Barrel, a speedy little acid, with Wordsworth's "Lines Written in Early Spring." Who doesn't? *I heard a thousand blended notes…*But he suddenly flashed on his paranoia. He was in a strange hippie house, totally tripping out and feeling weird. Were these people cool? Were they what they seemed to be? "I don't know, man," said Jamey. "Like you guys have been cool, but maybe I should get out of your space, man."

Tawny could dig it, but John didn't agree at all. "I wouldn't do that just now," said John, looking into *her* dilated eyes. There was none of the green to be seen, just a big round black moon over each eye reflecting whoever was looking into them. John's voice was very gentle, musical, loving. Jamey trusted John and related to him, musically and personally.

Danny and Sky were coming up the stairs. The basement door was almost closed, but not tight. Jamey heard it like an echo. "I must be stoned, man! She was flashing the beav, and it looked like there was stuff in there. Like a dick or balls. That's a pretty heavy illusion, man."

"You're one sick fucker," said Sky. "You should definitely put down, man."

When they tumbled into the living room, Danny made another announcement. "We're going over to the park. Want to come?" He was asking anyone, but he was looking at Jamey's legs.

"Oh, no, man. I should be finding my way home..."

"I think you should just trip out for a while and enjoy the high, Jamey," said John, who took *her* by the hand and led Jamey to his bedroom, installing Jamey on the bed. It was a water bed, and Jamey had never experienced that feeling. The bed rocked and surged with every move, magnified by the opened doors of perception. Jamey turned over on the water bed to get his bearings, unwittingly exposing his bottom for John. "Is there any music you would like to get into? I could put something on for you."

Jamey always claimed that it was cool and said so again. John put *After Bathing at Baxter's* on the tune table because it was the right thing to do. And the sky, through the window casing, did appear to be green today. At the end of the side, which seemed to take several lifetimes and about five minutes, John tip-toed into the room to turn the album over. Jamey was now in a ball on the bed. Sky and Danny had split the scene, and Tawny was in the kitchen. John next tried The Doors. Jamey was heard laughing *her* head off during Morrison's rendition of "Back Door Man." It was, for Jamey, no longer just the little girls who understood.

Jamey had been noticing some attractive flavors in the air the whole time that she had been in John's room. He eventually raised himself from the water bed, no easy feat in his condition.

When *she* appeared in the doorway, *her* eyes met John's, and he was looking back to Jamey in love. Jamey could feel the difference. It wasn't only the tits and ass, the short dress, the cool style. John was trying to connect on a more profound level. "I have to get back," said Jamey. "Rick is kind of short tempered. What time is it?"

John had to go through some effort, but he ascertained that the time was just before five. Now Jamey was sure that Rick would be back at the hotel, and that he had to be there. He flashed on the slap at the theater the night before. It was suddenly very urgent. But he didn't know how to get there, and he didn't have any money with which to do it. John was willing to take Jamey, but he didn't have the fare for either of them. Neither John nor Jamey could begin to figure out how to solve the problem. As they were discussing the difficulty, Jamey began to cry in frustration, though there was certainly no call for it. Jamey sensed that John was about to give him a reassuring embrace, but, out of sheer exasperation, Tawny came into the living room. "What hotel are you at?"

"Saint...?" said Jamey.

"Saint Francis?" said John.

"I think so."

Tawny continued, "And there's somebody there, right? You want to reach somebody at the hotel to tell them you're all right, right?"

"Right," said Jamey. Tawny waited. Jamey realized the point. "Um... Rick the Perv."

"You want to ask for Rick the Perv?"

"No," said Jamey. "Richard. Richard Altier. He's my boyfriend, at least for a few days."

"Richard Altier?" said John. "The photographer?"

"You know him?" said Jamey.

Tawny, having gotten this far, said, most pointedly, "Then why don't you call the fucking hotel and tell him to get his ass over here?"

That sounded like a simple solution to an otherwise insurmountable problem. But Jamey wasn't able to handle the mechanics of the telephone. He went back into John's room and put himself down on the bed, the cold water rocking beneath him as he settled. The sounds of the waterbed were calming, drifting freely through time, if not space.

John followed into his room. "Jamey." He had a golden tone, a rich beautiful baritone, surprising for one so young, though he was a year or two older than Jamey. Jamey already knew he liked older guys. "Jamey," he repeated. "Do you want me to call Rick for you at the hotel? You don't have to, if it's a bad scene."

Tawny was just inside the door. "You have to call, John. She's totally insane. He might be terribly worried about her. It's not her choice when she's this far gone."

Jamey heard the conversation, more or less understood it, and even had the urge to clarify several points, but he was also grooving on the sound of John's voice, the Doors music, and the sound of the water. Then she heard John go through what seemed an impossibly complex operation that involved calling the information operator for the number of the hotel and then using that number to talk to the hotel which then rang him through to the room. Voice to voice across space. But then, why not? There had been people walking around on the Moon. It was a new and different world. But there had been those murders in the canyons, too.

John was functioning like a champion, but he got no reply in the room. He went on to talk to the desk leaving an urgent message for Richard Altier to call the hippie house as soon as he came in. It all seemed like a lot of effort. When John put the phone down by the side of the bed, he leaned back beside Jamey. Jamey was closer to John than two guys would have been, but Jamey didn't feel repulsed by John either. "You smell like a guy," Jamey observed, putting his face in John's chest for purely scientific purposes.

"I guess guys smell like guys," said John.

"I don't," said Jamey. "I smell like perfume and soap and shampoo and laundry and lipstick and," he giggled, "and olive oil."

"You do," said John, allowing himself to drink in those smells with the permission she seemed to provide. "You smell nice. I'm not getting the olive oil."

"It's all an illusion, you know," said Jamey. "We're not who we seem to be. We can play Ulysses, but that doesn't make me Jack Bruce, does it?"

"You don't have to be Jack Bruce or Jack Cassidy or anybody else. You have to do your own thing," said John. "Hippie 101. Do your own thing. You're not Jack Bruce. You're Jamey."

The phone sounded again, and John was suddenly up and talking again, a take-charge guy. He introduced himself and explained that Jamey was with him and that if he wanted to come and get her, John would provide the directions. John tried to maintain his good humor when he explained three times that Jamey could speak for herself when he arrived. He assured Rick that Jamey was safe. John fell back down with Jamey. They pulled themselves onto the middle of the bed, both staring up at the ceiling.

"Your boyfriend is coming for you," said John.

"He's not a boy," said Jamey. "He's like forty or something. That's not a boy, is it?"

"Aren't you kind of young for a guy like that? How old are you?"

"I could be his daughter, or his son," said Jamey. "I'm claiming to be eighteen. But I'm sixteen. But I'll be seventeen in the fall."

"You could be his daughter," said John. "But then where would we be?"

He meant the question in jest, but Jamey was perplexed by it.

Tawny popped her head into the room again, finding John and Jamey looking up at the beautiful infinite space of the textured ceiling. "Everything okay? Is someone coming for her?"

"He's on his way," said John.

"Probably for the best," said Tawny. "Let's not say where the acid came from." Tawny had been prepping and cooking all afternoon. "You two. Get yourselves up for dinner. I want Jamey to try it before he gets here."

Jamey suddenly realized what those ambient smells that had been developing through the later hours had been. Jamey couldn't remember the last time he had eaten. Had it been the Italian bread from late last night? That was a long time ago! He had no memory of Zim's.

At the wooden kitchen table, Tawny served Jamey, the three boys, and then herself. It was meatless spaghetti with mushrooms and tomato chunks and some very tasty seasonings. Jamey didn't do vegetarian, but under these circumstances of profound hunger, all in the imagination, and intense stoniness, which was real, he declared it the best meal that had ever been served at any time since hominids had developed the science of the fire. The garlic bread that Tawny served with it was, in Jamey's opinion, extraordinarily tasty, crunchy, and satisfying. He was highly complimentary to Tawny and he could sense that her distance was rapidly closing.

Now that Jamey was beyond the first rushes and now that his hunger was put to rest, he was beginning to come down a little and groove onto a mellower plane, one which allowed more interaction with human kind. Jamey, in close proximity, perceived that John was lonely, that he was reaching out to *her* in a most gentle and kind manner. Jamey knew that it was impossible, even not taking Rick into account. He had been deceiving John about who he really was, and it was unlikely that what John needed was a pussyless girl with a dick. It was a pretty shitty thing to do, but none of it had been done intentionally. Jamey had just fallen among them as Jamey *herself*.

Danny, having eaten and having gotten beyond the rush, was beginning to pay attention to Jamey again. It seemed pretty fake to Jamey next to the seemingly real affection of John. "So, when am I going to see you again, Jamey?" Danny asked.

"Do you guys ever get to L.A.?" he replied, collectivizing the question.

There was general agreement from Sky, John, and Tawny that such a thing was highly unlikely. "No, we don't get down there," said Sky.

"Oh, no…" said Tawny. "Bad vibes." The very suggestion was over the line, a breach of etiquette.

"Lotta good bands come out of LA, man," said Danny, obviously open to the idea.

Jamey was saying nice things like how glad *she* was to have met them and how sorry *she* was to have inadvertently taken Danny's acid in the tea.

"Do that in your room," Tawny scolded him. "You'll get acid into my cooking. I don't want my baby to have two heads."

Jamey, turning to John, said, "You got me through my trip, John. Thanks. I feel like Dorothy in Oz. I'm such a baby, like I never took acid before. I love the waterbed. It was kind of weird at first, but I want one. I don't know if it would work at Rooms-for-Rent."

"You should try it for getting it on," said Danny.

"You did it on my bed?" John complained.

"That chick from across the street," said Danny. "You weren't home." This exchange was interrupted by the signal from the buzzer on the porch.

"Okay," said Tawny, "That's probably your boyfriend."

"He's like forty," said Jamey. "He's not a boy at all. And I'm not…"

There was another insistent buzz. "And he's got a girlfriend your age? I think that's illegal," said Tawny, again disapproving, but Jamey realized that this time she was a mother hen protecting Jamey, not pecking at him. Obviously, Tawny was one conservative hippie chick. Probably the motherhood thing kicking in. One of these days she was likely to ban pot from the apartment. And that would be the end of the party, man. Wo!

There was a third buzz. John went to the sound box. "Hold up, there!" he called. "She'll be right down, man." He turned the switch off. "Jeez, Louise."

Jamey gathered *her* hat. "Am I forgetting anything? Oh! Silly me! No purse." Jamey was just leaving, saying a silent good-bye when he had a flash. He tried to unhook his lapis necklace and had John help *her* to unclasp it. Jamey could feel the closeness of John, inhaling *her* hair. He half expected John to take him in his arms. Taking the necklace, he wrapped it under Tawny's hair and hooked it in place for her. "I want you to have it, for being so nice to me." Jamey petted the six month bulge, feeling the excitement of life within. "You're so beautiful," said Jamey.

"Wow!" said Tawny. "It's not materialistic," she said, turning to Sky. "It's like natural stuff, and very artistic, too. Like real artists made it."

"It's cool," said Sky. Jamey shook Sky's hand, kissed the side of Danny's face, and gave John a long close hug with no daylight between them, if only for a moment in time. "Okay, Scarecrow. Gotta go now. Wizards and all." Then he was into the hallway, down the stairs, and out the front door where Rick was impatiently waiting.

He looked up at Rick's angry face. "My dad is like that," said Jamey. "He's always mad at me, like I fucked up. I guess I do fuck up. Sorry." Rick could see the big dilated eyes.

"I don't say that you fuck up," said Rick. "But you are majorly fucked up. You dropped acid?"

"It was an accident," said Jamey.

"Tell me in the car," said Rick. The hippies watched as Jamey climbed into the waiting taxi. Rick, looking tall and cool, followed Jamey into the back seat. Jamey could see the hippies in the lighted window above as the car pulled away toward the hotels across town. Jamey explained to Rick, as best as he could recall, that he had been touring the Haight all of a sunny afternoon when his purse had been stolen and he had been knocked to the ground only to be taken in by a tribe of hippies. Sort of Snow White and the Hippies. He told how he had inadvertently taken acid with his tea and had come on in a jam session. Which was more Alice in Wonderland.

"It was really a trip," said Jamey. "And good acid, by the way. But it was American. Not commie stuff, like some."

"I could have taken you to some cool spots," said Rick. "I know some people. You don't have to ride the streetcar."

"I knew you knew people," said Jamey, not as impressed by Rick's reach as he had been. "But I had fun. I lost the expensive purse and your blue necklace."

"Did you have sex with that hippie guy on the phone?"

"How can I?" said Jamey. "The minute he got into my pants, he'd find a dick. If I were really a chick, I mean with a pussy, who knows what I would have done? But I'm not a girl. I'm not a guy. I'm a freak. And you like freaks, so I'm your girl as long as you want me. And I know that that's not very long. You're probably tired of me already, having to come and find me. You're a busy big shot, and you don't have time for me."

Rick pulled Jamey closer. He put Jamey's head on his lap, stroking his hair and his face. The car made its way across town. Jamey felt good. He felt protected when Rick was nice, which was most of the time. He felt like he felt with Mona. Mona always took care of Jamey. Most of the time. "What happens after I go home?" asked Jamey.

"What do you mean?" he asked.

"When do I see you again?"

"Jamey," he started. "Our deal is just for a little while. A little while away from home. You know I love you."

"You love my ass," said Jamey.

"Oh, yes!" Rick agreed. "But you can be so incredibly credulous."

"Maybe so," said Jamey. "But I don't think you answered the question about what happens after. Or maybe you did."

ANGEL OF THE MORNING

AT THE HOTEL, Rick poured wine for Jamey. Rick was in and out, making some meetings with people in the industry from up north. He wanted Jamey to dress up again in full form. Due to the drug, he wasn't as effective as he might have been. The whole drag thing was feeling strange to Jamey, not because it was drag but because it was a lot of detail and he preferred to trip out and pass over the details. Mona had kept him together in Hollywood and Molly in the canyon. Jamey just wasn't that good of a girl in terms of the detail work.

He pulled on the long evening dress that showed off his bottom. The hotel salon, despite the hour, touched up Jamey's hair and makeup, so he was in good physical form even if his mind was still under the strong influence of LSD. Rick had given him twenty bucks for expenses, but Jamey made no profit on that, giving the girls all the tip money. Jamey, the student, had always maintained pretty well on LSD, and Jamey, Rick's girlfriend, did as well now that the rush had passed. He was never quite sure which person he was. The mirror always caught him off guard. But it made no sense to do anything differently now. He had been Rick's pussy, and he hadn't minded it at all.

When Jamey returned to the hotel room, Rick was impressed with his little doll. At first it was just appreciation, but Jamey knew the plans were about to change for the evening when the kissing turned to shoving and Jamey's face was against the door, and his dress was being raised. Turns out that Rick was telling the truth when he told Jamey that he liked *their* clothes. Jamey didn't resist the advances. He was Rick's girl-boy, whatever he desired, and he liked it when the desire came out. That was the best thing about living as a freak. He was the center of attention and attraction. He closed his eyes and waited for, secretly begged for the penetration.

But then Rick pulled back. Jamey had given himself over to his fate in Rick's hands. When it didn't happen, he felt let down, a feeling of emptiness and unfulfilled desire. He had to put a cork in the bottle until later, so to speak. "Get your sweater," said Rick.

"But…" He slipped to his knees.

"We have to go out," said Rick, turning away.

In the city night, they went to several club scenes, checking out the local bands, drinking, and Rick greeting familiar faces from various strata of the business. Jamey was seldom introduced, though from time to time he was required to shake hands or smile at strangers, some important and some less so. Jamey enjoyed the musical part of the parade most of all.

Rick was guiding him as he had that first time at Jack's, but there was no resistance on Jamey's part this time. He liked the feeling of Rick's hand on his ass from time to time, though the padding made it less intimate. Dashing from club to car, the night was cold on his ankles and the sheer covering on his legs. When he shivered, Rick held him tighter. It was romantic.

Jamey had never been a dancer, a junior high school wall flower, maybe too cool at the time, but it was 1969, and there was not much structure to the dance. He looked pretty on the floor, and, in drag, he was more confident than he had been as a dude. Sometimes, Rick would hold him on the dance floor. And when Rick kissed him on the dance floor, Jamey was in love all over again. Rick was a weirdo perv, but he showed his confidence in everything he did. It wasn't the plastic confidence that comes from the money and the prestige that he certainly possessed. It was the same courage and confidence that allowed him to earn the money and prestige in the first place. He really didn't seem to care what they thought. All the pretty people at the same party wherever it was were trying to impress him. Jamey's idea of the nightlife had been hanging out at a coffee shop until all hours, walking Teri Ann home, and then walking around into the wee hours with Craig Roman. This party, drinking, and drugging scene was out of his scope of understanding. Without Rick, someone might have gobbled him up, but, with Rick, he was the princess in the night. He generally maintained his cool throughout it all, trying hard not to annoy Rick. It felt to Jamey that Rick was in love with him. Could it be?

Rick was a busy guy, sometimes leaving Jamey to his own devices, smoking Tareytons and taking a little wine, standing about looking cute, grooving on the tunes, watching the people. One person who kept smiling across the room at him was a woman in a red gown with long blond hair. She looked like a speed freak, but an elegant speed freak.

When Jamey looked around, she was next to him. "Nice outfit," she said, shaking Jamey's acid reverie.

"Thanks," said Jamey. "Yours is pretty, too." He knew that it was appropriate to return a compliment.

"I spent enough," she replied. Jamey's fashions usually came from

Mona of Hollywood and cost wasn't an issue. This stuff from Rick's wallet was just a fantasy to Jamey, and no cost to him, other than his manhood, but that was long gone. "Your boyfriend takes good care of you." Jamey was a little uncomfortable now. It seemed pointedly personal, but to what purpose? He didn't know what to say, so he took another sip of the wine. "You dress up very well," she continued. "Nine out of ten wouldn't know you were in drag."

"Well, it's not any of their business, either," said Jamey.

"Maybe not," she replied. "But I *am* interested." The voice was sort of Anne Bancroft in The Graduate.

"Are you coming on?" asked Jamey.

"Should I?" she replied. "Any chance?"

"I don't think Rick would like it," said Jamey.

"The question is, how would you like it?"

Jamey was always confused on that point. Even in full drag, he always wanted Mona. He liked girls. Always had. Thought about Teri Ann. He wasn't done with girls at all, even if he was a freak. And this girl seemed rather sophisticated and stylish. But, of course, there was Rick somewhere nearby. This would never do.

"Meet me in the girls' room in about ten, sweetie," she whispered, kissing Jamey's ear as she said it. In a few minutes, *she* saw Rick slip into one of the rooms in the company of some big shot *she* didn't know. When ten minutes had elapsed, Jamey made the journey to the second floor bathroom. The door was closed, but not locked. "Come on in, sweetie."

Jamey slipped into the bathroom, and there was her new-found friend. He wasn't at all sure that he knew how this would work, but his cock was making every effort to break out of the tight panties. They fell into each other's arms and began to make out in earnest. Jamey was trying to take control like a guy would, reaching behind to undo the buttons on her dress.

She didn't fight him exactly, but she didn't give in to him either. She was being aggressive with Jamey, and she was a little bigger and a lot stronger. For the second time in the night, Jamey had his face shoved against a door and his dress being raised from behind. Jamey was not quick about the ways of the world, but it eventually hit him that his new pal was packing a cock which he was about to shove up Jamey's backside.

"No!" Jamey cried, trying to slip away.

"You little tease!" Jamey felt pressure on his back pinning him in place.

"You're the tease," said Jamey. "I was going to do you..."

Jamey felt him in his underwear while the hand on his back slipped up to Jamey's shoulder. And that's when Jamey took a bite out of his hand. Jamey bit hard until he was out of Jamey's pants and they were separated. "Now I'm getting out of here," said Jamey. He could hear his voice ascending as always in times of stress, but he was a girl now and it seemed more natural. "I've been to rape school. Fuck you, Jack!" Jamey straightened himself up and replaced his pants and his dress.

"Well, you don't have to get all bent out of shape," he replied. "Just a little sex."

They were sharing the mirror as they both fixed themselves up. Jamey caught the other fellow's eye. And then they both started laughing. "It's weird, man…girl…whatever the fuck," said Jamey.

"Right. Like Paul McCartney thinks it's strange that the banker doesn't wear a Mac in the pouring rain."

"Really," said Jamey. "If that were the strangest shit going down, you know. Fuck. There's weirder shit than that." They were both laughing now, touching up their lipstick and rouge.

"Let me get that," said Jamey's new friend, doing Jamey's eyes.

"Thanks," said Jamey. "I'm Jamey."

"Patty," he replied. "Sorry about that. I thought you might want me to slip it to you."

"It's not that I don't," said Jamey. "But. You know. My boyfriend. I could do your ass."

"You're too dangerous," she replied. Jamey kissed Patty's hand where he had bitten it.

"I have to get back," said Jamey. And they parted at the door that took them back to the party.

Patty winked at Jamey as Rick escorted him out of the party. They stopped for a late supper at Zim's where Jamey experienced some way serious déjà vu, and then back to the hotel, and to bed. Jamey had to adjust his point of view back to his feminine side. It wasn't difficult to do. Whether Rick was in love or not, Jamey was. They fell asleep entwined, Rick breathing on his ear. Jamey liked it.

In the morning, there was a light breakfast with orange juice and vitamins to replenish and refresh Jamey after the inadvertent LSD sojourn. He thought about the Patty incident. The thing that made it all possible was that Patty had known his secret from the start, just as Rick knew all about him. Jamey could be himself, and that was when he had the most confidence and pleasure in his girlhood. He wasn't hiding who he was. He was enjoying it.

Rick rented a car, and they set out together over the bridge into Marin. They drove for maybe an hour and followed the roads to a little ranch in Larkspur which was, like the jet, the property of someone else. Rick had money, but he had a lot of friends and relationships to augment the lifestyle. It was a very elegant place in a beautiful setting. Though there was lots of greenery, there wasn't anything natural about it with its expansive manicured lawns and the gardens down the hill. Even in July, the lawns were green, at least for several hundred feet around the house at the top of the slope. They walked the grounds, Rick, with his camera slung over his shoulder. It was a beautiful and isolated setting, with a charming little stream that ran through the property. Jamey kicked off his sandals and walked in the water which soaked the bottom of his jeans. They looked at the plants and flowers, and Rick arranged flowers in Jamey's hair, taking photos just for fun, as he said. It was all very calm after the busy day and night before, a good place to recover from the trip. Rick took photos of Jamey in his jeans and peasant shirt. Jamey now liked to pose and was getting better. "My solo album!" he said. "After the band makes it big time." He posed, sometimes trying to express sexuality, sometimes expressing the innocence of the love generation.

"Lose the shirt and the bra." Rick spoke with authority, as if he knew what he wanted.

Jamey looked at him. "You don't want to shoot my real tits," Jamey protested, used to the packaging.

"Models don't talk, Jamey," said Rick. Jamey had seen Rick in this mode. He had his *artistic* vision going. When he was working, when he was creating, the model ceased to be a person. It didn't make Jamey feel good, but he knew how it worked. He dropped the shirt. He turned around for Rick to unsnap the bra which followed to the grass.

"I'll be back," said Rick, running toward the house. "Hey! May as well lose the jeans as well." After removing them, Jamey was standing in the middle of a gorgeous lawn that seemed to go on forever appareled in his pink underpants. There was a road with traffic in the far distance, but, most likely, the drivers could see Jamey no better than Jamey could see the drivers.

Rick had been gone for a long time. In the meanwhile, Jamey had been sprawled on the grass, a flower waiting to be picked. He felt the sun on his almost naked body, the breeze kissing him, and he stretched out looking up at the sky. Despite it all, life was gorgeously beautiful. His heart was filled with it. He felt a very fortunate hippie to be thus placed in time and space. It wasn't the acid. That was gone. He wasn't particularly high. It was just a moment in the sunlight, a part of it all.

He opened his eyes when he heard Rick's voice. "I knew they had this, but I couldn't find it at first," Rick was saying as he descended from the house across the grass, approaching Jamey and carrying a long rounded silvery polished piece of metal which was, in fact, a hood ornament from an old Hudson. He had also brought along a second camera. Rick had Jamey up again. He arranged Jamey's hair and had him hold the ornament to catch the sunlight.

"I'm sorry to speak," said Jamey, realizing his place, "But my stuff shows through the pants, doesn't it? I could put it away, if you want."

"It's not enough to impress anyone," said Rick. "I'm not shooting your stuff anyway. I just took off your jeans because I like boys without pants." He patted Jamey's pink backside, but Jamey felt a stab to the heart. Rick could have just said, 'I like *you* without pants.' Why bring the other boys into it? But, who's to say it wasn't done on purpose? Jamey's face was less giddy after that remark, more serious, more thoughtful, more vulnerable.

"This thing looks kind of phallic, doesn't it?" said Jamey.

"Go for it, if you want to," said Rick. "Meanwhile, shut up and be beautiful. That's why God made you." For about twenty minutes, Rick took shots of the bare-chested Jamey holding the Hudson hood ornament. "I got enough," was all the thanks.

"Shall I dress?"

Rick looked at Jamey now, not the model. "I don't think so," said Rick. There was an intention in his eye. The next thing, he was chasing Jamey across the lawn and the grounds. Jamey was giggling, being the object of the chase, and Rick was just a little winded these days. "When I catch you, you little tease..." Tearing around the corner of the house, Jamey ran squealing across a patio, almost crashing into a glass table, when he suddenly stopped. There was a gardener who had turned from the bush he was trimming to see Jamey, who didn't know what to do.

"Whoops," said Jamey, the laughter leaving him now.

"Excuse me," said the gardener, struggling for the appropriate English. He was a brown skinned short older gentleman with a nice smile and quick eyes. Jamey had no rejoinder, but Rick came running up behind in the next instant. He put on his dominant power face.

"Get your clothes, Jamey," said Rick. "Go around the front. I'll let you in." Jamey withdrew, embarrassed, red toned, and rather exposed. He walked quickly, no longer running like a nymph, and found his clothes on the lawn. He replaced his things and, carrying the car ornament, walked up to the front of the house where he was soon joined by Rick. He gave the *object d'art* to Rick, who took it inside. "I didn't tell you to put them on," said Rick, taking *her* by the hand up to a bedroom where they spent the next hour.

ONCE THEY HAD LEFT the grounds and returned to the public road, Jamey began to laugh.

"I don't think he expected that!" said Rick. "Pretty nasty blow to his psyche. A guy could go many many years and never have to see anything like that." He went on. "You're very beautiful. An angelic apparition! He was lucky to have been there." Jamey blushed sweetly.

Jamey had confidence problems, and he was grateful to hear compliments from Rick. Crossing the bridge, Jamey asked, "So why don't you want to see me after this? You said I'm beautiful. The sex is wonderful, at least for me."

Rick shook his head, almost incredulous. "You really are a girl sometimes," he said. "But, okay. I don't want to get that serious, Jamey, because what I love about you is very fleeting." He touched Jamey's face as he drove. "You'll need to shave in a few hours, just to maintain the illusion."

"But they have electric stuff now. Mona told me about it. You can afford that for me."

"Electrolysis," said Rick. "But, it's also the innocence of your age. As you get older, you'll have expectations. You're only sixteen. Your little brain will grow. It can't be helped."

"I'm not very smart," said Jamey. "My dad says I'm an idiot asshole. You should see my report card. Even Miss Curtis gives me D's, and she likes me."

"If I were still in love with my first he-she, he'd be a hundred by now. But, I like boys, not men. It's Peter Pan. You'll grow up. In a year or less, you won't be the Jamey I love. Maybe in a month. That's actually good for you, for you to grow up and be the person you're meant to be. You shouldn't get all hung up on me. And it's bad for me because I *will* miss you. I don't make a big deal out of it, but I really will miss you, Jamey. I know it, because I miss a lot of them. Not all, mind you. Some are just pretty little asses. But I like many of them. Do you understand that?"

Jamey thought about it and answered honestly, "Not really. I don't get any of it. I don't know why a man likes boys. I don't know why they have to be boys, and they can't grow up. And I don't know why I like it now when you kiss me and fuck me, and all of it. I don't understand that. I feel like a girl, as if I know what a girl feels. But even before, when I was with Mona, I don't understand why I turned into a girl in the first place. See? I don't understand any of it. Only that you don't want to keep me around. I mean, I get it. I get that. I won't be a problem." Jamey then added, "But won't you want someone to take care of you?"

"I have Zulema for most things. Molly for the others. And, every now and again, I have someone special like you. But it never gets old. Remember, Jamey. My wife thinks I'm an asshole. And she's right, isn't she?"

"But what about the boys? Fuck it. What about me?"

"You have your band," said Rick. "Molly said that that's what you wanted. You wanted to get a shot at being an opening act and maybe a chance to make a record. That's what Molly said you really wanted. That *is* what you want, isn't it?"

"I think Molly was talking to Mona," said Jamey. "But, yeah, that's what I want. I want the band to have a chance at the big time."

"Well, you got it. I called Jerry before we left, when you were upstairs, and he said he'd make arrangements."

"When?" asked Jamey.

"I don't know. Molly's been talking to him and, what do you call her? Mona. Whatever they've cooked up. So maybe it'll be the big time for you, and you won't care about me any more." Jamey would have protested, but Rick then went into a completely different rap. "Listen, I have to shoot The Doors concert tomorrow night at the Cow Palace. The next night, there's some gig in Wisconsin. Blind Faith."

"You're going to see Blind Faith?" said Jamey, impressed all over again.

"I was thinking, we could extend our little time together, and you could come with me to the gig on Friday. You could meet Jim."

Jamey wasn't sure if he was supposed to be a chick who was in love with Jim Morrison or a musician who admired him. But he wanted to be at the show, fer sure, man.

"Maybe you could have sex with him," said Rick. "He swings both ways, you know."

Jamey didn't know, but he knew Rick. "I don't want Jim Morrison," Jamey asserted. It was the correct response, even if he sort of did.

"And on Saturday in Wisconsin or Minnesota or wherever the fuck it is, you could meet the fellas, if you like. They'd like you."

"Until one of them found my balls."

"Well, I don't know. Maybe they're like Morrison. I wasn't suggesting that you have sex with them," said Rick. "You would have made a rather promiscuous young lady. But we could do Chicago. I'll take you to the blues clubs. Some Willie Dixon. How does all of that sound?"

"It sounds like a dream, but mostly because it would be more time with you."

"Promiscuous, but sweet..." said Rick.

"I mean it. I was scared at first. I never had sex like that, I mean, of course I never had sex like that. I like being your girlfriend, which is kind of queer. I'm impressed by all these people you know. Morrison and Winwood and Clapton and Mike Carl, and Jesus Christ! But for all of that, I like hanging out with you. But you know I have to be back by Friday. We're gigging."

"God damn it! Are you telling me that you would rather get back to L.A. to play a gig at a sweaty pussy bar than to fly across the country to see Blind Faith? Forget about me. Are you serious?"

"I know that's not too impressive, but we're a band. They don't have anyone to sit in for me. And, anyway, I don't want to lose my place in the band. I have to be back by Friday afternoon at the latest. I could see you when you get back, if you'd let me."

"You're fucking insane," Rick shouted. "You're coming with me."

"I'm not," said Jamey. Rick didn't push it after that. They crossed the bridge back into town, listened to Traffic, and things had settled back down. Going up the elevator, Jamey was laughing again. "I'll never forget the gardener's face when I came running up in my underwear, flat chest and painted nails. His mind was blown. Not even disgusted. Just blown away. I don't think he ever thought about such things. It's kind of new to me."

"Crazy world," said Rick.

Later, they had a nice dinner out on Fisherman's Wharf, including a lot of drinking on Rick's part. On the way back, Rick told Jamey most definitely that he would have to stay on for the concert, whether he would meet Morrison afterward or not. When Jamey finally got the message that Rick wasn't going to deliver him back to The Contortionist, Jamey said that it was cool. He usually did. He proposed to get himself back to L.A. on his own. He had $137. PSA was around twenty.

Jamey decided to take up the subject in the morning. He didn't want to fight about it, and Rick didn't like Jamey to say no to anything. They went to bed early. Rick had been drinking. Jamey wanted the sex, especially if this were to be the last time. He could show Rick that he was worth it, but Rick had fallen into a stupor, crashing on Jamey while making love. Jamey was a sensitive soul and wondered if he was already failing to interest Rick. Jamey was already feeling older, and that's what Rick didn't want.

OUT OF TIME

UPON AWAKENING, Jamey sensed that the room had a different feel. Rick's stuff was gone. He had split the scene. There was an envelope with five twenty dollar bills and a note informing Jamey of an airplane reservation and ticket at the PSA counter. He looked front and back for some sign of "I love you" or "I'll see you in L.A." There was nothing like that. "Which I think means Fuck Me!" Now he felt what Molly had expressed about the door suddenly slamming. Was Rick out of his life, just like that? Very strange!

He took a long shower and put himself in Mona style fashion, the hotel-refreshed yellow dress with the yellow underpants, along with his sentimental favorite earrings, the pearls from Rick the Perv. He wore the bra for shaping, but he skipped the extra hips. He dried his hair, put on the perfume, and a little bit of the makeup. It was back to L.A., back to Mona, back to Rooms-for-Rent and The Contortionist, and it sounded okay to Jamey after living the jet-set life. He didn't have to be anyone's girlfriend now. He might miss that and the jet setting, but, for now, he wanted to be the Hollywood chick he had been before. And he had a lot to tell Mona. Fuck. Bryan Cooper had had a handful of Jamey's ass! He couldn't wait to see his best friend. From Rick to Mona, once again!

Having lost one handbag, Jamey was suspicious of carrying the prop. He had a lot of money. With what he had just come into, he had $237. So he put $37 in the bag for busses and lunch and the like, and he deposited the bulk of the money into his bra.

Jamey packed everything into the various suitcases. He put anything that he wanted into one suitcase, more Mona style than Molly, just cramming in what he could, though he took along the hip forms to show Mona. The other bag, he left in the room. He carried his own bag now, not wanting to incur tipping liabilities. He stopped by Craig's desk again. "New look!" he remarked.

"Old look," said Jamey.

"Adorable," he commented.

"Just what a girl likes to hear," he said. Jamey, in his final imperious Rick Altier surrogate voice told Craig to make arrangements with Molly

Gifford about the luggage upstairs. Craig, in turn, told her how to pick up the hotel shuttle to the bus station and what bus he needed to take to get to SFO. After checking in and finding his ticket paid, he set about having some lunch. He was carded when the apparent young lady ordered a beer, forgetting that he was no longer under the protection of *her* important boyfriend. He settled for a Coke, which he generally preferred. He was a punk kid again, and a nobody—though hardly invisible with *her* exposed legs and rounded chest.

This was Jamey's first commercial flight, a distant cousin of his first flight in the Learjet. It lasted only about an hour, a blessing, because he was seated next to a handsome chap who couldn't keep his eyes off of her bare legs and who found any number of reasons to brush up against her. He tried to engage the girl in conversation. Why she was going to Los Angeles? What did she do for a living? Why was she traveling alone? Did she have a boyfriend? What were her favorite bands? Jamey wasn't interested, and he had a pretty good idea that the fellow wouldn't be all that interested in what Jamey had to say about any of it. You never know, but it was a good bet.

While Jamey had liked the attention before, it was becoming intrusive. Everyone wanted her, to get into her pants that is, but they hadn't the first idea about what he was really about, including the pants. He returned to his Officer Tanquerson revelation: being a chick is a gnarly business. Had he just been Jamey, the sixteen year old dude, he would have been ignored, not even a second bag of peanuts. "Love your outfit," said the stewardess. It being a Mona special, and not one of Molly's Beverly Hills selections, Jamey concluded that the fashion thing was less than scientific, more a matter of taste.

He touched down at LAX around three in the afternoon. It was late August, and the weather was very much warmer and smoggier than it had been in Frasco. Jamey was uncomfortable with the weather, but this was the reality he had chosen. He could have been with Rick, getting ready for The Doors concert. Instead, it was Maiden Head. He had no idea what to do next. He didn't know how to take the public transportation, such as it was, to the abode between Sunset and Hollywood where he and Mona comingled, to a point. He decided to take a taxi into Hollywood, and screw the cost and screw the hassles. He was rich enough. The trusty driver should know the way. Jamey was trying to organize the long, strange story that he wanted to relate to Mona, but there was also the gig to worry about.

In the back of the taxi, he daydreamed about still being with Rick, going to the concert tonight. He wondered if Rick had been serious about giving him to Morrison. That was bullshit, he concluded. He would go for it, but not if Rick had to know about it. Like he would ever encounter Morrison without Rick! Maybe just run into him at some party with Mona. He laughed. Time to forget all that. No more private jets to see the English rock legends somewhere in the Midwest. No more encounters with Bryan Cooper backstage. Not unless Maiden Head were to make it.

In the end, Rick would have had to drop him off somewhere. Today or next week. His relationship with Rick was like that moment on the lawn up in Larkspur, a beautiful interlude, but ever so fleeting. He had been a fantasy for Rick, an illusion, and one that wouldn't last as long as the fire on Zuma Cove. Like his Wednesday acid adventure, it would pass and all the intensity of love and life that he had experienced would be a very vague memory. He could regret what didn't happen. He could regret what did happen. It didn't matter. Time was rolling along.

Riding in the back of the taxi, he kept noticing the nagging clicks of the meter. He looked in the purse and calculated his expenses since the hotel. The shuttle, the express bus to the airport, the lunch, Jamey had about $25 in his handbag. The taxi was heading north on the 405. The driver, a hippie with a pony tail, rolled down the Santa Monica Blvd. ramp and proceeded eastbound. The meter continued to click past $15.

It was still early relative to the afternoon traffic, about 4:00 PM. The driver turned left onto La Cienega. It was quickly becoming obvious that Jamey would have to withdraw some cash from his reserves. He couldn't get into his top without unzipping the dress from behind. That would have been difficult even if he weren't in a car. The meter was relentless at $18. The tip alone would put him over. He had to get to the money from his clothes.

He moved to the side directly behind the driver in hopes of concealing himself, but he could see himself in the rearview mirror suggesting that the driver could see him, too. These maneuvers had probably got the driver wondering what was happening back there. Moving to the other extreme, Jamey was exposed to the mirror and the driver's peripheral vision which was sure to be on high alert once the zipper came down.

He tried getting on the floor behind the driver's seat, but from that position he couldn't reach the zipper. So, back on the seat, Jamey bit the bullet, reached behind, and zipped down the back. Unfettered, he was able to bring his arms through the arm holes of the tight dress and work his hands under the dress and feel under the bra for the bread. He saw the driver looking back through the mirror. There was next the honking of horns. The driver next to the taxi had stopped at a light to observe Jamey undressing. He missed the shift of the various colors on the light standard, and the cars behind him were complaining.

"Eyes on the road," *she* cautioned the driver, and to their neighbor, "Same to you, buster!" The two cars started up again. "Careful what you wish for, big boy."

The taxi man pretended to stop watching for a moment, but he wasn't very convincing. Jamey came up with the cash which he put in his purse. It took almost as much effort to find the zipper and replace it from the seated position. By and by, the taxi turned onto Sunset, eastbound again. Things were looking familiar. It was well past four. Jamey, with plenty of cash available now, urged the driver toward the club. He might be early, but he would surely meet up with the band, and with Mona, if he just hung out at The Contortionist.

The final bill was $26 and Jamey let go of $32 for the driver's trouble. "I won't charge you for the show," he said.

"Good!" he replied. "'Cause I never saw anything."

"Nothing to see," said Jamey. "Thanks for the ride, man."

"Cool," said the driver, looking up at the XXX Girls! Girls! Girls! XXX signage. "You sure this is where you want to be?"

He felt like answering, "More than anything!" but he thought it would have been as cliché as slapping Rick that first night for kissing him. A lot of his ideas came from the movies. Nothing is real. "Pull in the back here," said Jamey. There was no sign of Denise's brother's van.

"Well," mumbled the driver, "Come to think on it…"

Jamey entered the club from the back door, dropping his case in the corner where the band played. There was no set-up, so he figured he would have to wait for the van to show. He felt the eyes of a few patrons falling on him. Maybe they thought he was the next act punching in. That's what he felt like under their gaze. It was only late afternoon, and the first scheduled show was hours away. The juke box was playing for some dispassionate thrusting stripper who wasn't getting prime time tips and was likewise not putting on a prime time show.

Jamey found Tony. "What do you want?" he asked Jamey, and not in a friendly way.

"What?" said Jamey. Tony was generally rude, but this seemed unnecessary.

"What are you fuckin' doin' here? You quit. Get the fuck out of here!"

"What are you talking about?" asked Jamey. "I just got back from Frasco. What's happened?"

"Your little slut friend quit. She said you had a different gig tonight and she wanted the night off. Fuck that! I pay good money..."

This was all news to Jamey, but one point required an answer. "You don't pay us twenty-five dollars a head for three days, and that's before expenses. You don't pay good money. But where's this gig?"

"You don't know?" he asked. "They're doing a big show at Jerry Westerfield's pad in Beverly Hills. It's your big chance, cutie—unless they dumped you. Now, Tony—Tony could make you feel better..." He reached for Jamey, but he shook Tony off.

"When did they pick up their shit?" said Jamey.

"A couple of days ago. When she said she couldn't make the scene on Friday, I kicked her and her shit out of here. I got another band coming in. Not chicks. Chicks are trouble."

Mona wasn't there to say it, so Jamey did. "You live on chicks! You suck menstrual blood."

"Get out of here!"

If they were planning to do a show for Westerfield, then they would be practicing, especially if they were working in a new bassist which Jamey figured they must be. Maybe Rick or Molly warned them that he wouldn't be bringing Jamey back. No. It was entirely unlikely that Rick would care about the band. Whatever. Jamey knew where to go next.

He put out his thumb and, not surprisingly, he managed to flag a ride in his little yellow micro-mini. It was a lawyer. "Are you working?" he asked.

"Na—I'm just trying to get down the road. Is that cool?"

He reached over and squeezed Jamey's thigh. "I don't mind some company," he said. Jamey removed the hand gently, but clearly. "Can't blame a guy..."

"Guys are guys," said Jamey. The attorney tried a few more gambits, but he allowed that Jamey wasn't putting out, at least not for free. When Jamey saw the stop, *she* said, "Just right here." He didn't seem to be stopping, so *she* started pounding on his paint job. He pulled over with a laugh, and there was the necessary pinch on his ass as he got out of the car. "Thanks, guy!"

"Sure I can't take you somewhere?" he asked. "There's a little motel up the street..."

Jamey was already going into the practice studio. Isaac was there, but the joint was dead. "Are they here?" asked Jamey.

"They left. Practiced all afternoon."

"Who's they?"

"What do you mean? It was the same old band. You know, the other guitar player. The one with talent."

"Leslie King?" said Jamey.

"Yeah. She's pretty good. Chink's back on bass. I don't know what the fuck she's doing rockin' and rollin'. That chick can play piano."

"Piano?" Jamey was stopped cold.

"You should hear her sometime. Not that noise you guys do. Any idiot can do that. Say, what are you doing anyway? Did you quit the band?"

"What am I doing? That's easy. I'm getting fucked," said Jamey, who just figured out that she had been replaced for a reason. "Listen. I hear they're giggin' at Jerry Westerfield's place in Beverly Hills. You know where that's at?"

"How the fuck should I know?" he answered. "She was on the phone the other day, writing some shit down. Maybe she put it with her music?"

"Her music?"

"Yeah," he said. "She rents a piano practice room several times a week. Plays long hair stuff. I thought everybody knew." He took her into a dingy but well-lighted piano practice room with a ratty upright. On a shelf were several books of music, most marked with the name *Mary Wang*, though there were a couple marked by other pianists, pianists that Jamey figured had to buy new copies of Chopin's *Études* and *The Well-Tempered Clavier*. So Jamey realized that Mona's piracy in fact did extend to musicians.

"She plays this stuff a lot?" said Jamey.

"She comes around six. Leaves around nine. Six bucks for three hours. Plays pretty hard in here." He was looking at the papers on the piano top. "Hey! Is this the Chink's writing? She was on the phone a few days ago and she was writing some notes. Sometimes I let her use the phone."

Jamey looked it over. It was Mona's hand—or maybe Mary's—but there was no clue. A few phone numbers. Some names. Westerfield. Nichols. It was no help. "Thanks for the total blow-mind," said Jamey.

"Is it good for a blow job?" he suggested.

"It should be," said Jamey. "But I don't have time. Talk to Mona."

"I don't think so…"

Taking his suitcase, Jamey left the studio. They wouldn't be playing until evening. There had to be some way to figure out where a famous asshole like Jerry Westerfield lived. Mona could do it.

Jamey took the bus down to Rooms-for-Rent and dropped off the suitcase. "How's the rent, Jack?"

"Mona paid for the night. Didn't have enough for the week."

"So we're cool for now?"

"On ice," said Jack. Jamey went up to the room and dropped her suitcase in the door. The room looked as if it had been bombed, but he didn't take the time to check it out. He checked himself in the mirror, refreshed his makeup and perfume, and was heading out the door when it hit him. Rick had given him Westerfuck's card that first night. He went through his stuff, but he couldn't find it. So he went through Mona's stuff, and the card was right on top. Jamey was out the door, almost running to catch the next bus heading into Beverly Hills.

Once at Benedict Canyon, he walked about a half mile up the road and then put out his thumb to pick up a ride. It was eight-thirty by the time that Jamey arrived on the scene. There was a big house set way back from the road and the lights were blazing. Cars were parked on the estate and on the road. The place was packed presumably with the bright lights of the music scene. Jamey could hear the music as he approached. He recognized Karen's drumming, so he knew he had found the band. But it wasn't the same band. Leslie King was a natural star. Though Jamey was self-interested, Leslie's talent was undeniable. Jamey had to be impressed. They were playing "Foxy Lady" with Mona on the vocal. Leslie was cresting. Jamey had gone around the side of the house and made his way to the patio. On the opposite side of the patio, in a little gazebo, the band was entertaining the crowd. On Mona's count, the band cranked right up with another song, an original number, "Something about the Night."

All alone and in the zone
Digging on the scene deep in my stone
Something's wrong 'cause I don't feel right
Something about the night

Jamey had heard it mentioned and had heard some of the riffs. It was Leslie's song, and it was pretty hot stuff, especially on the guitar side. A waiter offered Jamey a drink, which he gladly took. He hadn't eaten, but with the drinking and drugs, it was all sort of catch it on the fly. The wine went straight to his head.

The audience didn't seem impressed one way or another by the music, though it was clear to Jamey that they were playing for their lives. If

Westerfield was in earshot, Jamey couldn't determine. The band went right into "Crossroads" with Denise singing the blues, and Leslie blowing away the leads. Jamey was hoping to stay undercover, but, despite the beautiful women in their multi-hundred dollar dresses, Jamey somehow stood out, perhaps because of *her* simplicity, a tiny dress and sandals. He tried to get across the patio to the band but was waylaid for dancing and some social mixing. Being with one of these bastards gave him cover, so he went with it. When the band jumped into "Honky Tonk Women," cowbells and all, sure enough, Mona and Denise traded vocals. And Leslie was killing the guitar part. In short, Maiden Head was a lot better with Leslie. It wasn't that Mona's bass was better than Jamey's. It was just that Leslie's guitar was so much better than Mona's—or pretty much anyone but Jorma, Clapton, or Hendrix. And Leslie was young.

Jamey could do the math. Mona had a chance at the big time, an audition with the big shots. Jerry Westerfield. Who knows who else? So Mona wanted to make the best impression possible. She got Leslie King back with the promise of a showcase. Something more tangible than week after week at the naked lady bar. Makes sense. Obviously, Mona wasn't going to kick herself out of the band, so she went back to bass, and that meant that Jamey was squeezed. Anyone who knew Mona, or Lisa, or Mary knew the process.

Jamey only ever got about half way to the gazebo. It was clear that there wasn't anything to talk about. He was stinging from the hurt, but even he knew that Mona was right, though it was a dirty trick. He took another glass of wine, and some food off of a tray. Had the deal already gone down before Jamey had left for shopping with Molly? He had asked Mona to fuck him in the ass, and she had definitely done it now. More, she had pulled right out and slammed the door.

He thought about complaining to Rick, their benefactor, but to what purpose without a band? The guy's hand was on Jamey's yellow ass. He had no business being offended. He was there to be used. He wanted to talk to Mona, but the tears were already coming. He didn't want to look and sound pathetic in front of Mona and the others. He didn't want to be Larry or Gary or Jack Bruce or John Lennon or even "Bobby's Girl."

The guy said he thought the band was pretty good, and Jamey agreed. On the third drink, he kissed Jamey on the mouth. He was obviously getting excited. Jamey told him that *she* had to find the ladies' room. The bastard pointed inside and up the stairs. Jamey disappeared into the crowd. When he thought he wasn't being visually tracked anymore, he walked through the party and out the front door to the sounds of "Honky Tonk Women."

He made his way down the hill to the canyon road. It made sense now. Mona had taken care of him, teaching him how to live, how to get into the scene, and she held his hand and blew his nose. She had also blown his mind. He had walked a long while before he was out of the light, out of earshot, out of range, and realized that *she* was out of time, kicked out of the band on his pretty little ass, facilitating as it had been. Without a doubt, he was out of there.

He was walking down the dark road toward Sunset, which might have been miles down the canyon. Walking down the road, he freely cried. No sense holding it in. He had been intentionally screwed by his best and only friend. She would fuck a big yellow dog if it would serve her, if it were for the band, but Jamey hadn't realized that he was Rovette.

His dreams of rock and roll fame, nurtured for five years, were over in a shaft. Maybe there was a shot at success for the girls, but even that seemed plastic to Jamey. The whole business was a put-on. Maybe he wasn't really meant to be a Bryan Cooper, a Jim Morrison, or even a Mona Ming—or Mary Wang. Maybe he was just a girlfriend or boyfriend or freak-friend. And maybe not even that. Maybe he was just a hippie kid from the Valley. Hollywood's full of them.

Jamey wasn't even thumbing, but a hippie dude in a micro-bus pulled over and offered the damsel a ride. Jamey had been doing nothing but dumb stuff, so he took the ride, really not taking any precautions now. The guy was preening to impress *her*, but Jamey seemed to give an aloof impression that kept him at some distance. Maybe he would take a sudden turn down a canyon road and rape and murder him? One can hope.

"What's happening, man?" he asked. "Why the tears?"

"I cry when I'm sad," said Jamey.

The dude thought about that. It made a lot of sense to him. Jamey quickly determined that the dude was no threat and that he wasn't going to deliver him from this miserable world.

Down at the crossroads, at Sunset, the dude was going west and Jamey was going east. No murder. But Jamey was still a long way from home. Dressed as he was, he was sure to pick up a ride on Sunset, if the Beverly Hills cops didn't grab him first.

Jamey started walking. What to do now? Always the clock. Always the next thing. No time to think. Should he give up his little room and take up residence on his own in some similar place? The room they shared wasn't anything to fight over. Mona could have it, unless she was going to go on tour with the band. He could go and pull out his few things, and move on to another place. He had almost $200.00. Without Mona, it would last long enough to get him started again.

He would have to think about what kind of job he would get. The El Portal was easy, but not enough hours at these prices. Without Mona, without the band, he would have to up the income. Barmaid? Waitress? Sounded like a lot of work. Or he could be a guy. There were a lot of options when he looked in his mirror. There was more than one carwash in town. He knew that drill. Hell, maybe he could go to work in a foundry, whatever that was. But then he'd have to cut his hair, all done in ringlets. Didn't sound like a place for a hippie chick with painted nails and tight dresses and lipstick.

And, whatever work he did to put brown rice on the table, whether as a girl or a guy, he was thinking he had to do something to break on through on his own. Like Rick said, maybe a solo act. There was the open mic at The Troub. He might have to work all day, but at night he had to keep working on the music thing. He had to make a name, and to make music. He wasn't sure if it would be Jamey Craig, the chick or the dude, but he—or she—was going to be somebody.

And then there was the immediate matter of the night at hand. If he went to sleep in their room, wouldn't Mona be along, sooner or later? She had paid the rent, so she would be there eventually. He wanted to be done with her. She had a way of making it sound all right, and it wasn't.

He understood that what she had done was, to Mona's mind, a reasonable thing to have done. Like Craig Roman said. If the Foresters had wanted him, he might have left Crazy Place for the hot shot gigs. You have to look out for yourself in this business. Mona wanted to make the most of her chance, and Leslie was the most exciting thing Mona had to offer to the big time. And Mona wasn't wrong about Leslie.

But Jamey was hurt nonetheless. The fact that it was logical didn't make it feel any better. She wouldn't let her use him anymore. He would work for himself now, as he should have from the beginning. He could manage the money a whole lot better without Mona. It wouldn't be so much fun, he had to admit. And he would miss her. Or miss having someone around, because Mona hadn't really shared anything, had she? Had she ever said a true thing in their whole time together? He never knew that she was still doing piano. Hard core piano. He never knew. It wasn't some other dude, but she just had to lie about everything. What was true? Portland? The rape? Her job? Was anything true? And what about this Leslie? Mona said that she loved Leslie. Were they in love, and that's why she didn't want sex with Jamey? Mona was a trip.

Anyway, he figured, he had to see her eventually. There was nowhere else to go tonight, and he wasn't going to sleep in the garbage. He figured that when he saw her he would just sort of play it real cool. As The Exciters might have expressed it, "Easier Said Than Done."

I'M LOOKING THROUGH YOU

IT HAD BEEN A LONG DAY of public transportation. Jamey hitched out of Beverly Hills and was dropped off without any significant incident at their hot dog joint near the pad. He had had some peanuts on the flight and some hors d'oeuvres at Westerfuck's, so a chili dog and fries was just the thing to inspire dramatic new dreams.

As he stepped, a little drunk, from the car onto the curb, he hadn't felt this alone on the boulevard since meeting Mona. It was going to take some time to get used to a Monaless universe. But there was never time to live. Life just kept happening.

The red lights hit him, and the siren whined briefly. It was the cops again. "Shit," was his first remark, having learned that from Mona, too. Jamey closed his eyes praying that it wasn't the same two assholes, and it wasn't.

"So, was that your last customer for the evening, or are you just getting started?" The tag read Officer Intveld.

"Customer?" said Jamey. "Oh, no…"

"You're not a prostitute?" the officer insisted. His partner was out of the car. Officer Morrison. Probably not related. Two on one. Jamey didn't like *her* chances.

"I was hitching," said Jamey. "Busses don't run this late. Really. I was just trying to get home. I'm not a whore." Given her outfit, she might have added that she admitted to being a slut, but how would that have helped? Anyway, Jamey's claim just didn't ring true to the officers, though he was technically correct, Molly's comment notwithstanding.

"Well, you're dressed for it. You're getting in and out of cars. I mean, should I believe you or should I look at the circumstances?"

"Really. I was just hitching home," said Jamey, trying out a smile and a laugh. Intveld wasn't biting.

"So, let's have your I.D."

"Well, I don't have any," said Jamey. "I lost it…at a party. I lost it at a party."

"Lost it at a party."

"No. Really. I lost my identity at a party. True story."

"How old are you?" the officer asked.

"I'm definitely eighteen," said Jamey. "Look. I just live down the block. I'm not a prostitute. I'm a musician. I'm in a band. I just live down there. We could ask the manager guy, Jack. Because I live there. It's cool."

Officer Intveld was impassive. It wasn't adding up. "You been drinking?"

"I had a little wine at that party. And I haven't eaten anything. So, well, I'm a little woozy."

"What's your name?" asked Intveld. He was a curious fellow, thought Jamey.

"Jamey," he answered. "Jamey—Jamey Joplin."

"Jamey Joplin?"

"Not related," said Jamey.

Officer Intveld asked her, "Jamey Joplin, are you carrying any drugs?"

"No drugs," said Jamey, feeling confident in that answer.

The officer reached for her purse. "But you can't..."

"But you said there's no drugs." Jamey opened his purse and the officer took possession of it. "No drugs," said Jamey. "Just my key and some cigarettes and junk." Intveld handed the purse to Morrison, who did a little rummaging. "And, sorry, I don't have any pockets..."

"Well, if I was a hippie girl," said Intveld, "Where do you suppose I could hide my stash? Any ideas, Morrison."

Morrison looked Jamey up and down. "Couldn't say," he answered. "But it might get a little damp..." Inside the purse, Morrison found a stack of money, almost $200.00.

"Pretty good for a hooker!" said Morrison. "Or are we dealing?"

"Look, guys, I'm cool. I wasn't doing anything. I don't have any drugs. I just want to go home. It's all the money I saved from working. I don't like to leave it at Rooms-for-Rent, if you know what I mean. Not exactly secure."

Intveld looked at Morrison. Morrison shook his head.

Jamey continued, "It hasn't been a super great day for me. I don't even need a hot dog. I'm cool, guys. I know you have to check out the scene, but I'm nobody to worry about. Please? Pretty please...sugar on top?"

"Well, you're a sweetheart," answered Intveld.

Jamey felt for the first time that he might get out of this one. "Come on..." Jamey begged, ever so nicely, going little girl on him, trying a different approach from what Mona had suggested the last time.

"The thing is," said Intveld. "If you had your I.D. If you didn't look like an infant. The money. Something happening here. I can't send you back on the streets not knowing who you are. If something happened, and it came out that I let you go... I have to check you out. If everything checks out, no charges. But I'm going to have to take you in. We need to know who you are."

Jamey wasn't a chick for nothing, so he decided the best thing to do was to turn on the waterworks, but it was too late for that. "Turn around," said Intveld. "Morrison."

Morrison took out his handcuffs. As he locked *her* wrists behind *her*, he addressed Jamey, for Intveld's benefit. "How long you been in drag?"

"What do you mean?" said Jamey.

"I can tell a dude from a chick," said Morrison. "And you may or may not be a dude. I won't argue. But you ain't a chick."

"Son of a bitch!" remarked Intveld. "The queer had me fooled!"

"So my mother dresses me funny," admitted Jamey. "All right. I'm a dude, sort of. But you could still let me go. I'm no threat to anyone. I'm just a fairy, right? Someone'll probably beat the shit out of me and that'll be the end of me—no problem. If they kill me in jail, paperwork."

"But if you're lyin' about that, sir," said Intveld, "I don't know what all else." The officer lightly frisked Jamey, above, below, in front, and behind. It was, at the least, degrading to be handled by these thugs. Passersby probably thought the scene a bit disconcerting. Jamey was lightly attired and the cops were convinced that he didn't have any weapons. The rest of the search could be handled in a more formal setting. With his hands locked behind his back, dressed in a micro-mini, it was a helpless feeling in the back of the cop car, and one that he had known before.

"I don't suppose you guys could use a blow job..." They were impassive now.

Somehow he rationally knew that this wasn't going to be an assault, but he felt the fear all over again anyway. And it was hardly a feeling of relief when the car rolled onto the police compound as it should have rather than up into the deserted Hollywood Hills as had Tank's.

Jamey was brought into a small interrogation room. He was in drag, and the cops didn't want to throw him into the general population. Even in a jumpsuit, he had a very young hairless body, painted nails, and a too sweet look about him that would do nothing but make trouble throughout the night. The officer wanted a matron to do the body search, but Jamey was a dude, and that point was evidenced during a detailed body search. "Not much of a dick," remarked the officer. "But for classification purposes..."

After the search, they gave him boys' clothes topped with an orange jumpsuit. Jamey didn't like that as it suggested that he might be a keeper. In the tiny room, he waited and waited. It seemed like hours. He was genuinely hungry now. Life was a lot harder without Rick.

Finally, a detective came into the room and spoke to Jamey. He carried a clipboard with some report forms. "Listen up, princess," he said, as if he were a P.E. coach trying to shame Jamey into being a man. "We need to know who you are. If you don't want to tell me, then you'll go to Eastlake on the morning bus. That's the juvenile facility over in East L.A."

Near the foundry, thought Jamey.

"I don't approve of this sort of thing, but I think you would find that you would be very popular. White boy. Obviously girly. Nails. Curls. Bare legs and ass. I think you'll be very popular, if you get me. Now I don't have a choice. I can't send you out to live on the streets. Can't happen. I don't know who your parents are, so I can't contact 'em. Now I'd say that we have a problem, but yours is worse than mine. I just have to go home to the shrew. You'll be going to Eastlake where they won't handle you with care." Jamey said nothing, but he was thinking. "So you have to explain why you got no I.D. Why you got two hundred dollars. Why you're dressed up like a whore."

Jamey was already convinced. The officer had him at Eastlake. But the detective didn't give him a chance to decide or to hesitate. "There's a bus leaving for Eastlake in the morning. That means that you'll spend the night here. I expect we can protect you here, but I don't like your chances over there. So, you can tell me who the hell you are or you can get used to life on the bottom. Any thoughts, princess?"

There was no way out of this. Mona wasn't going to come riding to the rescue. The great and powerful Rick didn't know where he was. He was either in Frisco or on his way to Wisconsin or where the hell ever. Jamey could hold out, but to what purpose? The cops would eventually find the bulletin with his picture that he knew must be out there. So, he could put off the inevitable, and suffer the ill-effects, but, in the end, they would discover his identity. So Jamey Craig spilled the beans. The detective filled in his reports. He asked Jamey to remain where he was. There was an element of humor in the request as the door from the little interrogation room was locked.

When the officer returned, he explained that Jamey's parents had already been contacted and that they were on their way to pick him up that same night. Jamey was advised that he had been given an appointment to appear before a juvenile court, but there were no specific charges. The court would make the determination as to whether he could be safely returned home on an indefinite basis or whether he needed to be made a ward of the county.

In Jamey's head, there was no reason to stay away from home any longer and no reason to return to Hollywood, except to see a movie or a band at a club. He already missed Mona, like you miss a drug habit. She was crazy, but she was the mainline from life to his heart. He sat in the little room, his head on the table, resting, but unable to sleep. Hungry besides. He had already cried it out. Had he stayed with Rick, he might have been at The Doors concert. He might even be having sex with Jim Morrison. But Rick had probably been bluffing. He was a jealous guy.

More than an hour later, an officer came into the interrogation room and told Jamey he was being released. It would, at least, end the boredom of sitting there. He was told that he couldn't take the orange jumpsuit; there were rules about that sort of thing, handing out county property. So the officer gave him a bag with his dress, his underwear, his sandals, and, maybe, some privacy to dress. Jamey transformed himself back into the Hollywood chick. There wasn't anything he could do about the hair and makeup. A *girl* likes to make an impression.

He could imagine Jim Craig meeting him in this cute little dress at midnight in the Hollywood station house. But, despite his apparel, he actually looked forward to seeing his mom more than maintaining his cool. He wished he hadn't hurt her, but how else could it have gone? Walking in the brightly glaring hallway, he was suddenly confronted by the unexpected presence of Officer Tanquerson, passing Jamey and Intveld and Morrison in the hallway.

Jamey, showing his visceral fear, observed the man who probably raped any number of frightened kids. He hadn't expected another encounter, ever. He had put Tanquerson in another world, a freaky place, like a bad trip. But it had been a real thing in the land of the chronically unreal. The escorting cops felt the tensing in Jamey's muscles. "It's just your folks," said one of them. "Never seen ya like this, huh?"

Officer Tanquerson gave them a wide passage. He nodded to his fellows and gave Jamey the once-over as if he were just another runaway freak. He went on his way without a sign of recognition, not even a triumphant smirk at having gotten away with it or some sign of contempt for the he-she-pansy. He pretended perfectly to know nothing about the kid.

Jamey wanted to say something. Tank had thought she had been an underage runaway girl, instead of the freak that he was. Instead of protecting her and getting her home or to safe harbor, he took advantage of her. And it was practiced. Jamey knew he might protect another kid down the road, but he was ashamed. He didn't want to tell his parents or anyone else. Only Mona knew, and she had already said that she wasn't going to hassle it.

YOU NEVER CAN TELL

A S HE PASSED THROUGH THE RELEASE DOOR in the thin yellow dress he had put on that morning in San Francisco, Jamey was given over to the custody of his parents. Jim Craig was stunned, disgusted, and angry in quick succession. Missy's jaw dropped. Jamey's mother approached the child and put her arms around him, kissing the side of his face, smelling the residual fragrance, and caressing him dearly. She said nothing about the get-up.

At the release window, his purse was returned to him. He looked inside it, and found no cash. He expected as much. He was surprised when he was handed an envelope. In it was the remaining $193.25. Another envelope had his earrings, his ring, and his key. He signed for it all and scraped it into his purse. His mother led him by the hand out of the police station's glass doors, with no sign or sense of shame or shock. They were followed by the old man and Missy, both of whom were somewhat subdued. Jamey asked to go back to his apartment to pick up his guitar and a few things. The old man said they absolutely weren't going to do it, but his mother said they would.

"Are you hungry?" Margaret asked him.

"Starving," said Jamey. They were almost at the Big Boy.

"Here, Jim."

"What the..."

"Jamey's hungry," she insisted. The family stopped at the Big Boy. It was crowded, but the Squaresville family got a booth. Jamey recognized a few of the waitresses, including Carrie.

"Hey, Jame," she said. "What's the haps, man?"

"Oh, it's cool," said Jamey. "These are my people, from home. My Mom and my Dad, and my sister, too."

"Far out!" Carrie smiled at Jim, who gave her nothing. She smiled at Margaret and then at Missy, and they were much nicer.

"All right," said Jim. "That's just fine. Now, the boy here is hungry..."

"Jim!" said Margaret sharply, eyeing *the boy*.

"Well, what the hell do you want?" asked Jim.

Jamey smiled and looked up to Carrie. "What do I want? I want a Big

Boy!"

"Me, too…" said Carrie.

On the way out of the restaurant, the Craigs passed by a woman with blond hair and a very intense look on her face. She stopped Jamey. "I didn't see you at the clinic. Did you go somewhere else?" Jamey was bewildered. "Same dress, honey. I hope you did something about that."

"I'm fine," said Jamey. "Yeah. Everything's…" Margaret was looking from Jamey to the lady. "Oh, this is my Mom. Yeah. Everything's fine."

"Oh, I'm so glad. I was worried about you."

"But you don't really know me," said Jamey. People were pushing past the log jam in the doorway.

"Nice to meet you," said Jim, pulling the family out to the car. "God damn it! I have a golf game tomorrow. What the hell time is it?"

In the car, going down the boulevard that Jamey had lived on these last two months, the old man started in. "We're gonna get you a haircut in the morning, and you're going to have to live by my rules…" When they got to the donut shop, Jamey directed his father to turn the corner. The old man started in again, but Margaret cut him off.

"Don't start *that* again," she said.

"What are you talking about?"

"Don't start," she said. "It was your bluster that made him run away in the first place. Now that we have him back, thank God—it's going to be different."

"What the hell?"

Jamey directed them to the shabby building. The old man parked out front. "I'll go in," Jamey said.

"I'll go with you," said Missy. "In case you need help carrying things…"

"I don't know…" the old man was starting.

"They'll be fine," said Jamey's mom.

Jamey and Missy went up the steps and unlocked the door for admittance to the lobby. Jack was nowhere in sight, but it was quite late. Jamey and Missy climbed the three flights. "No elevator," Jamey apologized, but Missy was young.

He half-hoped to see Mona in the room, but when he opened the door, it was just as he had left it, in a state of general disarray. The San Francisco suitcase was just inside the door. Jamey's and Mona's things were hanging in the closet or piled on the floor of the closet, spreading out across the floor of the room. There was washing in the sink and on the make-shift line, just like the first time Jamey had seen Mona's place.

There were more signs of life covering the bed, the bureau, and the chair: Bras hanging on doorknobs and bedposts and panties on the floor. With Mona's *girlfriend* out of town, housekeeping was even less of a priority than usual. Jamey's guitar case was open, but the instrument was sound. They had shared everything, so that was cool.

One of the bras was way too big for Mona. The leather pants with the studs that had always been in the closet from that very first day were on the floor. It wasn't Mona's ass that fit those jeans. There was also a strange suitcase on the floor. Detective Jamey concluded that Leslie King had been staying with Mona. Well, what of it? Mona always needed someone to bullshit.

Jamey rested on the bed for a brief final moment taking in the organic totality of his world with Mona. Maybe he was just another Jerry or Gary. It was a pleasure to have been of use. It just felt a little weird to be frozen out so suddenly. He wasn't at the Buddha stage and it wasn't so easy to shine it on. *A girl* has feelings. Jamey held Mona's little pink bear in his arms. It smelled of Mona, and pot, and the general depravity of Rooms-for-Rent. He hugged the bear and put him on the pillow for Mona to find.

As to his possessions, such as they were, there wasn't anything that he wanted save for his guitar and his photo of Lennon. He arose from the bed and went to work, starting by taking the dresses out of his suitcase and putting them on hangers in the closet for Mona. Missy was fingering her way through the dresses and various outfits. They were generally on the risqué side, but there were signs of other lives. For Mona, clothing was costuming.

He grabbed the photo from the mirror and put it under his guitar in the case. He returned to the dresser to open the small drawer where they kept the makeup collection. Using the mirror, he fixed his eyes, his cheeks, and his lips. "Good color for you," said Missy.

"Sexy," said Jamey. He put on his special pearl earrings and replaced the ring he had been wearing. When he opened the underwear drawer to show Missy, she looked at his treasure in fascination. "Kind of slutty," he apologized with a shrug. "Living on the street—and on stage."

"Pretty," said Missy, holding up a nice pair. "They're cute!"

"It's mostly Mona's stuff," said Jamey.

"Fer sure," said Missy, thinking that he was making some kind of excuse. He wasn't. From the suitcase, he took out the perfume bottle and daubed a little on his wrists, thighs, and neck as if he had been doing it for years, sharing a little with Missy. "Nice!" she exclaimed, impressed by his taste and his budget.

When he reached into the back of the drawer he came out with a small music box. Mona, or Leslie, had already been there, though. Empty. But he didn't need whites anymore. No more carwash. He was looking for their most recent lid, but found instead a heroin kit with a needle, a spoon, a rubber cord, some cotton, and some swabs. This was new to their little stash drawer. Too heavy for Jamey. But Mona had missed one joint in the very back. It was Tank's contribution. Jamey showed it to Missy with a wink. He slipped it into his purse. "We'll do it together someday soon." He snapped up the guitar case and closed the suitcase. "Anything you want?" asked Jamey. "Got some nice lingerie." She shook her head. "Then let's split."

Missy hugged Jamey in a sudden affectionate display. He returned the affection. She carried the guitar and Jamey carried his suitcase. They came down the stairs and crossed the musty lobby. Jack was passing through on the way to his room. "Hey, Jack."

"Hey, Jay," he replied in the same blasé voice. "Your twin?"

"My little sis," said Jamey. "Listen, I'm gone."

"You mean, Splitsville, daddy-o?" asked Jack. "Really? You still got a night, on Mona's dime." Jamey didn't seem to be moved. "Going home?" Jack realized.

"No choice," said Jamey. "Can't afford this classy joint. Here's my key. Mona has hers. I don't know what she's going to do. Can't speak for Mona."

"I saw her earlier today. She was in a fuck of a hurry."

"Didn't want to see me," said Jamey. "Well, probably not that. As if she would care. Okay," Jamey hesitated. "Peace and love, man." Peace sign.

"Peace," said Jack. Missy had moved to the door, holding it open now. Jamey turned from Jack to make the final exit. That's when he felt Jack's first and final slap across his bottom.

"You know better!" said Jamey.

"Hey, chick, you're not the only freak." Jamey followed Missy down the steps into the night, much cooler outside than in the building. They put the guitar and case into the trunk of the Bonneville. Jamey and Missy got into the back seat.

"You don't have much stuff, Jamey," said Margaret.

"Probably best," said Jamey.

"I thought you might change," said Jim, pulling away from Rooms-for-Rent.

"Don't start, Jim," said the Margaret. The Brougham was weaving through the late night traffic on the boulevard. Jamey could see in some detail the familiar freak scene as he went by. "Jamey, honey," she said, turning around to the back seat where Jamey and Missy were sitting. "If you want, we'll go to the Broadway tomorrow and we'll get you whatever you need. You can be anybody you want to be, Jamey, and I'll support you. Maybe we should think about a different school, just so you won't have to put up with so much teasing, but if you want to live like a girl, Jamey, that's fine with me. I can help you. That's one thing I know about. We can redecorate your room…"

The colors were not discernable in the dark car, but Missy turned a bright pink, while the old man was totally red. "Jesus!" he complained. "And he and Missy can share clothes. *Ooh! Can I borrow your pink sweater?*"

"I don't really mind," said Missy, reaching over and taking Jamey's hand in her own. "If Jamey wants to be a girl—I don't get it—but I don't see why he can't. Or she. I mean, I didn't know it was a choice. Maybe I could be a guy. I could go to work with *you*, Daddy."

The car was rolling up the onramp of the Hollywood Freeway. Jamey thought he saw Harry, the last of the Big Three, still trying to flag a ride at the crossroads. Couldn't be. They headed north toward the Valley. Jamey spoke next, cutting off the old man who had more to say. "That's so sweet of you, Mom. What you said about shopping," said Jamey. "That is so far out, man."

"*That's so sweet,*" the old man mocked, trying to get a fight going out of habit. He didn't have another strategy for dealing with any of this at the moment.

"It's cool," said Jamey. "I know I fucked up…"

"You don't talk like that in front of your sister and your mother!"

"You're right," said Jamey. "Bad habit. Look, I just want to go home now. I won't be a problem anymore. I think school will be pretty easy compared to living on the street and working at the carwash. I won't be a problem anymore. It's cool."

"You're wearing a dress!" the apoplectic old man shouted. "How is that not a problem? I mean, most families around town have a kid with long hair, but you're wearing a fuckin' dress!"

Before, Jamey would surely have mocked him by saying, "Let's not use that kind of language in front of my sister or my mother…" But he didn't bite. With a smile, he winked at Missy who squeezed his hand tighter. The car quieted down. It was very late now, and it was a long drive out to the west Valley.

Once at home, in the light of the family room, Mrs. Craig embraced Jamey again, touching his face and looking at him in the light, holding back her tears. She held to him, grateful to have him. She hadn't been sure he would ever be back. Now, standing in his yellow dress, bare legs, and painted toes, her son was home. "The dress is a little gaudy, and tiny," she said. "But those are nice earrings. And you smell good. Expensive perfume. Who wants cocoa?"

"It's three in the morning!" Jim complained.

"It's not," said Margaret.

"I'll have cocoa," said Missy. "Jamey, too."

"Okay," Jamey agreed. "Cocoa it is." Jamey and Missy sat down at the family room table. Jamey automatically crossed his legs in feminine style in the comfortable cushioned chair. With aplomb, he quickly removed the pearl earrings and presented them to his sister. "I don't need them anymore," he told her, trying to send a subtle message to the family. Communication wasn't their bag, and subtlety was hardly their thing. Missy knew expensive natural pearls in antique gold settings when she encountered them, and she was glad to get them.

"Wow!" she said.

"Dad," he addressed the old man. He still hadn't sat down. "I'm sorry I put you and Mom through all of this." The old man was listening, and Jamey went on, "It was pretty lame on my part. But once I was out there, I didn't want to just give up, like I couldn't make it on my own. I wanted you to know that I could make it. Well, whether you know it or not, I know I can. I supported myself. And, everybody, just let me explain about the dress and dressing up stuff."

"No, Jamey," said his mother. "It's fine. You can be who you want to be. I've heard about this sort of thing."

"In Readers Digest, no doubt," said Jamey. "Mom, it's so cool of you to want to accept me."

"Your mother is very *with it*," said Jim.

"But you really don't understand, Mom. It's like this. I was in an all-girl band. It was the only gig available. I made money by working at a carwash in the daytime, mostly at a theater, but, on the weekends, I was playing in the band, for cash, Dad—but I had to be a girl."

"Oh!" said Margaret. "Now I get it! It's like that movie with Tony Curtis and Jack Lemon!"

Missy and Jamey were all like "Huh?"

"With Marilyn Monroe!" Jamey knew who Marilyn was, sort of. But he didn't know her movies any more than he knew those of Bridgette Bardot. "Never mind," said Margaret, who was just happy within to have an explanation that she could actually process.

"I wouldn't have thought of it, but this girl, Mona, she dressed me up, and it worked."

"I'll say!" said Missy. "You look hot *and* sweet."

"My fake breasts are bigger than yours," said Jamey. "But you're catching up."

"Jesus Christ!" Jim complained.

"Well, I didn't say *tits*. Seriously. I'm not strange or anything out of whack." He was lying for his mother's benefit. He was pretty sure that he was stranger than he had ever thought himself. There were indeed any number of people to be. He explained, "I'm a dude. Like you don't have to worry about me. I promise you, as long as I'm not in an all-girl band, I won't be wearing dresses and high heels, okay? So, Mom, I can't believe how nice about it you were. I almost want to go with you to the mall just so we can bond over stockings and brassieres." Margaret blushed now. "But we really don't have to go lingerie shopping together. Not that I don't look hot in cute underwear, because I really do, you know. I have these pink pettipants that go practically to the knees…" A gesture brought attention to his bare thighs. A bad joke to top it all off was just what wasn't needed to restore confidence, but it showed that Jamey was home and somewhat his wise guy self.

"Well, if you're not going to dress like a girl any more," Margaret was saying, "Maybe we should get out the Super Eight. I don't think I'll ever have twin girls again."

"Jesus Christ!" Jim Craig complained. And then he quickly added, "We don't have no film. Used it up on the Fourth."

PLASTIC FANTASTIC LOVER

Before her junior year, Missy, now going as Melissa, had grown impatient with this courtly love business and had broken up with Craig Roman. It seemed plastic to her, these *thous* and that sort of thing. After all, in the end, Craig wanted to get into her pants just like any other hippie. She didn't object—to his desire, that is—but she didn't consider herself a candidate to star in the movie version of "Legend of the Girl Child Linda." The whole hippie thing was sexist, and Melissa was reading up on that and going through some changes.

As high school resumed in September, Jim Craig's son was missing Mona. She had been the life of the party, and now there was no party. As Mona receded, Jamey disappeared as well. Privately, he tried dressing up, but less as September became October and November. The materials were sweet, but he couldn't go out: mustache, sideboards, trimmed hair, and such. Except for his face, he wasn't shaving. No polish. Natural nails. Nothing fem. Down to the boxers.

Jamey gave up his stage name. When he returned to Knollridge High, he went by James. Miss Curtis was James' World Lit instructor the first semester of his senior year. "*What a difference a few months can make in a young man!*" He was writing papers, turning them in, and they were, in her terms, "reasonably cogent and occasionally lucid." There was less poetry, and that's usually a good thing. He was at last using that good head on his shoulders, as it seemed to his favorite teacher.

Not to take anything away from Miss Curtis, but Jamey knew that the turn-around was greatly enhanced by a decrease in the intake of psychedelics. He put down on acid, mescaline, and whites, but he still liked a little Maryjane, though far less often.

James and Melissa did their joint together on the back patio by the pool late one windy October evening after the folks had gone to bed. Melissa wasn't much of a stoner, but she had fun on that occasion. "Wow man!" She was glad to have her brother safe at home. The turn-around in school didn't hurt him with the judge who dropped the whole run-away business.

During senior year, James' beard and his long-delayed mustache started to grow in more discernibly, and there was more hair on his body in general. His upper body was less flabby, and his muscular system was increasingly defined, augmented by some daily running. James was never a Mr. Universe body builder type, but the testosterone was finally kicking in. He gained a few inches and his voice went lower. He could no longer reach the high notes, a la Stevie Winwood or Judy Collins. As his proportions changed, his bottom, once so fascinating to Mr. Altier, seemed to flatten, stretch out, and, in short, to have lost its charming appeal. On the upside, James was of the opinion that his unit had gotten both longer and thicker. It just seemed to hang better in his careful estimation. He wondered if Teri Ann Murphy might be willing to do a before and after analysis.

It was not to be. James thought fondly of Teri Ann, but he never scored with her again. She believed that going back to old sweethearts, even one she may have loved, was a sign of desperation, and she never would do it even when she wanted to—even when she was desperate. But she liked Jamey. In time, she was the only person who called him that. They had been each others' firsts, and she kept tabs on him for some time. He had a couple of girlfriends in the senior year, and surprisingly, even to himself, they weren't complete stony hippie chicks, charming as stony hippie chicks could be. He didn't need someone living in a dope cloud. James seemed more commanding than he had been before. He had changed, and Teri Ann was intrigued. But a girl just can't go back!

James kept his hair trimmed. The long locks were gone, and especially the cute ringlets, though it still reached just over his ears. Jim Craig could handle that, given the alternative that had been released to him at the Hollywood Division. Whether it was James' altered point of view or just the changing times, his personal safety was no longer in jeopardy at school. Nobody particularly wanted to pound on him anymore. He wasn't really a threat to the natural order of high school. He was playing by the rules, and he ceased to be interesting. He didn't have the need to be exceptional.

Jim Craig wasn't too sure about his boy at first, with a seared memory of the yellow dress and earrings. But, week after week, month after month, James seemed to be on the straight and narrow. As the calendar year ended, James asked his dad for some fatherly advice about taxes. Hoping to scare up some money, as a youth is wont to do, he asked about filing tax returns. On his dad's advice, James called the carwash and the El Portal and gave them his address so that he could receive the necessary W2 paperwork. When tax time came around, James had Jim Craig help him with his return.

Despite the very small sums, Jim was impressed that the boy had actually been working that summer, which, according to Jim, is what a boy should do. He couldn't file for the band work, the street musician gig, the panhandling, or the modeling, so all of that was left off the résumé and out of the story. None of it would have helped him with his college apps anyway. Jim wouldn't let James claim himself as a dependent, so his returns amounted to only about $22.00. But it was well received. James Craig, Jr., a tax filing American, had turned into a grown-up guy. That's what Jim, Sr. had wanted. It was a small step, but it made a big difference in bringing them into balance.

Though Craig Roman felt that things were different, James and Craig yet regarded each other as friends. James tried not to mention his feminine escapade with Craig, figuring that Craig would think the less of him, but Craig had seen Maiden Head in action. So it was he who broached it. James stayed with the story he had given his mother, that it was just to be in the band. Craig said he never would have done it, but James replied that Craig had never been living on his own. Craig accepted that, though it was still kind of weird to think of your pal in a dress and panties. Indeed, over the months, Craig came to believe that he was thinking about it *too* much. Jamey had looked like Missy, and Missy had looked majorly hot that summer. Anyway, James never put the queer moves on Craig or anyone else Craig ever knew about. James seemed just like a guy now. Growing up is always weird. It's all about the changes.

James had surrendered his rock and roll dreams of glory just as he had put down on drugs. They were both losers' games, though he still liked to play electric bass. After paying back Melissa, he used the remaining cash he had brought home from Frasco to replace his bass. He got a good deal when one of the Foresters was getting re-outfitted. James and Craig would jam in the old garage, and sometimes put together a pick-up band to play around the west Valley. But James no longer thought of himself as rock-star bound. He didn't dismiss the dreams of his musician peers since he knew that anything could happen. But he knew that he had gotten as close to the lightning as he was likely to get.

> *Now that I shouldn't touch you*
> *It's as if I never knew...*

The thing was that being close to the lightning wasn't going to get it; you had to be the lightning. Mona had once said that he was, but Mona had always been lying about something. The Gibson never got replaced. Some things can't be fixed.

Imagine Yourself
As the freak—takes you

JAMES THOUGHT ABOUT THOSE WEEKS in the summer of sixty-nine. The Rick thing, in spite of its brevity, had been profound on Jamey's side. He doubted if he had ever touched a girl as profoundly as Rick had touched him, especially the first time. He wasn't going to forget Rick, or Chris, or Tank, or Bryan Cooper's hand on his back. Or Patty, for that matter. Or John. John had been really sweet.

He did a fair amount of pondering, realizing that he had an appreciation, even a longing for certain guys. He almost killed himself driving by the pool one Saturday morning in senior year when he saw a squadron of male lifeguards in their tiny tight red shorts. Like the stories about Jagger, he decided he was, or had been, bi. But every day, he felt a little less beautiful and a little less special. He had enjoyed living as a girl: The intimacy with Mona; the feeling of the clothing; the wind up his skirt; the smell of the perfumes, the polish, the talc, and the lotions; the look of the nails; the jewelry; the hats; the hair with its ringlets, ribbons, and curls; and the attention—at times annoying, frightening, even life threatening, but so exciting and life-like. Jamey the chick had not been ignored. Now he was back to invisible, which was okay having lived both.

Given that James had blown the eleventh grade, high school turned to JC, and he tried on two occasions to find out if he had really lost his gay feelings. There was a handsome philosophy professor, maybe forty, and it did feel nice to have someone make love to him. But it was manufactured. There was no genuine affection in either direction. James surmised that it was more complicated than it was worth. It being a philosophy professor, that should have been expected.

The other occasion was a one-night-stand with a guy James met at a bar. He had taken James to his apartment in Sherman Oaks. He was older than James, but younger than Rick. He was reasonably healthy despite his drinking. He did James, and they fell asleep. James, most politely, had left early in the morning without leaving a phone number or address. It felt empty, and it felt wrong. Unlike Mona, he didn't rifle the guy's wallet. He gave up his queer activities, but the feelings were not so easy to be rid of.

He took up with a very nice young lady, a violinist, and they spent a couple of college years together. In the end, she found him a little distant and too guarded. She never knew about his big love with Rick though she instinctively knew that there was something in his heart that he wasn't telling. So, despite the good sex, she couldn't sustain the relationship. It was going nowhere if they couldn't share the truth. James regretted having wasted so much of her prime time.

As to the Hollywood side of things, Rick had been as good as his word. Westerfield got Maiden Head connected to Mr. Nichols, a music manager. They toured the U.S. and England in the latter part of 1969 and early 1970 as a support band for Indus touring groups. They hit the charts in 1970 with their first single, "Something about the Night." It was their first record and the best they ever made. Maybe not "Dancing with Linda," but pretty good. James liked it. He never knew what Rick thought about the fact that his little Jamey was ultimately not in the band that he had launched.

Maiden Head's success had been unintentional on the part of the genius squad at Indus Valley. Westerfield had asked Altier to shoot the cover, and it was the cover art that first got the attention, the cover with the portrait, on an endless green lawn, of a topless pubescent blonde with budding breasts holding the aerodynamic hood ornament from an early fifties Hudson. It was Jamey, altered by the air-brush, but who knew? Many a far out guru has meditated on the meaning of the Maiden Head cover. The innocent? The nascent? The virgin? Child pornography? Did it have anything at all to do with Maiden Head? Who was the girl? Shouldn't she be selling perfume or appearing in fashion magazines? What's with the hood ornament? Is it phallic? Check out her eyes, man. They had questions, perhaps, but they spent a lot of time looking at the Maiden Head cover to find the answers. Some still do.

The cover was so controversial that an alternative cover had to be released for some markets: A rough early photo on an L.A. club stage. Leslie was in leather, the girls in tiny dresses, and Mona was playing the orange Fender, the same bass that could be seen in old photos of Crazy Place. James didn't want to associate himself with the other cover—which may be why he wore trimmed hair, a mustache, and sideburns throughout his late teens and early twenties—so he didn't talk about either cover.

But, again, Craig Roman knew that bass, and he knew how it had gotten into Mona's hot little hands. He pointed it out to James and to anyone who might listen to his rant, keeping the rumor alive. Craig always said that Jamey had been a regular Pete Best. But that suggested sour grapes, and James really didn't feel that way. He was clear that he had probably missed a long ride on a bus—or a private jet—to Nowheresville. Even Leslie King, with all her talent and charisma, with their two singles, their hot first album, and world tours, was not so important in the pop culture story. Mona, her bass player, was less than that. Who wants to see The Noel Redding Experience? So to what would Jamey have amounted? Not really much more than he did: Another pretty face.

But, for a little while there, Leslie King got the hot reviews, and, because of her, Maiden Head, and Mona, finally got their Rolling Stone cover. Leslie was a heroin freak, and she died of an OD in Hong Kong less than eighteen months after Jamey left the band. Denise and Karen stayed in the music business. Jamey followed the trades, and Denise and Karen worked in various L.A. bands. They also did studio work and some touring gigs on the basis of their Maiden Head luster.

After Leslie died, Jamey didn't hear of Mona for many years. He was afraid she had drugged out, like Leslie. But the mystery was solved when Maiden Head was covered in a segment of a *Where Are They Now?* M-TV cable show. James learned that Mona's connection to Maiden Head had given her entre to the industry. Instead of performing, Mona had written several teeny-bopper seventies hits, including Pamela Priest's one hit wonder, "I Felt Good about You from the Start." In addition, Mona had married a big shot entertainment lawyer. The marriage hadn't lasted beyond a few years, but she had come out of it with a very good settlement, a house in Malibu, the income from her songs, and a son.

It might be reasonable to expect that Mona would have repaid Jamey for the bass once she came into a pile of money, but the two never had occasion to meet again. Anyway, if Mona were going to start returning everything she had stolen and to make amends for her wrongs, she would have been too occupied to care for the boy. She would have had to let those two girls out of the closet over at Immaculate Heart. How could she have made it up to Nick and Chris of the Big Three who were grounded and who lost the rest of their tenth grade summer due to her antics? She could have, at the very least, paid Larry, or Gary, his $50.00. But there were too many sins for which to atone. Mona left the past in the past. Many a woman keeps a strict line between her distant past and her children. It's probably a good idea.

If James would occasionally mention Mona with a shake of his head, he never mentioned his connection to Richard Altier. He was fairly sure that many of the guys he talked with over the years had not been penetrated as he had been, and he was just as sure that they had no idea what they had missed. Being Richard's girlfriend was not something one could discuss—or forget.

And Altier had become more controversial and harder to explain in the ensuing years. He famously published his coffee table tome, *Image of Love*. It never goes out of print as the love generation ages. He also published *The Gallery*, which still gets controversial reviews. The earlier stark scenes from Viet Nam of the often depraved carnage from the war never raised so much ire and vitriol as the pictures that Richard Altier published of the he/she-boy/girls that he had been shooting in the late sixties and early seventies: Boys dressed as girls, scant clothing, overtly sexual, obviously provocative, and none of it All-American. James recognized his former self in one of the pictures. He was dressed in pink and posing, his eyes pinned, and his face vulnerable and soul searing. Check out page 47, if you really want to know.

Jamey had looked too much like Missy for Melissa to miss it when she had *happened* to see the sensational book upon its release. She didn't confront him, but she knew. Some observers made the connection between page 47 and *the girl* who graced the cover of the Maiden Head album. So Jamey had achieved that moment of rock and roll immortality. That's what he had wanted, though this was not how he had pictured it when he used to play guitar and bass in Craig Roman's garage. He was more like the model on the cover of *Whipped Cream and other Delights* than Mike Carl, the piano player.

Interestingly, James encountered Saul Gary in the newspapers. Mr. Gary was arrested in connection with an attempt to take over the Wilshire Blvd. Federal Building in Westwood, an ill-fated mission that was completely botched. Nobody was hurt, and the Panthers absolutely disavowed any knowledge of, or association with, Saul Gary. Still it's always fun to read about your friends in the news. And Jamey had a chance to keep tabs on another of his friends.

In 1973, Richard Altier was charged with the rape of a young boy at the Laurel Canyon house. Among the detectives that were assigned to the high profile case was young Sergeant Tanquerson. He was involved in the original interviews with the fifteen-year-old boy at the center of the case, and he was present for the arrest. Tank let it be known that he was outraged by Altier's alleged depravity. Tanquerson was quoted as wondering how anyone could do such terrible things to the innocent children, the unfortunates of the street whom he was there to protect and to serve.

Altier's publicist and attorneys floated the idea that it was *only* a case of statutory rape. The ensuing brouhaha made it obvious that the public and the courts were not as hip, now, and on the edge as Altier had believed. The love generation had passed. Free love was a concept that had been dispatched. Then, whether to cash in or to seek some kind of justice, a second and a third boy appeared. As the attorneys say, "No bueno."

James followed the story in the papers. It was like reading his own life, but, even at a distance, he believed that what happened between Rick and himself was completely voluntary on his part. That made no difference since the accusers, and James, had all been under the legal age of consent. Altier had probably done everything that they accused him of, but James didn't think him the monster of Laurel Canyon.

When Molly Gifford, under pain of being charged as an accomplice, agreed to testify for the District Attorney, Altier decided that this was an uptight scene of the first order. With talk of rescinding his bail and prison hanging over him like a dark shadow, Richard Altier split the crazy scene in a timely manner on a private jet to Mexico. He made his way under cover of darkness to Europe, where, at great effort and expense, the extradition process eventually stalled.

The fugitive artist story fueled a second round of hot sales of all of his works. *The Gallery* took on a new meaning, and that helped to finance his legal expenses and to establish himself on the continent. His legal troubles made it difficult for him to travel as freely as he had, but he continued to work in a limited manner, and for even better money. He could no longer stay at the ranch in Larkspur, but there were villas in the south of France that served as well. His reputation as an artist was only enhanced, though the Pulitzer was probably out of his reach now. The important thing was that he could still pursue his peculiar interests—which he did, both in terms of photography and boys.

When people around the water cooler had opinions about the guilt, innocence, or general depravity of Richard Altier, as the story occasionally surfaced when a close call or a ruling by a French court was in the news, James Craig kept his testimony to himself.

If you really want to know, James Craig transferred to CSUK and graduated Liberal Arts in 1974. He took some time off before pursuing a double master's in economics and political science to work on the successful Jerry Brown gubernatorial campaign, hoping the new governor would restore the cuts to state mental health for Mitch and his comrades. James was invited to a victory party. The next morning, there was a photo in The Times which included James Craig in the crowd scene behind the triumphant Governor-elect and his sweetheart, Linda.

ONE SOUVENIR that James couldn't help but show off from time to time was his mind-blowing genuine original print of the John Lennon photo from 1967 photographed, inscribed, and signed by Richard Altier. James ignored the inscription. He claimed to have met Altier at a party in the hippie days. The photo never appeared elsewhere. James kept it sealed and in fairly good condition, though spending a month or so in a guitar case or hanging on the mirror in the pot laden room he had shared with Mona hadn't been the best treatment. By the early eighties, after Lennon's death, it was appraised at over $3,000.00. Not too shabby for a night in pink underpants.

ABOUT THE AUTHOR

RICHARD FEY knows Knollridge like Jerome Kern knew Broadway, like Janis could sing the blues, like Kerouac knew the road, like Harriet Tubman knew the woods, like Tom Eliot knew the futility of postwar civilization and the redemption of the Christian rituals, like Barbara Stanwyck knew how to come out blasting, like Jim Anderson knew best, like Dorothy Fields knew the way you look tonight, like Chucko the Clown knew how to Hokey-Pokey, like Jesus knew how to forgive, like Busbee Berkeley knew how to put together a little number, like Dionne Warwick knew how to sing a Bacharach-David song, like Sherriff John knew how to make a hat rack look like a Christmas tree, like Herbert Philbrick knew how to lead three lives, like Hobo Kelly knew how to confront mischief-makers, like McKeever knew how to get around the Colonel, like Donovan knew both the Roly-Poly Man and what he saw when he looked in his mirror, and he sometimes writes about it.

www.ingramcontent.com/pod-product-compliance
Lightning Source LLC
Chambersburg PA
CBHW050721180626
46814CB00002B/549